ADMISSIONS

In a strangled voice, Suzie said, "Want! *Want!*
You know what I want, Con? I want you to stop
with the fairy stories! I want you to go away! I
want to be dead! That's what I want!"

Con said, quite calmly, "Well, here comes your
nurse, so I'll just leave you for now, Suzie. But I'll
check back with you later." And, quite calmly,
she smiled at Carmen and said softly, "She's
upset, I'm sorry to say." And, still without fuss,
she let herself out of the unit, into the corridor
beyond. There was no one there now, no one at
all. Con leaned against the wall, trying to keep her
chin from trembling, fighting the tears that
threatened to overwhelm her. It hurt, it hurt; she
wasn't able to help Suzie at all! But that was
impossible, unthinkable! It was her job to help. If
she couldn't help Susan – someone she knew so
well; for God's sake, she had trained the
girl! – then who *could* help?

She straightened her back, took in a very deep
breath, and then let it out slowly. She would not
have hysterics here on the floor. Absolutely not.
She would calm down, and she would go back in
and do her job. Because that was what this was all
about, and that was the end of it.

ADMISSIONS

Marcia Rose

ARROW BOOKS

Arrow Books Limited
17-21 Conway Street, London W1P 6JD

An imprint of the Hutchinson Publishing Group

London Melbourne Sydney Auckland
Johannesburg and agencies throughout
the world

First published in Great Britain 1985

© Marcia Kamien and Rose Novak 1984

Printed and bound in Great Britain by
Anchor Brendon Limited, Tiptree, Essex

ISBN 0 09 939970 9

WELCOME TO CADMAN MEMORIAL
HOSPITAL

Welcome. You are in one of the country's most modern and up-to-date voluntary medical facilities. Our staff of dedicated physicians, nurses, technicians, and therapists is here to serve all your health needs. Please feel free to ask anyone on staff any questions or explanations you might want if anything puzzles or disturbs you. If your own doctor is not available, dial X 1790 for one of our volunteer patient advocates.

Cadman Memorial Hospital opened in 1890 as the Brooklyn Infirmary, located on what was then called Fulton Street. It was built just seven years after the opening of the Great East River Bridge (which we of course know as the Brooklyn Bridge) in order to serve the fast-growing suburban population in Brooklyn Heights, just across the bridge from Wall Street and City Hall.

For nearly a century, Cadman remained much as it was at the turn of the century. In 1972, answering the needs of a changing community, Tower A was built onto the original neoclassic structure; and with its addition, the hospital became one of New York City's most modern health-care facilities.

Today, Cadman Memorial serves the landmark neighborhood of Brooklyn Heights as well as Cobble Hill, downtown Brooklyn, Borough Hall, and the nearby Tillary Houses. It

1

is a primary-care hospital with 254 beds, 60,000 outpatient visits per year through its Emergency Room and clinics, and 25,000 admissions; 126 physicians (both residents and house staff), 158 nurses, and 87 physical and occupational therapists staff the hospital. Cadman can boast an eight-bed Intensive Care Unit (ICU), a ten-bed Coronary Care Unit (CCU), and shares a CAT scanner with Methodist and City General hospitals.

Cadman Memorial Hospital is accredited by the Joint Commission on Accreditation of Hospitals. Our high standards of care are well regarded, and we are proud of our special clinical services. Especially well known are the Earl L. Crawford Obesity Clinic, the Alcohol and Drug Treatment Center, the Birth Defects Clinic, the Genetic Counseling Service of South Brooklyn, and the All-Borough Arthritis Clinic.

Please be reminded that smoking is forbidden in all but specially designated areas; and we ask that patients and visitors be courteous to others in the hospital. We hope your stay with us will be as pleasant and comfortable as is possible.

H. F. X. Del Bello

H. F. X. Del Bello
Hospital Administrator

Chapter 1

ROUNDS WERE ALMOST over. Thank God, Bobby Truman thought, stifling a giant yawn. Oh, what he'd give for a cup of coffee right this minute! Even cafeteria coffee. He hadn't slept worth a damn last night; it had been weeks, months, since he'd had a good night's sleep. Hell, it had been six days since he'd been laid . . . but who's counting, right?

Wrong. Corinne had been so different since she got herself reborn or whatever the hell it was. If he was getting laid, he wouldn't mind being so tired all the time. If he was getting laid, he could take her preaching at him. He could take anything if he could only get laid once in a while!

He snuck a look at his watch: 8:23:45. God, he was tired. He was tired, and he was bored, and the patient they were gathered around right now was a tiresome, boring woman who seemed to think she was the first woman in history to have had a hysterectomy. She was holding tightly onto Adrian's hands, the tears streaming down her face. Dammit, didn't women realize how ugly crying made them look? It made you turn off so you couldn't even hear what they were saying. Although if he thought about it, he wouldn't mind at all if

3

Corinne would cry every once in a while. It was positively inhuman how calm she always was, no matter what. Yes, a few tears from that quarter wouldn't hurt a bit. In fact, it wouldn't hurt a bit if she acted more human, period. Smiling, chatting, coming on to him . . .

He really had to stop thinking about his wife and their troubles and concentrate on what was going on now, here, at this hospital bed, in this hospital room, in this hospital.

Now it was 8:34:32, and if Adrian caught him once more looking at his watch, he'd have something to say to him for sure. "Is your watch broken perhaps, Dr. Truman? Since you keep checking it, I can't help but wonder." Adrian Winter, Dr. Adrian Winter, chief of Ob/Gyn, would never actually yell, like some of them did, not in front of the patient; but he could needle you until you wished he would yell and let you off the hook.

Bobby had known Adrian Winter since he'd had him in medical school at Downstate, and that made it going on eight years. God, it was hard to believe that he was in his last year of residency, almost finished now and ready to go out into the big world: B. J. Truman, M.D. It was still hard for him to realize that he was really a doctor; chief resident, in fact. The first black chief resident in Cadman's history, in fact. Everyone was *so* damn nice to him . . . *so* polite and sweet. It was Dr. Truman here and Dr. Truman there. It gave him a laugh. And he knew damn well it never would have happened without Adrian on his side. Too many old-money families in Brooklyn Heights; too many old turkeys getting high blood pressure at the thought of black hands touching their white wives or daughters. Hell, he wasn't in Ob/Gyn so he could touch white women. He could have all the white women he wanted; he saw the way a lot of them looked at him. All the turkeys, he guessed, believed that old fantasy that black cocks were bigger and always a temptation.

No, he was going to be a gynecologist because Adrian Winter had convinced him that black women needed better care.

He was right. A lot of the problems in the black neighborhoods, at least in Brooklyn, stemmed from the unwanted pregnancies, the teenage pregnancies, the ill-nourished expectant mothers. There were horrendous statistics about child abuse and deaths in childbirth. Morbidity and mortality among black women and infants were unbelievably bad: it was a horror story. That's why Bobby Truman was doing his graduate work in Ob/Gyn, folks. Not to get his hands onto or into white women. . . .

Gary Weinstein elbowed him gently and whispered, "Bobby, please don't fall asleep while standing up. It makes the patient nervous." Bobby gave him a smile; Gary was okay. He was a second-year man; a good man, Bobby thought. He was smart, and he was always good-humored, and he had the light touch. Of course he tended to go a little too far sometimes. He'd have to watch it with the patients. Most Ob/Gyn patients didn't want jokes from their doctor. They wanted his entire attention—his or *her* entire attention, Bobby reminded himself. Hell, the patients were all women, weren't they? That's what all women wanted, as far as he could see.

Even Laura Cooper, their other second-year man. Or woman. There she stood, at his left elbow, watching Adrian deal with the patient as if it were a life-and-death situation, her gaze intent. Women just took life too seriously and too goddam personally.

Now he brought his attention to bear on the bed and the woman in it. She was a matron of fifty-five, a housewife, a mother, a grandmother and had never held a job. Private patient, of course. Most of the clinic patients were black. Of course. This was Dr. Winter's own patient, which was why he was presenting the case. She was propped up in bed, her hair uncombed, graying, tangled, her hands clutching the doctor's. "I'm not a woman anymore! No more babies!" she was moaning.

And when Adrian murmured, "Now, Etta, you know you don't want any more babies," she only sobbed harder. "You have your grandchildren."

"I know, doctor, I know. It's just knowing that all my female parts are gone. Everything that made me a woman . . . gone! My life as a woman is over, doctor, over!"

What histrionics, Bobby thought. The woman could have a complete and satisfying sex life until the day she died. What in the world did she mean, her life as a woman was over? And yet this was far from the first time he'd heard a woman in Cadman Memorial Hospital say that, in that tone of voice. A lot of women carried on. Of course, she was a bit young for a complete hysterectomy. Her body was youthful, though slightly overweight. He knew because he'd operated on her with Adrian. And she had talked it all over with them before making up her mind. Look, she'd been hemorrhaging for weeks at a time and was becoming weak from loss of blood. The operation was indicated. She'd been completely rational about it. Until this morning. Now, by all rights, Etta Schuster should have been smiling and relieved. Instead, there was Adrian, holding her hands and telling her over and over again that she had a whole lifetime ahead of her and women remained women long after their childbearing days were over. A continuous murmur of soothing words.

Now Adrian eased himself up. He'd been sitting on the edge of the bed—something a doctor rarely did at Cadman. It was felt that the patients needed their personal space in the impersonal hospital room. But sometimes, Bobby felt, you *had* to move in and cozy up to create the intimacy needed for a good recovery. Adrian still held her hand, still looked directly into her eyes, still smiled. Then he put his other hand on her head and said, "Etta, I understand. But you're making yourself suffer needlessly. This will only make the pain worse . . . and you're much too intelligent to do that. Come on, now. I need you calm. Tell me you'll try to be calm."

Through her tears, she gave him a radiant smile. "Ade, you're a wonderful doctor. Of course I'll try." Bobby gazed at his chief and marveled. The Old Man had done it again. He often told them that what most people missed in their doctor was the laying on of hands. It was the most important part of doctoring, bar none. "Back in the days," he'd say, "when doctors couldn't cure, couldn't even help most of the time, couldn't do a damn thing but pray, they cared for their patients by touching them. Never forget that, doctors. Touch really does heal."

The man was a genius; no doubt about it. They were all damn lucky to train under him. Most gynecologists were shits; everyone in medicine knew that. Women haters. Pain lovers. Heartless bastards. Like Nick Ponte, first-year resident, standing back there, dark and glowering and hairy as a bear, his arms crossed belligerently across his big chest, a supercilious look on his face.

It had taken Adrian the better part of a month to break Nick of his endearing habit of referring to all the patients as cunts. But break him he had. It was the one time Bobby had ever seen Adrian Winter beet red with rage; usually, he was cool and calm, stinging you with sarcasm. But that time, oh, boy, that time he could hardly speak. His voice had been thick with anger, every word measured out. "If . . . I . . . ever . . . hear . . . that word again as a *description* . . . If I ever hear any other gutter language used in connection with any patient . . . the person using that language can pack his bags and leave this service. Immediately."

Adrian walked out of Mrs. Schuster's room, and the rest of them—seven in all, two from each year except Bobby's because Alex Frank had left to go into research early last year—all walked out behind him, clipboards and pens at the ready. Out in the hall near the nursing station, Adrian stopped, waiting for them to cluster around him. Bobby thought for the millionth time what an imposing man Adrian Winter was. Well, if you were six feet four, you had a good start. But with Adrian, it went further than mere size. His was a commanding presence, even before he opened his mouth. His eyes, a light clear gray, were sharp with intelligence, and the rest of his face was lean, ascetic, clean-shaven, with an outjutting jaw marked by a scar. Graying hair, crisply curling but cut very short. Little half glasses that sat halfway down his hawk nose and managed to look glamorous, for Christ's sake. Glamorous! But they did. It was the hospital joke, how every new nurse an Ob/Gyn or pedes fell in love with Dr. Winter for at least a week. Some for longer; but by all accounts, he never fooled around, not during either of his marriages.

Bobby leaned against a corner of the nurses' desk, folded his arms across his chest, and gave Adrian all his attention. One of the nurses had brought a container of coffee up from the cafeteria, and the smell of it was making him weak. He'd been on call all night, and you'd think he'd have had more than enough coffee; but come morning, he still needed it.

Adrian gave his group a small smile and a nod and began quickly to discuss that morning's cases: hysterectomies, and tubes to be tied, D & Cs, uterine cancers, and all the stuff that was usual on the gynecological floor. Bobby realized that surgery was going to have to be part of his practice, but he had learned his first year of residency that he didn't really like it a lot. He'd much rather deal with patients face-to-face, on a personal level. When he'd been rotated to surgery his first year, he'd been put off when he discovered that discussions on rounds sounded more like a bunch of automobile mechanics talking about the workings of a Chevy than physicians talking about human beings. Another thing: on surgery, they never talked about pain. Yet every single patient was in pain, often terrible pain. And then he'd come to realize that, to surgeons, pain was not something pathological, something to treat. No, it was just a necessary and normal result of surgery that would eventually disappear.

Most surgeons just didn't concern themselves with pain. Adrian Winter did. Right now, for instance, he was locking horns with Laura who was saying that Mrs. Barton's D & C had gone perfectly and that the patient should be able to bear her discomfort because it was a natural result of the procedure. Laura, a woman, not having any more feeling than that! He had been noticing more and more that Laura didn't see patients as people but as cases, and it bothered him. He made a mental note to discuss her attitude with her, or possibly with Adrian first. Now Adrian was shaking his head. "We can't know anyone's threshold of pain, Dr. Cooper. We have to believe what they tell us." He smiled briefly. "A matter of faith." Laura made a face but didn't argue. "So we'll give Mrs. Barton the painkiller she says she needs." He went on, addressing them all. "Because if she says she needs it, she needs it. And personally I believe that if she's given five extra minutes of attention, she won't need any medication at all." There was a small ripple of amusement at this. Adrian Winter was very big on attention replacing drugs. Bobby happened to agree with this, but Laura muttered something about "coddling," and Nick under his breath whispered, "B.S."

It was a wonder, Bobby thought—not for the first time—how people decided to be physicians—people who had no more feeling for others than they had for a stick of wood.

"With all due respect, Dr. Winter," Laura was saying. "I don't think we as doctors should encourage these women in this kind of infantile behavior. Take Mrs. Schuster, for instance. The woman is totally unliberated . . . she's a throwback to all those old notions about a woman being only as good as her ovaries. In fact, I found it very self-indulgent to see a woman as young as she is thinking with her reproductive organs instead of her brain. She's a smart woman; I've talked to her. And here she is, moaning about her life being over. I mean, doesn't she know that the woman in the next bed has cancer and will be lucky if she lives another year?"

One of the first-year men, a nice kid but, Bobby thought, a bit of a wimp and more than a bit of an ass-kisser, put in, "Yes, Dr. Winter, I don't understand her problem, either. She's had the best possible surgery, she's healing well, no medical problems whatever. Isn't she just asking for sympathy?"

"Exactly!" Adrian said. He always stayed calm. Bobby had learned to watch the left eyebrow. If it quirked a bit, it meant that you'd just said something Dr. Winter considered unutterably stupid. The left eyebrow shot up now, but the stupid first-year guy couldn't know what that meant. He stood there, pleased with himself, grinning away like a goddam idiot. "The difference between you and me, Mr. Jacobs, is that I realize that the sympathy she's asking for is as necessary as any medication—maybe even more so." He held up a hand as Jacobs opened his mouth again and went on. "Let me tell you about Etta Schuster. She's the mother of five children— five bright, high-achieving and demanding children. It's small wonder that her role as mother is her prime means of identification. In a case like this, once the reproductive organs are gone, the identity is in jeopardy. With the proper care on the part of the physician and the family, this feeling does not last. Support is all, Dr. Jacobs. And let me remind all of you that this reaction to hysterectomy, while not as prevalent as once it was, is not at all unusual. Even in our enlightened, feminist age, Dr. Cooper."

Bobby thought that, of course, the most interesting part of Etta Schuster's story was the part Adrian couldn't tell his students because she was the wife not only of a doctor but of Cadman's chief of Internal Medicine. Possibly the most fascinating thing about Etta Schuster was her son-of-a-bitch husband. He'd found, during rotations, that Dr. Arthur Schuster was not above chewing you out in front of your peers and the patients. And he was not beneath taking all the credit for a good idea of yours and then grinning at you as he stole it. The nurses who had to work under him considered him a total shit. And Bobby happened to know, because in a moment of weakness Adrian had told him, that Art Schuster wrote out his wife's shopping lists, item by item, as if the woman didn't know what groceries to buy; and then, to add insult to injury, checked the fucking thing item by item when she got back from the market. The man was an unbelievable boor. Bobby would have believed any story at all; this one sounded apocryphal, but he was sure it was absolutely true. Art Schuster had reduced his wife, according to everyone who knew them, to a dependent, whining, egoless little woman who was now convinced that her only worth lay in her role as the mother of the children because that was the only area in which her husband did not meddle. It was sad. People thought every doctor was so holy, so wise, so compassionate. Well, they ought to meet Art Schuster . . . or Nick Ponte.

And as if on cue, Nick gave that strange little bark that passed for a laugh with him. "I'll take Mrs. Schuster out," he said, "and I'll give her a whole new identity."

The eyebrow flew up. "You, Dr. Ponte, will learn to think of your female patients in a somewhat different way, or I strongly suggest you begin to think about some other specialty."

"Yeah, Nick," Gary Weinstein said, "like veterinary medicine." There was some laughter, which Adrian cut off with a raised hand. Bobby stifled a yawn with his hand, wishing he were downstairs in the cafeteria, a cup of steaming coffee and a nice fresh Danish in front of him; a cheese Danish, he thought, his mouth watering. The last time he remembered eating was around two in the morning, half a stale tuna sandwich that had tasted disgusting. He was having trouble focusing on what was happening; it was always like this after his thirty-six hours on call. It was worse than jet lag.

He brought his attention back to the conversation. Cooper was mouthing off again. ". . . need education, so they know that hysterectomy isn't the end of the world."

Obviously, it was time for him to put in a word. "Look, Cooper," he said, "your education just isn't enough."

"Oh, yes—"

"Oh, no," Bobby insisted gently. He grinned at Laura Cooper. She was a pain in the ass but brilliant. More and more, he was beginning to think that all she needed was a different specialty. "Look," he said, pushing himself away from the wall, waking up a little as he spoke, "we saw an enormous difference between the behavior of Mrs. Schuster, who *had* to have a hysterectomy because of medical problems, and Mrs. Valentine, last week. Remember her? Barbara Valentine, divorced, two grown kids, and a new career, who was in to have her tubes tied? *She* wanted it; she chose to end her reproductive years, and she was very happy. My feeling is that each patient responds as much to their emotional state as to their physical state. And you can't educate someone out of emotions.''

Adrian smiled at him. "Exactly, Dr. Truman. I've found that ninety percent of recovery has to do with the patient's attitude. And, doctors, please remember that ninety percent of the patient's attitude often has to do with her doctor.'' Again, that quiet laughter, and then the shifting of feet that meant everyone knew the session was over and it was time to go for morning coffee.

Bobby checked his wrist; the watch read 8:59:55. He grinned and said, "Well, chief, you've done it again. Another five seconds to nine.''

In a tight little knot, they all stepped over to the elevators. This morning, one came almost immediately, and the group applauded its arrival. As they crowded on, two or three people got on from the other side, and Bobby recognized that trim little blonde Sandy Heller, for six months the head of public relations. She was some go-getter, Bobby thought. The old head of PR used to drink his lunch and doze away the afternoons. She was altogether different. Wherever he went in the hospital, it seemed, there she was likely to be. And Cadman Memorial kept appearing in newspaper stories. And some of the labs and doctors had even been featured on Frank Field. Bobby took advantage of the crowd in the elevator to look her over carefully. Very good-looking woman, one who took good care of herself. Not like Corinne, lately. He remembered when Corinne used to primp with makeup and pick out her clothes with an eye to looking feminine and sexy. Oh, hell. Sandy Heller, now, she knew how to dress. She was tiny and slender, her blonde hair hanging in a shiny straight fall to her shoulders, her skin all pink and white. She was wearing a fuzzy blue sweater with a matching skirt, and the blue brought out the blue in her big eyes. She was smiling as always. She had the most cheerful manner. Not to mention the nicest, neatest, roundest tits that ever filled out a fuzzy

12

blue sweater. They'd have those pretty pink nipples like all the centerfold girls.

"Ms. Heller!" The harsh edge on Adrian's voice made Bobby jump.

But she didn't seem to notice; her smile was even broader as she sang out, "Good morning, Dr. Winter!"

"What are you doing here so early?"

"The early bird catches the worm. I'm at my desk by eight-thirty every morning, doctor. And I've just taken Phil here to photograph Mrs. Martinez and the twins. What a beautiful woman! What beautiful babies! What a beautiful story!"

"I trust you've had all the releases signed."

"Oh, yes. And she's so excited to think she and the babies might be in the *Daily News*. Oh, Dr. Winter, don't make that face. Most people just love being in the *Daily News* . . . especially someone like Mrs. Martinez."

"What does *that* mean? Just what is Mrs. Martinez like, Ms. Heller?"

"Oh, you know. An ordinary housewife who's probably never going to amount to anything special in the world. And here she is, with the third set of twins in four years. This is her big accomplishment, doctor. And what's even nicer is she's so *cute*. It's going to be a wonderful picture. I promise."

The woman knew her stuff; she had already proven that. Why Adrian was so edgy with her, so hostile—and he *was* hostile, although he was hiding it as best he could—was beyond understanding. Some men, of course, hated to see women do well at high executive levels. . . . But not Ade. After all, he'd been married for eighteen years to a professional woman; his first wife was Cadman's own Doctor Ellie.

"I just don't like having the patients bothered," Adrian said, his lips tight.

Sandy Heller smiled benignly upon him as the elevator doors slid open to the main floor. "Oh, Dr. Winter, she loved it, and so will everyone else in New York City. And so, might I add, will Mr. Del Bello!'' She wrinkled her nose at him and swung off down the hall.

"You can dress Kelly now,'' Eleanor Winter said. She patted the bare smooth rump of the little girl who lay belly down on the table, and smiled. "Hop down now, Kelly, so your mommy can put your clothes on.''

"I can dress my own self, 'cause I'm big now.'' She was a tiny mite, very pretty, wth light brown skin, huge green eyes, and a halo of black kinky hair. And, Eleanor thought, you'd never guess she had been born with anything wrong. She laughed and lifted Kelly down to the floor. "Okay, then, you get dressed.'' Turning to the child's mother, she said, "She's just fine.''

Corinne Truman frowned, and, not for the first time, Ellie thought how much Corinne had changed since she'd got all involved with the Reverend Ezekiel Clayton. She remembered Corinne from before she had married Bobby—when she had been the receptionist for Downstate's dean of students. Lord, that had to be seven, no eight years ago. She'd been so elegant then, even on her tiny salary, and gorgeous. She was still a beautiful woman—well, come on, she was only about thirty years old—but she looked tired and worn and, yes, middle-aged. Ellie looked carefully at Corinne, trying to figure out what it was that made her look so washed out and plain; and then she had it. Corinne, who used to giggle all the time and flirt with the whole world, was now grimly serious. It was as if her religion had stripped her of all her humor along with her makeup. That wasn't really fair. A lot of the ladies from the Reverend's church were happy, jolly souls, and he himself had a wonderful sense of humor. No, Corinne had done it to herself, for her own reasons. Guilt. It had begun when she miscarried that first baby. That was back when they were all at Downstate, and Bobby was a harassed medical student, and she and Ade were happily married— She automatically stopped herself, as she always did when she thought about her marriage. Corinne's pregnancy had been the reason Bobby married her. And then, when she had miscarried so suddenly, just a month after the wedding, Corinne had been depressed for quite a while. Bobby, silent and seething, had almost flunked out.

Well, that was all in the past now . . . all of it. And here was little Kelly, three years old and doing just fine, bright and effervescent, just as her mother used to be. Ellie sat at the small desk and pulled the nursery school form over. "I'm telling them at Community that this child has the very mildest form of spina bifida—hardly enough to call it that. Her left foot—"

"Yes, I noticed that. It turns. We've been praying over it, and I think it's better."

Ellie bit back the disparaging remarks that rose instantly to her lips and said, "I hope you also continue the exercises I showed you."

"Of course, Dr. Ellie. I may be Christian, but I respect your medicine . . ." Unspoken was the rest of the sentence, "So why can't you respect my religion."

Mildly, she answered, "Between the exercises and the prayers, Kelly should be dancing a jig before we know it." The foot wasn't bad at all; it might need some bracing again. It had been braced by Occupational Therapy in infancy, and the weakness showed only when Kelly was very fatigued. She was a lucky little girl; some of the spina bifida cases in the clinic were heartbreakers. She might have been born paralyzed from the waist down, without sensation, crippled for life. Instead, there had been that hairy patch at the base of the spine and a foot that turned out, and that was it. She scrawled her signature on the bottom of the form and wrote firmly, "All normal activities," underlining it.

"Mommy, Mommy, help me with the socks. I have them on the wrong feet."

Both women laughed, and Ellie noted that for the first time that morning, Corinne was looking her straight in the eye. "Here, sweetie pie," Corinne said, lifting the little girl onto her lap and squeezing her. "Lemme just switch those socks around for you." And she winked at Ellie. Ellie felt a pang; it was so reminiscent of the old Corinne, and look at her, in her plain, shapeless skirt and blouse, her hair oiled and pulled back with what looked like three hundred bobby pins, not a smidgen of makeup, not even a little lipstick on that lush mouth. Even the shoes looked heavy and middle-aged, laced up tight and with sensible heels. "Here, baby," Corinne burbled, "just snuggle up to Mommy, and we'll get those shoes on . . . See, Dr. Ellie? We got new shoes . . ."

And the little girl piped, "With bells on them!" She laughed and wriggled around on her mother's lap.

"Watch that, baby," Corinne said and remarked to Eleanor, "Not going to be much lap left pretty soon." And again she winked conspiratorially.

Ellie stared at her, while the words sank in. "What?" she said.

"Oh, Dr. Ellie, you know what I'm talking about!" A smile lit Corinne's face. "I'm pregnant. At long last, praise the Lord, I'm pregnant. Two whole months, so I know it's true!"

"Corinne! I thought we'd talked about this!"

"Well, Dr. Ellie, God's will be done."

Eleanor fixed the younger woman with a direct gaze. "Come on, now, Corinne. God didn't make you pregnant."

"Oh, Dr. Ellie, you know that's not what I meant." She flushed a little, but there was no look of embarrassment on her face. She looked . . . at peace. She looked contented. "It's just that if it's God's will that two people make a child, then they do; that's all."

"I thought you were on the pill."

"When you put yourself into Jesus' hands, Dr. Ellie, you don't have to do the pill."

"But *Corinne*!" Oh, lord, this was frustrating. She longed to shake the girl, shake her until her teeth rattled. Couldn't

she remember back even three years ago—pre-Reverend Zeke—
when the words *spina bifida* made her weep! When the
thought that her sweet little babe wasn't perfect had put her
into another depression? Couldn't she recall those weeks of
self-doubt and self-castigation, when she'd wept constantly
and asked all the doctors, over and over again, "Is my baby
really all right? Are you sure? Is she going to be retarded?"
Back then, they'd reassured her, of course, but it had been
carefully explained to her that the next child might not be so
lucky. With each pregnancy there was always a chance of
having another spina bifida baby. The damage could be so
mild you couldn't see it or so severe that the baby would have
no brain . . . or any number of defects in between. And here
she was, pregnant, and babbling about God's will. "Corinne,
for the love of—! Don't you remember what the genetic
counselor told you about risk factors? I mean—have you
really thought this through?"

"Kelly needs a brother. Or sister." The voice was sweet
and calm and unyielding. Eleanor recognized that particular
tone of voice; it was straight from the Reverend.

"I'm sure she does, but what I'm asking is whether you,
you and Bobby, Corinne, have thought of all the possibilities?"

"Oh, Bobby!" She waved a hand in dismissal.

"He *is* one of the parents, Corinne. You can't leave him
out of it."

"Oh, I told Bobby."

"And what does he think about it?"

Corinne smiled. "Oh, you know Bobby. It always takes
him a while to get used to anything. He didn't want this one,
but now? He dotes on her, just loves her to pieces."

"But this time, Corinne . . . Well, it's different, don't you
see?"

"Dr. Ellie, the way I look at it, a baby is a blessing from
God. It's not for us to say that one baby is worth keeping and
another you have to throw away."

"Oh, Corinne, that's not what we're talking about. We're
talking about risk factors." Ellie looked up into the pale

17

green eyes that used to reflect laughter and life but now were as blank and smooth as glass. She could not find the person behind those eyes, and it made her both sad and angry. As gently as she could manage, she added, "But what did Bobby *say*?"

"Oh—" A vague wave of the hand and another one of those empty, meaningless smiles. "Something about how we can't afford it. But that can't be so, Dr. Ellie. He's a doctor now. We have plenty. He's so overworked lately, he thinks everything's impossible. But I know better." She gave Kelly another hug and stood up, holding the child in her arms. "I want to thank you, Dr. Ellie, for seeing us before regular hours. Now Kelly can be on time for school. The first week is so important . . ."

Eleanor nodded and smiled and gave the little girl a hug. She saw them out, locking the door behind them. When they were safely gone she said, "Damn!" hoping none of her anger had showed. Corinne knew damn well what the risks were; she just wanted that pregnancy. Why in the world, Eleanor couldn't figure. There were so many lovely black babies for adoption, so pitifully many. As a doctor's wife, Corinne could give three or four of them a good home and love and the proper care and a wonderful life. Why in hell would she want to take this kind of chance? Against this kind of odds? And what was Bobby thinking of, allowing her to become pregnant again? Well, come to think of it, Corinne had said she wasn't taking the pill. She might have stopped without telling him. Eleanor had always had a sneaky feeling that her first pregnancy had been achieved the same way—without his knowledge, for sure, and maybe even with a lie.

Eleanor moved about restlessly, tidying up her examining room. The Corinne she remembered had been gorgeous and ambitious. She had wanted to be secure, wanted all the things that money could buy and all the things she thought money could buy—respect and social position and even happiness.

Too often in conversation Corinne would laugh and toss her head and say, "Well, I'm only a poor girl from Newark, but . . ." or "When you grow up poor, . . ." She used her poverty as an excuse and as a reason and as a plea for understanding.

Eleanor had overheard her in the ladies' room once, as she put on her makeup, talking to one of the other secretaries. "I don't really like it here," Corinne was saying, with that little laugh she had. "But I figure a hospital is the best place to work if you want to marry a doctor."

The other girl said, "You want to marry a doctor?"

"More than anything!" Corinne had said, her voice shaking a little with feeling.

"Why?" the other girl wanted to know. "Most of them are jerks . . . noses buried in their books all the time, and when they come up for air, they don't even know how to talk to a girl."

"You're talking about the med students," Corinne said coolly. "I know they're pretty bad. But in the end they become doctors." Her voice became dreamy. "You ever notice," she asked, "how all the doctors' wives have such pretty fur coats? How their hair is always done? The jewelry they have? If only I can marry a doctor, I'll never have to worry again. Never!" And then the two girls left.

Eleanor, bemused, had come out of the stall and washed her hands, smiling to herself and thinking how naive Corinne was. Didn't she realize that a doctor's wife, nine times out of ten, could not depend on him to be around when needed? Lord, hadn't she had two of their three daughters all by herself—because Ade was delivering someone else's baby? And as for a social life . . . Well, that was laughable. And sadly, even when you got your doctor husband to a party, it was almost bound to be with other physicians, so that you were never free of shop talk. She thought, I really ought to talk to that little girl. I'd tell her . . . "Look, Corinne, I'm a doctor myself, and *I* find it difficult to put up with a doctor-

19

husband. It's not true that when you marry a doctor, you never have to worry again. You have to worry plenty because doctors are only human . . . but they often don't believe that. They're taught to feel they're godlike, and then they think they have to be perfect. It's a royal pain in the ass." That's what I'd tell Corinne, if I ever got the chance.

But of course she never had got the chance. And by the end of that year—Bobby's first year as a med student—Corinne had latched right onto him, was cleaning his room and typing his papers, cooking his meals and probably warming his bed, as well. And Ellie had figured. All right, the girl's a throwback. Well, a lot of black women were not interested in being liberated. They wanted first to experience strong men and stability . . . as she'd been told so often by her black women friends. But having a baby was not necessarily the way to achieve a stable marriage, especially not when you were at risk!

Oh, lord! the stupidity of it. People just didn't like to believe that the odds were ever going to be against *them*. No, the percentages would apply to everyone else; they and they alone were going to escape. She and Ade had discussed that attitude plenty of times. There was so much denial in patients, so much, and it was a damn shame. People just seemed unable to believe in things that might possibly happen in the future. Nobody ever stopped smoking because there was a possibility of getting cancer twenty years hence. She sighed. It was really difficult, dealing in statistical chance. She thought to herself. If something had a five percent chance of happening, it didn't sound like much. But if you were in that five percent, it was one hundred percent for you. Damn it, why hadn't Ade spelled it out for her; he was her gynecologist! It was a gynecologist's responsibility to make sure a patient like Corinne understood completely what was going to happen!

She looked around the waiting room and then laughed at herself. While thinking about Corinne and this new pregnancy, she had straightened the files on the desk, moved the chairs into precise rows, and turned all the plants a quarter turn, even though the examining rooms were inside and had no windows. The Birth Defects Clinic, she decided wryly, was, if anything, rather too tidy. And as long as she was getting annoyed with Ade, she might as well get over to the cafeteria and yell at him in person. She checked her watch; it was 9:17. She had to move her tail, or she'd miss him. And, as it always did lately, her heart began to beat faster at the thought of seeing him. Stupid heart; didn't it realize they were long divorced? And worse, he had a beautiful wife, a little son, and a whole new life, and he only thought of her as a friend.

Nevertheless, she stopped off in the clinic ladies' room, splashed some water on her face and reached into her hand-bag for a comb and a lipstick. Not that either would do her much good. With curly hair like hers, you could never tell when, if ever, it had been combed. Most combs, in fact, broke in her hair. The lipstick she put on without really looking. She didn't have to look in a mirror. She had a wide mouth with full lips; she could feel the contours easily. And anyway, the last time she had looked—really looked—at herself in the mirror was when she had been fourteen and had realized that growing up wasn't going to change the snub nose or the freckles or the dimple in her chin. She had realized that she was forever going to be what she'd over-heard her mother say to one of her aunts, plain as a post. That was the fate of Eleanor Norris— to be plain for the rest of her life, and in California, where every other girl looked like a beauty queen. Well, she had decided, maybe it was better than being almost pretty and always trying to catch up. Fourteen was the year she had decided to become a doctor, too. Funny, she'd never before quite realized the juxtapo-sition of those two things.

Now she glanced at her reflection, a fleeting checkup not on her features but on the whole picture. And she saw, as always, a tall, slender woman—angular, even a bit bony, but definitely a female for all that—with a lot of shoulder-length, curling titian hair, wearing a spanking-clean white coat and underneath, the flash of an emerald-green silk dress. There was her stethoscope in one pocket and her beeper in the other. She was all set to play doctor. Wasn't it funny that that's how she thought of it? Well, back when she had been in private practice, there had been no white coat, no trappings. She didn't have to have them; her office was in her home. Of course, she reminded herself, back then she had been a pediatrician and could never have allowed herself the luxury of a silk dress . . . not when babies were likely to throw up, pee, or worse, all over her. And often had, she thought, laughing a little.

Still smiling to herself, she stepped out of the clinic, into the busy main corridor of Tower A. Nearly nine-thirty and the joint was jumping. Most of the clinics opened their doors at nine-thirty or ten, but the pediatric clinic started at eight-thirty, and its brightly painted waiting room was already jammed with mothers and babies and young children in various sizes. There were two elderly men in Ophthalmology & Otolaryngology, a scattering of patients in Arthritis. She marched smartly down the hall, just catching glimpses through the series of open doorways. There were several hellos as she went along, and she answered, smiling, without slowing down.

And then, across the hall, a rich bass voice, absolutely unselfconscious and very loud, "Dr. Winter! Dr. Ellie, in fact. The very person I had hoped in my heart to encounter this morning!" Her heart sank. It was the Reverend Ezekiel R. Clayton himself, larger than life because the Reverend Zeke *was* larger than life. And on the rampage, it looked like, because otherwise, why would he be here so early in the morning? It wasn't a board meeting day.

He crossed to her and stood towering over her like an avenging angel. The Rev, as he was known throughout the neighborhood, was somewhat over six and a half feet tall and seemed equally wide. He was medium brown, with a large head, a halo of Afro-styled graying hair, and a flamboyant moustache to match. He always wore impeccable three-piece suits in pale fawn or pearl gray with a rather gaudy gold cross on a chain. Most important, the Rev had what you could only call presence. The moment he walked into a room, everyone in the vicinity looked smaller, paler, and less important.

He was pastor of the All Saints Tabernacle, a huge edifice, once a major synagogue, situated about three blocks to the east of the hospital. All Saints was a plain, square stone building, with only a few high round windows and a simple wooden doorway, set well back from the street. Two perfect square lawns of Kentucky bluegrass were separated by a walk made of white pebbles. The building looked rather incongruous, sitting by itself at the edge of Tillary Houses, a low-income city housing project of unrelenting drabness whose brick walls were being slowly covered with garish, painted graffiti. But nobody ever touched the tabernacle; its pale gray walls remained pristine, and the twin patches of lawn never felt so much as a footstep. Reverend Clayton was a power in his neighborhood. As often happened, he had found during the past five years that he was spending less and less of his time at religion and more and more at politics.

"Good morning, reverend," Ellie said, allowing her hand to be enfolded and squeezed. "Dare I ask what brings you here?" She grinned at him; actually, she liked the Rev. He could be a royal pain, but his community badly needed him to badger the local government, the precinct, the schools, the neighborhood hospital. And badger he did.

One large hand floated down from somewhere above her and came to rest gently on her shoulder. "The teenage mothers," he said and smiled broadly at her grimace. "I know, Dr. Ellie, I know we are at odds on the subject of teenaged pregnancy. But I cannot, you understand, allow anything that smacks of genocide—not on the very perimeters of my congregation." He sobered, and his dark, dark eyes, set deep into his head, glittered down at her. "We of the true Christian faith do not, in any case, believe in murder. Ah, excuse me, doctor, abortion is your word . . ."

Inwardly sighing, Ellie kept the tone of her voice friendly. "Reverend Clayton, I know that Dr. Blumenfeld doesn't push abortion to the girls in the clinic. And I wish I had time to discuss this with you this morning, but I have a meeting . . ." Meeting, she hooted silently at herself. She wanted only to bump accidentally on purpose into Ade in the cafeteria. "Tell you what, though. The clinic doesn't have hours until the afternoon, and someone else is taking my rounds. Can you come by at ten-thirty?"

"Expect me, dear doctor!" he boomed and smoothly moved away, heading for the little room at the very end of the corridor where Ted Blumenfeld had finally managed to place the Teenage Pregnancy Clinic. Poor Ted! So beleaguered on all sides. All he wanted was to help these girls. He wasn't trying to go against God, as the antiabortionists liked to say; he wasn't trying to commit genocide, as the black community hollered; he wasn't trying to encourage sexual behavior in young girls and destroy the traditional family, as the more conservative elements of the board tended to believe. He was caring for girls who were having babies when they were still babies themselves! He smiled at them, stuffed them with vitamins, suggested options, advised them to finish school . . . and still *everyone* was after him!

Ellie turned the corner by the Teenage Pregnancy Clinic, smiling a bit as the Rev's dulcet tones came floating right through the closed door. Then the automatic doors into the main building whooshed open and she hurried on, determined not to be stopped. She really wanted to see Adrian this morning; well, she had to, didn't she? She had to talk to him about Corinne. If she was honest with herself, and she prided herself that she always tried to be, she would admit that if she wanted to see him about a patient, she could call him any time during the day. She knew his extension, knew it by heart: 6584. His secretary would take the message. But professional consultation was not the reason she stood at the entrance to the cafeteria, craning to see down the length of the huge room, trying to spot a head of thick, prematurely gray hair.

She ought to be ashamed of herself, the number of times each week she just happened to accidentally meet him here. Accidentally! That was a laugh. She knew damn well when he went on rounds and when he had his hours; and she knew damn well he'd be in the cafeteria for that second cup of coffee between nine and nine-thirty come hell or high water. She hadn't been married to the man for sixteen years without knowing his habits, and he always had needed another shot of caffeine an hour or two after he got up and got going. When they had been students together, she used to bring him that second cup, in a paper carton from Rose & Sol's Luncheonette. Now, of course, it was all different. She fought off her disappointment; he was nowhere to be seen. She enjoyed these morning chats with him; more than that, she hungered for them. Funny, after the divorce—God, could it be six years already?—she had gone to a lot of trouble pretending she felt all friendly and amicable when inwardly she was a seething mass of hurt, bewilderment, and rage. She felt betrayed; she had had no idea he was being unfaithful to her, none at all. She had no warning. She had had no inkling, no little *frisson* of suspicion. Their marriage had been *ideal*—everyone said so. Two doctors, living together, sharing a life, three kids, working at the same kind of work, understanding each other and caring about each other! It just wasn't fair, that at the age of forty, with a whole new career just ahead of her, he should leave her so alone with three daughters to take care of!

For a long, long time after the divorce, she had put on a mask of civility, had pretended to be good friends. How it had hurt even to see him. Luckily, he'd then left Downstate, where she had been studying, and come here; so for a while she didn't have to see him on a daily basis. But the rage, the anger, the resentment was all in the past. Since she'd come to Cadman to head up the Birth Defects Clinic, they had been forced into each other's company. At first it had been difficult;

almost impossible. But once she accustomed herself to seeing him not as her husband, she found that all the old good stuff was still operating. And within the past six months or so, they had become once more the close friends they'd been even before their marriage, in med school. More and more, she had come to look forward to these morning meetings, which she knew damn well were not by chance. Sometimes, when she allowed herself, she even wondered whether he, too—

Chapter 2

A*DRIAN* W*INTER STRODE* rapidly down the hall toward the cafeteria, gritting his teeth but trying to smile. Sandy Heller of PR—the bitch—wasn't that important, not to him and not to the hospital and certainly not in the greater scheme of things. But dammit, she was part of that whole crew, those so-called business-oriented professionals, who had come into Cadman Memorial and got rid of Nate Levinson. Professionals, they called themselves. Professional killers was more like it. Nate was one of the best doctors ever, and he'd run Cadman for ten years and made it a place where sick people, rich or poor, knew they'd be treated with skill and heart. Rich or poor, you got only the best when Nate Levinson was in charge. Of course, that's when the hospital was very small . . . 150 beds, a typical community hospital, sometimes not totally up-to-date, sometimes not totally efficient. But it had always been totally committed to the patients. That's what medicine was all about, dammit. These new people had no medical background at all. A bunch of accountants and public relations experts. Ever since the board voted to build the two towers, beside the original Greek Revival building, ever since the first one opened, things had begun to change. Suddenly, good care wasn't enough. Suddenly, it was all computers and cost effectiveness and profit margins. And suddenly it wasn't enough to have a wonderful doctor as the head honcho. No, Nate was too old, they said. Nate was too old-fashioned. And so they just pushed him aside—semiretirement, they called it. And Nate hadn't been the same since. A feisty little fighter had been changed into a bewildered, depressed old man.

Dammit, he *hated* these politics. All during rounds that morning, his mind had not really been there. That wasn't right; it wasn't fair to the patients, and it wasn't fair to the residents. But he had a growing feeling that he was being eased out of the mainstream in this hospital. Nothing he could really put a finger on, not yet. But little details, little things. He'd given the keynote speech at the Brooklyn Community Dinner Dance every year for the past five years. He had been considered, next to Nate, of course, who had been chief of staff until they dumped him, the hospital spokesman. And here it was, the beginning of October, and nothing had been said about the speech. It was damned embarrassing, making him ask. Well, if he was going to be prepared, he'd just have to, that was all. But he hated it. That wasn't the way things used to be run around here!

Every time he said that to Ellie, of course, she laughed at him and said he sounded like a crochety old man instead of someone in the prime of his life. Was forty-six the prime of a man's life? Some prime, with this nagging nasty sickness in the pit of his stomach all the time. Ellie was the one who had said, "Look, sweetie pie, the old order changeth. I'm not so sure *I* love it, either, but the way I see it, you'd better changeth or leaveth. And if you have to kowtow a little to Hank Del Bello and say, 'Excuse me, sir, but am I to make the keynote speech?' well, you'll just have to."

Okay, he'd made up his mind. He'd go to Del Bello, who was the hospital administrator and in charge, and he'd find out what the hell was going on. Today was the day. He was sick and tired of worrying about it, wondering what it all meant, and finding his attention drifting during rounds. Of course, a lot of what he had to do on rounds didn't require his total attention, and thank God for Bobby Truman, who could run Ob/Gyn almost by himself now and who was in any case a wonderful doctor and a terrific right-hand man. But that didn't make it right. If there was anything he learned from his years with Nate Levinson, it was that concentration was all. You couldn't miss *anything*. Some patient might be giving you the subtlest possible signals that something was wrong, and if your mind was wandering—it was unthinkable. God knows, doctors were trained to take on enough life-and-death responsibility . . . too much, he thought. But when you made a *mistake*—oh, Christ, you couldn't live with yourself.

"Ade! Who are you planning to murder?"

He pulled up short, blinking a little, like a man emerging from a dark tunnel. Standing directly in front of him, her stocky body blocking his way, was Con Scofield, one of the few old-timers left around here and his favorite nurse. She'd worked Ob/Gyn for years, but she was head nurse in the Intensive Care Unit now. He missed Con on his service; she was the old-style nurse—a bit gruff, a bit tough, but thorough, observant, as good as a lot of doctors. And better than some, come to think of it.

"Sorry, Con. I was a million miles away. And angry, probably. Actually, I was thinking about Nate."

Con made a face and put a hand on his arm. "Yeah. Still makes me mad, too. The nerve of those characters, just throwing a good man into the garbage! Hospital boards!" Now her freckled face changed expression, from annoyance to concern. "Has anything happened to him?"

Adrian smiled down at her. Con Scofield was five feet ten, and he was one of the few men at the hospital who could look down at her. In the old days, he'd teased her that this was why she liked him. Not a pretty woman, no, poor Con, with her carrot-colored frizzy hair, her pale eyes, and round, homely face. But she was smart, and she was good, and he knew damn well that somewhere back in the dim mists of Cadman Memorial history, back when he had been a resident, something had happened between Nate and Con Scofield. They were a ludicrous-looking couple: God, Nate couldn't be more than five feet five, and some of the wags had allowed as how Con outweighed him, outsmoked him, outcursed him, and had more muscles besides. But he'd never joined in that joking. He had seen the difference it made in Nate. Something at home had been saddening the older doctor, had bowed his shoulders, and had clouded his bright blue eyes. And then he'd brightened and begun to laugh again. Who cared that he and homely Con Scofield both took a week off at the same time and came back looking smug and pleased and happy? When Nate fixed his home life up, Con suddenly went to Beth Israel for two years, and everyone knew the romance was over.

It occurred to him that maybe Nate could use some cheering up from Con right now. Why not? What could be better for a discouraged man than ministrations from an old love?

"No, no, nothing more than usual . . . Have you spoken to him lately, Con?" The nurse shook her head. "Well, he's down; that's the main thing. He's in a depressed state. I can't seem to shake him out of it. Maybe if you—"

She held up a hand and gave him a steady look. "Quit playing Cupid, Ade; you don't look good in a bow and arrow. Nate and I are both too old now, and besides— No, it wouldn't be a good idea; it really wouldn't. He might . . . misunderstand." Then she shook her head and hit him lightly on the arm with her fist. "And anyway, you almost made me forget what I wanted to talk to you about. I want your ear."

"You've got it, Con. What's the problem?"

"That Heller babe!"

"So what else is new? I just bumped into her on the elevator, all teeth and girlish charm. The woman's a viper, I'm sure of it. She's evil."

"Oh, come now, Ade, *evil*? Just pushy, *I* think. Well, you can't blame an ambitious woman for pushing herself; I mean, it's the only way a woman has of getting ahead in this man's world. You know that as well as I do, Ade. But she's getting to be a problem to me; she's pushing into places she's got no business in.''

He was instantly on the alert. "Not Intensive Care!" The ICU—Intensive Care Unit—was sequestered in a corner of the second floor, its walls superthick and soundproofed. You had to make your way through two sets of nurses and a guard, and you had to have a damn good reason for being there. Patients in the ICU were, of course, critically ill. Otherwise, they wouldn't be there. And, dammit, every single person in Cadman Memorial knew enough not to go there unless they had to! Even the cleaners crept around wearing bedroom slippers and not saying a word.

"She's been up there, all right. I keep telling her, 'Ms Heller, the ICU is full of stories, but they ain't printable until the people are *out* of the ICU.' But she doesn't get it, Ade. She just widens her eyes and says that Mr. Del Bello has asked her to get more human interest stories and the ICU is, get this, Ade, 'full of the human struggle to defeat death'!'' She gave a short humorless laugh. "Can you beat that? I told her that the only struggle I had was to keep sensation seekers the hell away from my patients and their families.''

Adrian laughed. "Good girl, Con. But tell me, why is she suddenly a thorn in your side?''

"Why else? She thinks she smells a story. And . . . you know what? She's right. But good God, Ade, I can't let her do it!''

Adrian thought a moment, visualizing the ICU with its eight beds, each one separated from the other by smoked-glass partitions; visualizing Suzie Palko lying there, so still. Just a few weeks ago, she had been totally alive, lively and quick and bright, a terrific scrub nurse. And then remembering that dark and rainy day, they called and told him she'd been in a terrible accident on the BQE. She had been thrown from a motorcycle and was in labor. She had been in only her fourth month, and she'd been so happy about this pregnancy,

31

happy as only a healthy young woman can be who looks forward to a life full of good things.

"It *is* Suzie you're talking about?" he said aloud.

"Of course, that poor child. Oh, Adrian, and that sweet boy, that Brian, he's so pitiful. I can't understand how they do it, tear around eighty miles an hour on a little bike! God! Oh, well, too late for that kind of talk . . ." She heaved a great sigh. "What is it, Adrian? Am I getting old? I find this case so hard to take. I'm constantly fighting the tears. Me fighting tears! But it's terrible up there. She hates it. She wants to die. If you talk to her, she says, 'Why are you feeding me? Why are you giving me medication? Let me die.' And I have to say, 'Suzie, you're a nurse; you know I'm not going to let you die. And too many people love you.' " Her voice was becoming quite agitated, although professional that she was, she never raised it. Adrian put a comforting hand on her shoulder. Con had been heading up the ICU nurses for three years now, and maybe it was time for a change. Burn-out was common up there among the nurses; so many of the patients died.

"And then there's Brian. He comes in, Ade, and he pulls up a chair, and he sits close to her and puts a big hand on her hair and sits there quietly. Hour after hour. They don't talk much, but there's such love there, Ade, such love! It's getting so I can hardly bear it. Just sits there with his hand on Suzie's hair . . ." She grimaced, and Adrian had a fleeting, panicked thought that she was going to break down. Yes, she needed to get away for a while; he'd have to talk to her about it soon.

"And here comes Heller," Con went on, indignant. "Labeling their suffering a human interest story. Human interest!" She sniffed. "So I went to Del Bello—I'm coming from there now—and I told him. Well, of course, I didn't talk to him the way I'm talking to you, Ade, but I told him in my best head-nurse voice that the patients in the ICU simply could not be disturbed. And when he gave me an argument, I said, 'Doctors' orders.' And do you know—that didn't mean a thing to him! 'Oh,' he says, sweet as pie, 'I'm sure we can get the doctors to agree to having just one picture taken . . . especially if it means a story in the *New York Times* or something equally significant.' Well! I said to him, I said, 'Mr. Del Bello, the only thing of significance in the ICU,' I said, 'is the comfort and care of my patients.' And he just laughed, Ade. He just laughed and said, 'Oh, Nurse Scofield, you are wonderful. We'll have to do a story on *you*!' Well!'' And Con looked positively scandalized. "I just left. Obviously, the man doesn't know diddly squat about care! And if you can't get action from the hospital administrator, then something's badly wrong around here!''

"Let's give the administration a little more time," Adrian said, not meaning a word.

Con laughed. "Never mind. I guess I just needed to blow off steam. Anyway, just talking about it has helped me make up my mind. Ms. Heller is not getting near Suzie or Brian. She's not doing any of her so-called human interest garbage with *them*—not while I'm head nurse! They deserve their privacy!''

"You're right, Con," Adrian said. But, having spoken her piece, she was already trotting down the hall, intent on the next item of business.

Adrian stood still for a moment, not wanting, really, to go to Hank Del Bello's office, not wanting to ask anything of him. The scene Con had just had with him was, he thought, pretty typical. Smooth and handsome, Henry Del Bello always made Adrian think of the hit man in a gangster movie: the one who goes home to a lovely wife and kids and the semblance of a normal life but is heartless underneath the slick exterior. And yet there was no reason at all to think this. Perhaps because he was good-looking and Italian? But no, it wasn't that; there was just something swinish about him.

Then he shook himself mentally and continued walking. The passageway was becoming more crowded as the secretaries and technicians came in to work, and he found himself saying good morning over and over again. But he didn't stop. He had to do this and do it quickly, or he'd change his mind.

33

Nate Levinson's office, he recalled with nostalgia, had been threadbare, messy, with piles of journals overflowing the tables and shelves onto the shabby oriental carpet. It had also always smelled faintly of cigar smoke. But it had been a comfortable place to drop by, to lean back in one of the four leather armchairs, and to discuss whatever concerned you. And it had been right in the middle of the building, too, its door facing you as you came in the main entrance, inviting you in.

Hank Del Bello had chosen a corner suite of three rooms. One was his office, one served as a conference room, and the other held his secretary and *her* secretary. It was still in the old building—what Adrian and most of the staff thought of as the *real* building, the *main* building—but off the beaten track and just the least bit hard to find for a stranger.

Well, I'm not a stranger, Adrian thought belligerently, rounding the corner and coming face-to-face with the secretary, an elegant black woman with a frozen face. The entire suite had been carpeted in thick, bright blue shag, with black leather furniture, chrome-and-white desks and files, and a lot of blobby-looking ''modern'' paintings and posters on the walls. Far too bright for his personal taste, and, he thought, it's all flash.

He had opened his mouth to say he'd like to see Del Bello when the door to the administrator's personal office opened. There, pausing in the doorway, deeply engrossed in their conversation, were Hank Del Bello and Dr. Art Schuster. Adrian's stomach muscles tightened involuntarily. Art Schuster—again! Again, Art Schuster with Del Bello! As he watched, Del Bello leaned close to Art, said something in a low voice, and they both laughed. It was the picture of chummy collaboration, and it immediately triggered his adrenals. Dammit! It wasn't his imagination. The post of chief of staff had been empty since Nate's so-called retirement— six months now—and it had been expected for years that he, Adrian Winter, was next in line. Once Nate had left, he'd had doubts—perhaps he'd only been the heir to Nate's particular throne—but Del Bello had called him in, chatted him up, and had assured him that no big changes would be made in the near future. Of course, nothing had been said about his taking the position, either, but he had been willing to bide his time and wait until the new administration shook itself down. Christ, he deserved the job! He knew this hospital as well as any physician in it and better than most. He'd been Nate's protégé since medical school. And if he now was beaten out by Art Schuster, the hospital's worst doctor . . . and the world's worst husband, as Etta Schuster had reason to know.

Then both men in the doorway caught sight of him and broke off in mid-sentence. "Adrian!" Del Bello boomed into the sudden dead silence. "Did you want to see me!"

"Yes, if you have a minute." Dammit, his heart was hammering like a schoolboy's.

"Well, actually—" Del Bello glanced at his heavy gold wristwatch and flashed him another broad white smile. "Could it wait . . . ? I mean, I can squeeze you in right now if it's something urgent."

"It'll keep," Adrian said. He gave a cool nod to Art, who looked uneasy, kind of guilty, he thought. Something was up, and that something was not to the benefit of Adrian Maxwell Winter, M.D., he was certain. Dammit! He didn't have time for this sort of thing. He didn't have time to worry and wonder about the look on Art Schuster's face, for Christ's sake! In the old days, there wasn't any of this nonsense. The hospital was for the patients, and it was run by doctors, and as far as he was concerned, all this other stuff was just so much bullshit.

"Good!" Del Bello said. The man had a marvelous voice—you had to give him that—deep and rich and powerful. "Talk to Nancy; she'll pencil you in."

"Pencil me in?" He was not going to dignify that phony executive jargon by understanding it.

"She'll schedule an appointment for you." Very patient, very superior.

"Forget it," Adrian said. "I'm pretty busy myself. I'll

catch you when I have a minute.'' He whirled and walked away, instantly regretting his impulse. Goddam childish, that's what it was. But the sight of the two of them standing shoulder to shoulder, giving him those condescending smiles, had just been too much. He'd bet now that Adrian Winter wouldn't be giving the keynote address that year; and what else that meant, he didn't really want to think about.

What he needed, more than anything else at that moment, was to get to the cafeteria, get himself a cup of coffee, and talk to his first wife. And never mind why that was so, either! He felt badly enough about Leslie and the baby; he knew he'd been impossible lately, coming home late, preoccupied and silent, too exhausted to even play with his little boy—or pay proper attention to his beautiful young wife. Anyone would tell him he was crazy to ignore his family and turn to Ellie for comfort. Maybe he was, just a little. He certainly felt disoriented. ''Pencil me in!'' he muttered to himself. Not only was it cant; it also seemed to say he could easily be erased. Too bad the cafeteria didn't offer anything stronger than the world's blackest coffee.

''Morning, Ellie.'' Even the sound of his voice gave her a strange giddy feeling. She damped down a surge of joy—she must not allow her feelings to get the better of her—and was able to turn to him with an impersonal smile.

''Good morning yourself, Adrian. A little late this morning, aren't you?'' She could have bitten her tongue. She might as well announce, ''I come here every morning looking for you.''

He grinned down at her. ''Wrong. I was already here for my breakfast and was finished by nine-seventeen. I was in Ted's clinic, helping him deal with our friend the Reverend—fat lot of good any mere human being can do with that man!—when I saw you buzz by. Well, I came right after you . . .''

To her dismay, she felt herself flushing. ''Oh, Ade—!''

He kept smiling. ''Well, it was the perfect excuse to get

away from the Rev. 'Excuse me,' I said, 'but there goes my ex . . . and I've got to talk to her about college tuitions.' "

And now she had to drop her eyes because, dammit, she'd been hoping . . . Hoping what, dope? Hoping beyond hope that he had come running after her because he— Well, never mind. There was no fool like an old fool.

"Yes, well, *I'm* not going to escape so easily. I have a date at ten-thirty for him to harangue me about Ted's clinic . . . and abortion."

"Oh, hell," Adrian said, running his hands through his mop of hair—a habit he had when thinking hard. "Send him to me if he wants to fuss about abortion. *I'm* the abortion expert."

"I know, I know, but he bumped into *me* this morning. And besides, you know I'm always counseling the at-risk mothers not to get pregnant, and if they do, to think about abortion. And he doesn't want *anyone* to think about it, not even someone who's about to have her fourth son with muscular dystrophy, not even someone who's—"

He put his hand on her shoulder and said, "I know, I know. Let's not waste our time together hassling about the Rev."

Dammit, she wished he would stop saying those things, those warm little comments that sounded so personal and probably didn't mean a damn thing. He never used to do that, when they first began meeting here. She gave him one of her best brilliant smiles and said lightly, "What's this about tuition?"

"Oh, hell, Ellie, it was just an excuse. I sent it, I sent it. Both Sonya and Paulie are bought and paid for. Let's get some coffee and sit down, o.k.?"

They walked the entire length of the room together, his hand under her elbow. She was so aware of his hand, too damn aware. She wished he would take it away; no, scratch that. She wished it meant something. She wished she would grow up. It was ludicrous for her to be mooning this way over a married man with a three-year-old child who incidentally happened to be her ex-husband. It was laughable! It was lunacy! Not to mention the fact that she was going out with a perfectly lovely man of whom she was terribly fond and with whom she had a simply delightful relationship.

The food lines were very long this morning. "You go find us a place to sit," Adrian said, "and I'll get the coffee. Deal?"

"Are you paying?"

He laughed. "I think I can handle that. Although maybe not for long." She recognized a certain tightness in his voice that told her he really meant something by that. It wasn't just a throwaway gag line. She'd be sure to ask him about it when they sat down.

She watched him walk away, this man who had been her friend and her lover and her husband for so many years and who was now lost to her. God, he was a good-looking guy. It wasn't just her infatuation; he really was. Not handsome, exactly; his jaw was too long and his mouth too wide. To be utterly frank, he was lantern-jawed and too gaunt by far . . . especially lately. But there was something very appealing about him. All you had to do was ask any of his patients; they all thought he was a cross between Redford and Newman, only better. She watched his long stride and the big shoulders and thought, He looks powerful, that's it. The face with the strong features, the frank creases, the crinkles around the eyes, spoke of inner strength and confidence. But, as she well knew, it was the contrast between the prominent bones of his face, the rawboned, almost tough look of him; and those eyes . . . Adrian had large bright blue eyes with long thick eyelashes and long heavy lids. His eyes were soft and kind and full of the sweetness of nature that was the Adrian she'd always loved.

And there she went again—listing all his attributes, for all the world like a teenager in love. God, it was a good thing nobody could read her mind, or she'd be out of Cadman Memorial in a minute. Who could trust their ill child to a pediatric neurologist whose secret thoughts revolved around her unrequited love? If her patients' parents ever got an inkling—! They came to her with impaired children, with terrible problems, and she was good with them. She knew she was good with them. Because she was honest without being brutal. Because she always told the truth, and they knew it, and they trusted her. Funny . . . this attribute, which gave her such a good reputation as a doctor, had always got her into trouble in her personal life.

She threaded her way through the tables, looking for one that was empty, waving to some nurses she knew and shaking her head at a gestured invitation from the new guy in the Neurology department whose name kept escaping her. He seemed like a nice person, but really she wanted to talk to Ade alone. There was Corinne to discuss. Corinne should immediately get a reading on her proteinase B level, and if it turned out to be elevated—well, abortion was the only answer for her. Corinne and Bobby shouldn't be having their own children—not after their lucky escape with Kelly. And my God, Bobby Truman was still a resident. Okay, he was in his last year, but he kept talking about working with poor blacks, and it took a load of money to take care of a spina bifida case. And time! And what about Kelly? What a mess! And it all could have been prevented by a little judicious tube tying, or at least, at the very least, an IUD. A woman could forget to take the pill and forget to put in the diaphragm, but there was no way not to use the IUD. There it was, and there it stayed, and if any little Freudian forgetfulness was in play, it just wouldn't work. Dammit, why hadn't Ade insisted? He usually took great pains with patients who were at risk. Dammit. He was one of the few guys around who really *cared* . . . and Corinne was someone he knew personally, too!

Ah, there was an empty table, covered with debris from six breakfasts. Without really thinking, she pushed the litter into a pile, dumped it all on a tray, and put the tray on the window ledge where one of the busboys could get it. It was a shame to have this kind of mess in one of the few public spaces in the hospital; but hell, when you had everyone—doctors, staff, visitors, ambulatory patients, salesmen—coming into the same place to eat, maybe it was impossible to keep up with the cleanup chores. She took a clean paper napkin and mopped the table, laughing at herself for being the good little housewife she had never been at home.

"What's so funny?" Ade put down two containers of coffee and a largish square object, wrapped in waxed paper.

"Oh, Ade, a bran muffin! How lovely!" In spite of herself, she was touched by his remembering. Nonsensical, wasn't it, when they'd been married for sixteen years and she'd had a bran muffin every single morning. But still, it was so thoughtful.

Taking a big bite of the warm buttery muffin, she smiled at him and said, "I wish you hadn't bought this."

"Why not? It's your favorite, isn't it?"

"The point is, you're not my favorite at this moment . . ." She was secretly delighted to see his face fall. "I don't want to be softened up, because I have a few harsh words to say."

"Jesus, Ellie, not you, too!"

There it was again, that little hint of something awry. "What do you mean?"

He waved his hand impatiently. "Agh, never mind. You go first. Do your worst; I'll try to bear up like a man."

"Don't charm me, Ade Winter. It won't work. Remember . . . I know you, and I'm immune. It's Corinne." She watched his face, alert for any expression that might tell her what she knew. It stayed bland, expectant. "Corinne," she repeated. "She's pregnant."

"Yes, I know. And—?"

"Oh, come on, Ade . . . *and*? You really have to ask? You know damn well, and what! She's one woman who shouldn't be pregnant at all, and you know it."

"Ellie! Ellie! I didn't make her pregnant!"

"Oh, didn't you? Well, in my humble opinion, you're damn well an accessory before the fact! Where was her IUD? You *know* what this can mean."

He sighed and took a gulp of his coffee. "I know. I tried; you know damn well I tried. You've talked with her recently—"

"Not half an hour ago."

"Okay then, Ellie, you saw who I've been dealing with. You think this new Corinne, this so-called real Christian, this born-again, sure-of-her-notions Corinne was going to allow an IUD in her body? Hasn't she given you the 'body is a holy vessel' routine?" His voice cracked just a little, a sign she knew signified anger he didn't want to display.

"Why didn't you have Bobby come in with her? He's not born again, is he?"

Adrian's lips tightened. "Don't you think I thought of that? Yes, they both came in. Bobby's at his wits' end with her . . . she's so calm and so certain she's right and so removed from reality. Christ, Ellie, I tried; I really did. Bobby and I both talked until we were blue; we gave her every argument in the book. And you know what she said? She smiled upon us as if we were two small children, and she said in her sweetest voice, "Now don't you men gang up on me. I'm putting my trust in the Lord and my life into Jesus' hands.' Well, we gave her all our patience; we didn't scoff. But we *did* tell her she had to take the pill—which would be noninvasive . . . And she agreed, Ellie; she agreed! Is it my fault she lied?"

"Oh, Ade, there must have been *something* you could do!"

To her amazement, he erupted at her. "Jesus Christ, Eleanor, who do you think I am, anyway? The whole world thinks doctors have got all the answers . . . but you're a doctor yourself. You ought to know better."

"I wasn't—"

"Listen, you think Corinne Truman is my only patient? You think even that she has the worst problem I have to deal with? Right now I have three cases with such high blood pressure—! Two of them are her church sisters, in fact! But at least they listen to me. They *take* their medication, and they follow their diets. They have a chance. I have an Rh I'm watching and a probable toxemia. I've got to measure out my

41

energy, and frankly, Ellie, I'm going to save the best part of it for those patients who will comply, goddamit! I haven't got unlimited time, and as far as I can see, trying to convince Corinne Truman to obey orders right now is a goddam waste of time!''

"I'm shocked. I never thought I'd hear you talk this way."

"What goddamn way!"

"To hear you putting a premium on *compliance*? You? You who are one of our biggest advocates of understanding patients' feelings? Oh, Ade, come on!''

He leaned across the table, fixing her with his gaze, his eyes dark and stormy. "You come on, Eleanor. We *all* put a premium, as you so delicately put it, on compliance. We can't take care of patients without it. And Corinne is just the proof!''

"Oh, fine," she said, willing herself not to drop her eyes, because doing so somehow would mean losing. "And what about this baby of hers? Doesn't *it* count?''

Adrian now leaned back and drew in a deep breath. "Okay, that's true," he said. "But now it's too late. So tell me, Ellie, have you managed to talk her into an abortion? Have you managed to even get her to the genetic counselor? No, of course not!''

"Are you telling me we're all going to have to sit back and wait for Corinne to give birth? And if it's hydrocephalic, an L-4, club-footed, and without a chance at normal life . . . you guys in the Neonatal Nursery will do your damndest to keep it alive, no matter what, put it on the respirator and turn its lungs into cardboard, operate on it, force it to live, and then who gets to take care of it? Me!''

"Whoa up there, Ellie." His eyes glittered, and his voice was totally icy; no hiding of his irritation this time, and her heart sank. She hadn't wanted to go quite this far. "*You* don't get to take care of it. Corinne does, remember? You're only the doctor; you're not the mother. No, nor God Almighty!''

And then, quickly, as if he, too, were afraid of treading on this particular ground, he added, "Look, I can't tell my patients when to make love or how to do it. I'm an obstetrician. My job is to take care of that fetus and its mother, to do my best to help create an optimum pregnancy, a safe delivery, and if all goes well, a healthy baby. My job is to keep life going. That's it, Ellie; it's all there in the Hippocratic Oath."

"Oh, screw the Hippocratic Oath! You know Hippocrates never dreamed of the technology we have at hand."

"Well, Ellie, we have to use the technology we have at hand; we can't turn our backs on it."

She took a deep breath. She longed to scream at him, to have him come into her clinic and see the results of using heroic measures to save—to salvage, because salvage was the term neonatalists used—these two-pound fetuses. Brain damaged, crippled, some of them without even the capacity to know who they were. Her heart was hammering with her anger and frustration. But no. She hadn't sought him out in order to do battle on this old battleground. She had to change the subject; she didn't like seeing him look so grim and, yes, disapproving.

"Agh," Adrian said, wiping all emotion from his face and smiling at her. "What are we fighting about? It's stupid. First of all, we aren't going to change Corinne at this table. We aren't going to change anything at this table. The way I feel about this place, nothing's ever going to change!"

Oh, dear. "What's wrong, Ade? I caught some comment of yours before. What's happening?"

His hands balled into fists on the table, and almost instantly, as if to hide his feelings, he put them in his lap.

"You'll laugh at me again!" He sounded like a hurt child, and she immediately leaned toward him and put her hand on his arm. "No, no, Ade. I won't. Really, I won't. I'm concerned. What *is* it?"

"Well . . . the keynote speech."

She waited. "Yes?"

"Well, dammit, Ellie, it's only a couple of weeks away,

43

and nothing's been said about my speech. I'm beginning to think I won't be making that speech."

"Oh, Ade, that can't be so. You've done it for years now. That spot on the evening's agenda has your name engraved on it."

His eyes moved nervously away from hers. "Not in Del Bello's book. Dammit, when he first took over, he called us all in, every chief of service, and promised—he *promised*, Ellie—that he wasn't going to make any major changes for another two years. Hunh! I should have known better than to believe him. He's nothing but an accountant."

"Adrian! You can't mean it's a major change if you don't make the speech to the community dinner dance!"

"Christ, that does sound small, doesn't it? But the speech itself doesn't matter. I mean, come on, the community board isn't going to fade away if Adrian Winter doesn't make a speech once a year. But it's . . . symbolic, Ellie. Art Schuster's the fair-haired boy now. Wait a minute, wait a minute . . . I know the antagonism between me and Art goes back a long way, and you know damn well why I don't like him, and it doesn't have anything to do with his popularity as a speaker or as a fund-raiser. Honestly, Ellie, my personal feelings about Art have nothing to do with this . . . well, almost nothing." He tried for a grin, which didn't quite make it, and her heart turned over. He was deeply bothered; she could see that now.

He went on. "I'm being shut out, that's all. I'm being forced out, in the slimiest kind of way. Jesus, Ellie, you can't imagine what it's like, having to deal with Del Bello, who won't stand up like a man and say, 'Art Schuster is the doctor I want to work with. Sorry, Dr. Winter, but your day is done, and why don't you look for a new job.' Hell no. I tell you, Ellie, I'd feel better if he'd just level with me. But instead, he's playing some kind of cat and mouse game, and it's making me crazy. I'm a physician! I'm not supposed to spend my time with this kind of shit!"

"Adrian, listen, honey. You don't like playing politics; I

know that, not this kind of politics. But Art does; he always has. Art loves the cocktail-party circuit; he thrives on it. So let him. He's good at it, and a damn good thing, since he's such a lousy doctor! You're a wonderful doctor, so let him work with Del Bello, and you work with the patients. And stop worrying about it. Go to Del Bello and say, 'Let Art Schuster do it, okay? Then I won't have to think about it anymore.' "

He shook his head tightly. "I can't do that. I should invite him to favor Art Schuster? I should have to *ask* about doing something I've always been begged to do?"

This was worse than she had imagined. "Adrian, listen to yourself. Do you really mind if Del Bello happens to like Art Schuster? Listen, Del Bello may be right: Art Schuster is perfect in administration." She tried for a light laugh. "It keeps him away from patients!" But he wouldn't laugh, or even crack a smile. "Oh, Ade, come on. What's one speech in a lifetime?"

"It's not just the speech, Ellie. Don't you see that? It's . . . it's just the first drawing of blood. There's more coming. I feel it in my gut."

"Oh, Ade!" But what could she say to him? She'd known him a long, long time. If there was one thing Adrian Winter was good at, it was instinctively knowing what was going on just under the surface. His instincts were sharp. If he thought something crummy was going on, it probably was.

In a much more serious voice, she said, "Did he do anything to your budget?"

A bitter laugh. "Not yet. But I've been left off some of the memos . . . not all of them, not even the big ones. Just . . . some of them. I can't explain it, but I know it's happening. Oh, hell, Ellie, I wish you'd been with me just before and you'd have seen what I saw. Schuster and Del Bello are thick as thieves, and when they saw me, they suddenly stopped talking. I don't mean they paused; I mean, they stopped dead. I'm sure they had been discussing me."

"I'm going to ask around. I'll keep my eyes open."

"Would you? Good. I could use you on my side, Ellie."
Now he really smiled at her.

Ellie swallowed and gave him her best just-friends grin.
"I'm always on your side, Adrian," she said.

Chapter 3

IT WAS ALREADY ten after ten, and Ellie fairly flew down the corridor, her mind running ahead of her. She didn't like what was happening with Adrian; she didn't like it at all. She would have to figure out some wonderful, clever way of getting information and handing it on to him. From the old days, she knew that an anxious Adrian Winter was a surly Adrian Winter. Oh what a bother. She couldn't help but feel sorry for the poor second Mrs. Winter, who probably had never seen him like that before. And then she chided herself because, goddammit, the poor second Mrs. Winter had neatly and deftly stolen the husband away from the poor first Mrs. Winter, namely herself.

"Dr. Ellie, I can see you have that look in your eyes, but I need you. I really need you."

She stopped short, feeling a bit frustrated. Del Bello stepped out of his office, followed closely by none other than Art Schuster. Now maybe, she thought, putting her very best smile on, she could find out if Adrian's fears were justified or off the wall.

The two men were a strange-looking pair, she thought: Del

Bello, sleek, smooth, heavy, handsome, overfed and over-groomed. With his large head and his fleshy face, he looked like an aging, pampered matinee idol. And almost hidden a politic two paces behind, the boyish-looking Art, slight and wiry, with a habitual slouch that always made him look as if he were hurrying, his head, with its cap of curling dark hair, thrust forward. It was like seeing a lion in company with a terrier.

"Mr. Del Bello," she answered in a kind of coo, "if you need me, how can I possibly say no." Oh, Ellie Winter, shame on you, she thought, watching as they made their way across the hall to her.

Funny . . . she and Ade both had distrusted Del Bello at first sight, even before Nate was dumped. He was almost too careful, almost too slick. But with a certain charm, she had to admit. And she couldn't help it. When he came on to her this way, all smiles and flattery and flirty looks, she played right back. It was like a fun adult game, in which only she knew she was cheating, because she knew all his moves ahead of time. For instance, right now, she knew what he'd do. He'd come up to her, put an arm around her shoulder, and call her "dear."

"Ellie, dear, how's it going?" The arm fell across her shoulders, and the hand gave her a pat. "You run a wonderful clinic there. I hear nothing but good. Isn't that right, Art?"

"The jewel in the crown of Cadman Memorial," Art agreed, and he gave Ellie a big conspiratorial wink. "It's the clinic I hear the most about from the board members," he added more seriously. "And someone mentioned it over dinner at the Casino the other night."

Ellie smiled at him. That Art Schuster! She and Art and Ade had all been in med school together. It fascinated her; Art was such a poor doctor and such a good fund-raiser for any kind of medical project. He was such a phony in so many ways but so tuned into what was really going on. He was adored by his middle-aged female patients and abhorred by his nurses. What a mixture! His comments just now were absolutely typical of him; first the little joke to show what a regular guy he was and then the serious comment to show he was sincere. Not only that, but he made sure you knew that (a) he was on familiar terms with board members and (b) he belonged to the Heights Casino and was therefore socially okay. All of this self-serving stuff while giving you a compliment. Talk about efficient! Well, that was Art Schuster. It made him irritating, but it seemed also to make him successful. She had been in his house on Garden Place, and it was *done*—all antiques and original art and actually quite lovely.

She acknowledged his praise with a smile and a nod as Del Bello leaned in toward her and said, "Speaking of your clinic, anything specially interesting happening there lately?"

"All the time. Why?"

"You know what I mean, Ellie."

She wanted to say, 'Don't call me Ellie; only my friends call me Ellie. It's Dr. Winter to you,' but of course you didn't talk that way to the head of the hospital. "No. What?" Make him say it; let's see what euphemism for publicity he'd come up with this time.

"Something . . . unique, you know . . . something like that wonderful story during the summer; remember? That kid, the patient of yours who won at the Special Olympics. Human interest."

"Oh, you mean some case with PR possibilities." But he didn't catch the tinge of sarcasm; he rarely did, she had noticed. He was too busy listening to the sound of his own voice.

Now he smiled down at her with genuine delight. "Good girl! Now you're catching on!"

"Oh, it takes me a while, Hank, but I do learn eventually."

She caught the edge of a sharp glance from Art Schuster, who swiftly said with a grin, "Oh, Ellie, still trying to maintain your reputation as the bad girl of the hospital . . ." He twinkled at her, and although he didn't move, his silent warning to Del Bello was almost palpable. "But your ability to express yourself so well is exactly why Hank here has decided you're just who needs to present the hospital's clinic programs at the next budget meeting of the board."

"That's right," Del Bello put in. "And I certainly hope you'll agree, *Dr. Winter.*" Honestly, sometimes she thought the man was capable of reading minds. It must be why he had come so far so young. The man wasn't over forty; that she knew. He seemed to have an instinct that time after time got him out of trouble and let him smooth over his own mistakes. The board of trustees, a motley crew if ever there was one, all certainly seemed to think the world of him.

"This is certainly an honor," she said in the sincerest voice she could muster, "but honestly, Mr. Del Bello, I don't think I'm the best person for that job. Art can tell you; I put my foot into my mouth at least twenty-three percent of the time—"

"Not true, Ellie, not true . . ."

"Oh, yes, very true. We all remember Dr. Eleanor Winter, interviewed by Frank Field on the subject of nursing babies . . ." She began to laugh. "I managed to irritate absolutely everyone, from the manufacturers of formula to the ladies in the La Leche League." And then, over more protests she could see coming, she added. "And anyway, I only know my clinic well. You know who you *really* need—the one guy here who has an overview of all the clinics because he was in on the beginning of the clinic program—is Ade."

There it was; no mistaking it, that tiny flicker between the two men. Ade was right; the knives were out, and they were after him. Oh, dear, this was bad, much worse than she had thought. But she couldn't show them that she had caught on. Del Bello answered, just a beat too late, "Oh, well, there's a thought! We'll have to give that, uh, our consideration. Right, Art?"

"You bet! Although . . . well, Ellie, we really were hoping for you."

"That's right. We need to hit them up for more money for the clinics, and the board always responds better to a woman!"

Oh, really, Ellie thought, this is too much. Didn't the man have any sense at all? Did he really think that was the way to her heart? "Do you want me to ask them for money?" she asked sweetly. "Or a dance?"

Del Bello laughed, just a shade too heartily. "Oh, you're a card, Ellie. You really are. She always been this funny, Art?"

"Always." Schuster gave her a careful look and a careful smile. "All kidding aside, Ellie, don't say no too quickly. Think it over. Remember there are 126 doctors on staff here at Cadman; Hank and I thought long and hard before we made the decision to go with you."

Ellie bit her tongue, almost literally, so as not to say what came instantly to mind: that Dr. Arthur Schuster's name was not listed on the administration staff of this hospital. Yet, during this whole conversation, she kept hearing over and over again that the chief administrator of this hospital was making decisions in concert with that same Dr. Schuster. She found herself getting angry. The nerve of them, pushing a political social climber like Art Schuster into the position her Adrian had always been meant to have—had been trained for years to have and certainly deserved!

She hardly heard the mellifluous phrases that fell from Del Bello's lips, until the very end, when he said, "I've found, Ellie, that it always pays to bring in a pretty woman."

And, as she turned from them to march off, she heard herself say, biting off each word, "Then go find one, why don't you?"

Chapter 4

DAVID CRADLED THE frail body in his arms and said, "There, now, sweetheart, I'm going to put you in the chair. I'm tying that pink ribbon in your hair, and I'm going to wheel you down into the solarium so you can flirt with all the fellas and drive them wild." As he talked, he was moving deftly, arranging her in the chair, strapping her in, making sure the left leg and the left arm—those were the ones affected by the stroke—were comfortable and supported. His hands were gentle; he was always supercareful with his Golden Oldies, because they were all so brittle, so fragile, so frightened.

He knelt in front of the chair and surveyed his patient. "Pink's your color, Mrs. Santucci," he said, "and if I had a free minute, I'd hang out in the solarium myself."

"Oh, David! Get outa here!" She laughed. "I'm too old for you!"

David grinned at her. "That's what *you* think!" he said, and laughed. "Wanna meet me later and we'll test that theory?"

"David, I'm a grandmother and the past president of the Sodality!"

"Oh, yeah," he answered, pushing the chair down the hallway, "I know all about your kind. On the surface, president of this and grandmother of that and a real lady. But I know you really drive men wild!"

Mrs. Santucci giggled. She loved his sexual banter. One of the other nurses had cornered him and had given him a lecture. "You can't talk that way to a patient! You have to show respect!"

And his answer was "Look, when you're old and sick and everyone treats you like a nonperson, the best medicine is to have someone joke with you or flirt with you. It lets you know you're still alive!" That's what he told her, and that's what he really believed.

He placed her near a window, overlooking the park, fussed at her a little—they all liked a little extra fussing; it didn't matter whether it was medically necessary or not—and rearranged the pillow behind her. He had already put three other patients here, and the chairs were arranged so they could talk together. He had a word for each of them, and a smile. He was pleased this afternoon; they all looked pretty perky. He liked it a lot when he got his Golden Oldies feeling good. He really liked working with old people. It surprised him a little. He had thought he'd be depressed. Everyone outside of Geriatrics thought that old people were all depressing. They weren't! They were scared—well, who wouldn't be, old and sick!—but they were full of jokes and full of stories, and what they wanted more than anything in the world, he had found, was someone to talk to. No, someone who would *listen*. Doctors could only do so much for them. Broken hips, strokes, high blood pressure, diabetes. Most of the illness and injury that brought them to the seventh floor at Cadman were incurable. Hell, old age was incurable. He was just glad—this week, anyway—that there wasn't a single Alzheimer on the floor. It was awful, that disease, what it did to the patient, what it did to the family, just awful. He hoped when he went it wasn't that way.

He hurried back down the hall, looking into the rooms,

making chat, smoothing bedclothes, checking charts—all those duties he could do from the top of his head. He was thinking, he liked Geriatrics, but he had *loved* working with kids. The kids—! he sucked in a quick breath. He really shouldn't even think about his two years at the Birth Defects Clinic. That was another time and another place in his life. It still hurt. He didn't like admitting it. Big boys don't cry. But the memory of Ellie was like a big lump stuck in his throat forever. It had been so special . . . he'd never find another woman like her.

He never thought, growing up in Inwood, that he'd ever find *anything* in life. He was a street kid. His father drove a beer truck; his mother whined and had female complaints and slopped around the mean little apartment. And he went out in the street with his buddies and broke windows and did a little shoplifting and leaned against the lamppost on the corner and made dirty comments at all the passing girls. He didn't spend a lot of time in school—none of them did—but somehow he kept getting pretty good grades. And secretly he liked to read. He and his two brothers were being brought up Catholic, his mother's religion, but he hated the Church; he hated the whole thing, except for singing in the choir. That he loved, though he never admitted it. And for a while he was the lead tenor in a rock 'n' roll group. But it never worked out. One of the other groups from the neighborhood actually got a few jobs, but theirs—the Expressway—just fell apart.

So when he graduated from high school, his qualifications for life were that he could sing, he could drink, and he could read. Period. A typical loser from Inwood. When he looked around at the older guys, the guys he used to admire and look up to, they were doing dirty jobs, or they were doing time. It was 1971, and there was no hope for him. Except the Army.

He hated the Army . . . Well, that was a laugh, because was there a man in the world who ever loved the Army? He hated it, but the Army was damn good to him. Made a man out of him. Also, made a medic out of him, which was more to the point. It surprised him to discover that he was damn good at it . . . at taking care of people. It seemed to come naturally. He just seemed always to know what to ask and what to say, which made guys clutch at his hands and thank him. He didn't mind the blood. He didn't mind seeing guts or gore or torn muscle; he didn't blank out or black out like some. He just got calmer. And he did mind when they died. He was always rooting for them not to die. One of the M.A.S.H. surgeons he got to know gave him a sharp look one day and said, "You ever thought of going into medicine?" His answer was a great big laugh. He, David Ewan Anthony Powell, a doctor! He wasn't nearly smart enough. And there was no money for that kind of fancy education. So the doc said, "Don't wanna be a doctor? Don't blame you. But you've got the touch, Powell. You've definitely got the touch. Paramedic—that's the new thing stateside. Paramedic; you could probably do that on the G.I. Bill."

That was his first push, that M.A.S.H. surgeon. After he got out of the Army, he actually got his paramedic training, and he actually got a job. He'd been working in a Cadman Memorial ambulance for two years when he got his next push. He had pulled a heart attack into the ER. He'd already given the guy CPR on the way in, and there was a weak little pulse. But he thought the guy was beginning to fibrillate, and he yelled to the head nurse on the run. She came right over with the resident on duty, and between them all they kept his heart going. At the end, the three of them—medic, nurse, doctor—looked at each other, not with smiles but with that grim satisfaction you only know in the ER. And the nurse, Con Scofield, gave him a narrow-eyed look and said, "C'mere, Powell. Let me give you a cup of coffee; I want to talk to you." She'd been watching him, she said; she'd noticed him almost right away. Funny, she even used the same words. "You've got the touch, Powell." But what she said made him laugh even harder than when the surgeon suggested he be a doctor.

"A *what*? You want me to be a *what*?"

Con thinned her lips and gave him a warning look. "A nurse, I said, buster. A nurse. N-U-"

"I know how it's spelled, Ms. Scofield. But that's for women! Come on!"

"No, it's not, David. This is 1976, not 1776. Get yourself liberated and join the twentieth century. Lots of men are in nursing. There are six men in the graduating class at Downstate . . ." She went on and on, and he made believe he was bored, yawned at her, and laughed. He was listening, really, but he still thought it was for girls. It took her three months of talking to wear him down.

He'd never forget the day he appeared at the door of the Birth Defects Clinic. It was a brand-new clinic, not yet open, and when he opened the door, the first thing he noticed was the smell of paint. And the second thing he noticed—shit, you couldn't help but notice—was a great pair of female legs, up on a stepladder, right at eye level, shoes off, tiptoe. Nice ankles, and the knees weren't bad, either. The woman was in a white coat, so she was either a nurse or the doctor he was supposed to see. Dr. Eleanor Winter, her name was. He was preparing to clear his throat—she was very intent on hanging up a large poster of *Star Trek* people, and he didn't want to startle her, when suddenly she shouted, "Oh, shit!" and the poster slid out of her grasp and fell to the floor. She twisted around, very irritated, dropped the hammer, and then said, "Oh, shit!" again.

And then she saw him. He was expecting her to do the normal woman thing: get flustered, apologize for her language, tell him how embarrassed she was about twenty-seven times. Instead, she said, "Oh, good. Now I don't have to get down again. Could you do me a favor and hand me the poster and the hammer?"

"I'll do you an even bigger favor. You get down, and I'll put the poster up." He grinned at her. Not your typical woman, he thought, and then he laughed out loud, because shit, he wasn't exactly your typical man, either. He was a nurse, for Christ's sake. It was still so new, he kept forgetting it. But of course that's what he was here for, to see about his first nursing job.

She laughed, too, very good-natured. "I don't know if I ought to take you up on that offer. I'm a doctor, and I'm supposed to be totally liberated. I mean, I'm *supposed* to be able to hammer a nail into the wall without dropping everything. I shouldn't have to wait until a man comes along—"

"Oh, that's okay, doctor. I'm not just a man. I'm a nurse."

She stared down at him, and then they both began to laugh and laugh and laugh. And then she said, "Well, if you're a nurse, then that makes it all right. Please, nurse, would you hang up the poster." And while he was up on the ladder, she leaned on it—in case it decided to topple over, she said—and asked him, "Are you David Powell, whom I'm to interview for a job here?"

"That's me. Nurse David Powell. And as soon as I get Mr. Spock up here straight, we can start the interview."

"Mr. Powell . . . the interview is over."

"What? But wait . . . I know I sound kind of fresh, but I can tone it down if I have to—"

"Whoa, Nurse Powell. Take it easy. You're hired, is what I meant."

"But you didn't even ask me anything . . ."

"I don't have to now. Con says you've got it, the school says you've done well. And as for the rest, I can see for myself that you're going to be very handy around here . . ." Then she got more serious and added, "Look, Mr. Powell. You're brand-new at nursing. Well, I've just taken my boards in pediatric neurology, so I'm new, too. I can do just about anything I want with this clinic, because *it's* brand-new. And that means I need the right kind of people working with me. I have a gut feeling about you, David . . . Can I call you David? . . . Good, and you call me Ellie . . ."

It was always easy to talk to her, always natural. Right from the beginning, there was a flow between them, something nice that had nothing to do with doctor/nurse or

Marcia Rose

woman/man or old/young. It went beyond any of that. She
hired him and then seemed to forget that she was the boss and
he was just the hired hand. It was more a partnership.

The Birth Defects Clinic saw everything from infants to
teenagers and treated every kind of imaginable anomaly from
webbed toes to Down's syndrome to microcephalia to some
esoteric genetic thing that hit one in a million. They saw cystic
fibrosis, and they saw Reyes syndrome, and they saw Tay-
Sachs—oh, God, how Ellie fought Tay-Sachs. And it was she
who brought Rita Schneider to Cadman; it was she who
insisted to the board that genetic counseling was the first
preventive in birth defects, that you didn't have to wait until
something happened, until a baby was born with problems.

She was a wonderful woman. The first time he saw her, up
on the ladder, when she turned around, swearing, his immediate impression was She's plain; she's not pretty. She's one of
those typical redheads. But with Ellie Winter, you just forgot
pretty damn quick that you'd ever thought that, even for a
second. She was too witty and too warm and too damn smart
for you to find her anything but beautiful in a very short time.

Well, of course he had to think she was smart, because she
thought *he* was. She watched him handle the children, and
she watched him handle the parents, and then she told him
she'd like him to take over on some of the less complicated
cases. "I need my time to look at the new patients and to deal
with particularly difficult cases. I don't see why you couldn't
take histories and look after some of them. You know, see
them on their regular visits and measure and weigh them and
tell their moms and dads what comes next . . . *Well*?"

Well? Well, most doctors did not allow their nurses that
kind of responsibility . . . at least not officially. Of course he
was pleased. It made his job that much more interesting.
After six months at the clinic, he had to admit it was the most
satisfying work he'd ever done. He told Ellie one evening
when they were shutting up shop for the day, and he added,
"The guys in my old neighborhood would just roll on the
floor, hollering, if they heard me. Jesus! The idea of a guy

being a nurse would give any of them a heart attack. Then lemme just tell them that I'm a nurse to little kids—'' He threw his head back and laughed. "Well, obviously, I'm a fag!"

"Oh, David! Nobody could ever say that of you. You're the most masculine man around this hospital."

He put a hand on her shoulder and said, "No, no, you don't understand. A fag in my neighborhood was just a way of saying sissy."

They both laughed, and then he pondered a minute and said, "You know, Ellie, my favorites are the Down's kids."

"I know. I noticed. Well, they tend to be very sweet and lovable."

"That's not why I like them, you know. Not because they're tractable. I know that's why a lot of nurses would rather take care of them than some of the other retarded kids. But that's not it, not for me. First of all, you can see improvement—they try so hard, they really do, and that's gratifying. Look how well Mary Lou is doing since we got her into the nursery at Plymouth Church. All it took was a little stimulation. I knew she could do it! There was such intelligence in those eyes. Do you know? She can write her name now!"

Ellie smiled at him and took his hand for a moment. "That's why you're so good at your job, David, dear. You *care* about your patients."

"I do care. But the reason I love it is because they care about me. Yeah, that's it. You know, Ellie, when I was growing up, there wasn't a helluva lot of hugging and kissing. Not around my house! My mother was too busy complaining, and as for my old man—well, come on, we were three boys. A Powell man didn't kiss his sons, not once they stood up on their own and began to walk." He laughed shortly. "To my father's folks, once you were a toddler, you were treated like a little man. You didn't need that baby stuff.

"Well, you know the Down's kids—they are big huggers and kissers. And I have to tell you, the first time one of them grabbed me around the neck and kissed me and said, 'Davie, I love you'—it was Luis Sanchez, in fact—I nearly jumped out of my skin.''

"You didn't show it. That's another reason you're so good at what you do. You're professional.''

"Thanks, doc. But what I was trying to say is, I realized a minute later that I liked it. It made me feel good. I smiled at Luis, and I thought, I wish I could hug him back and tell him I love him, too. But all I could manage was, 'You're my buddy, Luis.' ''

When he looked up, directly at her, he was amazed to see tears brimming in her eyes. She blinked them back and smiled a little and said, with only a slight quaver in her voice. "Well, good for you, David Powell. My former husband never did get even that far.''

He'd only been in the clinic for three months at the time of this conversation; but he knew damn well who her former husband was: Dr. Adrian Winter, the head of Ob/Gyn at Cadman. The gossip was he'd dumped Dr. Ellie for some dumb blonde who was young enough to be his daughter but was a sex bomb. Well! he couldn't see anyone being sexier, really, than Dr. Ellie. He never met the other Dr. Winter, but he was sure he wouldn't like him. The guy was probably a pompous ass, like most of them, self-important and self-centered. He didn't know what to say to her now. He didn't know what to do. He knew what he felt like doing; he felt like putting his arms around her and comforting her. But he didn't dare; she'd probably slap his face. So he didn't.

He'd been with the clinic for a year—it was his anniversary, as a matter of fact—when he read in the *Post* that a certain Dr. Jeffrey McClintock, twenty-nine, of Haddonfield, New Jersey, had gone berserk, taken a shotgun and killed his wife, his mother-in-law, his three kids, a visiting neighbor, and, finally, himself. The report went on to say that Dr. McClintock, a veteran of the Vietnam War, was a resident in emergency medicine at St. Agnes Hospital, and then David just stopped reading. He nearly stopped breathing. He knew Jeff McClintock, twenty-nine, of Haddonfield. Jeff had been his closest buddy for a while; but he got out six months before David and went right to medical school, and they kind of lost touch.

The thing was that Jeff was sensitive and intelligent and educated—everything. David had thought, *he* was not. He'd really looked up to him, and in a way, as a paramedic, he had copied Jeff's style. After a brief time, of course, he developed his own, but he always looked to McClintock if he was in doubt about what to do. And he had gone crazy? It was hard to believe, except that nothing was impossible to believe if it had something to do with Nam. But . . . to kill your own children? Your own kids! He had put the paper down—he was sitting in his apartment, a beer bottle open on the table—and sat there and began to shake. He wrapped his arms around himself tightly, but it didn't help. He kept shaking and shivering, and pretty soon he was crying. Fucking war! Not Jeff! Not McClintock! Who next! Him? Could it just come up out of nowhere and get you by the throat? Could he be going along nice and easy, and suddenly get up one day and go into the clinic and do something crazy? The guy was a doctor, for Christ's sake! A *doctor*!

Well, he sat there, and he kept drinking and kept staring out the rain-streaked window. Then he couldn't stand it anymore, and he got up and got dressed and went out to walk. Where, he didn't know, and he didn't care. He just couldn't sit there any longer.

He never could remember exactly what made him go to Ellie's house on Remsen Street. He had walked all around the Heights and Cobble Hill for what must have been two hours, in the rain. And then there was her house—he'd checked it out on his walks before; he knew which one it was, the one with the big bay window—and he stood there on the sidewalk, looking at it for a few minutes, and then said out loud, "Oh, what the hell." And walked up and rang the doorbell.

Her voice came through the intercom, sounding strange and squawky. "Who is it?"

And for a moment he hesitated. He didn't want to say. But then that got embarrassing, and he blurted, "David!"

There was no answer, and he thought he would have to go away when the door opened, and there she was, in a velour sweatsuit. "That's what I thought I heard!" she said. "But I couldn't believe it. Well, what are you standing there for? Come on in. It's okay. My kids are with their father. You're drenched!"

She pulled him into the hallway. It was so pretty; he wasn't surprised at all. If he had ever thought about it, he would have expected Dr. Ellie's house to be pretty. And comfortable. And filled with plants and artwork and cheerful things. Everything was polished wood and figured rugs and—he couldn't look at everything at once. She took him right upstairs to the parlor floor, past the living room and the dining room into the kitchen, a big room with a tile floor and huge windows.

"Here we go," she said. "I'm going to give you a hot toddy . . . no, on second thought, I'm going to give you some hot tea and a big towel and one of Ade's—a terry-cloth robe, and let's see if we can bring you back to life." She was brisk and friendly and sweet, just like always, and she turned her back and busied herself at the stove when he stripped. It didn't occur to him for quite a while that she could see him quite plainly, reflected in those big plate-glass windows. He had stripped right down to the buff and was toweling himself off when he thought of it, and then he looked up, and sure enough, she was looking at him . . . at his reflection.

So he just stopped what he was doing, dropped the towel, right onto the floor, and stood with his hands on his hips, staring back at her, in the window. He felt his cock getting hard, and he didn't care. Let her look at it; let her see it. He wasn't ashamed of it. He was proud of it! So let her stare!

Ellie clutched the edge of the sink and whispered, "David, please! Maybe you'd better get dressed."

He walked over to her. "And maybe I'd better not," he said, wrapping his arms around her from behind. He felt her body stiffen a moment, then shudder and relax. "You shouldn't—"

"Yes, I should." He tightened his grip on her. She felt so good, pressed in against him, so warm, so soft, so . . . right. It was as if something were happening that had been preordained. It had been there in the making, and finally it was happening. It felt predestined.

He put his mouth up against her ear and said, "I want you. I can't help it, and I'm not ashamed of it."

"Oh, David!"

"I know. It's impossible. It's ridiculous. It's unheard of. But let's do it, anyway."

"Oh, David!"

He turned her around then and bent his mouth to hers. She was like a furnace; glowing with heat. Her mouth, her neck, her breasts under the soft shirt, her belly under the soft pants, all burned against his mouth. She was delicious, she was succulent, she was yielding, burning, sweet.

They sank to the hard tile floor, on their knees, kissing avidly, hungrily. Through half-closed lids, he could see the sheen of tears on her cheek, and he bent tenderly to kiss the wetness. "Ellie," he whispered. "Ellie."

"It's been so long," she said in a low voice. "So long, David. And I was married . . . so long. I don't know what do do with this . . . feeling."

"I know, I know . . ." He kissed her throat and her shoulders, softly, sweetly. "I was walking the streets. I was feeling so low . . . so lost . . . so alone . . . You're so . . . I can't say, I can't say . . ." He bent and kissed her deeply, feeling such gratitude for her house, her warmth, her acceptance, the sanctuary of her body, which he knew she was offering to him. She was moaning deep in her throat, and when he pulled his mouth from hers, he held her in a grip of steel, not knowing what to do next.

And she said, "Come, David. Come with me." And they got up and staggered—literally staggered—into a little room off the kitchen, a little room filled with plants and flowers, smelling of the earth and of growth and of spring. There was a narrow couch there, shoved into the corner, heaped with soft pillows. She backed herself onto it, and he fell onto her, fitting his body to hers, moving himself until they were one instead of two and the stiff rod of him was deep inside her, where still she burned. She pivoted her hips to meet his, and she wept, and she screamed, and he yelled—both in a kind of delirium.

At the end, she smiled and cried some more and sobbed her thanks to him. And they fell asleep, locked in each other's arms. Sometime in the night, safe in the shelter of her embrace, in the warmth of her flesh, he told her about McClintock. He told her about Nam, the endless fear and the endless barrage of your friends blowing up in front of you, and carting and hauling people in pieces, bleeding and hurt. He told her he didn't blame McClintock for going nuts, but why now? Why not in Nam? Why now, after he'd done everything he wanted? "He was such a good guy. He was a doctor," he kept saying to her. "You understand? He was a *doctor*. He made it. He killed his own kids. Anyone could go crazy . . ." She listened, and she talked, and by some miracle she did understand. And it was the first night in two years without the nightmare.

They were secret lovers for almost two years, he and Dr. Ellie, the best two years of his life. She was more than just his lover; she was his confidante, his colleague, his best friend. Even though there were fifteen years between them. Even though she was his boss. He thought it would go on forever. He was even thinking about getting married. And then one day, over lunch in the cafeteria, she took a deep breath and told him they had to end it.

He turned Mrs. Whitman over expertly, helped her arrange herself on her other side, made sure all the IVs were working correctly, said a few words, patted her on the shoulder. He'd told himself he wouldn't think about Ellie, and look at him! Here he went again. It didn't happen too often . . . after all, it was four years since it ended, and there was a limit to how long a guy could hold a torch. And he hadn't been a monk; in fact, he'd even tried living with Sally St. Angelo for a couple of months, and it had been fine. It was Sally who left. Well, hell, she wanted to get married, and that wasn't part of the master plan, not now. Yeah, he managed to have a good time in life. Women liked him; he never had to go without for very long. His buddies gave him the business about it all the time. "Jesus, Powell, how do you do it? The ladies just love you!" And he would laugh and throw out his hands and say, "Why the hell shouldn't they? I give good dinner. I give good conversation." And they'd all laugh.

He was lucky. He still enjoyed his work, and nursing was good in that you could switch around when you felt burnout beginning. He'd been in the ER for a couple of years, and when it got to him, because there were too many gunshot wounds and knife wounds and torn-up bodies and screaming girls and kids OD'ing and god knows what, well, he asked for a transfer. And he got one, because, shit, there was a shortage of nurses in this city. He gave a quick eye check of Mrs. Whitman's room. Good, she was already asleep again. She needed that rest. Pneumonia was hell on the Golden Oldies. Most people thought pneumonia was one of those diseases that was no big deal anymore . . . a little penicillin and you were as good as new. But not with the old folks . . .

The new little nurse, Yolanda, went breezing by, calling out, "Almost time for TGIF, David! You gonna be there?"

"Sure thing!" He watched her cute little rear end bobbing down the hallway and thought, It's been a while, man, and that sure looks good. A little doll. He could use some action tonight, and Yolanda had been coming on to him, in a nice way, of course, all week long. Like Leslie Winter. The second Mrs. Winter. Leslie liked him. He didn't know what she meant by it, and she wasn't blatant or anything. But there was something in the air between them. Christ, *another* Mrs. Winter! If it wasn't so weird, it would be funny. He didn't know what he'd do if she ever really came on to him. She was such a beautiful woman; she was the kind of woman you saw all the time in magazines and in TV commercials, but you never expected to find that perfection in real life. Every Wednesday, when she appeared in that little pink smock, seeking him out and smiling up at him . . . well, more than once, he'd gotten a hardon. She was something else, that Leslie Winter! Women who looked like that didn't often come into *his* life. And then he had to give himself hell. He must *really* be horny, thinking every goddam woman who smiled at him was hot for his body. Forget Leslie Winter, the hotshot doctor's wife, he told himself. That cute little Yolanda . . . *that* he'd see about, later today.

Chapter 5

$B_{OBBY\ LET\ THE}$ steaming water beat on his shoulders. He flung his head back, eyes closed, trying to let himself relax with the rhythm, trying to ease that ache in the back of his shoulders, trying to keep his mind from racing around angrily. God, he was tired; now he knew the meaning of bone tired, because every fucking bone in his body felt as if it had been pounded by giant mallets for hours. Oh, sweet Jesus, what he wouldn't give for a few hours of sleep! He'd been on thirty hours straight, with a tough breech delivery around 4 A.M., his favorite hour, the favorite hour of suicides. He soaped his chest and turned to rinse it off, thinking, thinking, not thinking. It was so hard to concentrate when you were tired, but he had to. Mrs. Cameron was his patient, and she needed him to calm her down before her D & C. Goddam, it looked like cancer. She thought so, and she knew he knew she thought so, and it was up to him to convince her that he didn't know she knew he knew he thought so. Oh shit! He couldn't think straight at all these days. Not getting enough sleep was bad enough. Then they worked you like a galley slave. And on top of that, he had to deal with all the crap Corinne was handing out lately. And that reminded him . . .

Poking his head out between the edges of the shower curtain, he yelled for her. And then he saw it: the neat ham sandwich, with lettuce on rye, sitting on a plate on the stool Kelly used when she brushed her teeth, and next to it, a cup of coffee. Shit! She'd snuck in here without saying a word, when she *knew* he wanted to talk to her. Not only that, but the fucking coffee was probably already cold. Why the hell didn't she say something? "Here's your coffee, here's your lunch," *something*!

"Corinne!" he hollered again, and felt that strange little buzzing in his head, saw those strange little blobs of color swim in front of his eyes. He stopped and took a deep breath. He had to slow down; he had to pull himself together. Christ, it was so bad he couldn't even think whether Kelly was coming home from nursery school yet . . . couldn't even remember what time it was. Oh, yeah . . . around twelve-thirty. So she wasn't . . . home yet. Kelly, that is.

"Corinne! Goddam it all to hell, will you get in here and talk to me! You're the one who said you have to talk to me every day, goddam it, so for Christ's sake, get in here!"

In she came, sidling around the edge of the door in a way that made the hackles rise on the back of his neck. He remembered—well, he sort of remembered—when she used to prance around the apartment stark naked and proud of it, when she used to march in front of him and then give him a sideways glance. If he wasn't fully erect, she'd stop right where she was, put her hands on her hips, and demand, "*Well*!" And he'd laugh like hell, and that ain't all. Oh, yes, those were the days; and look at her now: dressed like he remembered his old aunties and not quite looking at him, as if his nakedness were disgusting. She used to love his body. And she used to say so in very explicit words.

"Bobby, honey," she said in that even, sweet voice she always used lately, "Please don't take the name of the Lord in vain. You know it bothers me . . . *Bobby*!" Because, furiously, he had parted the shower curtains and stood there in the tub, the water flying all over the bathroom, his legs apart, arms akimbo, and loins thrust out. He reached over and turned off the water and then stepped out, naked, dripping. He didn't even care, goddammit, ready to take her and . . . He didn't even know what it was he wanted to do with her any more: shake her, hit her, or fuck her!

And, fuck her, she smiled at him and handed him a towel. "Honey, you're dripping water all over, and now I'll have to clean the bathroom again."

"I don't give a goddam about the bathroom, Corinne!" He just kept on talking, ignoring her tightened lips. He'd take the name of the Lord in vain just as often as he felt like! It wasn't her exclusive Lord. She could leave if she didn't like it! "Never mind the fucking bathroom. Let's talk about *you*, Corinne. Let's talk about your delicate condition. Let's talk about why, goddam it, you didn't think enough of your husband to tell him you're *pregnant*, Corinne! Pregnant!"

"It's bad luck to tell before the third month, Bobby, you know that."

"I don't know any such goddam thing! But here's what I do know. I know about anencephalic babies, Corinne . . . you know, no brain at all, a tiny little skull. And I know about spina bifida, Corinne, with water on the brain and club feet and—"

"It's only a ten percent chance, Bobby. That's not so much!"

"You fucking idiot! Not so fucking much! If you have a badly disabled, badly damaged baby, that's one hundred percent for you, Corinne. And one hundred percent for that poor crippled child, one hundred percent for the rest of its life!"

"Well, to a Christian, life itself is enough. Why can't you just accept what is, Bobby? You'd be a much happier man."

"I'd be a much happier man if my wife had told me she was pregnant and I didn't have to hear it in the form of a lecture on spina bifida from Dr. Eleanor Winter!"

"Oh, Bobby. She just guessed. I didn't tell her!"

He grabbed her by the shoulders, trying to ignore the way she pulled back from his touch. "That's not the point, and you know it. The point is, Corinne, why the hell are you pregnant? Abortions are not the way to do birth control; God, we have to tell that to the kids in the teenage clinic. I didn't think *you* needed it!"

"You're hurting me," she said, but it angered him that there was no hurt in her voice, no real emotion at all, just the same bland sweetness. Sometimes it was like talking to a windup doll.

"Honey," he said, trying to meet her eyes, trying to see behind her eyes to the girl he married, the girl he used to laugh with and make love to and *know*. "Corinne. Ever since Kelly was born and we knew we were at risk, we've been discussing this. I thought we had agreed—no more babies."

"God's will be done, Bobby."

Again that anger surged up in him, clogging his throat and threatening to choke him, and again he had to swallow, pause, take a deep breath. It was a fucking nightmare! He let her go and backed away from her. Goddam it, she wouldn't even look at him. She'd never look straight at him anymore.

"Not God's will, Corinne. *Your* will be done. What the hell happened to your pills? Jesus come in the night and tell you not to take them?"

"Oh, Bobby, you never used to talk to me that way. You've become mean. If only you'd let Jesus into your heart . . ."

"I'm as decent a human being as you are, dammit! And until you got mixed up with that crazy bunch over there at that church, who think they have a special line into heaven, you thought I was a good enough person."

"Don't you call them crazy! If it weren't for my church sisters, I'd never have made it those first weeks with Kelly. Remember how upset I was, how depressed, how much I sat around and cried? Well, they all gathered round me and talked with me and helped me with the baby and prayed with me. They gave me strength and hope, and look how well it all turned out.''

"Oh, my God, get in touch with reality, would you, Corinne? You know as well as I that Kelly is in such good shape because of Eleanor Winter! She got the best care available. Ellie is a brilliant neurologist and an expert in spina bifida and a fine physician, and if you can't remember how supportive she was, how many times you called her and turned up at the clinic without an appointment, and she was always there for you . . . even your special early-morning appointment last week. Don't you give those holy rollers the credit for all her hard work! Don't you dare!''

His voice had sunk lower and lower until the last few words were nearly a whisper.

Stubbornly, she said, "I'm grateful to Dr. Ellie. You know I am." Finally, she lifted her eyes and looked straight at him. They were brimming with tears. "Bobby, I hate to fight with you. I love you. I wish—Oh Bobby, you used to understand about God's plan—!''

"Corinne!" If only he could reach out to her and hold her close, as he used to. But she was so far off, on another path, that was so far away. "Look, honey, you got to agree that God gave us the ability to think, right? And you've got to think about this, Corinne. Because we can't have another child. I won't be able to make it with another child—especially if it's a damaged child. I don't have the strength. Dammit, I don't have the *time*." He looked down at the cold coffee and the sandwich. The ham was already drying around the edges. He had no appetite. And he had to get back, goddammit! He motioned to her, and she moved away from the door and let him go by into their bedroom. She sat herself on the toilet-seat lid; she often did when they wanted to talk, because their tiny room had no space for a chair. He threw his clothes on. The clock said 1:03, for Christ's sake, and he had promised Gary he'd be back no later than 1:00 on the button. Shit! Well, he'd take one of Gary's night shifts sometime when he had a heavy date. Meanwhile . . . it felt good to get into clean clothes. "Where's my tweed jacket?"

"Front closet," Corinne said. He glanced through the open door at her, slumped and placid like a lifeless rag doll on the toilet. He pointed a finger at her and said, "Corinne, you've got to have an abortion. It's the only way we're going to make it."

"Bobby, honey," she said, shaking her head, "we've been all through this before."

He opened his mouth and then thought, Oh, shit! What's the use. He'd deal with it later. "I've got to get back. Weinstein has been covering for me." And he ran, grabbing the jacket from the closet, his mind already raging ahead to his patients.

Corinne jumped a little when the front door slammed. She'd told him a hundred times that these cheap apartments couldn't take it. She hated it when he left angry. It left her with a sick feeling in her stomach. She closed her eyes and prayed a little, prayed for guidance and for strength and for Bobby. Oh, Jesus, bring Bobby Truman back into your grace; show him the way. They were growing farther and farther apart, and it hurt her to see it happen. A few tears leaked out from under her lids. She loved him, and she wanted his babies. God meant for married people to have babies. And the thought calmed her. God *meant* for married people to have babies; so God wouldn't let this baby be born without a brain or some other terrible thing; she just knew it. But if it happens, Lord, she thought. I'll know I'm being tested, and I'll meet that test, because my faith is in Thee. Everything in this life was a test; that's what the Reverend always preached. Good people met all those tests and let life's problems make them stronger in their faith and better people. What had he said last Sunday? He told them that when you're faced with a building that's got no heat and the people in it, your brothers and sisters, are freezing to death, you don't pray to Jesus to make a miracle and get warmth in there. You go to the housing authority and to the mayor and to the lousy absentee landlord and to the lawyers, and you get that furnace turned on. "That's doing the will of God," the Reverend Clayton thundered, and they all cried out, "Yes, Lord!" and, "Amen!" If she had a little crippled baby, she'd take care of it and love it and give it the best of care. She would. God's will be done.

Smiling, Corinne got up. It was time to go to Community Nursery School and pick up Kelly. What a bright little thing Kelly was! And so pretty and so adorable; everyone said so. And what if somehow they'd known before Kelly was born that there was a chance of spina bifida? What if Bobby had insisted on an abortion *then*? Her hand flew to her mouth. No, no! It was unthinkable that there would be no Kelly to say, "I love you, Mamma," put her little arms tight around her neck, and smile so sweetly at her.

Well, no *way* was anyone going to make her have an abortion this time, either! No way!

Corinne closed the door to Kelly's room softly and tiptoed away. She'd sung herself hoarse tonight; Kelly just didn't want to let go and fall asleep. Bobby was on call again and sleeping at the hospital—if you could call catching those naps really sleeping. She thought it was a shame, the way they worked the residents half to death. Bobby said it himself; it was dehumanizing. If he would only come to Jesus, he wouldn't have to worry about that; he'd always have the feeling of grace within him, no matter what they demanded of him. He'd be so much happier, as she was. Why couldn't he believe her when she told him how different it was since she was born again? She knew, didn't she? because she'd been lost and now was found. It was so simple, really, if you just left your heart open and let Him in. And it would make a much better doctor of him; that she knew with certainty. Bobby had so much good in him, so much. Under his cool surface, there was such a loving, generous nature. Look how he'd forgiven her for acting the harlot the way she had when she first knew him. Throwing herself at him—yes, Lord, she

knew she was wicked, she had sinned most grievously, and
didn't the Lord punish them both by making her miscarry?
And didn't let her get pregnant again for a whole year and a
month, even though she tried and tried. And she lied to her
husband. She told him she was taking her pills, and she
wasn't. And still, God said, No, you can't have another baby
yet. And that's when she met Sister Rebecca, in the laundry
room right there in this building. Lovely Sister Rebecca, with
her beautiful singing voice and her calm goodness and her
words of comfort.

Sister Rebecca was so good—the goodness just shone right
out of her face—Corinne found herself talking to her as if
she'd known her forever. She told Sister Rebecca how she
couldn't seem to get pregnant, and Sister Rebecca patted her
hand and said, "Do you know when the Lord sends your egg
down to be fertilized? Yes? Well, then, do you make sure to
lie with your husband those nights? Yes? Well, then, Sister
Corinne, I'm going to pray with you, because that's what you
need." And she took Corinne's hand in hers and let her head
drop back and closed her eyes and began to pray in her
wonderful rich voice. "Lord Jesus, look down upon this your
child, this your servant Corinne . . . look down, sweet Jesus,
and take pity . . ." Corinne felt better right away. It was as if
Rebecca's goodness washed over her and cleansed her, that
Rebecca's prayers opened her heart and cleared her mind. She
could hardly wait to tell Bobby about her awakening. But
when Bobby came back from the hospital that night and she
sat up in bed to tell him all about it, he was impatient and too
tired to listen. The more she tried to explain her feelings to
him, the angrier he got with her. He said terrible things to her
that night. He told her it was all nonsense and that she was
crazy, and finally right in the middle of something she was
saying, he snapped, "This is all bullshit!" and turned over in
the bed with his back to her and never kissed her or said,
"Good night." She had had to pray with all her might to
forgive him for that. But she had; she had forgiven him
because he was lost and ignorant and exhausted. She cried

quietly so that he never knew. And God came to her in her dreams that night; she dreamed of angels, big, buxom ladies who looked like Sister Rebecca, their heads wrapped in white turbans, like Sister Rebecca, and big warm smiles like hers. She was on a trip somewhere, and they were helping her find her way. She went the next morning after Bobby left for work and knocked on Sister Rebecca's door. When she told her dream, Sister Rebecca threw her head back and said, "Praise the Lord. You been called to Jesus; it's a sign for sure."

That wasn't so long ago, her meeting Sister Rebecca in the laundry room, but it had changed her life so completely, she could hardly remember what it had been like before. Well, of course she remembered, but it shamed her. Reverend Clayton said she wasn't to be shamed. "A woman's love for her husband is a precious thing to Jesus, Sister Corinne," he told her. "And the children you bear from this union are blessed. Your *marriage* is blessed, sister. Never forget that. Marriage is a blessing from God, and a good marriage is precious beyond jewels." But sometimes when she thought how she used to flaunt her naked body—the things she used to say! the things she used to think!—well, it didn't bear thinking of.

Slowly, she undressed herself for bed, took a clean night-gown from the drawer, put it over her head, went into the bathroom, and brushed her teeth and washed her face . . . and all without ever looking into a mirror. When she was reborn, she made herself a vow: to put vanity behind her and to never again look into a mirror for the sake of admiring her own face.

She climbed into bed, missing the warmth of Bobby's body. It was lonely, sleeping by yourself. She missed all the good things they always had together. She sighed and turned onto her back.

She prayed silently, as she always did before going to sleep, and then her mind wandered a little, and she mentally told herself portions of the Bible that lifted her spirits, and then she began to think about how many of the brothers and sisters took Bibles to Cadman and brought the Word to sick people. Some folks didn't want them, but Sister Julia told her they were awfully nice about it. "They don't cuss you out or say ugly things," Sister Julia said. "They say 'No, thank you.' And then, there's them that wants to see the Good Book, and sometimes they're so happy to have you read to them." Corinne shifted a little in the bed and thought, Oh, my, I'd love to do that. That would be so satisfying . . . to make Bible visits to the hospital. But when she told Bobby, he nearly hit the ceiling, he got so excited and mad. "You've got to be kidding, Corinne! Over my dead body will my wife wander around my hospital, getting underfoot and interfering with patients' proper care . . . Oh, I've seen your so-called brothers and sisters pushing their way in where they're not wanted, I've seen them, and the answer is *no*, Corinne, no and no again. Don't you realize," he shouted, grabbing her by the shoulders and shaking her, "don't you realize I'm a *doctor* there? I'm on the house staff, for Christ's sake! If you make a fool of me, Corinne, I'll never forgive you. If I ever hear that you've been Bible thumping around Cadman, I'll leave you; I swear I'll leave you!"

Oh, sweet Jesus, please gather Bobby Truman unto your bosom and forgive him his sins. If only he'd come to the tabernacle just one Sunday and listen to the man speak and feel the love that came pouring out . . . Oh, he'd change his mind; he'd have to. He'd stop fighting it.

She smiled to herself, thinking of the Reverend's serene face, his beautiful white-toothed smile. Oh, that smile! it flooded your insides with warmth. She loved to look at his beautiful face while he spoke those beautiful words. And then, later, she would kneel before him, and he would reach down and put his big warm hands, one on each side of her head, and bless her. And the tears would spring to her eyes, and her heart would pound in painful joy . . . In her bed, Corinne squeezed her arms and legs tight together and tried to conjure up the feeling—the sweet joy—that wonderful feeling when you gave yourself completely. In her bed, Corinne drew in a deep breath, trembling a little, then relaxed totally and fell asleep.

Chapter 6

THE BROOKLYN ACADEMY of Music this Friday evening in early October was ablaze with lights and jammed with theatergoers. The main lobby was redolent of coffee and chocolate cake as late arrivals quickly bought supper or dessert at the snack bar in the center of the lobby. Ellie Winter bit into her piece of warm quiche and sighed with pleasure. "Oh, good," she said to her companion, a tall man with a dark, neatly trimmed beard and aviator glasses. "I had a last-minute emergency and never got to eat . . . not lunch *or* dinner."

"I had planned," her date said with a wry smile, "to stuff you with foie gras or steak, not stand in BAM's lobby drinking wine from plastic glasses and watching you make do with whatever that is—"

"Oh, Steve, it's fine. I'm just delighted that in this theater you can at least get something good to eat. It's all homemade you know. Wanna bite?"

"Depends on what." He smiled.

For just a moment, she didn't get it, and then she got it, and to her dismay she felt herself blush. She wasn't used to it. She wasn't accustomed to having it talked about, and she wasn't accustomed to having it done. Steve was the most unabashedly sexual man she had ever met. They'd been dating for a little over a year; you'd think she'd be blasé by this time. He leaned close to her and murmured, "I'll just take a little nibble right now," and bit lightly on her earlobe. Shivers ran right down her spine, and she looked around, flustered. But of course nobody noticed. People were not staring at her. In fact, there probably wasn't a soul she knew here tonight . . . and then, suddenly, she found herself looking at a profile she knew by heart.

As lightly as she could, she said to Steve, "Well, what do you know, there's my ex . . . Over there. Adrian and the second Mrs. Winter. Over there. Look, but don't stare, Steve. Be a good boy. He's tall, with a lot of white hair, see? And she's small with a lot of yellow hair."

"Oh, yeah . . . I see them. Good-looking man. Though dumb."

"Steve! You don't even know him!"

"Yeah, well, I know he let *you* go."

"Come on, Steve, enough of your flattery. Look, they're flashing the lights. Let's go in."

"Okay, okay." But he paused to give Adrian and Leslie another look. "Yes, very nice looking. The picture of the doctor—"

"How about her?" Ellie said. "Don't you think she's gorgeous? She's a model."

"She's okay. Yes, yes, Ellie, of course she's pretty, but the dumb-blonde look just doesn't appeal to me. *You* appeal to me."

"I came here to listen to music, not to your blarney." But as they made their way to the Lecerq Space, she couldn't help thinking, The dumb blonde type didn't used to appeal to Ade, either.

She hadn't known what might appeal to that adorable boy at the other side of the lecture hall, but she knew it could *never* be someone like her. There were only a few other girls in her class at NYU Medical—seven, to be exact—but two of them were real beauties. They'd be what he would go for.

Sure, she'd dated plenty at Berkeley; of course she had. She wasn't dumb enough to think you had to be Elizabeth Taylor to attract men. But that boy—that man, really—whoever he was, was something special. So handsome! Tall and nicely built and craggy, wth a lot of thick black hair already sprinkled with gray. And such a nice smile! He was in the middle of a bunch of guys, and it seemed he did most of the talking, and they were all laughing. Oh, how she wished she could get to meet him.

But they were all just too busy, those first weeks, to do much socializing. Margie, her roomie, was a nice gal, and they went to a couple of parties together, but he wasn't at any of them. She saw him in class, of course, and learned his name, but that was it. Adrian Winter; even the sound of his named seemed glamorous and out of reach.

It was rough, she found, being a woman in medical school. None of the boys was ready to accept her, not as a colleague and not as a date. She had never felt so isolated in her life. The girls in her class all discussed it endlessly; they were being systematically ignored, ostracized, and discouraged. "Well, I for one," Ellie said one day, "am absolutely not going to let them get to me. I'm going to be a doctor. Let them do their worst. To hell with them. I'm going to be a doctor." And she did her best to ignore the snubs, the snickers, and the condescension of all the professors—all men, of course.

There were nights, in spite of her brave words, when she cried bitter tears into her pillow and wished to God she'd never ever thought of being a physician. Often, it seemed impossible.

The turning point came sometime in November in gross anatomy. She and Adrian and Art Schuster and a guy named Jack McKenzie were sharing a cadaver. Art was a pain in the neck even then, always making sly comments about the build of the poor dead man. "Nice chest. Don't you think so,

Norris?'' he'd say to her. Or, ''These legs are the legs of an athlete. Don't you agree, Norris?''

She usually just smiled blandly at him and didn't bother to answer, but she knew he was out to get her goat. And in the meantime, there was Adrian Winter, directly across from her, making her heart beat faster every time she snuck a look at him. She certainly wasn't going to show how upset Schuster made her, not in front of her dreamboat.

It was a Tuesday, she'd remember that forever, a Tuesday at eight in the morning. She walked into the lab, feeling a little peculiar, because today they were going to dissect the male genitals. And there they were, the three of them, sitting back on their stools, arms folded over their chests, just waiting for her to get there. She never could remember exactly what was said, only that it was clear that she alone was going to have to do the dissection—and do it with them looking on.

She collected her instruments, her lips set tightly, and decided to hell with Schuster; she was going to do it perfectly. Because, of course, it was Art Schuster's idea. MacKenzie was too much of a grind to even notice she was a girl, and she was sure Adrian wouldn't have thought of it. So screw Schuster! She set to work, her right hand shaking ever so slightly, but she willed it to behave. And she began, carefully, slowly. The worst moment was the first time she had to touch the penis, but then she just concentrated on the job she had to do.

Through it all, Art Schuster—obviously delighted with himself—wouldn't let up. ''What do you think of that organ, Norris?'' ''Think you can *handle* it?'' ''Is it too *hard* for you?'' She bit her lips together and decided she would not say a word to him, although the angry words were boiling on her tongue.

Finally, it was finished. The skin on her face felt taut and hot, and her lips were completely dry; but she had done it and done it well. Now she looked up, thinking, if Art Schuster says one more word, anything at all, I am going to dissect *him*, organ by organ, beginning with the one I've just practiced on.

And when she looked up, tightly under control, the first thing she saw was his pale eyes—startling in that dark face—twinkling with malicious laughter. His wide mouth was in a big grin. That split second before he spoke, she knew he was going to say something perfectly dreadful.

"Well, I see you've had plenty of experience," he said and paused for a beat. "How about a date tonight?"

"Art Schuster, you are a—" To her horror, her voice quivered and broke into a sob. Oh, no! No! Damnation! She wanted to tell him what a pig he was, what a slob, what a lowlife, what a—

"Son of a bitch!" Adrian Winter said.

Ellie's head swiveled to him in surprise, even as those first hateful, unwanted tears of rage began to slip down her cheeks. "Schuster, you are a bastard," Adrian went on. "You've been lousy all the way through, and she's done a perfect job, anyway. She's a good sport. But you've gone too damn far! Come on, Ellie, let's get out of here. I'm gonna buy you a cup of coffee."

She couldn't believe that it was adorable Adrian Winter acting as her champion. But she didn't want him to fight her battles, either. And she absolutely didn't want to leave crying. They'd all say, "Isn't that just like a girl?"

So she held up a hand and wiped her face with the back of the other and smiled, smiled, smiled, at Art Schuster. "Now that I've done all the work," she said, "*you* can clean up." And, to her own amazement, she hooked her arm into Adrian's and said, "You buy the coffee. I'll buy the doughnuts."

He bought the coffee, and she bought the doughnuts, and they talked for hours. She discovered that he was the son of a doctor—only the doctor in his family was his mother, a pediatrician—and that he was going into medicine because nothing else in the world was as important as taking care of people. And he found from her that she was a California girl, something of a tomboy, and that she was going into medicine because nothing else in the world was as important as taking care of people. They stared at each other; she remembered that vividly—just stared at each other, grinning. And that was the beginning.

After the incident in gross anatomy, she noticed a change in the attitude of her fellow students, subspecie male. She was one of the guys, she was okay, she was a good sport. She was accepted. She was accepted by Adrian, too, and soon they were seeking each other out between classes. They did their assignments together, and they joined the same study group. And when the kids got together for some TGIF, he would always make sure she was coming along. Of course, this was nice, but on the other hand, it was awful. He'd take her hand and put his arm around her shoulder, all very casual and friendly, whereas she had to admit that her feelings were not exactly all casual and friendly. She had a crush on him. She felt rather silly about it—after all, she was twenty-two years old, too old for adolescent infatuations—but there it was. He made her dizzy just by being in the same room! She never told a living soul. It was too embarrassing, because he obviously considered her literally one of the boys. She could see no difference in the way he treated her and the way he treated, say, Art.

In fact, Art Schuster got interested in her. Once he got past his prejudices about women in medicine, he became very attentive. They went to a couple of parties together, and he was always offering to walk her back home. She found him quite attractive, and she wasn't exactly a virgin, but she wasn't exactly a pushover, either, and there was something about Art Schuster's attitudes—nothing she could put her finger on, but she had a strong feeling he'd kiss and tell. Normally, she wouldn't even mind that so much—let the fool talk if that's what made him feel good—but she didn't want, ever, for Adrian to hear.

It happened very suddenly at the end of their first year. Ade had been going out with a little blonde nurse, and Ellie had more or less given up on him. She'd already told Art to find someone else, and a couple of the other guys were coming around. She had plenty of dates if she wanted them, although mostly she was too damn busy studying.

And then, after their last final that spring, she was standing on a line at the A & P near school, pushing a cartload of beer, pretzels, and coffee cake, with Ade and Art and three other students—there was another girl there, she remembered. Ade was saying something about waiting for Millie, his date, and he made a joke and said, "Isn't that right, Norris?" and dropped his arm across her shoulder. She felt an actual physical jolt at his touch. She was so startled that she turned to look up at him without even thinking. And he was staring down at her with an expression of absolute astonishment. The whole thing couldn't have lasted for more than two seconds, but it was the most definite thing that had ever happened to her in her life. She knew right then and there that something was going to . . . to *be* . . . between her and this man. She dropped her eyes instantly, and at the same moment, he pulled his arm away as if he had been burned, and they stood there in the crowded supermarket, surrounded by their laughing, talking friends, both of them, as it turned out, tingling with anticipation and nervous excitement and trying very hard to appear normal.

They waited until everyone else had left the party. She made some kind of excuse to hang back, and he got rid of his date by saying he had to study. And then the door closed, and they were alone at last, and they looked at each other and burst into laughter, saying, "Study! Study!" Of course it was funny, because they had just been celebrating their last final. There was plainly no studying to be done! And still laughing, they fell into each other's arms, kissing avidly. She remembered thinking how strange it was that although she had never kissed him before, he felt and tasted familiar, familiar and beloved.

They tore at each others' clothes; she could hardly wait to know his skin, the feel of him, naked, against her nakedness. His chest was furry, she thought in a kind of daze, and she loved it. She rubbed against him, clutching at him as his hands on her back pulled her up against his erection. He was breathing so hard and raggedly, she pulled away in alarm. His face was suffused with blood, and his eyes were hot; he muttered something and dragged her close into him again. She had never seen this Adrian Winter, and it was exciting beyond belief.

Why in the world didn't he take them both over to the bed? He was so excited himself; yet they stood like two dummies, hugging and kissing and moaning and sweating, half undressed and wild with desire. It was crazy!

Then he pulled back from her, shaking his head. "We can't, we can't, we can't."

What did the man *mean*? "Oh, yes we can. We can, Ade. I want to. I've been wanting this for ages . . ." She lifted her head to his, and once more his lips surrounded hers, sucked them in, and he groaned. She moved them both closer to his bed, waiting there so invitingly, waiting for them.

"No, no, no," he mumbled.

And she said, her lips still on his, "I'm protected. I'm protected. Don't worry. It's okay. Oh, Ade . . ."

Another groan from deep in his belly and at last, at last, they were tumbling onto the bed together, rolling around, clinging, bumping into each other, ripping at each other's remaining clothes, grabbing and kissing and biting. She was wet with longing for him, so that when he rolled over on her and pushed into her, it was easy . . . although she felt a momentary pang of regret. They had been having so much fun. Why had he cut it off so quickly? And then the thought was drowned in the flood of sensation as he pounded into her. Oh, God, he felt so good. It was so wonderful; it was better than she had imagined. He was so big, so hard, so wonderful . . . And then she dissolved in a sea of lubricity, screaming at her joy, and it was over.

She stayed the night with him and then in the morning, when she woke up, raised herself on one elbow and gazed tenderly down at him. He opened one eye, smiled a little, and said, "What do you mean, you're protected!"

"What?" She couldn't for a moment focus on what he meant.

"You have a diaphragm?"

Oh. So it was going to be that old you're-a-bad-girl routine. "So what?" Tears pricked at the corners of her eyes. She thought this was different; she thought *he* was different.

"So you're probably more experienced than I am!"

"So what?"

"So maybe you'll teach me a thing or two?"

Her heart lifted. She smiled at him. "Oh, yeah?"

"Yeah. Like . . . right now?"

Oh, boy, oh, boy! And she fell onto him, hugging and squeezing him in her delight. This time, she figured, they'd take their time. But no. It was the same as the night before. Very nice, but . . .

She shifted in her seat and slid a sideways glance at Steve Gussov. Shame on her for not listening to the music! It was the Dorian Wind Quintet, one of her favorites, and instead of paying attention, here she was in a reverie about the sexploits of her youth. It wasn't even some long-lost all-night adventure, either, but that first awkward time with Adrian, of all the damn things! Funny . . . as much as she'd loved him—and she certainly had—they'd never experimented sexually, never gone beyond the ordinary. Oh, it had been good, all right. It had been fine. Well, she loved him! No, scratch that. She was crazy about him! He was her dream come true; even after three children, there were moments she couldn't believe her luck that he had chosen her.

And then came her decision to go back for a neurology specialty, and then came Leslie Fox, and then came the divorce. And then, ultimately, inevitably, came other men. How well she recalled the first. David Powell, delicious David! She'd never forget him. How could she? Warm, sensitive, kind David Powell, the kind of man women dreamed of finding and almost never did, a man unashamed of his gentler side, unafraid to be considered weak or feminine. She had had plenty of men friends through her life; of course, she had. But David was different. David would talk to her the way a woman might, focusing on feelings and on people rather than on statistics or things. It made them a terrific team . . . in the clinic and everywhere.

Particularly in bed. Ah, yes, particularly that. Of course, it was a young body, when she had become accustomed to the little sags and softnesses in the bodies of men more her own age. She had never known a man so muscular and powerful. He would pick her up and carry her to bed, and she would laugh and say, "You're the first man—and the only one, I'm afraid—who could make *me* feel delicate and tiny." And he'd laugh with such pleasure. Whatever she liked pleased him. It was one of his many many charms. Dear David, with his rather plain snub-nosed Welsh face, his silky dark hair, the heavy beetling brows, and almost like a surprise, the gentle soft eyes beneath. How beautiful he'd seemed to her.

They had such fun together, always. One golden October afternoon was etched into her memory. He had been so mysterious, he would only tell her that they were going to Fire Island for the weekend. He'd borrowed a house from his friend Wolf Masterman—a beautiful house, he told her, right on the beach. "Don't bring a lot of clothing," he warned her. "Just a bathing suit and a quilt." She had thought he was kidding, but as it turned out, she really didn't need much else. The weekened was one of those Indian summer miracles, all bright blue sky and fluffy clouds and thick sunshine, and they were the only ones for miles around.

It was perfect. It was paradise. She could not remember ever having been so completely happy . . . never. They had to be so careful in the city, so self-conscious, so constrained. If anyone at the hospital should ever find out she was sexually involved with him—! She could just imagine Nate Levinson's reaction to *that*! He'd be shocked and disapproving. "A woman in your position—" That's what he'd say; that's what anyone would say. "A woman in your position, head of a clinic, a physician, on your way up . . ." She knew the end of *that* thought; she'd heard it often enough. A woman in her position was not allowed to have an affair with a man who not only was her nurse—bad enough!—but who was so much younger than she! Never mind that the men doctors did it all the time! A woman in her position was not allowed that freedom. A woman in her position was not allowed period. And so she and David were forced to sneak around. They crept to each other in the dark, they lied, they pretended . . .

But not on Fire Island, not on the white sand, smooth and undisturbed for miles, where David tenderly spread out the quilt and then tenderly took her, making slow, careful love, kissing her everywhere, touching her everywhere, murmuring to her and smiling into her eyes. The sun was as warm and soft on her bare body as the quilt under them. She floated, and she melted; they floated and melted together, over and over. And when they stopped making love, sometimes they still clung together, holding on to each other tightly, deriving such comfort from each other . . .

She ought to be ashamed of herself, sitting there next to a man—a man she liked a great deal, in fact—and thinking not about just one other man but *two*! And about stuff 'way in the past at that, 'way in the past and over and done with. Foolish middle-aged memories, all sex and purple passion! Who needed fantasies, anyway, with a man like Steve? She snuck a look sideways at him. Nice Steve. With him, there was no ambivalence, no ifs, ands, or buts. It was friendly, good-natured lust—just the sort of thing she needed in her life. No great emotion, no problems. They were actually very open about it, too. They would behave quite nicely in public, smile at each other, be polite, make conversation. Like tonight. And after the concert, she knew, he'd ask her if she'd like something to eat, and she'd demurely say, "No, thank you."

And then they'd get to her house, and the door would hardly close behind them when they'd crash into each other at about eighty miles an hour, undressing as they went. Most times, they never made it to the bedroom even. And afterward—well, okay, no melting, no floating. But that wonderful physical release, that contentment that came with satisfaction.

She shivered a little; in a way it was a shame he lived and worked in Boston, but maybe it was just as well. It was like an eternal honeymoon. By the time he got to the city, they were both raring to go.

As if reading her mind, he leaned over and mouthed into her ear: "Shall we go now?"

"No," she whispered.

"No!?"

"I think we should wait for intermission." He gave her a nudge, and she could feel his grin even though she didn't look at him. Almost instantly, she became wet. Turning, she said very low, "Steve? I've changed my mind. Never mind intermission."

The clock by her bedside said 12:38 when he flopped over onto his back, whistled, and said, "That was a good beginning."

Ellie laughed. Not for the first time, she wondered why he felt it necessary each time he was finished to pretend he'd just got started. He was a fantastic lover, capable of going on and on for hours—which he had just done. So why the little joke? the little putdown? the little defensiveness? As usual, she told him she'd had more than enough to satisfy her, "and maybe ten or eleven other ladies," she added. "Although I'm not going to call them in to test my theory."

He patted her hip and groaned the groan of a man who has just finished a good job of work. "That was pretty good," he said. "in fact, that was very good. In fact, that was so good, I'd like to do it more often. In fact, I'd like to do it a *lot* more often. Get me?"

"If you're asking me to stay awake one more minute, the answer is no, no, and no. I'm bushed!" She kept her eyes shut.

There was a moment of silence. Then she felt him roll over

onto his side, facing her, felt his warm breath on her cheek. "I didn't mean anything so short-term as another hour, Ellie."

"Uh-oh." Her eyes flew open.

"That's right, lady. Uh-oh. The man's proposing."

"Oh, Steve, I wish you wouldn't."

"Hold on there, doctor. Don't get nervous. We don't *have* to get married. We could nicely live in sin; that would be okay."

"My patients . . ." she said weakly. Inwardly, she thought rapidly. Any other time but now! If only she could make him take those words back. Two months ago, she wouldn't have paused for more than a minute. He was a lovely man—at fifty-six, perhaps a mite too old for her, but still lively, still sexy, still in shape—and she was very fond of him. He was a successful businessman with plenty of money of his own; they could have such a good life. But that was before her heart started to misbehave whenever she saw Adrian Winter. That was before she admitted to herself that she was still in love with him. No, worse than that, that she'd never stopped loving him really. So now it was very complicated. No, it was simple. She couldn't have the man she really loved because he was married, and she couldn't fall in love with anyone else, either.

"Oh, Steve, I couldn't. Really I couldn't. You're lovely, I'm ever so fond of you—"

"Oh, Christ! As bad as that, is it!"

"Steve, please!" She was surprised at the pain she felt for him.

"Hey, doctor, no problem. Forget I said anything."

She paused, trying to think of the proper phrases. "I don't want to forget you said it, Steve. I just want . . . time, I guess."

"A year and a half isn't enough time for you?"

"Steve, please, you don't understand."

"Oh, yes, I do, honey. What's his name?"

"His name is Steve, and I don't want him to go away, but right now—"

89

He grunted, then patted her again. "Listen, Eleanor, I'm going to make you a proposition. You come to Boston to live with me, and I'll get you the top job at Children's Hospital."

She had to admit it, it was awful, but her mouth watered at the thought of being chief of service. Chief of service! To do all the things she wanted to, to have the money in her hands so she could make the choices! Oh, Lord, it would be heaven on earth!

"Bribery is beneath you, Steve," she said lightly.

"At this point, I don't consider anything beneath my dignity. Goddammit, Eleanor, I love you! There! I haven't said *that* to any woman since my wife died . . . and that's seventeen years!"

He hadn't moved a muscle, yet she felt as if she were being smothered, surrounded, pressed. If she had ever had any doubts— She listened to herself as she blabbed and blabbed at him about how good it was that they didn't see each other so often, how bad she was to live with, how erratic her hours and unpredictable her moods. But they were all excuses, all of them. And Steve was no fool; he must hear it in her voice.

"Tell you what," he said. "Let's cool it for a while."

"Oh, Steve!" Her heart hurt at the thought of giving up their good talks and their good sex and their good times. She'd have to start all over again, into that depressing singles scene . . . Oh, Lord, she didn't know if she could hack it anymore.

"Just for a while, Doctor. Then, when I come back to see you, how about giving me the straight story?"

He knew somehow . . . but she had no answer for him, no easy explanation. She didn't know herself whether her love for Ade was a fantasy for the purpose of keeping her uncommitted or whether she couldn't commit because she truly did love her ex-husband. Would she ever?

"I'm sorry," she said, finally.

She winced in the dark when he said, "I hope you're not even sorrier in the end, Ellie. It would be a damn shame."

Chapter 7

C*ON* S*COFIELD LOOKED* up from the record books spread out in front of her and twisted her head from side to side. Her neck was stiff. The big round clock opposite the nursing station said it was nearly 2:30 A.M. on Friday night. Well, Saturday morning, really, but in her head, still Friday night. And she always felt lonesome on Friday nights. Why was that? Probably because Friday night to the rest of the world was a release from the work week, a rest from labor, and a chance to relax and let go. But not here, not in a hospital. And especially not in ICU. Of course, she didn't really *have* to be there. She was head nurse; she didn't have to take night duty if she didn't want to. But her friend Margaret Kenney had a heavy date tonight, and she was covering for her. And anyway Con felt it was important for every nurse and doctor to take night duty from time to time. Things were different at night. You had to be extra alert . . . and she was. She might be deep in paper work; she might even be daydreaming. But a part of her brain was always up there, watching those eight little screens with their lines of light, their *beeps* and *bleeps* that signaled respiration and blood pressure and heartbeat and everything else a nurse had to know. You never really rested in the ICU, never. There the clicks and hums and buzzes of all the machinery—the testing machines and the measuring machines and the life-sustaining ones—never stopped, never ceased, never rested . . . except at death.

She rubbed her eyes with her knuckles, sucked in a deep breath, straightened her back. The nights kept getting longer and longer the last few years. And then she saw herself, reflected darkly in the glass entrance doors. Look at that old broad, built like a truck, with a haircut that might have been done with a hatchet. God she was a mess! What's the matter with me, she scolded herself. Just look at me, allowing myself to get old before my time, overweight, unattractive. God, would any man see this woman and desire her? Not on your life. No wonder nobody ever looked at her anymore in the halls. It had been years since she caught one of those interested doubletakes. Hell, it had been two years—no, wait a minute . . . make that two years, three months—since she had a *real* boyfriend. Those occasional onenighters with Tony Veldecchio didn't count. But she had to admit she could use one of them right now. Maybe she'd call him when she got home.

God, what happened to the years! Here she was, still a young woman—fifty-three wasn't so old, not really—and yet she had to call a man in order to get laid! It seemed like only yesterday that she was twenty-two years old, fresh out of nursing school, and having to beat them off with a stick. She'd been a cute thing, real cute, always on the plump side, but they liked that. And she was fun; she liked a good time, liked to drink, liked to laugh, and liked to make love. Still did. So what happened to the soft, round, sexy Connie Scofield? Where was she and when had she gone away, leaving this tired middle-aged woman, sitting there in the ICU in the middle of the night, waiting for people to die?

She gave that wavery reflection a good long stare now. Yes, it was too damn bad. She'd let herself go. Fifty-three wasn't so old! Come on! She'd go on a diet; she'd get a new hairdo. Tomorrow. For sure. Just because she wasn't in her twenties anymore, that was no reason to give up.

She was lucky. She had her health. Oh, it was a cliché; she knew that. Her mother had always said it: as long as you have your health. But she was an RN; she *knew* it was really true. If you worked ten minutes in the ICU, you got a new respect for that cliché. Look what she had here tonight. A bleeding ulcer; almost died because the man was bleeding from the rectum all day and was too modest to tell his wife. He had to have five transfusions; lucky his son and daughter both had compatible blood. An FUD—a fever of undetermined origin—a real bitch, 105°, 106°, and no reason for it that anyone could discover, the woman'd had every test in the book, and meanwhile, she was fading. The woman with toxemia . . . she'd almost lost her baby, and might still. And Susan Palko. She didn't like thinking about Suzie; it made her feel torn up inside. But she had to, because there was Suzie, just a few feet away in Room C, lying there helpless, ruined, destroyed. Her life over.

Dammit, she'd trained that little girl! Susan Palko, class of '83, cute as a button, a real winner. She cared about patients, she had endless energy, and she was always cheerful. Had her whole life ahead of her: a good career and a nice boyfriend, and a couple of months ago, she'd pulled Con aside and whispered that she was pregnant and so happy. And look at her now. Only her head really alive; the rest of her body dead, dead, dead.

Oh, God, what dirty tricks fate played on people. So many crooks out there, so many evil people; you'd think one of *them* could get paralyzed from the neck down, but no. It had to be sweet little Suzie Palko!

Con abruptly got up. The paper work could wait, dammit. And Arlene was watching the monitors. She went to Room C where the private nurse sat, knitting peacefully in the dim light. They'd managed to get Brian Fuller to go home at midnight. The first week Susie was here, he'd stayed round the clock, his face tight and grim, his shoulders tensed, sitting by the side of the bed, the chair pulled up close, staring at her. That didn't do anyone any good. The boy had a job; he couldn't stop living because of this tragedy. But they still had to kick him out at night.

Suzie's eyes were closed, and she looked asleep. Con spoke in a very low tone. "Carmen, why don't you take a break now? It's been a long night."

The little nurse put down her knitting needles eagerly and stretched. "Thanks, Miss Scofield. I could use a cuppa coffee about now." She yawned hugely. "This poor child doesn't take much work."

"Did you turn her?"

"At midnight. I'll do it again when she wakes."

"Good. And Carmen . . . take your time."

"Thanks a lot, Miss Scofield. But I won't be long."

Nice little girl, and a good nurse, too. Not nearly as good as Suzie Palko . . . as Suzie *had* been. Suzie would never again put her hands on a patient, take a pulse, hold a hand, give an injection . . . nothing. Con leaned over and pressed her lips to Suzie's forehead. Poor child indeed! Carmen was probably no older than her charge. Helplessness made children of them all, patients in the hospital. And Suzie seemed to look younger every minute she stayed here, her features slackening.

Con straightened up, resting her hand on Suzie Palko's inert shoulder. God, the patients she had bent over in the night, through the years! So many, too goddamn many! The night was treacherous in a hospital. Pain that was forgotten in the daytime came up to gnaw at you in the quiet hours. Fears that were stifled by watching television or reading a book sprang up to haunt you. You were vulnerable in the middle of the night when most of the world slept and dreamed and you were wide awake and hurting.

How many brows had she rubbed through the years of nights? How many hands had clutched at hers for safety? She had smoothed out and tucked in endless sheets. Oh, yes, she remembered. White faces, brown faces, men and women and little children, too, and what she recalled best were the eyes, so grateful for the footsteps in the dark, for the touch of her hands. And sometimes, for the warmth of her body. Oh, yes, it was never spoken of, never admitted, but she certainly couldn't be the only nurse who had eased herself into bed with a man who needed her.

Suzie's eyes opened unfocused, and then they remembered and filled with pain. Con kept herself from wincing, kept her voice calm.. "Hi, there, Suzie. It's Con."

"Hi, Con. What time is it?"

"Three in the A.M. I sent Carmen downstairs for a cup of coffee. You thirsty?"

"Yes . . . it's one of the few things I can still feel."

Con turned away, ostensibly to fill the glass with cold water. She held it for Suzie, placing the bent straw between her lips, hating every minute of it. It was no good, having these feelings. A nurse was supposed to be professional. It wasn't supposed to matter if it was your own mother suffering there on the bed. Just like a doctor, you had to stay objective and keep your distance. "The patient is suffering enough; your suffering added to it is only going to hurt." That's what she learned in nursing school.

"Brian's looking better, isn't he?" Con said, conversationally.

A wan smile. "I think he started to eat." She sighed. "Poor Brian. He doesn't know what to do with me, this way . . ."

"It's going to take time for him to deal with it," Con said, but Suzie shook her head as hard as she could.

"Don't talk to me about time, Con. I don't *want* him to deal with it. I'm no good to him now."

"Suzie, listen. You're still in shock, in a way. Do me a favor. Don't make up your mind about anything yet—"

The voice was harsh. "Don't give me that stuff, Con. I learned how to do it in class, from you, remember? I know what's going on!"

"I know you do, honey. It's just that your state of mind—"

"I'm very well aware of the state of my mind, Con, thank you very much! I've got nothing else left! You don't know . . . you don't know what it's like to lie here able to do nothing, not one goddam thing, except think. And cry. Oh, shit, I'm sorry, Con. I don't want you to feel bad. I promised myself I wouldn't pull any dramatics on anyone— But it's hard, Con; it's so hard! . . ." Then her voice cracked, and tears flowed from her eyes.

Con grabbed a tissue and mopped at the wet streaks, murmuring comforting noises, then held a tissue to Suzie's nose.

"Oh, shit! I can't even blow my own nose! You know what I want, Con?"

"What? Anything!"

"I want Brian to find himself somebody else. I want him out of my life. *My life!* Ha! This isn't a life!"

"Suzie, please, give yourself some more time. Try to take it easy. I know it's hard. But think of all you have left . . ." The girl on the bed made a deprecating noise. "No, really. First of all, you have a man who truly loves you. I know he wants to marry you. Everyone heard him yelling it at you the other day. He loves you. He wants to take care of you."

"Yeah. Feed me and change my diapers . . ." There was just a tiny pause, and then, in a changed tone, she cried, "My baby! I lost my baby, and now I'll never be able—" Again there were tears, and again Con wiped them away.

"Listen," she said, talking as fast and earnestly as she could, as though the sheer force of words would erase the misery and blot out the anguish. "Listen. I saw this fellow on television once. He'd been in an accident, just like you. And it was wonderful; they gave him this robot, this mechanical arm, like, that moved to the sound of his voice. It was terrific! He'd say, 'Up,' and it would move up, and then he'd say, 'Stop,' and it would stop and then he'd say, 'Right' or 'Left' or 'Continue.' And he had learned a whole bunch of code phrases, too. And damned if that thing didn't put a meal together from the refrigerator, put it in the microwave, and then feed it to him . . .''

Suzie bitterly said, ''Just my type!'' She turned her head away.

Con winced inwardly, but she went blithely on, her voice as bland as custard. ''And you know what he said, Suzie? And he was young, too, just twenty-one or twenty-two.'' He said, 'At first, you think it's all over. Then you have to recognize your limitations. And then you have to change them!' '' She paused delicately, waiting, but there was no response. ''Change your limitations! Think of it! What guts! It could be a lesson for anybody! Where there's life, there's hope, Suzie! They're inventing things every day: computers that move your legs . . . whatever you want.''

This time there was a long silence, through which Con could clearly hear the hands of the clock outside clicking their slow way around the hour and the hum of the respirator next door.

In a strangled voice, Suzie said, ''Want! *Want!*You know what I want, Con? I want you to stop with the fairy stories! I want you to go away! I want to be dead! That's what I want!''

''Oh, Suzie . . .''

''Get out! Get out! Leave me in peace, for God's sake!''

Con said, quite calmly, ''Well, here comes your nurse, so I'll just leave you for now, Suzie. But I'll check back with you later.'' And, quite calmly, she smiled at Carmen and said softly, ''She's upset, I'm sorry to say.'' And, still without fuss, she let herself out of the unit, into the corridor beyond. No sound there, either, nothing to see, just the tiny red lights over the doors and down there at the end, the red and green arrows on the elevators. There was no one there now, no one at all. Con leaned against the wall, trying to keep her chin from trembling, fighting the tears that threatened to overwhelm her. And then a sob wrenched itself painfully from deep in her chest, and in a moment she found herself weeping wildly.

No, dammit, she wasn't going to stand there in the hallway, crying like a madwoman! But the tears were uncontrollable; they came from so deep inside her. She shoved her fist into her mouth, clamping her teeth down so she wouldn't make any noise. The sobs hurt her throat, hurt her chest. It hurt, it hurt; she wasn't able to help Suzie at all! But that was impossible, unthinkable! It was her job to help. She was good at it, damn good! If she couldn't help Susan—someone she knew so well; for God's sake, she had trained the girl!—then who *could* she help?

Was she losing her touch? But no, that didn't bear thinking about. Because if she lost that, she lost everything. That was what made her a nurse! For years, ever since the beginning, it had been Con Scofield for the difficult cases, because Con Scofield could make them want to try. If that was gone—! If she was used up—!

She straightened her back, took in a very deep breath, and then let it out slowly. She would not have hysterics here on the floor. Absolutely not. She would calm down, and she would go back in and do her job. Because that was what this was all about. And that's what she was all about, and that was the end of it.

Chapter 8

*H*E WAS SUCH a beautiful baby. And he smelled delicious, too. Their housekeeper, Delia, had just bathed him and put him in those cute footed pj's that Leslie Winter just loved. They made Gregory look like a little elf . . . but much cuter than any elf, she thought, smiling at their reflection in the mirrored walls of the foyer. The baby smiled back. He was so good! All the other mothers at the Pierrepont Street playground complained about the Terrible Twos. He had never been a Terrible Two, not for a minute! "Gregory's a good boy," she crooned into the mirror, smiling at him, and he smiled right back again. He was very responsive to a happy face. The nerve of that woman in the playground today! "Doesn't obey very well, does he?" she had said. Well, she thought, she didn't want an obedient little robot. He had such concentration! She'd noticed that for a long time. Once Gregory got involved in playing, he was in another world. She always had to go over and put her hand on his shoulder. She was careful to do it gently; she'd never forget the time she picked him up when he was in the middle of something or other. How he had jumped! And then he cried all the way home; she couldn't seem to comfort him. So, ever since then, she'd been supercareful how she interrupted him. Today, now, he had been so intent on something he saw outside the fence, of course he didn't hear her when she called him. He just kept right on going, right out the gate. She was just about screaming when Delia laughed and said, "Now, don't you ruin your voice, Mrs. Winter. I'll just run out there and get him." Delia often said that when little Greggie made up his mind to do something, there wasn't nothing could make him change his mind. It had nothing to do with *obeying*! Leslie hadn't answered the stupid woman . . . it wasn't worth it. She didn't even *know* her, and anyway, she had an appointment back home with the upholsterer.

She nuzzled happily into the baby's sweet-smelling, soft neck and watched in the mirror as he giggled and wriggled around. He was so beautiful! All right, she was his mother, but he *was*! Everyone said he looked just like her, but she thought he had Adrian's mouth. The big hazel eyes were hers, without a doubt; and unless it changed later on, the little nose. The honey blond hair, too. Oh, she hoped it wouldn't darken on him. Her mama had lived in fear that her hair would turn mouse brown; she used to check it every couple of weeks. In good weather, she'd pour lemon juice on it and make herself sit in the sun until she was sweating like a pig. And it never had changed. Until just recently. Leslie walked over close to the mirror and peered at herself. Yes, there they were, those gray hairs. Were there more today? She thought so. It was coming in faster and faster. Well, she'd have to throw her pride out the window and get her hair colored, or she'd *never* get another job. Not as an ingenue, anyway. And those little squint lines by her eyes—she leaned practically into the mirror so she could see, and the baby whimpered.

She pulled back. "Oh Greggie, did Mommy frighten you? Mommy wouldn't bump your head, little boy." She gazed at the baby face, completely contented with what she saw, and pressed her cheek against his velvet one. "Just wish Daddy would get here," she said, "don't you, Greggie?"

"Da-da," Gregory said, and she whooped with delight.

"Good boy, good boy. Now say, 'Ma-ma.'" The little boy watched her intently in the glass and pressed his lips together in an exaggerated way.

"Ma-ma," he said, and Leslie gave him another hug. He was talking! What did Adrian mean, he was late to talk?

Dr. Blume, his pediatrician, laughed at that when she told him. "Ade's just playing the proud father," he said. "Particularly since this is his first son. Hell, Einstein didn't talk till he was four! Tell him that, Leslie! And tell him," he added with a hearty laugh, "to stick to his own specialty."

"You're perfect," she said to the baby's reflection. "Mommy's perfect little boy."

Where was Delia? Wasn't it his bedtime? And she'd have to get dressed soon for the dinner dance at the hospital. She had a brand-new white satin—got it on sale at Saks—and a white marabou boa. Adrian hadn't seen this outfit; she'd been saving it for the next black-tie affair. And they hadn't been to one for simply ages! When they were first married, they went to *everything* . . . all the hospital affairs and then all the parties at his medical school and all the conventions—she loved the ones in Europe—and she got to wear the most exquisite clothes. But lately he hadn't wanted to do much of anything. At last, she'd made him say yes to this one, and they were going to go, or her name wasn't Leslie Fox Winter! And she was going to have a wonderful time. She hugged the baby, holding his arm out, and twirled around the foyer, humming a Straus waltz tune. She loved to dance, she *loved* to dance, and that night she was going to dance until her feet cried ouch.

"Delia!" she called, and the housekeeper came in at a trot, grinning broadly, holding her arms out. Gregory immediately began to twist in her arms, eager to get to Delia. She was so lucky, Leslie thought. Gregory loved Delia, and so did she. Delia was that rarity of rarities, a genuine jewel. Everyone said so. She took care of the baby and the house; Leslie could go out on jobs whenever she needed. And modeling jobs often went into crazy hours. Of course, it had been a little while since the agency had called, come to think of it. She'd call first thing tomorrow. But right now—she relinquished Gregory and turned to scrutinize herself carefully in the glass—right now, it was time to fix her face and look beautiful for her handsome doctor-husband. Now that she thought of it, what could be better than a nicy icy carafe of white wine waiting! Good idea!

She went into the big kitchen and looked around with pleasure. When they got married, Adrian bought this co-op as a surprise present for her. It had been a mess; the kitchen, for instance, hadn't been done in thirty years at least. It was so old, the sink had legs, and the walls were painted dark green, and all the cabinets were wood. And the living room! Maroon! "Do anything you want," he had told her, lifting her up and swinging her around. "The sky's the limit for my beautiful bride!" And then they made love right then and there on the foyer floor; well, on the thick wall-to-wall carpeting that had been left. Leslie sipped thoughtfully from her glass of wine, staring at her ultramodern oak and white kitchen without really seeing it, seeing instead her husband's face as it had so often looked when they were courting and first married: suffused with adoration and lust.

She let her thoughts drift, and she thought how lovely it would be if the door would open and it would be him, smelling of the outdoors, his cheek a little rough and cold, calling her name, and when she went to him, he would be eager; he would sweep her into his arms and hug her close and kiss her long and hard. And when she said, "Oh, honey, don't, you're spoiling my surprise; I had a nice pitcher of wine all ready for us," he'd growl, "Forget the wine; you're intoxicating enough." And then they'd go right into the bedroom, and he'd make love to her . . . as it used to be.

Leslie sighed and took a deep drink from the wineglass, refilling it from the carafe. She mustn't finish it before he got home . . . and she certainly didn't need the calories, God knew.

What time was it, anyway? She drifted into the huge living room, only half admiring it. What good was it, with its beautiful furniture and its beautiful art on the walls, all arranged so they could entertain twenty people without crowding, when Adrian was just too darn busy and too darn preoccupied. They hadn't had a party in ages! They hadn't *been* to a party for three weeks, and it wasn't for lack of invitations, either. When your husband was a well-known doctor and chief of Ob/Gyn at a hospital, you got invited to a lot of things. No, they hadn't been going out, and they hadn't been making love very often since . . . since when? Since forever, it felt like. At least since Nate was kicked out as chief of staff at the hospital. When was that, seven months ago? Well, it seemed like a million years to *her*. She was young, she needed to go out, and she needed her sex.

The phone rang, and she ran to pick it up, checking the time as she did so. Ten after seven. Good, that must be Adrian; it only took him fifteen minutes to walk home from the hospital. Let's see, that would make it about seven-thirty, and the dinner dance began at eight. So she could entice him into bed, and they'd still make it back to the hospital by eight-thirty. That was plenty early, and—

"Hello, darling," she said. Oh, wasn't it silly how breathless she felt.

The answering voice was a shock. It was female. It was saying, "Terribly sorry, Mrs. Winter, the doctor asked me to call. He's in the labor room. He says he'll be home as soon as possible."

"What about the dinner dance? Did he say anything to you about the dinner dance?"

"He told me not to call Mr. Del Bello yet, so I imagine he hopes to make it, Mrs. Winter. But this looks like a tough one, so I don't know . . ."

It occurred to Leslie that she could go to Cadman with his clothes and go downstairs to the party herself to wait for him, maybe have a couple of drinks and a dance or two with Art Schuster or Jeff Boynton or maybe that cute new doctor in pediatrics. But oh, no, none of the young interesting doctors would be there; this dance was for old crocks only. Oh, well . . . the last party they'd gone to at the hospital, back in June, Hank Del Bello had all but propositioned her. It would be interesting to see what he'd do tonight. "You tell Dr. Winter I'll be dressed and waiting for him," she said, and hung up.

Ten o'clock. Damn. Damn, damn, *damn*. She had to squint to read the little numbers; she'd finished the whole carafe herself and had refilled it, and now it was gone again. Whoops, she was a little bit high. But who cared? they weren't going to go to the dance, so she might as well make her own party. And she'd spent so much time bathing and perfuming herself and doing her hair. Foo on him. Who told her it was nice to be a doctor's wife? Carefully, she took off the white satin and hung it in the closet. All her undies were pure silk and cluny lace. The bra was just a wisp, designed to push her breasts up, with just a hint of pink nipple showing . . . and the panties were just as weentsy. She sucked in her stomach, turning from one side to the other in front of the large mirror in their bedroom, striking poses easily and naturally, as if she were in front of the camera. Her hair, which she had twisted into a Grecian knot, she let loose and shook it so that it covered half of her face and then looked through its golden curtain. *Any* woman would love to have that blonde! If she wanted to, she could get dressed right now and go to Aesop's Fable on Montague Street and sit at the bar, and in six minutes she'd have every man in the place swarming around. She eyed her image, considering. Should she pull on a pair of jeans and a sweater and try her luck? It would serve him right if she ended up being fucked by some hot young bearded stranger. Maybe someone who looked like Joe the pharmacist—he was always coming on to her, and he was adorable . . .

ADMISSIONS

But she knew she wouldn't. She was chicken. What if he found out? It was unthinkable. A doctor's wife didn't go around letting strange men pick her up and screw her, not in Brooklyn Heights. The Heights was like a small town; everybody knew everybody. Especially a doctor's wife. All the big shots at Cadman Memorial lived there, and all of them were well known to everyone. She could *never* . . . ! Of course, she didn't really want to. She was just miffed right now. She gave herself a cute little nose-wrinkling grin in the mirror. Of course she didn't mean it! She loved her husband! It was just that lately he had been so . . . so . . . Well, how long since they'd made love? Five days! Five whole days, and the last time he'd really only been doing it to please her. She could feel his lack of interest, and it was just like not having it at all.

Leslie yanked at the panties. She heard them rip, but she didn't care. Off with the bra! Off, off, off! Naked, she danced herself around the room, singing loudly, wishing she'd brought another carafe of wine into the bedroom with her. Adrian didn't pay enough attention to *either* of them lately! What was his problem? They loved *him*! She told him all the time, and Greggy just beamed whenever he saw his daddy appear.

She walked herself over to the mirror and stood with her nose practically on it, looking herself over. Oh, God, I'm getting old. Just *look* at me! Her eyes filled with easy tears, and she blinked them back. Look at that belly. It was positively gross—she could grab a whole handful! And her breasts! They were *sagging*! She frowned at herself. What was she going to do? You couldn't get them back up once they started to go! And then she caught sight of her face, all screwed up, like Greggy's when he was getting ready to howl. Instantly, she smoothed it out. Scowling made wrinkles. She was already getting them; she didn't need any more. Oh God, she was really truly getting *old*. How many years to the big four-oh? Not many, not enough! No wonder Adrian was ignoring her . . . no wonder he was late so often!

She peered at herself with great intensity. Am I—oh,

God—too old for him now? Had it been her youth he fell in love with? He was a gynecologist, for God's sake! He was with women all day long. And didn't women always fall in love with their obstetrician? And how about all those nurses? Not one of them was over twenty-three. Well, except maybe Con Scofield, but she didn't count. Everyone knew that the young nurses were always falling in love with the handsome doctors . . . especially if they were chief of service! Oh God, what if some little nurse was after him and he was liking it! It wasn't impossible. After all, she told herself, *I* was the other woman. I took him away from his wife, and *she* was a doctor herself! He fell in love with me at first sight. All my friends said, ''Forget it, will you, Leslie? Those guys never leave their wives.'' But he did because he was so crazy about me. Oh hell, he can't be fooling around with someone else, not when he has me at home. Can he? She smiled bravely at herself. Of course not. He was late, that was all. Some woman was having problems, or it was a first baby and taking a long time, and Adrian was the kind of doctor who believed his place was with his patient. He was so wonderful, she should be ashamed of herself even thinking about fooling around, or even flirting. She had a wonderful idea; she'd just climb into the bed all naked and wait for him.

Adrian had let himself into the house quietly. He ached all over, and after he hung up his coat, he stretched and pulled his shoulders back. It was no good; they hurt, anyway. What a night! Seven hours in labor and then a breech presentation. The fetal heartbeat had stopped three times. But in the end they did it, without doing a C section, he and the nurses and Bobby and a gutsy mother who was awake every minute. She'd been great; it was the husband who thought he would faint. Adrian grinned a little, remembering it. Well, it had been a light touch in the middle of everything. And now there was a new person in the world, Ronald Adrian Tyler, eight pounds four ounces, 17½ inches long, breathing just fine and perfectly alert. He got nine on the Apgar. Again, Adrian stretched. Deliveries were always satisfying . . . well, almost always. When there were problems or there was a stillbirth, that was rough; rough on everyone. Not this time, of course . . . although it had taken a helluva long time.

But if he was perfectly honest with himself, he had been just as glad to have a genuine reason not to show up at the dinner dance. He started down the hall, carrying his shoes. The apartment was totally quiet; Leslie must have fallen asleep. She'd be sure to give him hell the next day about missing the dance. He sighed deeply. He was sorry for her sake; she was such a child in some ways, and she loved to dance and flirt. But shit, why couldn't she realize how awful it would have been for him to sit through the whole program and listen to Schuster give *his* keynote address and have to smile and smile and smile. The trouble with Leslie was that she was too young to understand, too young for a lot of things. He sometimes wondered if their marriage had been a mistake . . . but, oh hell, he loved her, and she worshiped the ground he walked on. He was lucky. And then of course there was Gregory. His heart filled at the thought of his beautiful little boy, and he carefully opened the door to Greggy's room. The night light—a sleeping Snoopy—was on, casting a faint pink glow over the child who lay on his stomach, his knees pulled up under him, his little rear end up in the air, his plump little cheek looking like pink and white satin, the long eyelashes sweeping down. His breathing was calm and even, and he didn't move a muscle. Adrian smiled at his son, bent to pick up three stuffed animals Greggy had thrown to the floor, put them back into the crib, and stood there staring at this unbelievable creature, this perfectly formed little person who was flesh of his flesh and blood of his blood. His son. A flood of emotion rose in his chest, and he reached down to pat Greggy's smooth cheek. The little boy stirred, and he instantly pulled his hand back. Best not to wake him; he'd be up half the night.

He went down the hall to their bedroom. He wrinkled his nose; it was filled with the smell of stale wine.

Leslie was under the quilt, fast asleep. He tiptoed around; if she had been drinking all evening, she'd be less than pleased if he woke her. He had his pajama bottoms on when she stirred and mumbled, "Adrian? That you?"

"Go back to sleep, sweetheart. I'm sorry I woke you."

"I'm not." Her voice was heavy with meaning, and he thought, Not now, honey. I need my sleep. "Ade? Come on over here."

"Uh . . . Leslie. Listen, sweetheart, do you know what time it is?"

"Don't care. C'mon . . . I saved a place for you." She giggled.

He slid under the quilt, and she immediately moved close to him. "Leslie." He gave her a light kiss, searching a moment for her lips in the dark. Her mouth opened provocatively; she tasted of stale wine. "Honey," he said. "I'm very tired."

"Let me rub your back, sweetie. Come on, roll over."

"Not now, sweetheart . . . I'm very tired."

"Come on, Adrian. It'll make you feel *so* good."

Dammit, didn't she know how to take no for an answer? He shifted a little on the bed, irritated; she misunderstood and burrowed down under the quilt, trying to push his pajama bottoms down, kissing his belly and making crooning sounds. Oh God, he thought, but his penis stirred a bit, aroused in spite of his fatigue. Leslie smacked her lips and tugged at his bedclothes. She bit lightly at the skin on his belly, then moved her lips down, her mouth open. He could feel her warm breath, and he wished he were awake enough to enjoy it. She was very good at it. Her mouth enveloped the penis, licked at it, sucked on it. And he was falling asleep. He couldn't help it; he was drifting off. He could feel his prick soften and go limp even as her tongue curled around it in the way she knew he liked. His head was so heavy; his eyes felt weighted. He wanted to say, "Tomorrow, honey, tomorrow I'll make it up to you," but he couldn't find the strength to open his mouth. His lips would not move. He was falling asleep; he was falling asleep . . .

Leslie felt the cock go soft, and at first she couldn't believe it. It couldn't be! He always responded eagerly to anything she decided to do. That's what he had always loved about her. She was his sexual adventure, he told her. She didn't wait for him to make all the moves; she was avid and eager. "God, but you're primitive," he told her the first night they made love. He'd *always* got hard for her! All men had always got hard for her! What was wrong?

She lifted her head and whispered, "Adrian? Darling?" There was no answer, just a suspicious evenness to his breathing. She wriggled up the bed. He was asleep! He'd fallen asleep while she was coming on to him! The bastard! How *could* he? She could always get him hard by using her mouth, always! What, did he think that every single time he rolled on her, she was as eager and willing as she seemed? Was he kidding? Plenty of times she was worn out; plenty of times she was damn mad at him for spending all his time in that dumb hospital and ignoring her. She could have been out having a good time for herself if she hadn't got married and had a baby. Plenty of times she felt like pushing him off and saying, "Not now, Adrian." But did she, ever? She did not! He never knew, not even for one minute, that she might not be perpetually turned on to him. And he had the goddamn nerve to fall asleep while she was giving him head!

And now he was starting to snore, goddammit! And she had been so good, never complained one word. She hadn't bitched at him when he finally called to say their evening was off. She'd been sweet as pie and so fucking understanding! And furthermore, she hadn't even said she'd go without him. She'd tried that once, and he'd become terribly upset. She'd realized then that he was jealous. He was scared to have her at a party without him, where she could flirt and dance and drink when he wasn't there to keep an eye on her. In a way, it pleased her that he was so possessive. A big important doctor was jealous of little Leslie Fox from nowhere! Well, but this time she could have easily insisted that she was going to go; she had bought a new dress and the shoes to go with it and a beautiful little pewter bag. Oh it was such a stunning outfit, and dammit, Adrian hadn't taken her anywhere for weeks and weeks! She was only thirty-six years old, dammit. That was *young*, too young to sit around this apartment with a baby while everyone else went out and danced and saw plays and had a good time!

Not to mention their love life! But he'd better watch out, because she was getting awfully horny. It was more than a week; she knew that. A week! At her age! What a waste, what a waste!

She sat in the bed, shivering a little, yet unwilling to curl up next to him. He had really made her mad this time. He was so self-centered. He hadn't even said he was sorry about her missing the dinner dance, about messing up her evening . . . her weekend, as a matter of fact.

Oh, it made her so mad! She'd thought that being married to a doctor would be wonderful. She'd imagined that everyone would envy her because she was the doctor's wife. The doctor's wife! That was the top of the heap! Well, and look at her now . . . sitting shivering in her bed while her husband snored away next to her, ignoring her completely. Oh, she had all the clothes she wanted, all the help she needed, a beautiful little baby, a lovely apartment—everything she'd ever dreamed of, really—and yet she had nothing. It was all a waste.

She finally lay down next to Adrian, being very careful not to touch him. To hell with him! If he didn't want her, there were plenty of men who did! She curled up into a ball, trying to get comfortable. Plenty of men!

She could be in bed with anyone she *wanted*, and no other man in the world would be asleep next to her! David Powell . . . She smiled a little to herself, thinking about him. David was a beautiful man, a giant of a man. He towered over everyone. He must be well over six feet and broad . . . Oh, those shoulders, those great big broad hands with the dark hair curling down from the wrists. She got weak whenever she looked at his hands, imagining them on her body, eager and strong. She drew in a deep, shuddering breath, her own hands playing the part of David Powell, running over the soft breasts with their erect nipples, over the flat belly and the smooth inner thighs. Oh God, he would be wonderful. Everyone loved David, everyone. They all said he was the best nurse in the whole hospital; they said he could lift the patient together with the bed and not even sweat. Sweet David Powell, who took care of the geriatrics, even the Alzheimer's patients who were so difficult and childish and acted crazy so much of the time. He was patient and gentle. He called them all by name, he listened to them, he put his big muscular hands on them. They must feel so good when he did that! Oh, David! Leslie stifled a moan and wrapped her arms around herself tightly. Her heart was beating very fast; she must stop this . . . Sometimes he touched her. When she wheeled the book cart onto the geriatic floor, if he was around, he'd give a big grin and come over to her. "Need help today, Mrs. Winter?" And he'd let his hand drop onto her shoulder. It felt like something scalding her; she felt the breath catch in her throat. And yet his touch was so light; it wasn't as if he were coming on to her, as the others always had. But he liked her; she knew he did. When she looked up, his eyes seemed to bore right into her, right through her head and into her thoughts. She could always feel herself blushing whenever she met his gaze. It wasn't slimy, as if he were undressing her mentally; his look was tender and sweet.

At first, she'd been flattered and enjoyed the little flirtation they had. And then she thought he was around more than usual. She thought she noticed that he appeared more and more often in the rooms she was visiting. And she found herself, every Wednesday—that was her volunteer day; every doctor's wife had one a week—every Wednesday she'd put on her makeup with extra care, trying to erase the signs of age. She wanted to look extra special for him. And young. He was young. She wanted to see his eyes light up when he spotted her; she waited, almost holding her breath for him to come up to her, to look her over the way he did, to grin down at her and say, "Lookin' good, Mrs. Winter." Or, "You certainly brighten up the place, Mrs. Winter." He had the deepest dimples, the whitest teeth!

She knew; she knew. She wasn't dumb; he couldn't fool her with his "Mrs. Winter" this and his "Mrs. Winter" that. He liked her; he wanted her. Lately, she had such a strong feeling whenever they were together that all he needed was a sign from her and his big muscled arms would reach out and crush her to him. And lately she had to fight herself not to lean up against him, rub up against him, feel him get hard with wanting her . . .

In her bed, wide awake, she felt the throbbing between her legs. Oh God, she was really horny! Why couldn't Adrian seem to understand how she needed it! It would be so wonderful with David Powell . . . she just knew it. He was so big, so tall, so broad. And the size of his hands and feet! Isn't that what they said? You could tell the size of the prick by the size of the feet . . . If that was true . . . She bit her lower lip, imagining the thickness and the heft of him, stiff and hard and bulging out . . . Oh, God!

Leslie hurled herself out of the bed. This had to stop! It was crazy! And it wasn't nice, picturing herself in the sack with another man while she was lying right next to her husband. Her poor tired husband, who had to deliver women's babies no matter what time it was or how exhausted he was . . . or no matter how badly his wife needed him. She really ought to be more understanding. She really ought to be more patient.

She glanced at the glowing green numerals on the bedside clock. Only 10:56! Unbelievable! So early! Why, they were still eating at the dinner dance. She could get her clothes and still go if she really wanted to. Oh, that was silly . . . of course she didn't want to appear at the dance at this hour, alone. She grabbed for a robe in the closet and belted it tightly around her waist. She was really wide awake now.

Dammit, she wished she hadn't thought about David Powell. That was no good. No good could ever come of it. And it didn't even soothe her and put her to sleep. No, it just made her hornier than ever. She heaved a great sigh. She wished Greggie would wake up. That was a funny thought, but she'd enjoy playing with him now. It would give her something to do, to take her mind off other things.

She'd go watch the news. She liked the news. Her daddy was a news freak; well, all those years he'd spent in the wheelchair, that was his preoccupation. He read every newspaper he could get his hands on, and he watched all the news shows. And he liked her to sit with him and discuss the news with him. So now *she* had to watch the news; it was something about her that tended to amuse Adrian, as if he couldn't believe that someone so pretty could care about the world.

Well, maybe she had more than one surprise for Dr. Adrian Winter . . . if he didn't wake up and start paying attention to her one of these days very soon.

She wandered into the den and turned on the set, snooping around for something to snack on. Sometimes the housekeeper left little dishes of candy or nuts around. Yes, there was one . . . chocolate-covered mints. Oh, yum. She grabbed a handful and started to nibble. She'd diet tomorrow.

The picture sprang to life on the screen, and she let out a little cry because it was Cadman Memorial. Wasn't it? Yes, of course it was. You couldn't mistake that tower, stuck onto the old-fashioned main building. But my God! What was going on? They couldn't possibly be covering that dumb dinner dance. They had *that* every year. TV coverage. Wouldn't it just be her luck that they'd have it the year she wasn't there! She'd kill Adrian if that's what—

And then she began to listen to the announcer. ". . . Police are inside, and I'm told there is no danger to any of the patients . . . Wait a minute, ladies and gentlemen, I've just been handed a bulletin . . ." The camera shifted to a rather harassed-looking Connie Collins who was trying to look into the camera and read at the same time. "A hospital spokeswoman says that there has been a shooting in Cadman Memorial and one person is dead, but that the police have it under control . . . The alleged killer has surrendered and is—''

Leslie didn't wait to hear anymore. Oh God, a shooting! She'd have to wake Adrian right away; would he be mad? He was so tired. But he'd be furious if she didn't. A little smile curled her lips. It'd serve him right if she let him sleep, let him wake up tomorrow and go to the hospital knowing nothing.

Shame on her! What a horrible thought! Her own husband . . . No, no, she couldn't do that to him. And what if it was one of his own patients? He'd never forgive her.

She ran down the hall, calling his name loudly as she went. He'd be very irritated to have to get up. Too bad. If he'd made love to her, he'd still be awake.

Chapter 9

B*RIAN* F*ULLER WALKED* slowly down the corridor, his head bowed. He didn't have to look where he was going; he knew the route from the elevator to the ICU by heart. He'd walked it every day for the past three weeks. The nurse on duty barely glanced up when she heard him approach the station. She nodded without speaking. She knew who he was. They all did, he thought. He was Suzie Palko's fiancé. He was the son-of-a-bitch driving the motorcycle the night of the accident. He was the stupid bastard who didn't know enough to watch it on the Brooklyn-Queens Expressway when it was raining. He was the criminal who'd crippled the woman he loved, made her lose their baby, and ruined her life. Hell, ruined *both* their lives. Made a total mess of everything. That's who he was. Brian Fuller, the total mess. Here it was! Saturday night, when he and Suzie should have been dancing at the Olympus. And instead . . .

Maybe, Brian thought as he walked quietly down the hall, maybe he'd be able to make it up to Suzie tonight. Help her. Make it up to her. His lips twisted in a grim smile. But he didn't want to think too much. When you thought too much, it stopped you from action.

He'd junked his bike. He got rid of it the next morning as soon as he'd found out how badly off Suzie was. He never wanted to see the goddam thing again. He'd never ride again. But that was nothing; he would give up anything for her. He owed her. The question in his mind was how much did he owe her. She'd asked him to do the Big Thing. She'd asked him last week sometime. But he told her, you didn't do something like that without giving it a helluva lot of thought. He'd been chewing on it all this time. Well, of course, the first thing he said to her was no. No, absolutely not. But she'd begged him. Shit, it was horrible, sitting in there looking at her wanting so badly to move and everything, and her body was dead. Even her face and the look in her eyes. She lay there and wouldn't look at him and begged him over and over. Shit, he'd asked her to marry him right there in the hospital. He promised he'd take care of her the rest of her life. And she laughed in that bitter way and said, "But, Brynie, you don't understand. That's what I'm asking you to do, don't you see? To take care of me the rest of my life." And she gave him a look so full of meaning, he could hardly bear to look her back in the eyes.

But now he'd made up his mind. He'd thought it over nearly a full week. Tonight was the night. He stopped outside her cubicle and took in a deep breath. It was always hard, going in there, at least at first.

She was lying there, her eyes closed. Was she breathing? Yes. She was breathing. If you didn't know, you could swear nothing was wrong. She wasn't hooked up to any machines or anything. She just looked like any other pretty girl, sleeping. Like if you called her and woke her, she'd jump right up, ready to go. He winced and said softly, "Suze?"

Her eyes flew open. "Hi, Brian. What time is it?"

"Ten-thirty."

"Day or night?"

"Night."

Silence. He cleared his throat. "Suze?"

"Mmmmm."

"I've decided."

Now she really looked at him, and there was a spark of life in her eyes.

"Listen, Suze. Are you sure?"

"I'm sure. I've told you a million times."

"I know that. But you could change your mind. I wish you would change your mind."

"Brian, you know I can't live this way. You're a good man. You're strong. I knew you'd come through for me. Goddam!" She began to cry, twisting her mouth and turning her head away.

"Suzie! Please!"

"No, no . . . I love you, Brian. I love you, Brynie. I do, I do. I just was thinking . . . the way I am now, I can't even hold your hand. I'd love to . . . go, holding your hand. And I can't even do that!"

"Suzie!" The sound wrenched out of him. Tears began to leak out of his eyes. He ran to her bed and flung himself down over her body, hugging her fiercely. "Suzie, Suzie, you're my best girl. I love you, I love you . . . I can't, I can't . . . I said I would, but I can't."

"Listen to me, Brian." Her voice was ice cold and determined. "You have to. If I could do it myself, I would. But I can't. So you have to. You *have* to."

He choked back the tears. She was right. He had to be strong for both of them. Hadn't he spent the last week, night after night, day and night, thinking about it, mulling it over, changing his mind a million times? But he always came back to the same thing. She wanted it; she really did. And he understood. If it was him, lying there, helpless, no longer really a man, he'd ask her the same. Yes, he would. If it was him . . . Oh God, it should have been him. He was the motorcycle freak. She told him a million times to give up the bike. She said it scared her. But would he? No, no, of course not. Brian Fuller was too damn smartass. And she was so

117

good; she was scared, but she always climbed right on behind him and wrapped her arms around him. Jesus, that was good . . . to feel the warmth of her, close in behind him, pressing in against him, till she felt like part of his own body. And now—! Look what he'd done to her. Yes, he'd do it. He had to. She was right; he had to. He loved her. He owed her.

"Okay," he said, pulling himself up and wiping his face with the back of his hand. "You're right; of course you're right. I'm sorry I broke down."

After a moment's silence, she said, "You have it? With you?"

"Yes."

"Let me see it."

"No, Suzie, don't ask me to do that."

"I want to see it."

Wordlessly, he reached into his leather jacket and drew it out: the Colt .45 revolver. He held it where she could see it, trying to keep his hand from shaking, and when she smiled, he put it back.

"I told you," she said. "I told you it wouldn't be any problem getting it in." She smiled. "You'd have more trouble bringing me a milk shake!"

How could she joke? His insides were quivering from the tension, and he wanted to throw up. But he had to be strong. It was up to him to be as brave as she was.

He cupped his hand around the top of her head, and she rolled her eyes up to him, smiling. "That feels good."

He wanted to bawl. But instead he bent over and kissed her tenderly on the lips. "You always did have the nicest hair," he murmured. "Like silk."

"Is it still streaked from the sun? From when we were on the Cape in September?"

"Yes," he lied.

"That's what I'm going to think about, before—you know. I'm going to think about the beach and the sand and the sound of the gulls screaming and the surf when it hisses up on the beach. And I'm going to remember you, all tan and smelling of coconut oil and sunshine . . ." Her voice drifted off off and was quiet so long, he gave her a sharp look to see if she was okay.

"No, I'm all right, Byrnie. I was just thinking . . . thinking about our little boy."

"Oh, Suze! Don't!"

"No, it's okay. It doesn't hurt so much now, now that I know it won't hurt much longer. Now I can think about him. Four months along . . . well, it's probably just as well it wasn't six months or seven because then the poor little thing wouldn't have a mother."

"Suzie! Don't!"

She took in a deep breath. "Brian, listen. I love you. And I'm ready. Don't wait any more, okay? I'm ready."

"Oh, Suze—!" His voice broke, cracked, and the tears started again. She seemed not to notice.

"I'm ready," she repeated, and her voice sounded remote, as if she had already moved on. Her eyes opened, and she smiled at him. "Kiss me good-bye, Brynie. Kiss me good-bye."

He obeyed, his lips quivering. "Good night, angel," he whispered, his voice was all shaky.

She answered, "Good night, angel," and closed her eyes. Brian took the gun from his inner pocket, cocked it, aimed it. He had to hold his right arm tight with his left hand, it was shaking so.

"Suzie," he whispered.

"Good night, angel," she said in a voice softer and lighter than feathers, and he pulled the trigger.

He stared at the blood on the white sheet, the spreading pool of blood, at her wide, vacant eyes. He was sobbing like a baby, his ears reverberating from the sudden deafening noise. Suddenly, he realized. She was gone. He had killed her. And he raised the gun to his own head.

Chapter 10

THE OLD MAN'S hand slipped down, inch by careful inch as they danced, until it rested on the curve of her ass. Sandy Heller smiled to herself, thought briefly of shifting a bit so it would slide right off—because, of course, he was pretending it wasn't there at all and so held it very, very lightly—and then thought, Oh, what the hell. It's Van Zandt, and he's chairman of the board of trustees, and if he wants to cop a feel while his wife is busy talking with the other old biddies, well, okay. She'd had worse. *Much* worse. She'd give the old crock a little thrill for a minute or two, and he'd always remember her with pleasure. She'd get it back from him, one way or the other.

Only a small part of her attention was on Howard Van Zandt, anyway. Hell, she could dance and keep up the chit-chat with him at the same time and *still* look around and see everything that was going on. For instance, she'd made note of the fact that several doctors had come on to Dr. Ellie Winter. What in the world did they see in her, anyway? She was not a beauty by any means; in fact, you could even say she was plain. But that Dr. Ellie Winter was having none of them. She'd also seen Hank Del Bello make a move in that direction and had been pleased when Ellie Winter turned that cool, uninterested smile on him. Sandy was saving Hank Del Bello for herself. And she'd been watching with interest as the Reverend circulated, turning on the charm for every single person in the room. He'd pressed her own hand with that extra little oomph and had twinkled at her—he was a huge man, and he used his size to dominate—and what had he said? Something about lunch together. "I know a place, makes the best soul food," he'd said with a big grin. "You like soul food, Ms. Helier?"

And she gave him a sassy smile and said, "With you—? I'm sure anything would taste terrific." And was rewarded with a big belly laugh. The Reverend Zeke was kind of cute . . . For a fleeting moment, she wondered what it would be like to be in bed with him, with that big black thing— She might just pursue that thought one of these days. But not now. Now she had to keep her eyes and ears open and also keep Van Zandt's hand from wandering too far afield.

It wasn't much, just a little tiny ripple of movement over there in a far corner of the room. But she noticed it, and she was instantly alert. She craned her neck to see, and sure enough, Hank Del Bello had stopped dancing and had bent to one of the security guards who was whispering in his ear. Neither of them looked very happy. In fact—she nodded and grunted agreement with Van Zandt without really hearing him—Hank was looking greener by the second. Oh, boy. Something was up, something big.

"Oh, Mr. Van Zandt . . . I mean, Howard . . . would you mind terribly? I just . . . well, fact is, I've got to run to the ladies." She didn't have to say another word; he didn't want to hear about her having to pee or anything else real. He let go of her, all flustered, and she positively ran out of the ballroom, because the guard had left in a big hurry, and she didn't want to lose him. By the door, Hank was already in conference with Art Schuster, talking very quietly and fast. But you couldn't hide a story from Sandy Heller!

She had to hustle. Glancing around to make sure nobody was watching her, she walked as fast as she could—damn these stiletto heels!—into the lobby. It was totally deserted except for just the guard at the front desk, so nobody knew anything yet. She turned to the right and followed the green-clad back to the elevators, slipping in casually just behind him, looking into her bag as if hunting for something so that she wouldn't have to meet his eyes. Once she looked at him, the chances were he'd ask her where she was going. This way, she was virtually invisible.

Second floor! Better and better! All the really dramatic and interesting cases were here because of the intensive care and cardiac care units. And there he went, down the hall toward the ICU. Oh, God! Let it be the nurse, the paralyzed nurse with the bearded boyfriend. She'd been trying to get a story out of that case for weeks now. Con Scofield was the original gorgon; she didn't let anyone anywhere near her precious patients. Especially the nurse—what was her name again? Oh, yes, Susan. Susan Palko. Oh, please let it be her. . . . Had a miracle happened and she moved or something? Wouldn't that be fabulous? God, it would be the story of the year, and Cadman would look better than Jesus doing the loaves and the fishes. And so would she, of course, and that never hurt.

To anyone who had ever been in ICU, it was immediately obvious that something was going on. The nurse on duty, while appearing calm, was chalky, and her eyes kept shifting nervously over to one corner of the room. And no wonder. In that corner were at least four guards, surrounding some poor guy in blue jeans slumped over in a chair, his head in his hands. Quickly, she moved closer, and as luck would have it, he lifted his head. It *was* him, the nurse's boyfriend, the motorcycle freak. Instantly, almost without thought, she reached into her little bag, got out the Minox, and began clicking away even before she had taken in the fact that he was weeping, tears just streaming down his face. She got off six shots before anyone in the room could have known what she was doing, and then, smooth and swift, she tucked it back into her bag. By God, she had gotten away with it! She stifled the smile that sprang to her lips. What in the hell had happened, anyway? Had Susan Palko died? It sure looked like it. If she'd got better, he wouldn't be sitting there crying with four guards around him. What the hell had happened?

In her head, she began to figure it. The nurses had stopped watching the monitors, and she died without anyone knowing it, and he'd found her that way. He looked absolutely stricken, in agony. Or they'd forgotten to give her something, some medication she needed. Or worse, they OD'ed her. What *was* it? Very quickly, she moved in as close as she could get. In a minute for sure someone was going to notice her and kick her the hell out. Hospital people were funny sometimes about publicity; they didn't seem to understand yet that her job was to make them look good. Hell, if anything went wrong, she could cover it up! Didn't they realize that?

"She asked me to. She asked me to. She *begged* me! You understand? You understand how she felt? Christ, she wasn't alive from the neck down! My poor baby! My poor baby! Oh, Suzie! They didn't let me go with you. They stopped me, baby! They stopped me! I'm sorry. I'm sorry." He paused a second, swallowed, and said defiantly, "I'm not sorry I did it. She wanted it. I'll take my punishment, but I'm not sorry I killed her."

Killed her! Oh, my God, what a story! Oh, my God! Her mind racing, Sandy quickly moved up to the little group and in a low but authoritative voice said to one of the guards, one she recognized, "Gary. Sandy Heller, head of PR. What's going on here?"

The guard turned, startled, but he immediately responded to the voice of authority. "Well, Miss Heller, this guy just shot his girlfriend. He had the revolver to his own head, but George here"— he pointed to another guard—"got there just in time to grab it."

"Have the police been called?"

"Of course. We always call the police right away with something like this."

"Good." Her mind was really racing. She had the picture. Had she been too far away? Could she risk taking some more? No, not necessary; it could be cropped quite nicely. She was almost positive that she'd gotten a few shots after he lifted his head so you could see his grief and the wetness on his cheeks. The point was How did you do the story so that the hospital didn't look negligent?

Now there was a commotion outside in the main corridor. The sound of footsteps, agitated voices . . . She recognized Hank's, he had a really gravelly voice. And in a second, in he came, almost at a dead run, scowling like crazy. "Jesus Christ, a gun! a gun!" he was saying. "A guy got into *my* hospital with a goddam gun!" And then he stopped, looking at them all with surprise, as if he hadn't expected anyone at all to be here. He opened his mouth as if he were about to say something to her, then changed his mind and turned to the duty nurse. "Okay, what happened? Tell me the worst. How many did he get?"

The nurse frowned at him. "How many? What do you mean, Mr. Del Bello?"

"The guy, the guy, the guy with the gun! How many?"

"How many people did he *shoot*, do you mean?"

"Jesus, how many times do I have to ask you? Of course how many people did he shoot, for Christ's sake!"

Her lips tightened just ever so slightly. "He only shot Su—!" She broke off, her voice quivering a little, and then continued in a much tighter tone. "He—Brian Fuller is his name—he shot his girlfriend, Mr. Del Bello. She begged him to kill her. She was totally paralyzed, you know, and very depressed."

Some of the tension went out of Del Bello's shoulders, and he almost smiled. "Oh, Christ. The story's all over downstairs that some nut case got in and went berserk up here—shot up the whole place, they're saying. I'm sorry about the girl, but I've got to say it's a relief. There's a big difference between a mercy killing and somebody just going bananas.''

It was time for her to step in. He didn't know a damn thing about how to handle this! Well, okay, that's why he hired her, so she could do it.

She stepped up then, putting a hand on his arm and standing very straight. "Everything's under control, Mr. Del Bello," she said, "publicity-wise. Nobody else knows what has happened. I already have half a dozen absolutely beautiful pictures . . . and I know the story. I've been following it for weeks, and I have lots of background notes. He's a very sympathetic young man, not a nut at all.''

"But Jesus, Sandy, a guy got in here with a gun! What kind of security have I got if a guy got in here with a goddam gun!''

"It was a handgun. He could have gotten into anyplace in the world with it except an airplane. The hospital can't be blamed for that. And, as you said yourself, this was a mercy killing.''

"Doesn't matter. If one guy can get in with a gun, then ten guys can get in with ten machine guns, for Christ's sake. They're gonna crucify us, Sandy!''

He was sweating. Smooth, slick Hank Del Bello was greasy with sweat. Sandy gazed at him thoughtfully. It was not becoming to him; it made him look as if he had no class. She put that thought away for when she needed it.

In a soothing voice, she said, "No they're not. Not with the two of us handling it. They're not going to crucify us . . . they're going to sanctify us. Oh yes, they are. We're going to smell like a rose!''

He gave her a look of such gratitude and childish trust that it was all she could do not to laugh aloud. "Really?" he said. "How?''

"I've had years of dealing with the media, Hank. I know most of the reporters in this town, for openers. And as for the rest, between the two of us we'll figure out exactly how to handle this so that Cadman Memorial becomes the most respected, beloved hospital in the history of medicine.''

He blew air out of his mouth and threw his head back. After a moment, he said, "I think I'm going to be very, very glad that I hired you for this job." There was an extra layer of meaning in his voice, and she felt that old familiar lift inside, the one she always got when a deal was going through, when everything was working just right.

"Oh yes," she agreed, her voice a murmur. "I think you are."

More footsteps pounding down the hall; only this time she knew it was the cops. Their voices were loud; they made no attempt whatsoever to hush themselves. They just wanted to do what they were supposed to do and to hell with the rest of the world. In a minute, they burst in: three of New York's finest—God, they were getting young! They looked like babies, all three of them!—more or less led by one of the security guards.

Hank was quick; you had to give him that, Sandy thought. In a flash, he had turned to them and was saying, "It's under control, officers. I'm Del Bello, head administrator." And he was suddenly completely in charge, keeping them from the bearded boy, telling them the whole story and asking them just what they were going to do—all at the same time.

The security guard came right over to her, flushed with excitement and trying hard not to show it.

"Say, you're the lady in charge of public relations, aren't you?"

"Yes. What's happening?"

"It's getting wild down there. The lobby's crawling with reporters and TV camera crews. I've got two guys down there helping me, but I don't know how we're gonna keep them off the elevators. They smell a story, and they want up!"

"Oh, lord! I hope they don't make their way into the dinner dance . . ."

"Don't you worry about that. I made sure they don't even realize anything's going on in there. I got them all in the waiting area, but they're insisting they have to talk to somebody."

"You've come to the right person. What's your name?"

"Leroy Jennings."

"Well, Leroy, your boss is going to hear from me what a good job you did tonight." She watched, pleased with herself, as he straightened his shoulders. She'd seen him around; an older man with a big gut and a small enough ego so that a compliment really set him up. He'd go home tonight and brag to the little woman . . . and he'd be Sandy Heller's friend forever.

"Tell you what," she said. "I'll come down with you now and— I know. We'll put them all in the cafeteria and give them coffee. Can you get a few of your men in there?"

Seriously, he said, "I think I can round up a couple."

"Good. Then I'll hold a press conference and then . . ." But she didn't have to tell this guy what she was planning. Hank Del Bello, now, was a different matter. She took a deep breath and went over to where he was with the three young policemen and began to burble, looking just as earnest as she could manage and talking in the biggest words she could dig up from her memory. And sure enough, in a moment, she had him extricated. The three young men, it seemed, had to wait for their detectives, or something like that, and he was free to go downstairs with her.

In the elevator, she briefed him very quickly. "The lobby is full of newspaper and television people. Don't worry about them. I'm going to hold a press conference in the cafeteria and—"

And then the elevator doors opened. When the press saw two people in evening dress, they surged forward. She heard someone holler, "That's Del Bello. The head honcho." And then they were all pressing in on them and yelling questions, one on top of the other. "How many people are dead?" "How'd the killer get in, anyway?" "Mr. Del Bello! Has the guy been caught?" "How did he get in?"

Sandy watched as Hank blanched. He looked really sick. She realized all of a sudden that he'd probably never had to face this kind of crowd before. He was the kind of guy who

127

was always prepared and well rehearsed. Off the cuff, she realized now, was not his style. "Listen, Hank," she said to him, "I'll be hospital spokeswoman. As soon as I get them all into the cafeteria, you go to your office and wait for me. Start drafting a statement, and I'll be with you in a minute." Without missing a beat, she stepped forward and raised her voice. "I'm Sandy Heller, ladies and gentlemen. Head of public relations and the hospital spokesperson. We want you to have the full story . . ." She had to pause when they all began talking at once. She held up a hand, and to her delight—it never ceased to delight her when it happened—they stopped. "No, no, I can't go into it here; it's rather complicated, and I think we should all be more comfortable. There's plenty of room in the hospital cafeteria, and we can all have a cup of coffee. I know *I* could sure use one at this point." There was a small ripple of amusement. Good, she thought. "The security guards will show you where to go, and I will be right there. When I have filled you in, Mr. Del Bello will have a statement for you."

They murmured, and they bitched, but they went. It was wonderful how, with the right kind of psychology, you could get a group of individualists like these guys to just go along with whatever you said.

She turned to Del Bello. He really looked frazzled. She'd have to powder him up a little for the cameras. Otherwise, he looked fine, rather dignified in his evening clothes. As a matter of fact, he was a damn good-looking man. He'd come off very well, if she could just get him really calmed down. Look at him right now. He was turning to her, indecisive, waiting for her to tell him what to do next. She realized, with a bit of a jolt, that she really was in charge. If she worked it right tonight, she could firm up her position here at Cadman. She'd just have to be extra careful not to threaten his *machismo*. She put a hand on his arm and tipped her head back just the littlest bit. "Now look," she said, "I want you to go splash water on your face. Yes, that's very important. And brush your hair. I'm going to give them the whole background. I know the story. I know who Susan Palko is—was. I'll come and get you, and then, here's what you'll say to them—"

"I'm going to tell them that the guard who let that guy in with a gun is already fired and that the head of security will be gone tomorrow."

Her jaw dropped. The idiot. He couldn't mean that! But oh yes, he could. "Oh. Mr. Del Bello," she said in her sweetest tones, "I don't think that's the way you want to handle it. No, no. See, what people are objecting to is that hospitals are becoming more and more inhumane, too big business in their outlook. That's not what they're going to want to hear. No, what we have to say is that we care, see? We're the hospital that *cares*. Firing the guard will accomplish nothing, and besides, what it does is say that we did something wrong. See? We're not going to admit for one minute that our security was lacking in any way. Because, Hank, you know you could fire everyone in security and it could happen again. You can't have metal detectors in a hospital. Our security is very good. They don't let in strangers. This guy was no stranger. He'd been coming to Cadman every day and night for several weeks. He was very well known. No, it's not a question of security. It's a question of *heart.*"

"Heart. That's good, Sandy. The hospital with heart. Yes, I think that's a good idea. The hospital with heart."

"Yes, that's it, that's it. You don't want to come on all tough and vindictive, not when there's a tragic story to be told. I see you as the big strong leader, showing them that we're affected by this human tragedy, that we care more about the *people* involved than with any petty problems of blame or denial or what have you . . . And then, of course, at the end, you can assure them—"

He grinned at her. "I get it. I'll assure them that I'll be meeting with our head of security first thing tomorrow to discuss whether or not the hospital needs any changes in its present system and procedures." He grinned more broadly. "Did I get it right?"

Oh, that devil! Yes, it was going to be very interesting, dealing with Hank Del Bello. "You got it just right, Mr. Del Bello. You're going to be absolutely perfect. I promise." She gave his arm a little squeeze and ran off toward the cafeteria. God, he was muscular. She hadn't realized it. He looked big and well padded, even soft, but he was hard as a rock. Very nice!

She heard the murmur of their voices in the cafeteria, like the surging of the surf, long before she got to the doorway. There they all were, just waiting for her. Waiting for her! The New York press corps! God, this was wonderful! She planned swiftly in her head. She'd give the background, then she'd go back to Hank's office and look over his statement and make changes. It didn't have to be a long statement, just a few well-chosen sentences. They were damn lucky to get the chief administrator in person at all, and that's what she'd tell them. And then she'd come back to the cafeteria with him, and she'd stand right by his side the whole time so that if he needed her to fill in with a statement or field questions or something like that, she'd be there. Oh God, this was exciting, the most exciting thing that had happened in a helluva long time!

Del Bello's office was really very comfortable, Sandy decided. In the daytime, it looked a little . . . stark, a little bare, she had always thought. But then, her taste ran to antiques, not Bauhaus modern. But now, in the dim lights, it was very nice. Elegant. She stood at the bar in one corner—a very nicely stocked bar it was, every possible thing anyone would ever want to drink—and decided that what they both needed right was a stiff straight shot of whiskey. "Scotch or bourbon?" she said.

And he laughed, saying, "Vodka."

"Straight? You drink vodka straight?"

"Any way I can get it," Del Bello said. He took off his dinner jacket and threw it onto a chair and stretched hugely, grunting and groaning. The back of his shirt was soaked, she noted. And she also noted that he had muscles in his back, too. How deceiving he looked in his clothes, kind of pudgy and paunchy. He let himself drop into a corner of one of the couches and leaned back. "Jesus!" he said. "What an ordeal! But I think we pulled it off . . . Oh, listen, put an ice cube in there, will you?" She complied and poured herself one, too. Not her idea of something delicious to drink, but she might as well keep him company.

When she handed him his drink, he slanted a look up at her and said, "Just what the doctor ordered . . ." She knew what she was supposed to do; she was supposed to laugh. That was a witticism. If for no other reason, she knew *that* by his expectant look. So she laughed. Never let it be said that Sandy Heller didn't know how to handle a man, any man, under any conditions.

"What time is it?" he wanted to know, and when she checked her wristwatch, she was shocked to discover it wasn't even eleven. It felt as if days had passed since she had looked over Van Zandt's shoulder and seen Hank with the guard. "Ten to eleven. Almost time for the news. They were all there. Which channel do you want to watch?"

"Any. Doesn't matter."

She decided on Channel 4 and Connie Collins. Collins was pleasant and didn't bitch at you just because you were a woman, like some others she could name. And then she stood, undecided, in the middle of the room, wondering whether she should sit beside him or, businesslike, take a chair across the coffee table from him.

"Poor son of a bitch. To have to see his girl like that every day . . ." He breathed out loudly and shifted on the couch as if he were uncomfortable. "That's a bitch, you know. That's a real bitch, the worst. You can't know what it's like unless you've gone through it." He stopped talking and rubbed his eyes with his fingers, and then suddenly he sat forward, tense. "You know, Sandy, I hated to see him taken away by the cops. My feeling is that he did the right thing. He shouldn't have to go to jail for that."

"I'm glad you didn't say that to the press!"

"What? Oh, no, of course not. I'm talking personal now, Sandy. My father . . . he died very slowly. Of the big C, you know? With chemotherapy and radiation therapy and every other goddam thing. And then even that didn't do any good. His hair fell out, and he was weak, and his mind would wander off. So he lay there in a hospital bed, in pain most of the time. You know, it was strange. He wouldn't dose himself up, not for a long time; said he wanted to be in his right mind." Again, he let out a gusty sigh, and his fists clenched up. As he continued to speak, he hit his thighs lightly with his fists. "He was a dead man for four months, Sandy, a dead man with a heart that wouldn't quit, just wasting away and suffering . . . Jesus Christ, if I'd had the guts that Fuller kid had, by Jesus, I'd have brought a revolver myself!" He waved a hand at her. "No, no, don't say anything. I'm not grandstanding. I mean it. My poor old man who had always been so big and strong—I look like him, you know, he had this same heavy build—my father, strong like an ox, down to eighty-five pounds before he finally went, crying with the pain until he got so bad he couldn't say no to the painkillers anymore. I wish to Christ I *had* put him out; it would have been the best thing I could do for him." His voice cracked, and Sandy immediately turned away; she knew she shouldn't look at him or say anything. Now she turned the sound up on the big set and put a careful smile on her face before she turned back to him.

She needn't have worried. He was completely under control; maybe just the hint of mistiness in his eyes but nothing definite. He gulped at his drink and smiled at her and held his glass out. "Well," he said as she took it from him, "I didn't do it. I didn't have the balls, and that's that. It's five years ago, but you know, every once in a while something brings it back to me."

She poured him a generous amount of vodka, thinking to herself that Hank Del Bello seemed so focused on ambition that it was almost weird to hear him talk about a personal

132

relationship. In the hospital, he was always very aggressive and sure of himself. Her dealings with him, up until tonight, had always been totally impersonal. Up until tonight, it had always been "Mr. Del Bello" or, occasionally, "Mr. D." She had always known that he liked her work all right, but she'd never had any sense of his seeing her as a person, a woman. Well, all that had changed. He had put himself into her hands tonight, and guess what? He was going to stay there if she had anything to do with it.

And there was Cadman Memorial on the screen, looking positively stately with the lights on it. She hadn't realized how impressive it looked . . . but then, when had she ever taken a good hard look at it. Tower A was modern, but it really fit right in with the original building, which had been built when architects thought public buildings ought to look like Greek temples. And it did look like someone's notion of a temple of healing . . . She made a mental note to suggest they have a drawing done of the facade to use as a logo.

A drink in either hand and without taking her eyes from the screen, she backed up and eased herself down on the couch next to Del Bello—next to Hank—handing him his glass without looking at him.

They panned the building with a voice-over giving some background. "Cadman Memorial in historic Brooklyn Heights . . . scene tonight of a real-life tragedy . . . story of a boy and a girl . . . alleged mercy killing . . . life-support systems . . ." At that point, Sandy thought, Oh, bullshit, you guys; she wasn't on any life-support systems. But what the hell, those details probably didn't matter. They certainly didn't matter to the average viewer.

And then there was the reporter herself, mike in hand, her hair blowing a bit in the wind. And then a cut to some tape of the boy leaving with the police. And then—

"Here we go!" she exclaimed, excited in spite of herself. Hank's face looked bigger on screen than she had expected, and paler. But he looked calm; he looked calm and in charge. Good.

"Oh, you look good!" she murmured, sipping at her drink. There was something to be said for straight vodka; it made a nice warm glowing spot in the middle of your belly. And then she concentrated on what the man on the television screen was saying.

"A great tragedy has occurred here tonight," said the chief administrator of Cadman Memorial Hospital. His voice was deep and low, and his eyes were calm but sad. "The victim— whom we here at Cadman all knew—was a young nurse. She had been severely injured in an accident and was in our Intensive Care Unit, paralyzed from the neck down. Totally paralyzed."

The man on the screen paused, and his eyes misted over. *His eyes misted over!* Sandy grabbed Del Bello's knee and squeezed it in glee. She murmured, "Oh, beautiful, beautiful!" He clamped his hand over hers.

And then the man on the screen continued. "The young man, who has been arrested, was her fiancé. He was distraught, grief stricken. The young woman had begged him to free her from what she saw as a living prison. And so he did so. Whether or not his action was justified will be decided in a court of law. Tonight, at this hospital, we are not sitting in judgment. We are mourning . . . grieving the loss of a life in a place dedicated to preserving life . . ." And one tear, just one tear, glinted as it tracked down his cheek.

"Oh, shit!" Del Bello groaned. "Would you look at that! I look like a goddam fairy!" The hand over hers clenched.

"Oh, no!" Sandy exclaimed, wrenching her eyes from the screen to give him a intense look. "That's *fabulous*! One tear. Oh, my God, it's . . . *perfect*!"

"You don't think it makes me look weak?"

Now she turned and grabbed him by his shoulders. If he weren't so big, she'd shake him. "Let me tell you something, Hank. Not only does that *not* make you look like a weakling; it makes you . . . Oh, hell! It makes you look like Dr. Schweitzer! That, my dear man, is a million-dollar tear! And tomorrow morning, first thing, out goes a press release, and we're the Hospital with the Heart." She began to laugh from sheer nerves and exultation. "A million-dollar tear—you couldn't have done it better if you'd been coached!"

He looked dumfounded but pleased. "Yer kiddin'!" he said, and then he, too, began to laugh. He pulled her in to him and gave her a big hug. His cheek was harsh against hers, and he smelled of something very citrusy mixed in with his sweat. She snuggled in, her arms curling around his neck, waiting, knowing. And of course he turned his head and bent to her lips, his mouth already open.

He put his mouth over hers and thrust his tongue into her mouth, searching with it, while his arms went around her, crushing her. She felt lost in his embrace; he was so big. He had bent her back, his body on top of her, the weight of him pressing down on her, forcing her back into the soft leather cushions. All the breath was sucked out of her; for a moment, she felt totally helpless, her head swimming with sensation. She struggled a little, but he was lost in his own excitement, and he tightened his grip on her.

When he lifted his head and looked down at her, whispering, "Jee-sus!" she put a hand on either side of his face.

"Now my way," she murmured, and brought his head down to hers. She kissed him softly, licking his lips and nibbling at them. He had a wonderful firm-lipped mouth. She let her lips soften, then part, and he drew in a ragged breath, opening his mouth again. But this time he waited for her to explore him with her eager tongue.

A groan came from deep in his belly. He held his body very still for a few minutes, as if he were holding his breath, while she played with her tongue and lips, grabbing his thick wavy hair with both hands and finally grinding their mouths together.

Then he could control himself no longer. With a grunt, he pulled his mouth away from hers, his eyes glittering, breathing hard, his big hands under her satin blouse, tearing eagerly at the wispy chemise, rubbing her already erect nipples, pinching them lightly. Quickly, he stripped the blouse over her head and flung it somewhere. She looked up at him through slitted eyes, feeling the surge of heat that climbed over her breasts up into her throat. She flung the chemise away herself, panting a bit in anticipation as she watched his head come down to her breasts, his lips eager.

He was hot as hell, and so was she. She'd been wondering about him for months and lately had started a few little fantasies in which he took a major role; but she hadn't expected her reaction to be so quick and so overwhelming. She couldn't wait for his lips to cover the nipple, to draw on it, suck on it . . . and as he did so, she felt herself getting wet in a flood. She was close to orgasm, and they hadn't even done anything yet, not really. She dug her fingers into his hair, saying, "Yes, yes, yes, yes . . ." Her loins were quivering. His mouth was beautiful; it was warm and wet, and it was loving her body. It was adoring her, and he was moaning with his pleasure. Now he pulled his lips away a little and moved his head wildly, licking at both nipples by turns, his hands digging into her back, kneading her, pulling her so close to him, so close . . . The muscles in her loins began to quake; she was right on the edge, and he knew it; he knew it. He sucked at her avidly, and her back arched as she spasmed over and over, yelping, hearing herself and telling herself to be quiet but unable to stop.

As soon as she had quieted a bit, he pulled away and bent to kiss her lips again, running his big hands over her naked back and down under the satin skirt, down under the satin panties, rubbing at that sensitive spot at the base of the spine between her buttocks, moving lower. She moaned a bit, smiling, and then she felt him pull away from her. "No!" It burst out of her, and her eyes opened in alarm.

He had pulled back and was stripping off his clothes as fast as he could, just letting them drop on the floor. When her eyes met his, he laughed out loud and said, "You are crazy! Hotter than a pistol, by Jesus, and not afraid to show it. And let me tell you, baby, I *like* the way you show it." And he paused to put out a hand, which he lightly ran over one breast and down to the top of her belly. "Take off the rest of your clothes," he ordered, his voice rough with heat. "Hurry!" And he laughed again, shortly.

Her heart was pounding furiously. Wordlessly, she pulled off the skirt with the panties all at once and faced him on the couch, kneeling, pulling in her stomach and thrusting out her round, pink-tipped breasts. Her eyes never left him. She was dying to see what he looked like. And when he stood, letting his pants drop and stepping out of them, she licked her lips with pleasure. He was not terribly long but very thick and very, very stiff. It stood straight out, curving up, almost purple, it was so engorged. "C'mere," she ordered.

His eyes just gleamed. "You really are crazy," he said, but he came close to her, his cock pointing right at her. She put her hands around it, caressing it. She'd never met a man who didn't like this. And he was no different . . . just a bit hornier. She could feel his eyes on her, watching her every move, and she could hear his uneven breathing, feel his excitement growing. When she leaned forward to take him in her mouth, though, he pulled back, saying, "I'm too close to coming. I don't want to come yet."

And she looked up at his feverish face and smiled at him and said, "Me, neither."

She let him lift her and lay her down and position her on the couch. His hands were trembling as he pulled her legs apart. He loomed over her. He had a nice body, with a chestful of graying curly hair, the body of an aging athlete, a little on the fleshy side but underneath, what was left of well-developed muscles. He was very broad, with a deep chest and wide shoulders, and as he lowered himself onto her, pushing his penis into her, she held her breath at the anticipated weight.

As soon as he was in her, he became too excited to think about what she needed, pushing in and out of her in a frenzy, grunting with each move and sweating. Maybe he wasn't smart enough to satisfy a woman, but he was terribly hot, babbling every dirty word he could think of. Good, she thought. He'd be wanting her all the time from now on, all the time. And maybe she'd let him, and maybe she wouldn't. Depended on how good a boy he was going to be.

She wanted to laugh out loud with her pleasure. Now she was set; she was really set! Inside her, she felt him stiffen that extra little bit, and she thought, Good, he's ready. All she had to do was wriggle her ass a little. She'd make him come real fast, and they could catch the late news on Channel Nine.

Chapter 11

THE WOMAN IN the bed was quite beautiful but rather colorless, Bobby thought; and then he had to laugh at himself. Because, considering his own coloration, who *wasn't*? But she really didn't look well at all, Mrs. Kingsbridge, not at all. Not that she was *ill*, but she had reactive depression. And Bobby just didn't like the look of her.

Apparently Adrian didn't, either, because he was holding her hand, sitting on the edge of her bed. "Are you sure you don't want something to help you sleep? It's all right for a night or two, you know. You won't become addicted." His tone was light, and he smiled.

He got a tight little try at a smile back. "No, doctor, thank you. I'm fine. Really. And this . . . situation . . . is something I must deal with, not all doped up but fully conscious."

"You look very tired. It's important for you to get your full night's sleep. I know you feel . . . so sad right now."

"Not at all, doctor." She blinked rapidly, and Bobby marveled at her self-control. "I cannot allow myself to feel sad. First of all, Bernard—my husband—is quite upset, and I must be strong for us both. And next . . . well, Dr. Winter, you know it was not a good pregnancy right from the beginning. This is the second time I've been unable to carry full term. At least this time, it was seven months and not four. So you see, I really want to focus on finding out why this is happening and take every precaution against it happening the next time.''

"I've told you, Mrs. Kingsbridge, that we are certainly going to find out everything we can. We're going to work on this problem together. As for becoming pregnant, perhaps you'd wait a week or two?"

Now there was a real smile, weak and wavery but genuine. "I want to thank you again, Dr. Winter," she said, "for showing me the baby."

"Of course. Of course."

"The first time . . . well, they kept it from me. They wouldn't show it to me, and I had nightmares for months. I thought it was some kind of . . . monster." And at last her voice broke. It would do that lady a world of good, Bobby thought, to have a good old-fashioned cry. She was far too rigidly controlled.

When they all clustered in the hallway. Adrian quickly said, "Before any of you become too impressed with Mrs. Kingsbridge and her intellectual approach to her own stillborn child, let me point out that she can't sleep and won't eat. There's a great danger we doctors face in putting a premium on quote good behavior unquote. This woman is what too many of us consider a model patient, because she is able to intellectualize. Let me tell you, yes, she's able to tell you her symptoms and her thoughts; but her difficulty is that she hides her emotions to such an extent that she will develop symptomology from her repressed anxieties."

"I know that kind," Nick Ponte put in. "They don't *have* feelings."

"You're quite wrong, Dr. Ponte. In fact, you're totally wrong. Mrs. Kingsbridge hides how badly she's hurt because that's how she was brought up."

"Yeah, well, where I come from, the more you hurt, the louder you yell. And as far as I'm concerned, that's much better. At least you don't have to *guess* how your patients are feeling, for Christ's sake!''

"Okay. You may be right there. It's easier to deal with emotions that are out in the open. But we don't always get easy in medicine, Dr. Ponte. You, for instance, can't count on always treating women of a Meditteranean background who respond in a way you instantly understand.''

"Yeah, well, if I practice in Bay Ridge, I will.''

Bobby watched the left eyebrow arch ever so delicately, and then Adrian turned to Laura Cooper, who burst out, "I don't get it! How could this woman really care about a child who was stillborn? Of course, I realize she's disappointed. But she never bonded, and that's what counts, isn't it? What I'm trying to say, Dr. Winter, is that I don't think Mrs. Kingsbridge is hiding anything.''

"Would you care to explain her sleep disturbance?''

"Well, I—''

"This is the second problem pregnancy for this patient, lady and gentlemen . . . doctors. Let's forget Mrs. Kingsbridge's feelings for just a moment and let me ask you, What do you think is the next step in treating her pregnancy difficulties? Because she *will* become pregnant if she possibly can. And then . . . the chances are excellent that there will be problems again. If you were to suggest a course of action to her, what would it be?''

Gary Weinstein answered quickly. "Genetic counseling.''

"Right, Dr. Weinstein. Genetic counseling, doctors, is our newest diagnostic tool, and I suggest to you that . . .''

Genetic counseling, Bobby thought, his mind drifting, Right on! I wouldn't mind going to see the genetic counselor right now myself. He crossed his arms on his chest and set his face in a serious and listening expression, his eyes focused on the miniature Christmas tree at the nursing station. He defied anyone, even Adrian, to tell he wasn't thinking about the case at hand at all but about the soft belly and pink-tipped breasts of Rita Schneider, Cadman's genetic counselor.

The last time he'd looked down on that beautiful terrain

had been last Sunday in her apartment on Henry Street, bouncing around on her water bed and laughing like a pair of loons. She had $100-an-ounce pot, sinsemilla from South America, and they'd shared a joint, so they were feeling no pain whatever. That was some brunch hour! More like two or three; he stopped looking at the clock once they got started. What a woman, that Rita! Well, he'd guessed it from the first moment he walked into her office.

She had been bent over some paper work, totally absorbed. He stood for a minute or two and then cleared his throat loudly. She looked up, did a double take—it was the first real double take he'd ever actually seen in his life—and then she gave him a grin that said, more loudly than words, Hey, you look good to me! He found it very exciting; it had been so long since a woman had looked at him that way, and this was a very sexy lady: small and cute with big brown eyes and big soft tits.

"Good morning," she said. "What can I do for you?"

What sprang to his mind couldn't be said out loud, he thought. But he was wrong, because he *was* saying it out loud not ten minutes later. He was sitting across from her, leaning over her desk and agreeing with her that the very best idea for both of them was for him to visit her the very next Sunday and get better acquainted. And the twinkle in her eyes left no doubt what she meant by that.

He had gone to her office hoping to get her to call Corinne. Corinne was adamantly refusing to go in for counseling. "The Lord will provide," she kept saying in that maddeningly righteous way she had. It was obvious he was going to have to intervene, and so here he was, in one of his few free moments . . . and damned if that Rita didn't make him forget completely what he had come in for. He'd never met a woman like her before, not ever.

Rita Schneider was a free spirit, totally without self-consciousness. Within two minutes of her looking up, looking him over, and giving him that lascivious grin, she had already

142

told him she found him adorable. "You remind me of that O. J. Simpson," she said. "Anyone else ever tell you that?" And she laughed.

"A few," he admitted.

"Yeah? Well, here's a new one. Whenever I see O.J. on one of those television commercials, you know what I do?" She waited a beat or two and then said, "That's right; that's what I do. Just can't help myself. Handsome black men like O.J.—and you—just turn me on." To his amazement, he had a sudden erection at her words. She laughed again and said, "I didn't know black men could blush!"

"We can blush," he heard himself saying. "But there's other stuff we do a helluva lot better."

She lowered her voice and said, "I hope you mean what I think you mean." There were bright pink spots high on her cheekbones.

"I do mean what you hope . . . or think . . . or . . ."

They both began to laugh, and then she just said, "Look. I find you very attractive. Do you wanna try it on?" He licked his lips, feeling nervous, but he nodded. His heart was hammering in his chest. "Good," she said and licked *her* lips. He nearly jumped out of his chair. She was for *real*. "Here's my address. Come Sunday . . . for . . . ah . . . *brunch* "

And that next Sunday, there he was—Corinne would be in church for hours and hours, he could be sure of that, and Kelly would be in Sunday school—and there *he* was, holding onto Rita Schneider's round buttocks, shoving his frantic cock into her as far as it would go, shouting over and over again, "I love it, I love it, I love it!" And when he came, it was like an explosion; he rammed into her, his muscles quivering with the release of his orgasm, light flashing behind his closed lids.

He collapsed onto her, struggling at first to catch his breath, and stayed there for a long long time, just feeling good. He opened just one eye after a while and was startled to find that he was looking at pale skin. He'd fantasized it, sure, but she was the first white woman he'd ever laid. Of course, there had been one or two girls who called themselves black but were actually fairer than Rita Schneider. But this was different.

And then he had to think again. Because he hadn't been conscious of her skin color for a single second while they were making love. It hadn't made any difference whatsoever. So much for all the theories. And so much, too, for his black consciousness, for all those years of telling himself that like should stay with like, and that mixing it up was nothing but trouble. This hadn't been any trouble at all!

That was the first time . . . and last Sunday was the fifth. Or maybe the sixth. Who cared? Because each time it just got better and better. When he appeared at her apartment door, it swung open as if by magic, and when he got inside, she was hidden behind it, stark naked and giving him that grin. It never took them more than two minutes to make it to the water bed.

Bobby shivered a little and forced himself back into rounds. The first thing he noticed was that Weinstein was giving him a wiseass look; dammit, he knew Bobby had been wool gathering. But when their eyes met, he gave him a big wink. He was a good guy, that Weinstein. Of all the residents in this group, Bobby thought he would make the best doctor. If he learned not to be *too* funny. The latest Bobby had heard was a rumor that Gary was working on a play, a comedy . . . writing the damn thing! It made you wonder; I mean, you looked at Weinstein, and you saw a skinny little guy with a big slice of nose and a wise mouth. And the guy was trying to write a play at the same time he was taking his residency. The two things just didn't seem to go together.

And now Adrian was saying, "Thank you, doctors, and I'll see Cooper and Kalchuk in the OR at three o'clock, and Dr. Truman, it would be nice tomorrow if you could stay with us . . . okay?"

Aw, shit! He just hoped he wasn't blushing like a stupid kid. "Sorry, Dr. Winter."

"Just get some sleep, will you, Dr. Truman?" And he all

but ran off, leaving them to straggle to the elevators for their morning coffee ritual in the cafeteria.

Bobby went with the group, but his mind was not really on anything they were saying. Ever since he'd started in with Rita, he found himself daydreaming whenever he wasn't involved with work. They'd made a pact to avoid each other in the hospital—he got in touch with her by phone—but right now he was wishing he could stop by her office. They'd lock the door, and he'd grab her and give it to her—!

He had to quit this constant preoccupation with sex. It was crazy. He had to finish this year without fucking up, and then there were his boards . . . shit, there was his whole fucking future to think about! And instead he was thinking about fucking. It was ridiculous.

On the ground floor, the first person he saw was Sandy Heller, and right next to her, as happened more and more often later, so everyone said, was Del Bello. Bobby wondered if the two of them— Oh, but come on, Truman, he chided himself, you've got sex on the brain. Del Bello was too smart to dip his quill into the company ink. He laughed a little. How many times had he heard that expression from his old man?

The group found a table right away, which was lucky, and also unusual. Gary offered to play waiter if someone would pay for his coffee and donut. Gary was perpetually strapped, and Bobby hadn't figured out whether he was really poor or just cheap. As always, the cafeteria was a hubbub of noise and color and motion, and yet it was the place they always migrated to when they wanted to relax. Because he suddenly realized you weren't being tested in the caf. You could talk with anyone—the doctors or nurses or administrative people. The cafeteria was like neutral territory. You could say just about anything you wanted to, and it didn't count, as it did on duty upstairs. In spite of the unbelievable din, it was actually restful here.

Bobby sat back in his chair, letting the general conversation wash over him, and looked around the huge room. In spite of all the people moving around and chatting and calling to each other, it was less hectic than it had been for the whole month of November—right after poor Susan Palko died. God, that had been a circus.

"Newspaper and television reporters," Adrian had said with a grim little smile, "are not like you and me, Bobby. They have no sense of shame." And Bobby had to agree. Right after the shooting, okay, he could understand that for a day or two they'd be milling around outside the hospital, trying to talk to everyone who'd ever known Suzie or Brian or to the doctor in charge or the nurse in charge or whoever else they thought could give them a juicy story. They had to earn a living; he understood that.

But it went on too long, and every time something happened on the legal end—like when Brian made appearances in court—there they all were, back again, like a pack of vultures, shoving mikes in everyone's face and asking dumb questions. "Are you a doctor? Well, doctor, what is your reaction to the bail set for Brian Fuller?" What the hell was his reaction *supposed* to be? He wasn't a lawyer or a judge. He didn't even know the boy!

Finally, it had got so bad that Con Scofield asked for a leave to get away from them all, and Del Bello had called a huge meeting, with all the chiefs of service and all the head residents and head nurses—everyone. And he told them. "You have one answer, ladies and gentlemen, to any question put to you by the press. *No comment.* Is that clear? Yes? Good. If pressed, please tell them to speak to the hospital spokeswoman . . . that's Ms. Heller, here." And that's what they had all done, and after about a week of that treatment, the reporters all gave up.

Now when he looked around, he could see one of them, a guy from *Medical World News* named Joe Crawford . . . but that was all. And he was probably on a different assignment, anyway, since he was talking to Dr. Singh, who was Arthritis.

"Hey, you guys, can a refugee sit down here?" Bobby looked up, surprised to see one of the Medicine residents, a first- or second-year man, standing by the table. Chuck Cardin, his name was, and the only reason Bobby knew that was because he was black and, in the beginning, had come to Bobby to complain that he felt conspicuous.

"Does it ever get any better?" he'd demanded.

"Your color?" Bobby had answered with a laugh. "Nope. That won't change. You gotta face it, man. Even though you're a fucking doctor, you're always going to be a black man trying to make it in the white man's world. So what you have to do is, you have to change your head." He'd kept tabs on Cardin for a while, and then, apparently, the kid calmed down, because he kind of disappeared.

Bobby reached over, and they slapped palms lightly. "How you doin', man?"

Cardin made a face. "Oh, man, that Schuster!"

Now they all turned their attention to him. Even on the lowly level of resident, you had to notice that Art Schuster was becoming a power around the hospital. "Yeah . . . what about him?"

"What a pain! Always throwing his weight around. You guys get to say something once in a while!" There was a murmur of agreement. "Sure. You're trying to learn, right? I mean, you're here to learn, right? That's what you're here for. Well, Schuster grandstands all the time . . . never gives any one of us a chance to say word one. Man, he doesn't care what any of us thinks. I don't think he cares if we learn. All he cares is that his rich patients think he's wonderful. He holds *their* hands a lot and makes them feel good. But not us. He's only interested in shooting us down. Never a word if you have a good idea; just steals it and pretends he thought of it himself. But make a mistake—any kind of mistake, no matter how minor—and he's all over you in that nasty sarcastic way he has. In front of the patients!"

Bobby put a placating hand on Cardin's shoulder. "Tough luck, man." And silently he thanked whoever was responsible for making a man like Adrian Winter head of Ob/Gyn.

Now Gary came back with a tray loaded down with plastic cups and plastic knives and plastic-wrapped goodies, and they got off the subject. Then Laura said, "Oh swell, Gary, everything but a corn muffin!" and Gary bent from the waist, proffering it to her as if it were a bouquet of roses; and despite herself, Bobby thought, she had trouble hiding a smile. "Oh . . . well . . . thanks, Gary."

"I'm a sweetie pie, aren't I, Laura, darling?"

"You are a sweetie pie."

"See?" he said, pulling a chair up from another table, "And I didn't forget, even though I was in the labor room all night." He grinned around the table and said proudly, "A seven-pound two-ounce little lady!" And they all applauded. "You know," he added, biting hugely into a cheese Danish, making half of it disappear, "deliveries are really much better when the patients take the Lamaze course. It's amazing, the difference. She was awake the whole time."

"Who, Gary, the baby?"

"No, nitwit, the mother. Oh shit, you know what I mean!"

"As far as I'm concerned," Laura said, "I'd rather be in OR, even a delivery room, than playing mommy. I don't like—I dunno, I'm beginning to think that what I really want is surgery. But surgery isn't a woman's game, is it? They fight it all the time."

"Who's *they*?" somebody said. "Come on, Cooper. There are plenty of female surgery residents. There's one in renal surgery!"

"That's right. That's my friend Marilyn. Marilyn Chen. Ever see Marilyn? She's a teeny little Chinese girl, just about five feet tall, and you know, weensy. So of course all the scrubs in Renal Surgery are men's sizes large and extra large. She has to roll up the sleeves a zillion times, and they keep flopping down. Oh, it's more than just a pain in the ass, Gary, so stop with the smirking. It's really a message that they don't want women, that women don't belong there, and that they aren't going to do a single blessed thing to make any woman comfortable."

Bobby put in, "Are you sure, Laura? No, no, don't get all in a snit at me. The reason I'm asking is I'm thinking about all our Oriental doctors, not to mention some of the Indians. I mean, they run pretty small. Men's large and extra large would be uncomfortable for them, too."

Laura gave him a sharp look. "Better and better . . ." she said. "So they might really *have* smaller sizes. That's very interesting."

"Don't quote me."

"Don't worry, Dr. Truman. I'm not out to get anyone in trouble . . . except maybe Dr. Freidman." She was referring to the chief of Renal Surgery. "I think I'll just do a little detective work. Wouldn't it be fabulous if they were saving the small scrubs for the guys and—? Well, in any case, there's never one for her when she needs it. Never."

Cardin nodded his head gloomily. "The establishment is a bunch of turds."

"Not always," Weinstein said. "Dr. Winter is fantastic. At least I think so. Do you know he was one of the first doctors in the city to encourage his patients to do Lamaze. He was telling us stories last night about how the hospitals used to fight it and fight it. Why, I can't imagine, since it makes everything easier for everyone. When the woman is wide awake and cooperating in the birth, you don't have to dope her up, knock her out, strap her down, and you've got the husband right there with her, helping. What a difference! I wish *all* our patients would do Lamaze."

Nick Ponte gave a laugh. "Only one thing wrong with that idea, Weinstein. To do Lamaze, you gotta have the husband, right? And most of our patients . . . shit, they ain't got no husband!" He did not add, "Because they're black women," but he didn't have to, Bobby thought. He just gave Bobby a look across the table that dared him to make something out of it. So he decided he damn well would.

"Yup," Bobby drawled, "the black women ain't got no husbands . . . and the Eye-talians, well, they're laying there, shrieking and cussin' out the son of a bitch that knocked 'em up." And he gave Nick stare for stare.

"Aw come on, you guys," Gary moaned. "I can't take that stuff from you this morning. Give a skinny, tired Jewish guy a break, will ya? So the other day a Jewish broad brought her hairdresser. Do I care?"

"Wait a minute," Laura said, half laughing. "What's the joke. Why'd she bring her hairdresser?"

Gary gave her a look. "*Shiksas!*" he said, fondly. "She brought her hairdresser so she could look good all the way through the birth, of course."

Laura pursed her lips. "I think ethnic jokes are in bad taste."

"Oh no," Gary persisted. "Bad taste is when you bring your manicurist, too!"

"Ethnic *and* sexist!"

"I'm not sexist. None of us at this table is or are sexist. Right, guys? Right."

"Oh, really? Would you like to make a small wager, my dear Gary?"

He grinned. "Sure. A date."

Now Laura grinned back. "That's if you win. What if I win?"

"You get a date with *me*."

She ignored the general laughter and said suddenly, "Oh, look! It's Dr. Winter with an arm around that pretty young nurse from pedes!"

"I don't believe it!"

"Where is he? I don't see him?"

"This I gotta see!"

They all craned their necks, twisting and turning, while Laura sat and smirked. Bobby was a little surprised: Adrian was particularly warm and very supportive of nurses, whom he felt were the unsung heroes of every hospital, largely ignored or put down by most doctors. But he'd never, ever, been known to fool around with any of them! It wasn't his style. He didn't even flirt. Bobby, of course, did not deign to make himself conspicuous or obvious, but he cast a surreptitious look around. Adrian was nowhere in sight.

"Come on, Laura. What are you talking about? He isn't even in here!"

Now she allowed herself a big self-satisfied grin. "Typical! Typical! Typical! Same old story. You say 'doctor' and everyone in the place assumes it's a man!"

"Oh, shit!"

"That's right. *I*, of course, was referring to the equally intelligent, equally eminent, equally beloved Dr. *Eleanor* Winter, who at this very moment is patting Nurse Halverson on the shoulder and seems to be saying, 'Nurse, you're okay.' "

"That's dirty pool, Cooper."

"No, it isn't. You're all lousy male chauvinist pigs, and I've proved it. So there."

Gary shrugged and threw up his hands. "Oh well," he said with a mock sigh. "I've lost! Now I'm just gonna have to pay off! Dr. Cooper, I'm about to take you out for the meal of a lifetime."

"I know you'll be eating crow, Dr. Weinstein, but I plan to order lobster."

There was general laughter at that one; Gary had a reputation for being cheap.

"Well, she's going to be disappointed today," Nick Ponte said.

"Who?" Bobby said. Nick had a habit of grabbing subjects out of thin air.

"Dr. Ellie, of course. I heard Adrian say he was meeting Del Bello about something or other." He barked that harsh laugh. "So she won't get her feel-goods today."

"Watch that mouth, will you please?" Bobby found himself fighting an almost irresistible impulse to punch Nick in the face. The guy was incapable of any sensitivity whatever. What the fuck was he doing in gynecology? Or even in medicine, for that matter? "Dr. Ellie is not only a good friend of mine—and a good friend of her ex-husband, too, I might add—but she is also a wonderful physician."

"Sure, sure." Nick waved a deprecating hand. "That still doesn't explain why she meets him every morning of the week for coffee, does it?"

"I think," Bobby said in carefully measured tones, "that they discuss medicine and their three daughters and other areas of mutual interest."

"Yeah, well. She can't hold a candle, far as I'm concerned, to the second Mrs. Winter. Va-va-voom! Know what I mean?" And Nick's big hairy hands described a super curvaceous shape in the air. "I wouldn't kick her out of *my* bed!"

"She wouldn't have you, you asshole!"

"Nevertheless, she's some sexy broad. I've watched her walking around in her little uniform with her little book cart and her little ass wriggling so nice from side to side—"

"Good God, Nick," Laura said, rising to her feet, "can't you lay off for even a minute? Do you have to be gross every single second of the day?"

"Bug off, Gloria Steinem!"

She tossed her head. "To use that name as invective is a sure sign of low intelligence."

"Agh! That's the trouble with you overeducated broads. You don't know how to be women anymore."

Bobby, too, got to his feet. "Ponte, I don't want to have to tell you again. Come on, man, there must be two dozen women doctors in this hospital, if not more; and Ellie Winter is head of the Birth Defects Clinic. And she was perfectly wonderful as a wife."

"So how come he left her?"

"To tell you the truth, I never could figure that out. To leave a terrific woman like her for that empty-headed blonde—"

"You couldn't figure it out? Well, I can. And it's spelled S-E-X."

Bobby scowled down on Nick. "Sex! Sex! You know, Ponte, I'm beginning to think Cooper's right about you. You have to be gross every single minute, it looks like."

"Agh . . . you married guys. You can get it whenever you want. The rest of us have to go looking for it. And yes, man, it gets to be important. It gets to be *numero uno*, you know?" He tipped his head and grinned up at Bobby. "Aw, hell, you know what I mean. You people like it!"

For just a moment, Bobby literally saw red: little flashes behind his eyelids. One day, he thought, one day . . .

Now Laura Cooper scraped her chair back angrily. "You guys make me sick sometimes," she said. "Nick, you've really done it this time. What a supergross thing to say. '*You people like it*.' That stinks! Bobby Truman is the straightest guy in this hospital. He's married, settled, has a little girl. His wife is pregnant again. Did you know that, you horse's ass!" In disgust, she walked off, followed almost instantly by an embarrassed Gary Weinstein.

Bobby stood, clenching and unclenching his fists. Ponte *was* an ape, but goddammit, he happened to be right. I'm a phony, Bobby thought, a gold-plated triple-A fake. Married, settled, ha! He was really just like Nick Ponte, obsessed with fucking.

Chapter 12

Court Street near Borough Hall in Brooklyn was not the place to be at high noon if you were in a hurry. The sidewalks were jammed with slow-moving, serpentine streams of pedestrians traveling at a snail's pace in order to look over the merchandise. The dozens of temporary booths were highly illegal, of course, but overlooked by the occasional cop on the beat. The black vendors sang out praises and descriptions of their wares: "Check it out, Sony tapes!" "Big beautiful boots!" "Designer jeans, half the designer price!" hardly pausing to make change and dicker over prices. Here and there on the sidewalk stood huddles of Court Street lawyers, nose to nose and belly to belly, plotting, planning, mapping strategy, destroying reputations—all at the top of their voices. And then there were the thousands of secretaries, bookkeepers, and legal assistants, subclassification female, marching along as fast as possible, eyes darting about for the best bargains.

Adrian plowed his way through the throngs, oblivious to everything, just hoping he wouldn't be very late for lunch with Nate. Nate was depressed, to put it mildly, and he didn't want to do anything to add to that. But of course when he passed 44 Court Street, he gave it his habitual little salute. Planned Parenthood. The busiest and oldest Planned Parenthood office in New York . . . and wasn't it the original one? Or was the original in Brownsville?

He smiled to himself, recalling himself as a younger man, new to the Heights, standing on this corner with Art Schuster, also a new resident. They had been friendly back then, friendlier at least than they were now. They had each bought a hot dog from the cart that always stood at the corner, watching the passing scene. And Art said, "Ade, look at that! Tell me if I'm imagining things!"

"What?"

"Over there. See? The gray building with the big revolving doors. Just keep your eye on those doors for five minutes, and unless I'm mistaken you'll see a parade of the best-looking girls I've seen in a long time."

They each got another frank and stood there in the sunshine, letting themselves be jostled, counting girls. And Art was absolutely right! Practically no men went in or came out of that building; just girl after girl after girl. "What do you suppose—?" Adrian mused.

And Art quickly said, "What in hell do you think? It's a fancy cathouse."

"Oh, come on, Art. In the middle of downtown?"

"Why the hell not? And it's lunchtime, isn't it? They must have a *hell* of a lunchtime trade in this neighborhood! In fact, I saw a little cupcake walk in there just now I wouldn't mind taking a taste of. You game, Winter?"

Adrian couldn't help making a face at the suggestion. Casual sex turned him off. But to Schuster he only raised his hands and smilingly said, "I'm a happily married man, my friend."

"Jesus, so am I. What's that got to do with it?"

There was no use discussing it with Art Schuster. Art was that old cliché, the notorious womanizer, ready and randy all the time and always looking for opportunities. Adrian found it pretty slimy behavior . . . tasteless, really. Stupid, even. The man could easily end up with a venereal disease. Not to mention the fuss that went on every time he ended a liaison with a nurse. It was actually disgusting, he thought.

Later that week, it had given him enormous pleasure to say, casually, "Well, Art, it's a good thing you didn't try to go upstairs to that 'brothel' and seek out your little . . . ah . . . cupcake the other day."

"Why? They raid it? Jesus!"

"That's no brothel, Dr. Schuster. That's the main office of Planned Parenthood! That parade of pretty young things was going upstairs to get their birth-control." He had to laugh. And of course, Art Schuster being Art Schuster, he had to have the last word. "Well, at least then you know she's safe!"

Now, so many years later, he was still shaking his head over Art. Maybe he shouldn't. Maybe he shouldn't bother; and maybe Art's constant preoccupation with sex wasn't considered so unusual in today's so-called open society, so why even think about it. But he knew why he was still bothering with Art. He had always considered Art a bit laughable, a bit of a boor. Admit it; he'd always considered himself a cut—or maybe two—above Schuster. And hadn't their careers just proved his superiority? *Up until now* . . . and even thinking those three words put a clutch on his belly.

Dammit, any other time he'd have talked this whole thing out with Nate. Dammit, he'd have been grateful for Nate Levinson's ideas and support! But how could he now? How could he? Nate needed cheering up, needed good news; and that was Adrian's mission right now—to bring good news and to cheer the old man up. He had to laugh at himself; he was going to do some good job of that if he kept thinking about Art and not something interesting and amusing to engage Nate's attention . . . And here was Rose & Sol's right now, so he'd better come up with something—

"Adrian! You're late!"

He turned with a smile and then had to fight to keep it on his lips. God, Nate had aged in just these few short months!

He'd seen Nate in his apartment before, deep in one of his beloved old leather armchairs. But now, fully dressed, walking in the bright daylight, it was suddenly obvious how much weight he had lost, how bent he had become. And he needed a haircut . . . hell, he had needed one at least a week ago.

"So are you!"

"Yeah . . . well . . . you'll forgive an old man."

Adrian winced inwardly. Nate Levinson had always seemed rough-and-ready, pugnacious, feisty. He was a man built like a block, almost as broad shouldered as he was tall, with the chest of a tenor, a big head with a monk's fringe of curly hair, and a large slice of nose. In the old days, there had always been the stump of a cigar clamped in his teeth; but he'd given up smoking ten years ago. Today he looked shrunken, somehow, small and worn out. He did look old . . . he looked like an old man, and goddammit, he was only sixty-two. For a physician, that was prime time!

"Did you bring an appetite, Nate? 'Cause I'm buying."

"Agh, I'm not so hungry. Maybe a bowl of Rose's soup!"

"Soup! Come on, Nate. You don't like soup; you've never liked soup, and it's too late to start now!"

While they bantered, they had walked into the luncheonette, a brightly lit, long room that looked much as it always had, except that the old blue marble formica counter tops and tables had been recently replaced with bleached oak formica. But the floor was the same terrazzo, and the same collection of forties neon signs hung behind the counter, saying, "Coke 5¢" and "Alka-Seltzer" and "hot coffee." Donuts and Danish were piled high under clear plastic domes; there were six different homemade pies with cuts in them; and all the salads— freshly made each morning by the proprietress, Rose, as a hand-lettered sign announced—were under a clear plastic cover, in plain view. There was the good smell of soup and coffee and melted cheese in the air and the happy babble and clink of people eating well and enjoying themselves.

The two men stood for a moment, looking for any empty table, when out from the kitchen came a large round whirl-

wind wrapped in a clean white apron and topped with a head
of curly strawberry blonde hair. "Dr. Levinson! Dr. Winter!
What a pleasure!" She gave each of them a quick hug,
beaming upon them. To a young couple waiting just behind
them, she said, "These are the two biggest doctors in Brooklyn.
And they're old friends. Been coming here since we opened
in—no, no, I'm not telling. I'm not giving away my age! So!
Why are you standing? Come, we'll find you a cozy table for
two . . ." She led them down the length of the room, pausing
only long enough to call into the pass-through: "Sol! Just a
minute of your time! Look who's here!" And in a minute,
Sol was grinning at them, bending down to see them clearly;
his broad, beefy face was red with pleasure. He wiped his
hands on his apron and stuck one out to them. "Doctors are
always welcome; you know that. But especially . . ."

Adrian gave him a wink. "Listen, Sol, make the pastrami
lean enough, and I'll try to be nice to your grandson. I only
said I'd *try* . . ." Sol laughed, and Adrian and Nate moved
on. After they had seated themselves at a little table in the
rear, Adrian said to Rose, "He's a good boy, Rose."

"Who?"

"Come on; you think I don't remember the baby pictures
and the bar mitzvah pictures every time I look at him on
rounds? Not to mention the pony pictures and the prom
pictures and the first bicycle pictures and the graduation
pictures . . ."

She laughed heartily and waved him away. "Okay, okay,
I'm proud of my Gary. The first grandson. And soon he'll be
a big doctor like you. Of course I'm proud. Who wouldn't
be?" She made a gesture around the place and added, "You'll
notice a few additions on the wall next to the cash register.
Myrna! These doctors need menus!"

Adrian was so busy laughing and watching Rose's pretty,
animated face as she talked that it took him a few minutes to
notice that Nate hadn't said a word. In fact, Nate was not
even smiling. Adrian said lightly, "We should come here

more often, Nate. A doctor gets more respect at Rose & Sol's than in any hospital in the metropolitan area.''

Nate gave him a weak grin. ''Yeah. They're nice people.'' There was a moment of silence, and then, with what looked like a mighty effort, he said, ''Tell me what's new. They stopped hounding you about that little nurse, right?''

''Oh, sure. Although it was hot stuff for much longer than I would have guessed.'' The waitress offered them two giant menus, and he waved her away, smiling. ''No need . . . we'll have two hot pastrami specials, double potato salad on one, two coffees right away. And, uh . . . did Rose make a lemon pie this morning?''

''Lemme see . . .'' The girl stood on tiptoe, craning her neck. ''There's cherry and three apple streusels, and yup, I see a lemon meringue.''

''Two of those . . . but later. And the two coffees right away, okay?''

''Sure. I gotcha, doc.''

''I remember,'' Adrian said, smiling at his old friend across the table, ''when you warned me that one of the bad things about the practice of medicine was that every Tom, Dick, and Harry would think he had the right to call me doc.'' Again, no answering warmth, just a wavery kind of smile that never got anywhere near Nate's eyes. Dammit, he was going to have to get the old man to a shrink if this kept up. So far, the only thing Nate had expressed any interest in was the shooting. Lord, was it really two months ago? Just about. Here it was, almost Christmas, and that had been the week before Halloween. He remembered Halloween because all the little girls who marched around the streets dressed like nurses gave him the willies.

''Poor Suzie,'' he said. ''The little nurse, I mean. She kind of got forgotten in the brouhaha. The media only wanted to talk about the right to die!'' He made a face and took a sip of his coffee. ''Right to die! When we're there every day fighting to keep people alive. But no, they don't want to talk about that!'' He shrugged and tried for a less heavy tone.

"Did I ever tell you how I got the news? No? Well, there I was, fast asleep, and my wife—Leslie, that is—"

Dryly, Nate said, "I remember."

Adrian felt himself flush and hated it. But doggedly he kept on, not quite looking the older man in the eye. "Anyway, Leslie came bursting in—she'd seen a news flash on the television—screaming, 'Your patient is dead!' You can imagine . . . ! I'd just finished a tough delivery, and of course that was the first thing that popped into my head, and I ran for the bathroom to throw some cold water on my face, trying to figure what in hell could have gone wrong; and I was half dressed before I finally saw the news myself and found out what it was really about."

Again, uneasy silence descended. And then Nate said, "She was right."

All Adrian could think of was Leslie. "What? Who was right?"

"The little nurse . . . what was her name, Palko. She was one hundred percent right. That's why the news people homed in on it. The right to die. Don't knock it, Adrian. You don't know what it means until—"

"Nate, I don't believe what I'm hearing. Since when does a physician even *think* like that. We're too busy saving lives!"

Now he saw a glimmer of the old fight in Nate's deep-set, dark eyes. The old man stared at him for maybe a full minute, and then he said, very clearly, "Bull*shit!*"

"Nate!"

"No. Listen to me, Adrian." Nate hunched forward, over his plate, his face finally animated. "The right to die—we don't believe anyone has it. We think we—and I mean doctors—we think only we get to say who lives and who dies and when. But that's not right, Adrian. No amount of training gives anyone the capability of knowing who deserves to live and who doesn't."

"Nate! No doctor ever says he knows who deserves to live and who deserves to die."

"Yes, we do. Oh, yes, doctor, we do, we do. We make those decisions all the time, confident that we're right, that we know, that we have the inside track. We say that all babies should be salvaged . . . even if their little brains aren't working. No, no, don't try to shut me up. I'm not talking that loudly. In fact, I feel better at this moment than I have felt in weeks . . ." He paused and took a gigantic bite of his sandwich. "Remember my Sadie? Agh, never mind, of course you remember her. A massive stroke, right? You and I, Adrian, we know what that means. That's death. Even if she's breathing, even if an occasional moan comes from her mouth, the EEG is flat; there's nothing going on in the brain. What is a man or a woman without the ability to think, Adrian? Dead. Everything that makes a person a person . . . dead. And yet . . . you remember, huh? Sure you do. And so do I. She lay in the hospital and never again spoke to me or opened her eyes or knew who or where she was. And I didn't have the guts. I didn't have the strength to pull that plug. Oh, yes, I could have. Very easily, more easily than you know. But you know, Adrian, fear makes cowards of us all. I could never be absolutely sure she wasn't awake somewhere. Even though I *knew*. Agh! six months! Six months, you remember? I visited her constantly. . . ."

His voice drained away and with it all the vitality. Now he looked down at his half-eaten sandwich in his hand, eying it as if it were suddenly spoiled; and he put it down on the plate, pushing it all away.

"All I can say, Adrian, is . . . Palko was right. She wanted to die; she didn't want to live. And goddam, we didn't have the right to *force* her to stay alive."

Adrian cast about in his mind frantically for something to change the subject. Nate now looked more than animated. He was agitated; out of control. And Adrian didn't like it. But he couldn't let his worry show, not to Nate. Nate would certainly pull back and become impossibly defensive.

"You're right, Nate, of course. I didn't mean—"

"Agh, what do I know? It's so easy to second-guess. I've been out of it now for so long . . ."

"You're on the board. You have an office up there."

"Agh! Board! Office! What does it mean? My teeth have been pulled! I've got no power over at Cadman, and you know it!"

"Power! Power? I can't believe what I'm hearing. Nate Levinson, talking about power? Shit! We need you!"

"Who the hell needs me anymore?"

"*I* need you. Jesus Christ, Nate, things come up all the time. And goddam it, I don't have anyone to talk to anymore!"

Now Nate's big head came up, alerted. "What's his name . . . Del Bello. What's wrong with talking to him?"

Adrian took a deep breath. "God," he burst out, "I wish you were still there." He did not see the look of pain that crossed the older man's face. "God, it's all falling apart! Del Bello doesn't talk to me, Nate. Del Bello wants to get rid of me. Oh yes, don't shake your head, don't look like that, it's absolutely true. Can you guess who is Del Bello's pet doctor? No? Think of the most incompetent, selfish, self-centered ass in Cadman . . . no, in Brooklyn . . . no, in the world!"

"Art Schuster!"

"You got it!"

"Good!"

"What the hell do you mean, good?"

"That's where he belongs. That man is a natural wheeler-dealer. And if it keeps him away from patients, then I say, *Good*! Let him do what God intended him to do: to charm the money right out of their wallets. Don't you worry. Art Schuster will get Tower B built!" And then he sat back, apathetic once more.

Adrian had a few horrible moments, a stab of hurt in his guts. Did Nate mean that he, Adrian, could not have got Tower B built? And then he calmed himself down. Nate was a depressed person, a man who felt betrayed and left behind. It was up to him, to Adrian, to make Nate feel better. He repeated those words to himself several times; and then, with a laugh, he said:

"Remember how we thought Del Bello was a prig? Well, we were wrong. He's turned out to be . . . well, a womanizer."

"I could have sworn," Nate said, interested once again, "that he was more in love with his Catholicism. . . ."

Adrian grinned. 'Remember that little blonde public relations girl. Well, he's carrying on with her. Sandy Heller."

"I remember who she is . . ."

"Jesus Christ, Nate, I didn't mean—!"

"I know, I know, you didn't mean anything. Goddam it, Ade, why do you waste time with a bitter old man who's no good for anything anymore?"

"That's not true!"

"It's true . . . Don't argue; it's true, and it doesn't matter."

Adrian put his own sandwich down on the plate. He felt as if he had been there in Rose & Sol's forever, working hard to pick this man up, to carry him, to make him feel that life was worth living. He was having such doubts about his own life. How in the hell could he possibly help anyone else?

"Goddammit, Nate, I'm here as your friend. I *am* your friend. Goddammit, Nate, I love you!" He stopped abruptly, unable to continue. "Oh, hell, you wanna sit around and feel sorry for yourself? Go ahead. Be my guest. I've had it. Look . . ." And he stood up, uncaring what anyone else in the place thought of him or thought about the little scene. "I'm telling you, we need you at Cadman. Are you coming with me or not?"

The older man set his jaw. "No."

Adrian pulled out his wallet, searched through it rapidly, and pulled out a twenty. Slamming it down, he gritted, "Look, Nate, you're needed. I've already told you. I haven't got the time to tell you over and over. When you're ready, why don't you call me?" And without waiting for an answer, he stormed out, heading blindly up Remsen Street. He'd better walk, to cool off. When he got to the corner of Henry and Remsen, he was completely taken aback to see Bobby

Truman—Bobby?—coming at a dead run out of 275 Henry and heading back toward Cadman.

Adrian stopped where he was on the street. He felt completely disoriented. What, he wondered, what the hell was Bobby Truman, who lived at the other side of Cadman Park, doing in the middle of the day on Henry Street?

For some reason, he knew he didn't want to find the answer.

Chapter 13

LESLIE WAITED FOR the elevator doors to slide open, smiled prettily at the two young doctors next to her, and graciously allowed them to let her get out first, pushing the book trolley in front of her. She knew she looked pretty today—particularly pretty. When she woke up that morning—no Adrian in the bed next to her, of course; he'd taken to getting up earlier and earlier, and it had been weeks since she'd seen him before evening—she was already filled with a floating feeling. Excited. Elated. Like remembering it was your birthday, and there'd be presents waiting for you downstairs.

And then, when she glanced in the mirror after she got up, she was delighted to see how well she was looking. No dark circles under her eyes. She gave herself a big smile, wanting to laugh aloud. Today was going to be a special day; she just knew it. She giggled to herself and, for the first time in just about forever, took down the makeup kit with anticipation. She was going to do a super job on her face that morning . . . and when she got finished, nobody would ever guess she'd spent a whole hour. The natural look, that's what she wanted today; natural with a little polish. Natural and sweet, for sweet David Powell. And she crinkled her nose at herself in the mirror and shivered a little. Oh, he was going to be so surprised!

Oh she was being naughty, and it felt so good! When Mrs. Wittaker called and asked if she could do a favor and fill in on the book cart this Friday, at first she'd felt resentful. A doctor's wife, and all she was good for was to push a cartful of books around! And then it came to her in a flash: if she worked on Friday, she could see David Powell again . . . .and even better than that, she could see him when he wasn't expecting her. He'd been getting more and more interested in her. He tried to pretend it was just friendly, but who did he think he was kidding? If Leslie Fox Winter knew one thing in this world, it was men. She knew he was turned on! She just wished her husband would happen by and see what was going on, see how some men still found her attractive, see how David Powell touched her arm all the time when they were talking, gazed down into her eyes, smiled in that special way.

She had it all planned out. She'd put herself on the geriatrics floor around three-thirty or so, right at the end of David's shift. And then she'd ask him to help her back downstairs to the volunteer office on the main floor, and of course, he'd do it. And then she'd smile at him and say, "Oh, David, that's so kind. Do let me repay you by buying you a cup of coffee." Or was that too stiff? Maybe she should say, "Would you like a cup of coffee?" Just plain, like that. What if he said no . . . Maybe she should say that *she* wanted a cup of coffee, and then he'd have to come with her. How she'd love walking into the cafeteria with him, chatting and laughing and tossing her hair a little and making believe she didn't know full well that Adrian was there at a table with his students. Not that he ever told her. Oh, no! But a couple of Fridays when she tried calling him to ask him if he could come home early for the weekend, his secretary told her, "Oh, Dr. Winter always meets with the residents from four o'clock to five on Fridays, Mrs. Winter." So now she knew, and she was going to parade in there with David Powell and sit across from him and let him kid around and touch the end of her nose with his finger—something he had started doing recently. Oh, how she'd smile and dimple and look happy. And maybe they'd talk about poor Mr. Poznik with the two broken hips, and then she'd look serious and intelligent. Just let Adrian happen to look over and see her and stop and wonder what she was talking about so intently that she didn't even notice he was in the room!

Down the corridor she padded, smiling to herself. She had it all figured out. Adrian *had* to be jealous when he saw her with David Powell. Everyone in the hospital knew David and loved him. Every single nurse in Cadman had been rumored to be in love with him. He was so lovable, so sweet, and yet sexy. She couldn't quite understand that, but of course wasn't Adrian both sweet and sexy? Well, but she'd never really thought of Adrian as exactly *sexy*. That's not how you thought of a man his age. Not sexy, exactly . . . more like protective.

It was a cocktail party. That's where she met Adrian. At a party she hadn't even wanted to go to. But she had gone because she had nothing better to do that Friday night. It was in a beautiful brownstone, all modernized and gorgeous but absolutely jammed with people. You could hardly move. There were two good things about it: plenty of men and plenty of men. She nibbled on some shrimp and got herself a glass of Perrier and lime and began to beat them off. She was accustomed to having men make a beeline for her at any party, and she had long ago learned the art of the vague smile and the nonanswer and the drifting-away move. So there she was, holding her drink and trying to escape some nerdy little guy who kept putting his clammy hand on her neck, when she saw this tall, good-looking man standing all by himself in a corner, sipping at a short drink and looking the place over as if he were king of the world. Across the room, their eyes met briefly, and she saw a flash of interest in his. Her heart gave a little lurch of excitement; she remembered thinking to herself, Well, well, look at that; that handsome older man just gave me the eye, and I like it. She kept looking at him, and after a minute she said to herself, You know what? I'm not letting *that* one get away.

She wasn't planning to marry him; she wasn't planning anything at all, really. It was just that they looked at each other and something clicked. Before they even said a word to each other. It was so romantic! She walked over to him, and without a word they went out onto the terrace, and without a word, she lifted her lips, and he kissed her, and she felt a thrill go down her spine. And then he pulled back and said, "I don't believe I did that. I think I've had too much scotch, and I apologize, lovely lady."

"Oh, don't apologize. It was so nice. It was super! Oh, I'm so sorry you're sorry!"

He laughed, swaying a little, and she could see now that yes, he was a little looped. But very attractive. You had to look very closely to see he'd been drinking. Very attractive, oh yes. She twined her arms around his neck and pulled his mouth down to hers. Oh, yes, very nice, lovely, lovely. He kissed her hungrily and wrapped his arms around her tightly. It felt so good, so secure. He was so nice and tall.

When he lifted his head, he was laughing again. "This time I'm not sorry," he said. "I'm just sorry I don't even know your name."

Then they began to talk, and she discovered he was an important doctor, the chief of something at a big hospital. A doctor! Doctors were rich and respected. Doctors *were* the kings of the world; she knew that very well from her childhood. The most awesome and powerful figures from those early memories were the doctors who came to the house to see her father. The doctors in the hospital where her father went for treatment. The surgeons, oh yes, the surgeons, with their cold eyes and their way of looking down on you. Absolute rulers.

And here she was, on a balcony overlooking the Manhattan skyline, with a handsome, successful doctor who looked at her with hot eyes, who kissed her with eager lips, who moaned a little when he pulled her hips close in against his. If she wanted this man tonight, she was pretty sure she could have him.

By the time the party was breaking up, she had decided she wanted him. He was by far the most intelligent, terrific, exciting man she'd met in a long time. Everyone at the party knew him, and they were all asking his opinion on everything. He belonged to the tennis club, and he was a member of so many big organizations. He was just wonderful. And he never let her leave his side. But when it got to be eleven o'clock, she had to go, because she had to be up early the next morning for a shoot, and she told him. "Of course," she said, leaning up against him just the littlest bit, "you could take me home. That would be nice. And we could keep on . . . talking."

When he had hailed a cab and they were snuggled into the backseat, he said uneasily: "Leslie? There's something I should tell you."

She smiled in the darkness. "You're married, aren't you?"

"How did you know?"

"Nothing as good as you could still be on the loose, doctor!"

He threw his head back and laughed. Oh, he liked that; he liked it a lot. He kissed her all the way across the bridge, all the way up the FDR Drive to East 86th Street to her building. And then she said, "Not good night, doctor, not yet."

He looked deep into her eyes and then said, "You really mean that?"

"Oh yes, I do."

"Oh, God!" he breathed. "You are a dream!"

"Just get out of this cab, doctor, and I'll make your dream come true."

Oh, he liked *that* even better than what he had liked before. When they got upstairs and she locked the door behind them, he just stood there as if he were hypnotized. He was quivering, like a kid.

And then she realized what she had. What she had was a faithful husband. She'd bet any amount of money he'd never screwed around on his wife. Oh, no, it took Leslie Fox to go get him excited enough! So she'd have to take him by the hand and lead him down the hall and get them both undressed, and then, she thought, they'd see some fireworks!

He was so hot that as soon as she lay down beside him, he seized her, his breath rasping in his chest, and with a grunt, thrust deep into her. She let out an involuntary cry. There was nothing gentle about him; he was horny as hell. He pumped into her crazily, mindlessly, moaning without words, grabbing handfuls of her hair, biting at her shoulders. She could hardly catch her breath. She was just surprised that he didn't come right away, just kept going and going . . . and then suddenly he let out a yell and slammed into her, and she could feel his orgasm, shuddering inside of her.

He left her right after, and she lay for a long time in her bed, thinking about the way he fucked. He had possibilities. He was horny, he was well hung, and he lasted quite a while. No subtlety, of course, no great technique. All that pushing in and out was okay, but it wasn't everything. She was going to have to take him and teach him how to make love. He could take her to the best places, and he was so nice-looking. And a gentleman; not like some of the slime that came into the studios to see what they could find. And not like some of the cruds she'd had to date for the sake of her career. It just so happened she had time to work on him; she happened to be between men at the moment. Smiling to herself, she slid down under the quilt and fell happily asleep.

He called the very next morning. He said, "I think I'm crazy, but I want to see you again."

She did not say, "Of course you do," although that's what she thought. Instead, she put on her very best voice and said, "Then I must be crazy, too, because *I* want . . . to see *you* again, too."

It seemed so long ago, long ago and far away. Another life, another world. It had started out so exciting, so full of promise. He'd been so eager to see her and to touch her and to get her into bed. He'd been so ardent, so consumed with desire. The other models warned her. They said, "All these married guys are alike; they never leave their wives. Forget it, Leslie. Have your fun now, Leslie," they said. "Have him buy you some stock. Ask him for some real pearls. Get what you can, honey," they said, "because these married men never leave their wives." But the miracle had happened! *This* married man, *her* married man, had left his wife . . . his wife, a doctor herself! And for whom? For her, for Leslie Fox from Atlanta, Georgia!

The day she came into the agency with that big diamond on the third finger left hand, she felt so . . . proud, so complete. It was the payoff; it is what you got for being beautiful. And for holding out. She could have become Juanito's mistress the previous year. He begged her; he wanted her there, in an apartment in the Dakota, when he came up from Rio. She could have been the playmate of a very big gambler and been taken to Atlantic City, to Vegas, even to Monte Carlo. She could have married Charlie Gold, who owned the big coat house on Seventh Avenue and was rich, rich, rich; but Charlie could never get it up, and she decided no, thanks. She turned them all down, no matter how rich, no matter how glamorous. And she got the prize, all right, an important doctor, a sweet man, maybe not the world's most imaginative lover but at least straight, not kinky, not weird, and he loved her. What else could she possibly ever want or need?

Well, now she knew the answer on that one. She could possibly want and need some attention, for pete's sake, some human contact, some understanding, some company, some love, some warmth, some affection . . . ! Oh, hell. She stopped just before the Geriatric nursing station to collect herself. Living with Adrian lately was like living with nobody; and if she couldn't shake him up today with David Powell, well, then she didn't know *what* she was going to do!

And there he was! David! Leslie's heart began to hammer painfully. Oh, why did he do this to her? He wasn't anyone's fantasy, not to look at, though he was big and strong

enough; she'd seen the easy way he lifted patients and carried
them. But he was so cute! He was so adorable! He was
smiling at her right now, and that smile could make you do
anything in the world. That smile said you were the only
woman in existence, and it also said he was very happy that
was the case. She couldn't help it; she was drawn to him.
His black floppy hair was always falling over one eye, and
he had a habit of tossing his head a little to flip it back
. . . and she loved that. She left the book cart by the nursing station and walked to him. He had big capable hands
with black hair curling on the strong wrists. She loved his
hands.

She stopped directly in front of him, feeling all breathless
and expectant. And she could tell by the glint in his eyes that
he was feeling it, too. The notion of going to the cafeteria to
tease Adrian now seemed childish. How could she have
thought of such a silly idea?

"Hello, David," she said. She felt hypnotized, waiting,
waiting for him to do something.

"I'm almost through with my shift," he said.

"I know."

"Will you . . . meet me . . . after?"

"Yes," she said.

He swallowed visibly. "At my place."

"Yes."

"I live at—"

"I know where you live." She recited his address and
apartment number, and he whistled softly. She stood, silent,
still patient. After a moment, he put out his hand and touched
the end of her nose with his finger.

"See ya!" he said.

Half an hour later, she lay on his bed, while he explored
her body with hands, lips, tongue; her mind was reeling.
Never before, never before had anyone made her feel this
way. He was fabulous, he was fabulous, she was floating,
she was in heaven, she couldn't think, she couldn't breathe.

Oh, my God, oh, my God, it was so wonderful, so delicious. What had she done! And somewhere in the back of her mind, in a quiet, isolated place, she told herself, "*This* one. This is the one. Go get him."

Chapter 14

I_T WAS THE_ third morning in a row he hadn't come to the cafeteria for coffee, and she was disappointed . . . more disappointed than she would admit to anyone. Ellie drank her own coffee, cold and bitter as it was, and thought her own thoughts and hoped nobody could read her mind. For days she'd been saving her anger about Del Bello and Schuster in order to bounce it off Ade. He'd understand! She'd been looking forward to it; it would give them something to work on together, to figure out together . . . Oh, hell! she really felt like crying in her frustration. Where the hell was he? They'd been meeting in the morning every single day for months and months. All right, so it wasn't prearranged or anything. It was a tacit understanding, but still he had to realize that it had become a regular rendezvous! Didn't he? She hated this; she _hated_ this! First, she hated counting on seeing him every day when she had absolutely no right to do so! Second, she hated reacting in such a stupid, dependent way. And last but hardly least, the waiting and the disappointment and the silent treatment reminded her a bit too clearly of certain aspects of her married life with him. Her married life with him—her *former* married life—was not something she liked recalling. It was too painful. She had gotten a raw deal! After sixteen years of devoted wifedom and motherhood; after all those years of being a pediatrician because it meant she could have a home office and be available; after all those years of having her practice in the house so she could make her own hours and take care of the kids, as well as him—he dumped her! Yes, he dumped her, as soon as it got uncomfortable. Anyone who thought a professional woman was lucky, was considered by her husband as an equal, was crazy! And plenty of people did think so and had said so to her over the years.

And here she was, six years and three lovers later, sitting in the goddam cafeteria with a lousy cup of coffee in a paper cup and a lousy *Journal of Neurology* for company, all hurt and bleeding inside because he hadn't shown up. Screw him! Come to think of it, screw waiting around in the cafeteria for one thing and another. One thing and another . . .

David had loved their meetings in the cafeteria. It tickled him to sit side by side, close together, all but holding hands. "Right in front of God and all these people," he would say; and nobody in the world would ever guess. They would meet whenever they could during the day, after clinic hours, barricading themselves behind a pile of papers, charts, and books, pretending to be working. David would look into her eyes very seriously, very earnestly, his face the picture of professional concern and calm, and he would be saying things like "Come home with me now; I'm so hungry for you." Or "Last night was the most wonderful sex I've ever had . . ." Or "Don't smile at me that way; it makes me want to jump on you and bite your neck!" He delighted in saying things like that, because she couldn't object, and she couldn't respond. She was a prisoner of her rank and her upbringing. He knew damn well how hard she had worked to become a doctor and to get her own clinic. He knew how important it was to her. Hell, in the end, she had sacrificed her *marriage* to her career, hadn't she? And how easily she could lose it all. The Cadman medical establishment was a bunch of reactionary, WASPy, uptight men who were scared to death of having a woman be the boss of anything. One breath of scandal, and she would be out on her ear. David knew that!

Of course, secretly she loved his saying sexy things to her when nobody else could hear, or even guess, what he was saying. She loved the titillation of knowing he was excited and feeling her own excitement swell knowing that later, later, it would all become a delicious reality. Those heady moments of anticipation in the crowded, noisy, busy cafeteria were the most erotic experiences of her life. And the best part of all for her—middle-aged, middle-class mother of three, matron, physician, and pillar of the community—the very best part was fooling the world!

Except it seemed she had really been fooling herself. Because one afternoon, late, when she was at her lowest, finishing up some Medicaid stuff in the clinic and hating it—math had never been her strong point—the door opened, and in walked Art Schuster, smiling and smiling.

She was smart enough to ask herself what the hell he wanted but too dumb to realize what he was up to. He just oozed charm all over her nice empty office, and she was so tired; all she wanted was for him to get to the point, say his piece, and get out. And she said as much—with a bit more tact.

"All right, Eleanor, since you insist. I *wanted* to take you out for a drink. But if you won't, you won't . . . Very well, then. But I insist that you put those papers away. What I have to say requires your complete and total attention." He sat down, facing her, leaning forward across her desk. Too far forward. She felt invaded, somehow, and leaned back away from him. And then she knew; she knew absolutely that he was going for her where it would hurt the most. David.

"It has come to . . . ah . . . our attention that you're seeing a . . . well . . . a . . . uh . . . Eleanor, we've known each other a long time, and I've always had the utmost respect for you, and affection, too—"

"Art. Get to the point. It's David Powell, isn't it?" He nodded, looking a bit embarrassed. "That's my personal life, and I don't think it's the concern of anyone outside my family. In fact, Art, in my opinion, we have nothing to talk about."

"You will forgive me, Ellie, but we *do* indeed have something to talk about. And that something is your career."

He had a terribly sincere look plastered onto his face, so blatantly put on that she longed to slap it off. Instead, she gave him a tight little smile and said, "Have it your way. Go ahead." She hoped she looked calm; she hoped he could not see the pulse hammering wildly in her throat or that sweat was gathering under her armpits. She needed to stay in control . . . if she possibly could.

She didn't hear every single word he said; there was a humming in her ears. But she caught enough and stayed silent until he said, "Everyone is talking, Eleanor. Everyone knows, and everyone disapproves. The idea! Why, it's ludicrous! Not only is he a nurse—a nurse!—but he's just a kid! You're carrying on with a man young enough to be your *son*!"

Then she exploded. "You damned hypocrites! All of you! That is the most unbelievably sexist thing I've ever heard in my life! I'm carrying on with a nurse, and it's a scandal, right? When plenty of male doctors in this hospital do it . . ." She looked him straight in the eye and added, "Married men, too. At least I'm not married! I can carry on with anybody I please. I find this absolutely unconscionable, Art! Just because I'm a woman—!"

He threw up his hands. "Ellie! Ellie! I can't argue with that. You're absolutely right. But, sweetie, it's a sexist world we live in; that's a fact. And it's a fact that yes, we do judge women differently than men."

"The fact is, Art, you've no right to judge me at all. Do you speak for the administration? For the board?"

"Luckily, it hasn't come to that yet. No, I speak as a

friend. A friend who wants to warn you before you get into trouble.''

"Trouble! What kind of trouble, for God's sake? You sound medieval, Art. I don't believe what I'm hearing. You want to call me on a morals charge?'' She stood up, too agitated to sit.

"Ellie, Ellie, calm down, sweetie. Nobody's calling anybody up on any kind of charge. But listen to me, would you? There's enough gossip around and enough negative feeling— even my wife, even Etta, has heard something—to harm your career. Okay, maybe it's not fair. But it's reality. I know you want to keep your clinic . . . I know you love pediatric neurology. And maybe you have your heart set on being chief . . . ? *Whatever* . . . this . . . ah . . . relationship isn't going to help you.'' He held up his hand again in mock surrender. "Calm down. Don't kill the messenger.''

He was right, of course. It wasn't just him. She knew he had enjoyed being the bearer of bad news, especially if the subject was prurient. She was only sorry that self-preservation kept her from facing him with his own reputation as a notorious womanizer—usually with his nurses. On the other hand, the powers that be were exactly like him, no different. In a weird sort of way, Art Schuster had actually done her a kindness. She'd just been fooling herself, thinking they'd kept it a secret. She could feel the blood rush to her face whenever she saw him. Others must have noticed. Of course they had. And all those secret little touches in the cafeteria . . . someone was bound to have seen. She'd been living in a fool's paradise. Art was right; it was ludicrous. She and David were a ridiculous couple.

For three days—and three sleepless nights, as well—she wrestled alone with it, sometimes squirming at the thought that she and David had caused titters and whispers. And then she would remind herself of how good she felt whenever she was with him—even working in the clinic. He had been so good for her; when she had been feeling low and abandoned and unattractive, he had come along and said to her, "You look good to me." How could she care what others said? Or, as was likely the case, what Art Schuster thought that others said. And then she would picture a board meeting and the little smirks as people discussed Dr. Eleanor Winter and her nurse-lover. Could they ever give chief of service to a woman who was besotted with a man young enough to be her son, almost? And so she twisted and turned and argued with herself and got up every morning feeling as if she had been beaten, her throat and her nerves raw.

Finally, she asked David to meet her in the cafeteria right after clinic hours. It was one o'clock, and it would be horrendously noisy, but she liked that idea of all that tumult around them. If either of them was tempted to become emotional, that large audience would force them to stay cool.

As soon as they sat down, styrofoam containers of coffee ignored in front of them, David said, "Okay, supposing you tell me what the problem is?"

"What makes you think there's a problem?"

He laughed. "Ellie, Ellie, you think I don't know you? Come on. For the past few days, you've been walking around like a zombie, doing your work, answering questions, but totally preoccupied. Totally preoccupied. I figured, okay, I'd give you a few days to work out whatever it is. And now it's been a few days. So . . . you want to tell me about it?"

She had thought it would be so simple, telling him. But it wasn't, not at all. She opened her mouth, she closed it, she said, "Well, um . . ." several times, and then in the end, just blurted it out. "People know."

David frowned. "People know . . ." he repeated, puzzled. And then he grinned. "Oh, Christ! You mean people know about us . . . that we're lovers! Is that all that's bothering you?"

"What do you mean—is that *all*?"

He laughed. "Come on! Of course people know! They'd have to be blind *and* stupid not to see it!"

"Dammit, David, don't be so insouciant. I've worked hard

to keep it a secret . . . *you* know that. We've never been to so much as a movie together! Maybe it doesn't matter to you—everyone finding out—but it sure as hell matters to me!''

''I understand that it matters to you. In the beginning, sure, it pays to be careful. But, Ellie, now we've known each other long enough to know it's going to last. Now if people are finding out, so what?''

Ellie heaved a great sigh. Patiently, she said. ''David. Darling. Listen. I'm a doctor, on the staff of this hospital . . .''

''You're not answering my question.''

''Let me finish. As a doctor on the staff of this hospital, I have to maintain a certain decorum, a certain standard of behavior—''

''Oh, Christ, Ellie! This can't be you talking! I don't believe what I'm hearing.'' He gave her a wink and said, ''I know what your problem is. And I'm suffering from the same deprivation. It's been five days, Ellie. What do you say we leave right now and continue this discussion in bed . . .''

Ellie stared at him, just a bit stunned by his attitude. ''You're not taking me seriously,'' she said.

''That's right. Because it's not serious. So people know about us. So tell me. Did the sky fall in? Were you called to the principal's office?''

''As a matter of fact—''

''Oh, Ellie,'' he groaned, and put his face in his hands. For some reason, that particular gesture maddened her. It was as if he were hiding from her, from her words, from her concerns.

''David,'' she said crisply, ''it is obvious that you are incapable of understanding my situation.''

He looked up, straight into her eyes. ''No, no. I'll listen. I'll be good.'' And he smiled; but she was not going to allow herself to be charmed, not this time.

''Good isn't the issue. The issue is this: it has been made very clear to me, by a colleague, that our relationship puts my career in jeopardy.''

''You don't mean this, Ellie!''

''Yes, I do.'' And, to her own amazement, she realized

that she really *did* mean it. Sometime during the past few days, without being consciously aware of it, she had come to a decision. After all her sacrifices—including her marriage— she was not about to give up her future just to get laid. That's what it all boiled down to. And now she gazed at him, seeing him as if for the first time. He *was* a kid, a very young man with a very young face and a very young outlook on life.

"Ellie, darling, why are you getting so upset? We're lovers, not murderers. You don't get a scarlet letter any more for it, Ellie. It's okay!"

"It's not okay with the powers that be."

He made a noise that dismissed the powers that be; and she found herself growing impatient. Really, it was like talking to an adolescent! And then it came to her, the crux of the whole matter. "David," she said, "do you know what we have here? We have a generation gap!"

"Ellie, don't—"

She shook her head, feeling so calm and so peaceful, it was like floating above all those moiled emotions she'd been struggling with the past few days. The answer was clear, and amazingly, it didn't seem to bother her. It just showed what you could do, once you put your priorities in order.

She smiled very sweetly at him, watching his face crumple as he realized what she was saying. "It's over, David. We have to end it." And then she stood up very calmly and very calmly turned and walked away.

A week later, he had transferred out of the clinic, and that night, in the dark, she awoke suddenly and burst into heartbroken tears. She wept endlessly; she could not stem the tide. It was horrible, and she clenched her fists and made a promise into the darkness that she would never, ever allow herself to feel like that again.

Ellie shook her head, annoyed with herself. Of all the damn times to start raking over the purely sexual relationship she'd had with David! Funny how sometimes memories came flooding back, complete and intact, when you least wanted them; and other times you could try and try to conjure up how someone looked or tasted or smelled, and it eluded you.

Well, to hell with all of them, she said to herself with a laugh. She pushed the tasteless coffee away, picked up the journal, and headed for Del Bello's office. Dammit, before she had this confrontation, she'd really wanted to chew it over with Ade. Couldn't he have picked up a phone? How long would it have taken him to call her and say, "Ellie, I'm busy. Ellie, I'm going out of town. Ellie, don't worry if you don't see me for a while. I've gone underground." Good grief, he could tell her any damn thing! But simply not to show up after months and months of being there the same hour every morning! Well, she was a damn fool. She'd begun to think that he was making a point of being there each morning—as she was, of course—and all the time he was probably not thinking about her at all.

She marched down the corridor, fuming and storming inwardly, and damned if he wasn't marching right toward her, a frown between his eyes and a determination in his step. "Ade!" she called, and he walked right by. For one horrid cold moment, she stood there in the hall with the bottom falling out of her stomach. He was ignoring her! And then she yelled at herself. That was stupid. She remembered her Adrian; when he was preoccupied, the whole world could call him at the top of its collective voice and he would be oblivious. So, cursing herself for a damn fool, she turned and ran after him.

"Ade! Ade! Are you deaf?"

At her voice he turned, and when he saw her, his face lit up with a sweet smile that turned her heart over. "Ellie! Just the person I wanted to see!"

She found anger rising in her throat. "Oh, really? Just the person you wanted to see? Then why haven't you tried to see me these past three days?"

A look of stupefied perplexity crossed his face, and he frowned. She recognized that look; that was the look that said, What in the world is this female up to now? What crazy female notion am I about to hear? She'd seen it on her father's face, and god knows, she'd seen it often enough on every other man's she had ever come into contact with.

"What?"

"You haven't been in the cafeteria at all this week."

"Oh, Ellie. I've been very busy. I've had . . . more important things on my mind."

"More important? More important than *what*?"

Again, that perplexed little scowl. "Why . . . than a cup of coffee. What is bothering you, Ellie? Because I don't really have time to play guessing games."

"No. More to the point: what's bothering *you*?" Oh. That was different, she could see that right away. Because now they were talking about important things; they were talking about *him*.

"Jesus, Ellie, that Del Bello . . ."

"Yes, he is a pain. I'm on my way to see him now. Took me a week to get an appointment, for God's sake!"

He waved her words away as if they were of no import, and in revenge, she talked even faster. "I'm having a problem with his girlfriend, and I'm about to face him with it. In fact, that's why I was so eager to talk with you. I wanted to see what you thought—"

"That's small potatoes, that woman. She's just a minor irritant."

"I'm glad *you* think so." Ellie stood very still, hoping the rage climbing through her chest, through her throat, into her brain, was not showing. If she had followed her impulse at that moment, she would have neatly strangled him and left him on the corridor floor without a backward glance. Her father had told her that men are selfish. Daddy, she thought, you were right. I'm sorry I thought you were joking!

"Well, of course I think so. Christ, Del Bello has ripped through my budget with his knife . . . has just cut the heart right out of it . . . and what's worse, *he* won't make any of the cuts. I have to fire people. I have to tell wonderful, hard-working people that there's not enough money . . . Jesus!"

"I'm very sorry about your budget, Ade. I really am. But

do you realize that you haven't heard a word I've said? Not one word?"

"That's crazy.I've heard every syllable. Listen, I'll repeat it all back to you. You're on your way to Del Bello and—"

"Goddam it, that's not what I'm talking about, and you know it. Dammit!" Tears were hovering just under her lids, and she was dipped if she was going to give into them. She'd first walk away rather than let him see her cry. "Nothing ever changes, goddammit. I see you every morning for months, and then suddenly you have other things on your mind, and I might as well not exist . . ."

"Oh, for Christ's sake—! You know I have to put my work first."

"Why?" She felt pugnacious. "You always used to say that. Now I'd like to know. Why? Why does work have to come first?"

He looked down at her as if she had suddenly announced that little men from Mars had just landed on the roof of the hospital. "Why? Why! I'm a doctor, that's why. What kind of a doctor would I be if I didn't put my patients before everything else?"

"My kind, Ade. I'm a doctor, too, you know. And yet I always managed to put *you* first, the marriage, the children, the house, the meals, the friends, the entertainment . . ."

He looked away from her and squirmed uncomfortably. Normally, she would have tried to make him feel better and backed off, but she was furious. She was more than furious. "That's right," she said, her voice still low and even but very, very angry. "You chose pediatrics for me—remember? —so I'd be available for wife-and-mothering. You were the one who pointed out that I could practice at home—I didn't need to spend all my time in a hospital—so I could arrange my hours, so I could have as many babies as you deemed necessary to a full family life— Oh, yes, Ade, and it was *you* who decided that I didn't really like surgery and that women were not really suited to gynecology and that we could have a double practice and feed patients into each other . . .

Remember? And I was . . . I was available, and I was home, and I was wife and mother first and doctor second. Until guess when, Ade? Remember that? Remember when I said I'd like to go back and study for the neurology boards? Remember how you fought me? And when I decided it for myself, you wouldn't talk to me for *weeks*! When I finally made a choice on my own, you dumped me.''

"I—I never! What are you talking about? That's ancient history. And besides—it had nothing to do with your career. You shut us all out! It was your doing.''

"Adrian Winter! I don't believe I'm hearing that again!" She'd heard those words too many times, starting with the night she faced him with the fact of Leslie Fox and he answered her tearful accusation with a muttered "You made me." He repeated that refrain many, many times, never able to face his own responsibility, always throwing it off onto her: her new career, her going back to school, her being busy all the time, her new colleagues, her new interests . . . all of it. Everything was her fault. He was the victim. At the time, she found it utterly crazy and totally painful. "I can't believe it," she repeated now.

"Well, it was! *I* never wanted a divorce!"

She stood, slightly breathless, staring at him, at his very handsome, very earnest, very serious face. What a dope! The sad part of it was he believed what he was saying; he meant it with all his heart. He never wanted a divorce! Oh sure! "Funny," she said, "you never wanted it, but you packed up and went straight to a lawyer and got it.''

She turned quickly away from him—she really couldn't bear talking to him one minute longer, not about this—and she strode away quickly, almost running, so that he would not see the angry tears.

Chapter 15

ELLIE SETTLED BACK into the leather couch and looked around while Del Bello talked rapidly and effusively into the white phone on his desk. She had a very strong feeling that just about everything he did was an act for her benefit. She gazed at him, a baroque man in a motel-modern setting and wondered if it was Sandy Heller's idea of an important man's office. She glanced at her watch, thinking, I'll let him keep me waiting for exactly five minutes and then—but she wasn't quite sure what she would do. Just walk out? Give him a high sign? Go talk to Norma? She wasn't sure. But she was sure as hell not going to play his little game and waste her valuable time.

Just then Art Schuster sidled in, dapper as always, moving along the wall—or, anyway, giving that impression. He always looked sneaky, even when he wasn't, because he insinuated himself into a situation rather than announcing it. All he lacks, she thought, is the loincloth, the turban, and the palm fan. Yes, indeed, he was Sabu in the flesh, the perfect ingratiating servant, the white man's burden right down to the swarthy skin.

Oh swell, she thought, too bad she didn't think to bring reinforcements. She should have known Schuster would show up. He was being mentioned in tandem with Del Bello more and more often in the memos, and hadn't Schuster just given him a new title recently? V.P. for Hospital Affairs, or something like that? She'd much rather have it out with Del Bello alone. It wasn't really fair, making her battle both of them. But since when were these games played fairly?

She gave Art a tight little businesslike smile and in return got the big wink and the semihard squeeze on the shoulder. So it wasn't going to be hail-fellow-well-met friendly it was going to be serious faces, and they'd call her Dr. Winter instead of Ellie. Inwardly, she sighed, wishing she wasn't able to tell ahead of time what they planned to do. She also wished, for instance, that she didn't know Art Schuster so well, so long, in so many ways.

Now that she thought of it, she had bumped into Art Schuster during every change in her life. Med school, and they dated a bit then. And right after her divorce, she kept seeing him in the cafeteria at Downstate. At first they just waved at each other. She was just as happy not to talk to him. She was hurting, she was hurting badly, and every reminder of Adrian, no matter how tangential, was something to be avoided. Art brought back memories of medical school, and medical school didn't bear thinking about. So she waved and smiled and hurried on.

But after a week or two, he began to appear on the line behind her, insisted on buying her cup of coffee, took her arm and led her to a table to sit with him. She couldn't figure it out. It was nice enough to have someone paying attention to her, although she felt too numb to enjoy any attention . . . but really, Art Schuster? They weren't really friends, and he was only at Downstate to give a series of lectures and would soon be gone.

And then she realized that in his own cautious way he was coming on to her. The intent blue-eyed gaze . . . the little intimate smiles . . . the little touches on her hands . . . She began to recognize the moves. When he finally asked her out for dinner, she hesitated. She hesitated long enough so that he cleared his throat and mumbled that he hadn't wanted to bother her with it but he and Etta were separated again; otherwise, of course, he would never . . . He looked up at her finally from under his heavy dark brows, and his eyes were sad, and she capitulated.

He took her to the River Cafe, which didn't particularly surprise her. Art would only frequent the best, most expensive, most exclusive places. She wasn't surprised when he spoke to the bartender as if they knew each other. She wasn't surprised when they were given a table by the window and could look out on the harbor and Manhattan across the water.

She also wasn't surprised when he took her hand over coffee and lifted the fingertips to his lips. She remembered that move from the last time he tried to get her into bed. It hadn't worked that time, either. And then she got her first surprise of the evening: when he kissed her fingers, a chill ran down her spine, and her gut tightened. Damn! she thought. Just because she'd been sleeping alone these three months . . . Did that mean she was ready to hop into the sack with any guy who bought her dinner? She looked over at Art and thought, He's really quite an attractive man. Could I? Would I? He nibbled at her fingers and looked deeply into her eyes, and she tried to imagine how it would be. But how could she? She hadn't been to bed with anyone but Adrian in about a thousand years. Any other body, any other technique, was unimaginable.

"You know what I'd like more than anything?" he said huskily; and she shook her head, thinking, I'll do it. I'll do it. Why not? I've got to start the rest of my life sometime and with someone, so why not this man I know and don't find repulsive? "I'd like," Art said, holding both her hands in his, "to take you home with me . . ." She eyed him for a moment or two, uncertain now that it had been put to her. What did she do? Did she get up? Did she say, "Yes, thank you very much, I'll go home and to bed with you." Did she smile mysteriously and say nothing? She'd never played this particular game with Ade, or with anyone, for that matter. She didn't know how.

Apparently, she waited too long to say something to him, and he got impatient. Because he smiled then and said, "Come on, Ellie. You know you want it." And boom, just like that, she was furious, totally turned off. That was the end; no way would he ever get near her. *"You know you want it!"* What an ugly thing to say! But the stupid fool was going on. "We could get a good thing going, Ellie. Look, we know each other. We don't have to pretend, play little love games or any of that crap. Think how convenient it would be! Lunch hours. I mean, our hospitals are only fifteen minutes apart . . ." And he squeezed her hands meaningfully and gave her an extra-soulful look. And she remembered thinking, You are a turd, Art Schuster! And furthermore, you are totally out of your mind if you think telling me how conveniently we could screw is going to make me want you. Funny, she never could recall exactly how she got out of it . . . only that he did see her to her house and that he was coldly annoyed.

And then he insinuated himself once more into her life— didn't he?—to tell her she'd better not continue her affair with David.

And here he was again, unwanted and unasked for, but what could she do? She checked her watch again. Del Bello's five minutes were up. He was still crooning into the phone . . . Well, he could sing love songs into it for all of her! She was going to get back to work! And to hell with Schuster, too! A pox on both their houses, she thought, irritated and amused at the same time, and began to get to her feet.

Almost immediately, Del Bello ended his telephone conversation and turned to her with a broad smile.

On her feet still, she said quickly, "Look, Hank, I realize that we're living in a public relations age, and I'm the first one to say let's get Cadman into the news. But let's face it. There's a difference between using the Heart Exercise Clinic, for instance, and the Birth Defects Clinic . . ."

"Dr. Winter," Del bello boomed, his arms spread as if in embrace. "We're all very proud of the work you do in the Birth Defects Clinic!"

"I'm very sorry, but we simply can't have Sandy Heller coming in with her camera, asking my patients personal questions . . . No, no, let me finish, please. I've had complaints from the patients, Hank. Serious complaints."

"See here, Dr. Winter, I've got to look at the *broad* picture. I understand your concern for your patients, and I'm with you all the way . . . However—now let *me* finish, please—it's the one clinic that's never been written up or been on television. And as for complaints, now I admit that maybe director of public relations isn't on exactly the same level as director of one of our clinics . . . but maybe it is, come to think of it, maybe it is. And anyway, Sandy Heller is a pro, Dr. Winter. She's not a newcomer, a dummy. We should depend on her good judgment . . ."

Art chimed in before she could say anything: "What's the sense of having such a marvelous clinic if nobody knows about it?"

She rounded on him. "What's the sense? The sense of having it, my dear Dr. Schuster, is for the patients. P-A-T-I-E-N-T-S. Remember them, Art?"

Del Bello moved out from behind the big desk. "Ellie, listen, when I came to Cadman, nobody in this city knew we were here. There was no direction to the hospital. Excuse me, I know you're a friend of Nate Levinson, and he was a wonderful doctor, none better. But facts are facts, Ellie. We had no public relations at all."

"We've always been known as a wonderful hospital, Hank. We've always done a bang-up job taking care of our patients. Which, unless I'm sadly mistaken, is what we're here for."

"Look, Dr. Winter." Not only was the title back, but there was that icy edge to his voice that meant he was getting tired of this conversation and of her notions. "Taking care of patients is of course our first priority. But this hospital has to make money, like any business. I know you medicos would love to forget that . . . but *I* can't. Cadman has to increase patient load and fill up those empty beds. Like it or not, Dr. Winter, one of the ways we increase patient load is through publicity.''

"You talk about increasing patient load so easily, Hank. I can't handle any more patients.''

"You'll get help as soon as you need it.''

"And in the meantime—? Look, all of this is beside the point. The point is Sandy Heller. She comes into my clinic without prior warning. She points her camera at the Down's syndrome kids or some poor child in a wheelchair . . . and maybe the parents are sensitive, maybe they don't want people's pity, maybe the kids are sensitive and embarrassed. You people have no idea how difficult the adjustment is for them . . .'' In desperation, she turned to Schuster, who was lounging against the wall in a typical Art Schuster attitude. "Art! You're a doctor! Surely you understand?''

"I understand; I understand. Of course I do. But you shouldn't worry so much. Sandy Heller knows what she's doing. She told me, when you got that spina bifida case—''

"Don't call them cases! Goddam it, they're *people*. That so-called spina bifida case is a little girl named Joanna.''

He put his hands up in surrender. "Please, Ellie, don't murder me! I'm sorry. When you put Joanna on her feet and walking and the physical therapy department came up with a big cake to celebrate, that would have been one helluva good story. And I think Joanna's family would have loved it. But you wouldn't let Sandy in even for that!''

"Oh, Art. She never asks. She just announces.''

"And because you were standing on ceremony, because Sandy Heller didn't use the right words or the right tone of voice, we missed one of the great human interest stories in the hospital? For shame, Ellie. For shame.''

Del Bello quickly said, "Now Art, don't be too harsh. You know women. They just don't have the same sense of business or opportunity as men.''

Ellie kept her mouth shut. She was afraid if she opened it,

something was going to come out that she might regret forever. Something like, Fuck off, both of you.

And then Art started in on how she should act as a role model for all the little girls in Brooklyn and the greater New York Metropolitan area, and she began to laugh. "Oh Art, honestly!"

"No, no," Del Bello pressed. "Art's right, Dr. Winter. How many women have your credentials? And you know what? Maybe what this hospital needs is a . . . pardon me . . . a mother figure. I mean, look at me, with my five o'clock shadow by ten in the morning. What kind of a nurturing image could I give!"

"I've got to get back to work," Ellie said. She was laughing openly now. "And Sandy Heller *still* has to give me a week's notice. I mean it!"

"Now, Ellie—"

She turned at the door. "And let me tell you something else, gentlemen. Next time, I'm bringing Con Scofield with me."

Chapter 16

"MEN!" ELLIE SAID with disgust. "Honestly! They are so impossible!"

Con sipped at her coffee and smiled. "It's David, isn't it?"

"David!" Ellie slid into her seat across the cafeteria table and stared at her friend. "Whatever put *that* into your head? David? That's ridiculous!"

Con raised an eyebrow. "Ridiculous? Well, I for one think it would do you good—"

"*What* would do me good?"

"You're blushing. You know that? You know darn well what I mean. You were *happy* with David Powell. You were . . . content. You were . . . *serene*."

Ellie began to laugh. "Serene! Me? The closest I've ever come to serene is when I've been under anesthesia . . . Come on, Con! Let's not create a myth here in the Cadman cafeteria!"

"Laugh away, girl. He's one helluva sweet guy, that David, and you were damn lucky to have him! Why in hell did you let him go, anyway?"

"How do you know he didn't let *me* go?"

"He cried on my shoulder, that's how."

"Oh, Con, he didn't!"

"Oh, Ellie, he did! And I mean real tears. He was real torn up when you two split."

"So was I," Ellie muttered.

"Well, you sure didn't act it!"

"Look, Con, David and I had a nice thing . . . All right, all right, we had a *terrific* thing. But it was never serious. I mean, it couldn't be."

"I don't see why not!"

"Oh, Con! A young man like him, carrying on with a middle-aged woman who's his *boss* . . . There's no future in that, and you know it!"

"Here's what I know. He was crazy about you, and you broke his heart. In fact, he still misses you."

Ellie flushed again. "I know you think the world of David," she managed. "And I know you have only my best interest at heart. But it's over and done with, long in the past; and let's not discuss it, if you don't mind."

Con sighed gustily. "Okay, okay. But you started it. You're the one came in fussing about men." Then she grinned. "So it must be Adrian, right?"

"I'm not talking about Ade, either. He's none of *my* business anymore. Oh, stop it, Con. The cupid routine does not become you. No, it's Del Bello. The man is so uncaring, so slick, so business oriented. I can't deal with him; I really can't. He thinks all he has to do is pay me some sort of ridiculous compliment and I'll fall to the ground so he can walk all over me. As far as he's concerned, the patients don't exist . . . except when they can be useful to the hospital. I just can't get used to it! They're so power hungry . . . that's all they're interested in . . . power, power, power! It was so different when Nate was in charge."

Con gave a bark of derisive laughter. "Oh, you guys, you make me laugh! Nate Levinson was a wonderful doctor and a workaholic. But you seem to forget that he was a lousy administrator. You don't remember the schedules that always came out late, the mixups in the OR, the incompetents he was

always giving 'just another chance'? He was a great guy—
you know, Ellie, you know damn well I always loved him—
but come on, let's not allow our nostalgia to cloud every
issue!" She gave a sigh and drank her coffee. "Look, Ellie,
you know as well as I that, often, the man who manages to do
everything and be everywhere for his work and for his community . . . that man has nothing left for his personal life. All
that compassion and sweetness; you'd think, wouldn't you,
that he'd make the ideal lover. Well, you'd be dead wrong,
Ellie. Because all that compassion and sweetness got used up
on the job. I guess I'm bitter because I never did get my fair
share—oh, forget it. I'm just being foolish!"

"No more so than all the rest of us, Con. Goddammit, you
and I are supposed to be really liberated, independent, self-
sufficient, and all that stuff. And here we are, talking about
guess what?"

Con threw her head back and laughed. "Boys!"

"That's right. We might as well be in the high school
cafeteria, wondering why the boys prefer their basketball
practice to us . . . All those years when I was practicing part
time at home so I could be there for the girls, he thought
nothing of coming home at nine, ten o'clock, because something interesting had come up at the hospital. He felt very free
to get involved in research because it was important to his
career. I mean, anything went, anything at all. And the
minute I decided to do something for myself—! Well, you
know what happened, Con. He couldn't hack it. He felt all
lost and lonely and alone and neglected. I didn't get any
support, and there he was, holding his patients' hands—for
hours, if necessary—giving them his total understanding and
attention. Not that I would deny his patients what's due them,
but where was *my* understanding and attention? Oh, never
mind! I don't know why I even bother thinking about it
anymore . . . since I have to think about my immediate future
. . . Yes, Steve's proposed."

"Do I congratulate you?"

"That's the trouble . . . I'm not sure. I like him well

enough; that's not a problem. But . . . I don't know. Something is missing.''

Con shot her a look. "And I think I know what that something is! Oh, come on, Ellie, stop ducking your head like a naughty kid. Look me straight in the eye and tell me the guy rings your chimes!''

Ellie couldn't help grinning. "As it happens, Ms. Scofield, you are totally wrong. The man rings my chimes, all right, but— Oh, hell, I don't love him! It's as simple as that.''

"Hunh! Yet you let David go, easy enough!''

Ellie sighed. "In fact, it wasn't easy, Con. I was forced to it. We were . . . very fond of each other, Con. But we had to sneak around; we had to behave as if what we were doing was dirty.''

"I never knew common gossip to stop Eleanor Winter!''

"You misunderstand. It wasn't the gossip alone.''

"Well, then?''

Ellie sighed again. "I was given the ultimatum by Art Schuster. He put on his most pompous expression, held my hand, and announced that he was my Dutch uncle.'' She made a face. "Dutch uncle! He loved playing the part of the condescending, morally superior male giving it to the weak-willed, mushy-brained little woman. Oh, yes, he was in his glory, Con. 'Ellie, you know I consider you one of the finest female physicians I have ever known . . .' And, 'You must know the board has its eye upon you . . . You are a woman of great promise . . .' All that baloney. And what it all added up to in the end was that my relationship with David was a matter of concern to the board, to my colleagues, to the administration, to my students—to the whole goddam world, in fact. I was given a simple warning, Con. Dump David or forget any future at this hospital.''

"What did that matter? You were already head of the clinic.''

"Oh, it was everything, Con. I'd lose everyone's respect, I wouldn't be able to command the funding my patients deserved . . . Oh, God, I can't remember every word! It's years now; it's water under the bridge . . ."

"I just can't believe that Art Schuster was able to browbeat you into submission . . ."

"My daughters were giving me a hard time, too. They found out, and it made them crazy. 'Oh, Mom, how gross!' And, you know, he *was* too young for me. He was just a kid. It was crazy . . ." Ellie felt anger tightening like a band around her head. Why was she getting angry? Over something so long ago? Con was opening her mouth to say something else . . . she didn't want to hear any more, Ellie decided, and she blurted, "He would have left me for a younger woman sooner or later— Hell, Adrian did, and I was his age!"

Con's eyes widened. "Oh, Ellie! Don't do that to yourself. It was Adrian's loss; we all know that."

Ellie blinked back sudden tears and said, "I'm overtired, I guess, and overreacting. You know, all the girls are home from school and it's chaos at 577 Remsen Street these days. Hot and cold running boys—mostly hot, I'm afraid—and something sticky cooking on the stove at all hours and never a free telephone line . . . not to mention the three separate stereos blasting . . . And worst of all . . ."

"Yes?" Con prodded.

"Well . . . when the girls are home, Ade's around a lot . . . to pick them up or to leave them off or to just say hello . . . Seems like every time I open the door, I see him."

Dryly, Con said, "And you just hate seeing him."

A sigh. "No, dammit, as you well know, I don't hate seeing him. And yet I do. The trouble is, I know what he's going through. Del Bello and Art—yes, even his dear old friend Art—are sniping at him all the time. They won't say anything definite, oh, no, but he gets left out of this and left behind on that . . . And the latest is, he's had massive budget cuts . . ."

"Well, maybe that explains it."

197

Ellie nodded at two nurses who walked by with their trays and said, "Explains what?"

"Oh, his general impossibleness lately. We had a meeting yesterday about that new nurse-midwife program I'm interested in . . . Well, a week ago, he was all for it. Now? Forget it. He's got seventy-seven reasons it won't work. They aren't trained completely. They can't handle emergencies. Our particular patient load is often undernourished and not in optimum condition for anything less than a physician's care. That's it, you know, Ellie. Forgive me for saying this, but the bottom line is they don't have that all-holy M.D. degree."

"Don't apologize, Con. You know I think nurse-midwifery is the wave of the future."

"Well, it damn well ought to be the wave of the present! And when push comes to shove, Adrian Winter is just like the rest of them: holding on to his own little bit of power for dear life! You know what he had the nerve to say to me? To *me*? Not to mention Marge Babcock, who started the nurse-midwife program at Seaton General and who was sitting right there! He said, 'You ladies want to deliver babies? Go to school and get a medical degree. Then you can deliver babies without arguments from me or anyone.' I couldn't believe it!"

"I can't believe it myself. That's not like Ade . . ."

"Well, the fact that I restrained myself from punching him in the nose is—"

"You, Ms. Scofield. So violent?" So intent were they on their conversation that both Ellie and Con jumped a bit at the voice from just above them.

"What? Oh, good afternoon, Ms. Heller," Con said. "Can we do something for you?"

"Is that chair empty?"

"You can see that for yourself."

"Good. Then I'll have my lunch and have your company, as well."

"Oh, that's a double treat, for sure," Con said, ignoring Ellie's warning look and leaning back in her chair with a little smile on her lips.

Sandy Heller might have been blind and deaf, Con thought, because she seemed oblivous to any of it. She settled her trim little bottom neatly onto the molded plastic cafeteria chair and arranged her tray in front of her. It held a container of lemon yogurt and a bowl of soup. Might have known, Con thought with some asperity, wishing she could hide the remnants of her submarine sandwich and potato salad. Dammit, she really *was* going to go on a diet. She'd start tonight; at the latest, tomorrow. The woman was amazing; she even ate daintily, chatting all the time. She talked about the number of doctors who had been appearing on "Straight Talk" and Frank Field and "Live at Five" and how many calls they'd gotten from people all over the country. "It's so exciting!" she said. "Well, why should people always think of Mt. Sinai or Montefiore or Doctor's or New York Hospital . . . We're as good as any of them . . . Right, Dr. Winter?"

"We try, we try."

"Well, I think it's just a shame; people in the rest of the country think Brooklyn is a joke. Well, I must admit, before Hank hired me, I felt the same . . ." She went on and on. Con only half listened; she was amused at the way the woman said Hank. Kind of savoring it, licking at it, in a way. You didn't have to hear any of the hospital gossip to know they were lovers; she told you by the very way she pronounced his name. And then Con came quickly to attention.

"What? Did I just hear my name and tv in the same sentence?"

"Well, I *do*," Sandy Heller said. "I think you'd make a wonderful human interest story, Con. I mean, you've been here forever . . . Oh, dear, I didn't mean it *that* way . . ."

"Not interested," Con said with a snort.

To her utter amazement, Ellie said, "You should, Con, you really should. You deserve a lot of credit. And besides, think what it would do for your nurses! Don't you think it will make every nurse in the hospital feel good?"

"Absolutely!" Heller said, and Con said gruffly, "That's not the point. I don't want personal publicity . . ."

"Oh, Con, stop being so stubborn," Ellie said. "Of all the people who deserve recognition—Oh, all right, never mind that part . . . But you'd be so wonderful on TV, and then people would see a caring human being and know that's what Cadman stands for."

Sandy Heller's eyes rounded for a moment, and then she quickly covered up her surprise. She was a slick one, Con thought. "Dr. Winter, I want to tell you how pleased and grateful I am to hear you talk that way. You understand what it is we're after . . . which is more than I can say for most of the doctors around here!"

"You will have to be patient with us doctors," Ellie said, and there was an edge in her voice, barely discernible, which Con recognized very well. Watch out, Ms. Heller, she thought.

"Oh, I've *been* patient, Dr. Winter. I think I've been very patient." Delicately, she licked the last of the yogurt from the plastic spoon. "I have a job to do. I may be wrong, but I think it's a pretty important job. *Public* relations . . . and if a hospital isn't there to serve the *public*, well, then what *is* it for?"

Con gave a snort. "Come, come, Ms. Heller, public relations doesn't have anything to do with the hospital serving the public. It's really the other way round, isn't it?"

Sandy Heller's lips tightened. "No, Ms. Scofield, I don't think so. I really don't. And I don't understand everyone's . . . attitude around here. I really don't. I'm not trying to do anything but make the hospital look good and bring in more business."

Now Con hooted, so loudly that heads turned to look at her. "Bring in more business—!" she mimicked. "That's not what health care is about!"

"You're as bad as some of those doctors, Ms. Scofield, and I'm—I'm surprised, that's what I am. I thought it was because they were men . . . You'd be surprised how often I'm talked down to just because I'm a woman. It's not easy, especially not in this hospital, let me tell you! The condescension! And I thought it was bad, working in government,

with that civil service attitude. But the attitude of doctors . . . !
Hunh! They think they're God! They think they know just
about everything. One of them—you must know him; he's
been here a long time—Tom Duffy, chief of thoracic surgery—
had the nerve, the utter gall, to put an arm around me after
I'd interviewed him for a news release and say, "I know
there are a lot of big words in there, but don't worry honey.
I'll help you write it!"

Con and Ellie both stared at her in disbelief, and she
nodded at them vigorously. Con couldn't swear to it, but she
thought she saw a tear in the corner of one of those impecca-
bly made up blue eyes.

Ellie said, "That pompous ass! Well, listen, Sandy, if it
makes you feel any better, three wives have got rid of him.
And next time, you know what you say to him? You say,
'Oh, all right, doctor, that would be nice. And the next time
you're in the OR, I'll help you operate.' "

"Yes, I thought of that. But I can't afford to make these
guys mad at me. But one day—!" She paused and dragged in
a deep breath and then gave them a brilliant smile. "But
enough of my troubles. I'm going to make those guys come
to *me* one day and beg me to get them publicity." She gave
Ellie an extra little twinkle. "And that goes for you, too, Dr.
Ellie. Your clinic has everything: birth defects, kids, hope, a
woman doctor, success stories, drama—everything you could
want for wonderful human interest stories. And, you know, it
could help someone. There must be so many people out there
who have these kids and don't know what to do or where to
turn. Public information—that's a big part of my job, you
know."

"That sounds very nice," Ellie said in her coolest, calmest
voice. A dead giveaway, Con thought, at least to someone
like me, who knows her. The more moved Ellie Winter
became, the more she pulled away and put distance between
herself and the subject. It was her way of not becoming
emotional; but to a lot of people, it looked a lot like amused

condescension, and Con winced inwardly, "Yes, very nice,
Sandy. But I'm still against your just walking into my clinic
unannounced. There are procedures, you know. The appro-
priate way would be for you to send me a memo or give me a
call, and then I'll have time to look through the files and
check with the parents and—''

Sandy Heller, whose face had become quite pink, interrupted Ellie with an impatient wave of her hand. "You're just
like the rest of them!" she burst out. "That clinic is your
special territory, and you'll be damned if any of us lesser
mortals, who don't happen to be doctors, can get in without
begging. You don't have any respect for *my* profession. You
think it's laughable. It's 'only public relations.' It's even a
little bit shameful, right? You think anyone in PR is a tough
little broad without any real credentials and no sensitivity.
Well, let me tell you something. I didn't come from money,
and I didn't marry it. Anything I have I've had to get for
myself! And I have feelings! I've suffered! I've suffered
plenty! I've had people sneer at me and leer at me and treat
me like dirt. But I keep going . . . in spite of it all! Don't you
make the mistake of thinking I'm dumb. . . .''

Con looked over at Ellie. Ellie's face mirrored her own
stupefaction. Then Sandy Heller got up, scraping her chair
back loudly and drawing in a deep, audible breath. Once
again, she flashed them that bright meaningless smile.

"If you'll excuse me . . . I really must run before I go
too far!'' She turned to face Ellie. "All right, Dr. Winter,
you'll get your memo, all proper and legal, the way you
want it. And it'll be signed by Mr. Del Bello himself, and
believe me, I will explain to him exactly why it's deemed
necessary all of a sudden.'' She paused, looking as if she
had a number of other things to say, and then flashed that
smile again and said, "Be seeing you!'' in a bright cheery
voice.

They watched her make her way out of the cafeteria,
showering smiles upon this group and that as she went. Con

and Ellie turned to each other and gave each other an identical shrug.

Gathering the papers she had earlier spread on the table, Ellie remarked: "You know, Con, for a minute I almost thought she was a human being."

Chapter 17

Con walked into the big room and let out an involuntary whistle. Oh, my Lord! she thought, why didn't someone tell me? What looked like five thousand glittering silver balloons, with white and silver streamers fluttering from them, floated high up near the ceiling. More balloons festooned the walls, and at the far end of the room was a huge buffet table draped in silver and white and loaded with platters and chafing dishes of food. And by God, it was catered! The bar, instead of being the usual tableful of bottles and plastic glasses, was a *real* bar with three elegant black bartenders in dinner jackets mixing drinks and flashing big smiles. And waitresses! Actual waitresses were flitting around sticking trays of food under your nose . . . and here came one right now. The girl smiled at Con, and Con smiled back and said, "Sure," and grabbed three little pastry puffs of something or other that smelled wonderful and said, "I'm hungry . . . five-thirty's my usual suppertime." But the waitress had already scuttled off.

If she hadn't known where she was—at Cadman's annual New Year's party—she wouldn't have known where she was. Other years, there had been platters from Rose & Sol's and a

table of booze and a couple of med students to serve and
maybe some music for those who got looped enough to do
some dancing and, oh, yes, those beat up cardboard figures of
Father Time and Baby New Year . . . where the hell were
they? Nowhere to be seen at this fancy dress ball! What a
change! She'd bet anything it was Sandy Heller's notion
of how to make people feel appreciated. Well, for one thing,
she'd like to tell Ms Heller that what would have been
appreciated by yours truly was a little warning. Here she was,
still in uniform, and she got a run in her stocking on her way
down here, and when was the last time she checked to see if
she had any lipstick on . . . And, on the other hand, there
was Sandy Heller, resplendent—no, scratch that—positively
regal in red velvet. It wasn't a long dress, but it was velvet,
and it was definitely without a doubt red. As were her pointy-
toed shoes. She looked gorgeous, but really, wouldn't it have
been nice if she'd let the staff know this was a dress-up
affair? Oh hell, there was plenty to drink, anyway, and she
felt like drinking plenty, so here she went. Right over to one
of those big black beautiful dudes, and when she said, "Dewars
on the rocks," he gave her a big beautiful smile and handed
her a big beautiful glass half filled with Scotch.

With the first sip, she immediately felt better. What the
hell difference did it make what she was wearing as long as
there was an adequate supply of Scotch. Besides, Sandy
Heller was the only one there who had dressed up specially
for the party. The men were in their usual dark conservative
suits—all the guys from administration and accounting and
the drug salesmen—and the women in their working clothes—
skirts and sweaters or uniforms. Another one of those little
girls with a tray bounced up to her, and this time there were
those tiny little franks on toothpicks, so she grabbed a few of
them, thinking with an inward laugh that she and the waitress
were dressed alike in their white nylon dresses and white
no-nonsense oxfords. And as far as most of the doctors here
were concerned, they were interchangeable. Handmaidens,
slaveys . . . Oh, hell. She drank some more, letting its

warmth soothe her, and looked around the room. Used to be a
time when she knew everyone in the hospital. That was
before Tower A, of course; now Cadman was too big for
anyone to know everyone else. She didn't know which way
she preferred it. She didn't really care at this particular moment.
She took another belt and noted young Dr. Truman over there
in a corner, nose to nose with of all the damn people, Rita
Schneider. But on second thought that wasn't too noteworthy,
was it. He had that spina bifida kid; she remembered Ellie
discussing it a few weeks ago . . . What had she said? Oh
yes, the wife was pregnant again and at high risk. Stupid
women! No imagination, that was their problem. "I want a
baby"; she'd heard that one many times. Like Suzie Palko,
wanting it so badly that she said, "He doesn't have to marry
me." She took a healthy belt of the booze, feeling that grip in
her belly. Poor Suzie . . . even now, so many months later, it
hurt to think about her, that poor baby. And she hadn't been
able to help her. But don't think of that again now; enjoy the
party. And look at that! She almost whistled again. Bobby
and the genetics counselor were standing awfully damn close,
and his hand was on her arm in a way that wasn't casual; no,
not at all. They couldn't fool Con Scofield; she knew intimacy when she saw it. And to think she figured the poor guy
must be worried out of his mind—! As she had the thought,
Rita said something to him, and he threw his handsome head
right back and roared with laughter. Con watched Bobby
laugh, wondering for a moment why she found it remarkable,
and then she realized that she had never, ever seen Bobby
Truman laugh out loud before, and she'd known him for all
four of the years he'd been here. She had sat at lunch with
him and Ellie and Adrian plenty over the years, had talked
with him, joked with him, discussed patients with him. But
she'd never seen him laugh like that. Well, she'd just tuck
that information away for now. That's what she always loved
about this party: people let down their guard for New Year's,
and you could find out what was *really* going on around here,
if you were sharp and kept your eyes open. The trouble with

most people was that they were too damn intent on their own
little affairs and never bothered to look around. And then she
had to laugh at herself . . . That was some justification for
being an old busybody, wasn't it?

She continued to watch the scene, thinking, It doesn't
matter how you dress the place up, the same stuff goes on.
Lee Royce, for instance, over there by the bar, surrounded by
women as usual. Lee was a drug salesman; Cadman had been
his territory for quite a few years now—eight, she thought.
He was always around and often upstairs because he peddled
antibiotics to the surgeons. Lee liked to drop by the nursing
stations and chat up whoever was on duty, maybe leave his
case with them for a while if he didn't need to carry it
around. He was a charmer; well, he was a salesman, wasn't
he? He had the gift of gab. But added to that were his good
looks. Con gave herself another silent laugh for that one.
Good looks, huh? That was an understatement. The man was
stunning, no two ways about it, with that handsome sculpted
face, the head of thick salt-and-pepper hair, and those shoulders!
Some little gal was always falling for him. Why, just a few
weeks ago, she'd had to talk to Mary De Vito, one of her
nurses—to talk her out of going out for drinks with him.
Come off it, she'd told her, Lee's a married man, makes no
secret of it, so don't pretend you don't know! And now,
today, here he was with Lucy Strang gazing up at him as if he
were the answer to all her prayers. And speaking of praying,
here came the Lord God himself, Del Bello, his arms outstretched as in blessing. You could hear the little hum even
before you saw him, the little hum of people murmuring.
"Look! there he is!" That swell of sound you always got in
the wake of a big shot . . . And she guessed that Hank Del
Bello was the closest thing to a big shot they were going to
get at this party.

Not only that, but he was out of his office and out in the
open, where if you were lucky you might get to grab him and
talk to him for a minute or two. She'd like to get his ear
herself. The ICU was so understaffed. She really needed two

or three more nurses. Turnover was the highest in the hospital, except maybe for the neonatal nursery. Anyway, she needed those nurses. She'd like to tell him, "Come on, Del Bello, there's a good reason the ICU is known as Burnout City." Oh, hell! He was so encircled by petitioners, she didn't have the strength or the patience to battle her way to the front.

And of course, right nearby, hovering behind him, was Dr. Art Schuster, God's gift to the healing profession. And hovering right behind him, as she had on every single social occasion at the hospital for umpteen years, was Etta Schuster. Con regarded Etta with interest. She wasn't so old, barely fifty if she was a day, and yet there was something resigned and ready for senility about her. Hard to figure. Was it the thickened body that she didn't bother to exercise or even to pull in with a good girdle? Was it the stiff hairdo, at least ten years out of style? That ridiculous pink chiffon ruffled number she was wearing? Con narrowed her eyes and really gave Etta the once-over and decided, No, it was all of those, but it wasn't really any of them. It was the cowed, beaten look of her. She could have been—hell, she once *was*—a good-looking woman, but she didn't bother. She didn't *do* anything to fix herself up. Well, who could blame her, really, married to Art Schuster? Everyone knew how he kept her on a tight rein, treated her like the idiot child, and expected her to cater to his every whim. So there she was, as usual, hovering that half step behind her dapper husband, always looking as if she were standing on tiptoes, trying to see over his shoulder to what the big people were doing. And *that*, Con said to herself derisively, was the president of the ladies' auxiliary. No wonder they couldn't seem to get any of their fund-raisers off the ground this year. Etta Schuster was bright enough, but she was a ditherer, poor thing. Not for the first time, Con wondered why in the world Art, with his overweening ambition, his hunger to belong to the best of Brooklyn Heights society, had stayed married to her. She couldn't be any kind of social asset . . . although, of course, that wasn't quite true, was it?

She came from an old, old monied Brooklyn family; she was his entrée.

And that probably made up for everything. Oh, hell, Con decided, she'd just get another refill of this good Scotch. She was feeling a helluva lot better. There was a short wait at the bar—the room was rapidly filling up now—and she leaned against it, looking around and letting herself relax. Then she heard a voice she recognized—who *didn't* around here?—and whirled around. The Reverend Ezekiel Clayton himself, in person, in the niftiest three-piece white suit you ever saw, was leaning across the bar, his big, blunt-fingered hand on the shoulder of one of the bartenders, laughing and saying, "Now, Brother Daniel, I want to see you on Sunday more often!" while he accepted a large glass of something.

"Reverend Clayton," she said, putting a hand on his arm, and he immediately turned, beaming with pleasure. He was always forthcoming; he always gave you both barrels of whatever he was feeling and thinking—after the barrage of flattery up front.

"Nurse Scofield! My favorite angel of mercy, whose healing hands have given immeasurable comfort to many of my poor flock . . . whose ministrations—"

"Rev! Quit that now!"

"My dear Ms. Scofield, I am most sincere, as you well know. It is the New Year; it is the time when we are all beholden to say those good words that are in our hearts."

"You know full well, Reverend, that I was about to yell at you . . . And you were trying to charm me. Oh, yes, you were. Don't bother to deny it."

He took a sip of his drink and moved a few steps away from the bar to a quiet spot . . . a spot, she realized instantly, where no one could easily overhear them. "Well, perhaps, I was trying to charm you just the littlest bit. But only because I find you charming."

She couldn't help it; she had to grin. That devil! And, reverend or no, he *was* a devil. "It's all very well," she said, "that you send your good people to the hospital with Bibles for the patients and words of comfort. A lot of folks welcome it.'' He ducked his head in thanks, but she saw the flicker in his eyes that said he knew what was coming next. ''But,'' she went on, ''a lot of folks *don't*.''

The Reverend Clayton frowned and pursed his lips thoughtfully. ''Now, Nurse Scofield, I could say at this point that some folks don't know what they want until it's offered them.'' He held up a hand. ''But I'm not going to say that, because I know that's not what you want to hear. All right—''

''Look,'' Con said, relentless. ''People are awfully sick in Intensive Care, and their families spend a lot of time with them. Sometimes a lady in the waiting room with a Bible in her hand means death to them and—''

''Say no more, Nurse Scofield; say no more. I'm with you all the way. I already talked to my flock about that very thing. I thought I had explained it well enough so that everyone understood. Sadly, it seems, not everyone did. But never you fear, there'll be no more ladies with Bibles anywhere near the ICU . . . unless, of course, invited to be there.''

Con touched the Reverend on his arm. Softly, she said, ''Look who's coming . . .'' And she barely had time to say it before Hank Del Bello was upon them, his hand extended.

Shit, Hank thought, striding over as fast as he could. Am I the only one here who runs around putting out fires? That little ballbreaker, Scofield, was wagging her finger and looking tougher than usual . . . and damn the Rev, anyway. He's always making trouble . . . And there they were, at each other, nose to nose. Between the blacks and the women around here, it was amazing the buildings were still standing.

But he got to them; they were both smiling. Damned if it hadn't looked like a fight brewing, but no, the Rev was giving him the glad hand and saying how Ms. Scofield had just set him straight, and that was quite a job, but she was the one who could do it, and Con Scofield was laughing, ''Oh, come, come, Reverend. You're not that crooked.'' Not fighting at all! Well, good, that was a relief. And now he could just make them both happy at one time, make himself a hero, and get the hell out before Scofield started blabbering to him again about her needing more nurses in the ICU . . . Dammit, every goddam department needed more nurses. Didn't the woman know there was a shortage of nurses? Didn't she realize they were in the middle of a nurse *crisis*, for Christ's sake? He was doing his best! But he couldn't get nurses out of thin air, could he?

"Look," he said, taking each one of them by an arm, "I'm about to do a wonderful thing here. I'm about to make the two of you very happy . . ." He had to smile, the way they looked at each other, dumfounded. "You remember that Psychiatry's needed a new chief for about six months now . . . Well, I've just finished a series of interviews, and the leading contender is Dr. Joyce Hunter, a brilliant black woman . . . Yes, I think we'll have our first black *and* female chief of service at Cadman very, very soon."

"That *is* good news," the Reverend said, and began to talk about the lack of black professionals in the hospital. Dammit, the man was a pain in the ass! Nothing satisfied him. Give him a mile and he wants another inch! He kept smiling at the Reverend, but he turned his head off and out of the corners of his eyes tried to spot Sandy. Goddammit, where was she, anyway. She knew she was supposed to hang around close by all during this thing and get him away from people. Instead of that, just like a woman, she was sashaying all over the place, showing off her boobs in that tight dress to every goddam lech who wanted to sneak a look.

And then he had to yell at himself. Jesus! He was a happily married man with a family and a big house in the suburbs—thirteen rooms, six phones, three and a half baths. He couldn't afford to get himself tangled up with her . . . Lately she was getting under his skin. Christ, he'd "worked late" twice every week since the shooting, and he just gave her a gold watch for Christmas! A fucking gold watch! He could hardly believe it. It had cost as much as the present he got for his wife, for Christ's sake! He'd never done that with any of his

ladies before. Oh, shit, she turned him on; she turned him on!
Like he'd never been turned on before! Well, no woman had
ever before liked it so much with him. None of the others had
moaned like her, writhed around like that. Sometimes she
acted like a bucking bronco. None of them said the things to
him that she said; none of them had ever been so hot—and for
him, for him! He knew he didn't have the biggest dick
around, but it didn't seem to matter to her. She just loved it!
She loved it! And she was a clever one. She said to him,
"Small? Ah, come on, Hank, it's terrific. And I like being
able to get it all in my mouth." She killed him! Shit, he'd
promised himself he wouldn't let himself start thinking about
it today. One of his resolutions was to cool it with her. And
where the hell was she? Goddamit, he got himself worked up
just thinking . . .

Hank took his eyes from the Reverend and openly looked
around the room, searching for the bright red velvet dress.
Was that her, over in the corner, surrounded by those residents?
If he caught her coming on to anyone else, he'd break her
legs. Enough of that! He reached out an arm and snagged
Adrian Winter's chief resident, his pet black boy. What was
his name again? . . . oh, yeah.

"Reverend, I'd like you to meet one of our best. Robert
Truman, Ob/Gyn chief resident . . ."

To his surprise, the young doctor stiffened a bit; in fact, for
just a minute, he thought Truman would pull away, but he
didn't. But he was damned tense. "Not Robert. My name's
Bob. That's right, Bob. Bob Joseph. It was my great-
grandfather's name, a slave name. He was called Bob when
he was a little boy, but after they discovered he was teachable
. . . Actually, what happened was, he taught himself to read.
Anyway, they made him a house slave then, and Bob wasn't
dignified enough, so they decided on Joseph. He was Bob
Joseph, and so am I!"

Holy God, what am I mouthing off for? Bobby asked
himself. To Del Bello, of all the damn people! Del Bello, the

Big Man himself. What's the matter with me? Do I have a secret suicide wish?

But Del Bello only smiled more broadly and said, in a mild tone, "What a great story. You must be very proud to have come such a long way. Listen, I'm the son of poor immigrants myself, the first college graduate in my family. And they renamed my father and mother at Ellis Island. The inspector they got couldn't handle Annunciata and Archangelo, so it's been Nancy and Archie ever since!" He laughed.

The Rev grinned and seemed to stretch himself even taller and broader. Bobby knew immediately that they were in for one of the Rev's little lessons in black history. He loved this kind of thing, the Reverend Clayton, just loved it. Well, it might be interesting, and it might be funny. It would have one major attribute as far as Bob Joseph Truman was concerned; it would get his mind off Rita Schneider and the mess his life was in right now.

"One of the grand things about our black people," the Rev intoned, "we have always felt free with the language. We have always felt creative. We are a creative people. We love to name our children pretty names . . . beautiful, lyrical, musical words. Sadly, there are those who would take advantage.

"Before affirmative action, Mr. Del Bello," Reverend Clayton said in a slightly different tone, turning his eyes to the hospital administrator, still smiling but with a grim set to his mouth that Bobby recognized. He got one hundred percent; a lesson was forthcoming.

"Before affirmative action, when there were no black doctors, not even in the middle of a large black neighborhood such as my very own, a young doctor from this very hospital delivered one of my flock—a poor, uneducated woman—of a baby daughter. She was so happy, so grateful. Had the child been male, she surely would have given it the doctor's own name; that's how she felt about him. But it was a female, and so she said, 'Doctor, tell me a name for my daughter. I want to name her in your honor.' And the bastard—excuse me,

213

Ms. Scofield, but I must be honest, I must be forthright—the son of a bitch smiled and said, 'Name her Placenta.' And the mother did, because it sounded so pretty, she told me, and wasn't it nice of the doctor to give her such a lovely, fancy name.''

The Reverend paused dramatically and took in a deep breath. By this time, his very powerful, ringing voice had attracted quite a bit of attention. ''Yes, Mr. Del Bello, you heard me right. A doctor in this very hospital, an educated, trained, you would think civilized man, did this dreadful and cruel thing.'' How his voice sank to one of those ministerial whispers that could reach to the second balcony of his tabernacle church.

''Placenta,'' he repeated. ''*Placenta.*'' A pause just long enough to keep the focus where he wanted it, and he went on. ''That sweet little girl would have had to go through her life with a joke for a name, with an insult for a name, with a *betrayal* for a name.'' There were quite a few people gathered round—the Reverend, in Bobby's experience, had only to project his voice the littlest bit and he instantly had a crowd—and from them came a collective murmur of sympathy. The Rev turned his gaze upon them and smiled upon them like a benediction. What a man! He was too old-fashioned for Bobby's taste, too much the cliché'd charismatic black pastor. But, Bobby thought with a secret grin, you had to call a spade a spade, and the Rev could work a crowd like nobody he'd ever seen.

''Of course, that never would have happened to a white woman, Mr. Del Bello, now would it? I was just a young minister then, Mr. Del Bello, and it made such an impression upon me that I made a vow to God at that moment that my mission in this community would be to get decent, humane medical care for my people . . . *Decent*, Mr. Del Bello, *humane* . . .''

The man was right, Bobby thought, and that was the trouble. The black community *had* been robbed of proper health care for generations. It was true. But he had a strong feeling that the Rev's so-called mission had more to do with the fact that Cadman was a convenient symbol of the white man's supremacy in this neighborhood than with any solely altruistic motives. The hospital served extremely well as a symbol, with its entrance fronting on mostly white, mostly well-to-do Brooklyn Heights, while its rear—service entrances, garbage cans, and furnace room—was turned toward the mainly black and poor Tillary Houses.

But Cadman was not terrible. Cadman was not a villain. Cadman was trying. Holy shit, the Reverend sat on the goddam board of trustees, didn't he? And you could never say that he wasn't listened to . . . because everyone knew you couldn't have him in the same room and *not* listen to him. He wasn't just a figurehead, a token. He wasn't even the only black member, in fact. And there were a lot of black nurses and technicians in this building; there were hundreds of black faces in the corridors.

Actually, Cadman was the largest employer of blacks in the entire area. To listen to the Rev, you'd think they were all cleaning personnel and laundry folders. It just wasn't so! And it made Bobby angry whenever the Reverend began to make stuff up just to get himself looked at. Yes, it was admirable, to watch him do his thing so easily, so naturally . . . but look at him, so pleased with himself. What did he have to be pleased about? Making a bunch of people uneasy and guilty? Man, this was a *party*. If he had real class, he'd never climb up on his pulpit in the middle of someone else's party. Actually, for all his glamour, the Reverend Ezekiel Clayton was a bullshit artist and a manipulator—no better in his way than Del Bello.

"Reverend," Del Bello was saying at this very moment, "that's a very moving story. I'm touched every time you tell it." There was a great deal of laughter, and the little crowd immediately began to disperse.

Del Bello moved off, with the Reverend calling after him. "That was very sharp, Mr. Del Bello, but it doesn't alter the truth." Swiftly, before Bobby had a chance to escape, he turned to him, grasping his arm, and said, "Isn't that right, brother?"

"I'm not your brother."

"Come, come now. In the eyes of Jehovah, we're all in the same family, my boy."

"I'm not your boy, either."

The Reverend's lips tightened, and his eyes lost their friendly, cocker spaniel warmth. "I know very well who you are, Bob Joseph. You're Sister Corinne's husband. She's one of my best, Bobby, one of the most devoted helpers we have. You know that lately she's been most generous of her time, and when your little girl is in nursery school, she comes in and works in the office. A fine secretary, a fine organizer."

No, I damn well did *not* know that lately my wife's been hanging around the church doing free office work for you, Bobby thought. Bile rose in the back of his throat. So that's why she was always too tired lately to bother about him! And why the hell hadn't she told him? She'd probably say she was scared he'd get mad; she was always saying that nowadays. Putting him on one guilt trip after the other! No time to cook him a decent meal or fix herself up to look like a real woman. Oh, no. But plenty of time to run to church and to pray and now free secretarial work! No wonder he couldn't get Rita out of his mind. She was totally tuned in to him. Every man needed *that*, didn't he? Every man deserved it. When he took off from the hospital every Wednesday and from home on Sunday and ran over to Henry Street, he knew he was going to get only good, only happy, only enthusiastic from her. It was something he could be sure of and look forward to. As soon as he was in the door, she was on tiptoe, her arms tight around his neck, her sweet mouth against his, whispering promises that set him on fire. That's how it was supposed to be, goddammit, between a man and a woman. That's how it used to be with him and Corinne, dammit. Dammit.

The Reverend Clayton moved just a tad closer and took Bobby's hand between both of his. "Yes, Sister Corinne is a fine mother, a devoted mother to your sweet little girl. You must be proud of both of them . . . and so happy that you have been blessed with another child on its way . . ."

He's got to be kidding, Bobby thought. He was one smart man, the Rev. He had to know that Corinne was high risk. But . . . maybe not. "You may not know this, Reverend, but that child on its way is on its way contrary to all medical advice."

"God's will be done," the minister intoned.

Bobby pulled his hand away. "Bullshit!" he gritted between his teeth, keeping his voice low. "It wasn't God's will! It was Corinne's. She stopped taking the pill—without telling me. Now you tell me something, Reverend . . . If our next child is born horribly deformed and retarded, is *that* God's will?"

"We are all part of God's plan, my boy. We mere humans cannot hope to know what is in God's great plan. It is not for us to know."

"Agh!" Bobby turned his head away, disgusted. In the end, you couldn't talk to people like him. Or maybe it was just that they couldn't listen. "Look, Reverend, every time the doctors around here try to get your people to take responsibility for their own lives and the lives of their children, that's the answer we get. *God's plan*. Well, it may be God's plan, but guess who has to clean up the mess? Guess who has to take care of all those pregnant teenaged girls from your parish who said it was God's will when it was only their ignorance . . ."

"Exactly, Doctor. The people need you, don't you see, to help educate them. Why don't you come to the tabernacle on Sunday—"

Bobby exploded. "I'm *doing* my job, Reverend, and my job is in the hospital! Why don't you do yours? Tell those girls you pray over all the time about how birth control works and about how they can come to the hospital clinic and get it. In other words, teach them how to be responsible for their own lives! Instead of encouraging them to throw their hands up and excuse everything as God's will."

"You are not doing your job unless you are giving back to your community—"

"My community! My community! Your church is not my community. For your information, I plan to practice in the ghetto after I leave Cadman. But that's none of your business. Your teenaged girls *are* . . . And we keep getting them, by the dozens. Not just the teenagers, either. Over half the obstetrical patient load is black women, and just about all of them are without husbands, without men at all. Without money. Without proper nutrition. What the hell are they doing, getting pregnant under those conditions? And then you give them a prescription, most of the time they forget to take it! Or decide to take twice as much so it'll work twice as fast! No wonder the doctors all complain! I'm sick and tired, Reverend Clayton, of defending those ignoramuses just because I have brown skin!"

The Reverend's voice was quite even, quite calm. "I suggest, Dr. Truman, that you are attracting . . . unwelcome attention."

Oh, Jesus! There he went again, blowing his cool. And wouldn't you know it, Adrian was approaching with what looked like blood in his eye. Oh, shit, now I'm gonna have to hear about short fuses and how it's unseemly in a doctor.

Adrian tried not to look in a hurry, but he was concerned. Bobby was scowling and frowning and had thrust his head forward the way he did when he was ready to explode. It wouldn't be a good idea for him to explode all over the Reverend Clayton, not here, at the largest gathering of the year in the hospital. He'd told Bobby more than once that he had to watch that short fuse of his. You had to learn in this life to hide your real feelings. Oh, you could *feign* anger when it served your purpose, but if you were intelligent, you knew enough *never* to show real fury—which might get out of hand.

Bobby didn't seem to be able to learn it. Just a couple of weeks ago, he was making rounds of his private patients on the Gynecology floor when he came upon Bobby and Nick

Ponte head to head, fists and voices raised, right outside a patient's room and in full view of the nursing station and the waiting room.

Of course he ran right over and separated them as quietly as possible and then gave them hell, also as quietly as possible. Ponte muttered insults under his breath so nobody could hear him and then, Nick-like, refused to admit he'd done anything. Truman, Bobby-like, was much more open. He shook off Adrian's restraining hand and spat. "Just give me five minutes with this crud . . . I'm gonna kill him. I'm gonna kill him."

"You're not going to kill anybody, Dr. Truman. You and Dr. Ponte are going to come along with me to my office, and we're going to have a short seminar on creating disturbances in front of the patients, the nurses, and the visitors." But the cool tone belied his worried thoughts. Bobby was very nearly finished with his training, and he was one of the finest physicians Adrian had ever taught. He had heart, Bobby; he hadn't allowed the dehumanizing hours and the dehumanizing demands to dehumanize him.

Adrian, over the years, had watched too many compassionate and idealistic young doctors become hard and cynical by the time they were ready to go out into the world and deal with patients on their own. Maybe it wasn't their fault; maybe it was the system. But the public was fast becoming disillusioned with medical care in this country. People were complaining bitterly that their doctors didn't care, and women loudest of all, that their gynecologists and obstetricians were self-centered and unfeeling. Look at all the nonsense lately about nurse-midwives and nurse practitioners! All a result of doctors whose sensiti... .es were systematically burned out of them by overwork and fatigue. The system of training doctors, he was beginning to feel, actually rewarded callousness.

He had had such high hopes for Bobby Truman who had seemed too strong and too tough to be destroyed in that way. But, good Lord, the man was going to jeopardize everything he had worked for if he didn't learn to hold that temper in check.

He was thinking all of this as the three of them made their way down the corridor and into his office. As soon as he closed the door behind them, Bobby rounded on Ponte once again, pinning him against the wall and hissing. "I ever hear of you doing a shit thing like that again—I ever get a *whisper* of it—I swear, Ponte, you'll be out of here so fast you won't know if it's Wednesday or 1946."

"Lay off, Truman. You're making a big deal over nothing."

"*Nothing!*" But Bobby allowed Adrian to pull him away once more and to push him down into a nearby chair. "Jesus Christ!" Bobby appealed to the walls. "*Nothing*, he says."

Nick rolled his eyes. "Agh, you're supersensitive, Truman. You roll over and die when they complain."

Adrian held up his hand and said, "I'd like to hear what happened. Who wants to go first?"

"There's nothing to tell, Dr. Winter," Nick insisted. "Nothing happened!"

So in the end he heard it from Bobby.

Nick was on duty, and one of the private patients had just been admitted for a routine D & C. Today she would have all routine tests and examinations to determine that she was okay for surgery. It came to Nick, who was on duty, to give her a rectal examination.

Apparently, Nick breezed into her room, without even introducing himself by name, and announced that he was there to give her a rectal. She told Bobby later that she wondered why he didn't explain anything but wanted to be a cooperative patient and not make trouble, so she rolled over to allow it.

"Does this bother you?" Nick asked.

And she said, "No, doctor."

"Does this hurt at all?"

"No, doctor, it's fine."

"Oh," he said lightly, "you like it, huh?"

She told Bobby that she froze, unable to believe she'd heard correctly. But as soon as Nick left the room, she called a nurse and demanded to see her own doctor . . . or, that failing, somebody who was that young man's superior. The more she thought about it, she told Bobby, the more upset she became. "It was such a violation," she told him. "It was like a kind of rape. I mean, Dr. Truman, the man had his hand in my body, and he said that disgusting, suggestive thing . . . ugh! What does he think—that he can do whatever he wants because I'm lying in a hospital bed?"

"My blood began to boil," Bobby said at the end of his recital. "Of all the goddam stupid things Nick Ponte has said and done since he started working with us—and he's said and done *plenty*—this takes the goddam cake." And he twisted around, furious all over again, screaming at Ponte. "What the hell are you doing in gynecology, anyway, you ape!"

"My wife died when she was twenty-two from an ectopic some lousy fuckup didn't find!"

There was a momentary silence, and then Bobby, with an obvious effort to calm himself, said, "I'm sorry."

Well, of course, Adrian had known before what drove Nick Ponte into a speciality he obviously really didn't belong in. He'd spoken to Nick about it, on several occasions, but Nick was adamant. He was going to make up for that death; he was going to beat back the ghosts with his own two hands. He was, technically, really not bad; it was just that antediluvian attitude about women's bodies. In the end it was going to get him into terrible trouble, Adrian felt. But, more important than Nick, no matter what he did, was Bobby Truman, a man of whom Adrian was fond. He saw himself reflected in Bobby Truman; he saw his own youthful ideals and his own youthful excesses. In a way, he guessed that he hoped to mold Bobby Truman into a better Adrian Winter.

As he reached the Rev and Bobby, Adrian said, "Could you excuse Dr. Truman for a moment, Reverend? We have a small emergency."

The Rev wasn't fooled; he could see that. But punctilious as always, he smiled sweetly. "Of course, Dr. Winter. And Dr. Truman, I hope you'll think about what I said. We could use you."

"Jesus, the man never lets up!" Bobby exclaimed.

"And neither do you, apparently."

Bobby ducked his head and held two hands up in surrender. "*Mea culpa*, boss. You caught me again. But he frosts me; he really gets me."

"Look, Bobby, in order to do much of anything around this neighborhood, sooner or later you'll have to work your way around or through the Reverend Clayton. Not only is he on the board, but he is one very powerful political guy. Smarten up! Don't let him get you . . . get what *you* want out of *him*."

"The first thing I want out of him is my wife back! Corinne used to be smart and competent and had a sense of humor . . . And now he's brainwashed her, and all she can do with her mind is quote the Bible and mouth off all those slogans they're so fond of over there . . . Ah, shit!"

They were walking and talking at the same time, and Adrian deftly steered them to the bar. "Take it easy, Bobby. *You* have to be in control, or you lose."

"Yeah, but don't you think that sometimes being able to feel is more important than control?"

Sharply: "What do you mean by that?"

"I mean that I'm worried if I shut off my emotions and control them too much, I'm going to be out of touch with my patients. And I'm not going to be very much of a doctor then, am I?" Bobby took another drink and slid a glance over at Adrian. "I'm sorry if that sounds too personal. I didn't mean it to pertain to you. I only meant myself."

Adrian laughed shortly. "I didn't think you were insulting my abilities as a physician. And of course, in a large sense, you're absolutely correct. The doctor who becomes too distanced and too objective becomes heartless . . . and cruel. I hope I haven't done that."

"Oh, Jesus, no! Every time we go on grand rounds, I think all over again how extraordinary you are . . . how you touch your patients and empathize and allow them their dignity."

To his amazement, Adrian felt a stinging sensation in the corners of his eyes. The boy meant it, and it warmed his heart. That's what this training of young physicians was all about . . . that sometimes, every once in a while, you could reach out and make real contact with one of them, you could transmit what you felt was important—not the techniques but the essence of it all, the *taking care* of people. God, this was splendid. You could never be quite sure how much of what you said and taught and lectured and showed them was really getting to them. So much of it was so murky and amorphous. He'd been low lately about one thing and another, and this was a real lift.

He put a hand on Bobby's shoulder and said, "Thank you very much, Bobby. You have no idea how much I appreciate those kind words." Bobby gave him a sharp look, and he added, laughing, "Oh, yes, even the Old Man has his bad days, Bobby." He took another sip. "Don't worry; it's not terminal."

Bobby, of course, would never ask what he meant. And he wasn't about to tell him, either. But God, between the political crap around there and the hell that was breaking loose at home, he wasn't getting much joy lately.

He had to face it; his marriage, his new marriage, his second marriage, was in deep trouble. Leslie was—oh, God, he didn't really want to face or think about it or deal with it—but Leslie was boring. He only felt drawn home these days by his son. He found himself not looking Leslie in the eye; he hardly could bring himself to make love to her, although she was very seductive, very provocative. Of course, when she ran her hands over him and caressed him in their bed at night, he couldn't help but respond. But afterward, he felt cold and empty and depressed. That was no way to be married. And it was driving Leslie crazy; he knew it was. She was so miserable these days, so short-tempered and pouty. He knew it was his fault—he never should have married her, and he also knew that one of these days, they were going to have to face the truth. It wasn't going to be easy; it was going to hurt them both.

She was being so careful, as careful as she could be. But he made her crazy; he made her wild. There he was, not five feet away, drinking and talking to a group of people, laughing and joking and pretending he didn't even see her. She got all dressed up for the party so he wouldn't be able to keep his eyes off her, and she just knew that he saw her, all right; he was very well aware of her presence. Well, she knew how the white knit dress clung, how it accentuated the positive, as they used to say . . . Lord, every other man in the room had given her "that look" at least once. How could he be so cool and uncaring? He was making her absolutely crazy.

Oh, David Powell, why am I running after you all the time? I've never had to run after a man in my entire life. I've always had all the men I wanted . . . *more* than I wanted.

Why, before she married Adrian, her phone was ringing all the time, *all* the time. And David just never bothered. Oh, when they were together, he was hot as he could be; he was all over her. Why, sometimes they never got to the bed. Once, it was on the floor, and another time he couldn't even wait that long and took her standing up, against the front door. He was such a good lover, better than anyone in her whole life. Just thinking about him made her want it . . . even if she'd just had it an hour before. He was no sooner out the door than she was horny all over again. God, men loved her! Didn't he realize that? If she wanted to, she could pick any man in the room and have him following her like a puppy dog in about two and a half minutes.

Leslie sucked in her belly— Lord, she was getting fat—and turned so that when he glanced over again, he'd get the full profile. He loved her breasts, he loved to fondle them and kiss them, and he told her over and over again how beautiful they were. So come on, David, stop acting so laid-back and look over this way. How she hated this; she *hated* it. When Leslie Fox smiled at a man, that man smiled back. When Leslie Fox crooked her little finger, that man came running. And when Leslie Fox gave her body to a man, the man was hooked! She'd always had her own way with men; that's why girls were born beautiful, so they could make it in this man's world. What was wrong with David Powell? Why did he hide his feelings? Why did he deny he was crazy about her?

All right, at this party it wasn't a good idea for him to be seen with her; he'd already explained that, and he didn't have to. She wasn't exactly dumb. She wasn't going to hold his hand or anything, especially not when her own husband was at the party. But some little sign from him, that's all she wanted! Some little signal that said, "Yes, Leslie, honey, I see you there, and I wish I could be with you."

Oh, she should never have said anything about love that noon, when they were screwing. She knew she shouldn't; she just got carried away. He was pounding into her, gritting his teeth and getting that wild look on his face that she loved, and she just couldn't help it. She cried out, "Oh, David, I do love you, I love you, I love you!"

And later, after he came, he propped himself up on one elbow and said, "Leslie, sweetheart, I like you a whole lot. But listen, I happen to *love* my job, and there's a guy I happen to like a lot, and it happens he's not only a doctor and could get me fired, but he's your husband. So . . . listen, sweetheart, take it easy. Don't push it so hard."

He was right; he was right. She had no business feeling this way about him. She was a married woman with a little boy and a position in Brooklyn Heights; a doctor's wife, the wife of a well-known doctor! But no one had ever made her feel the way he did: he was so warm and loving and tender and caring . . . No, no, she had to fight it; she was a married woman, and her husband was in this very room. She glanced around, and sure enough, there he was over by the bar, with that PR person Sandy Heller.

He always says he hates Sandy Heller, she thought, gazing

at them. But they seemed very friendly from there, and Sandy Heller kept touching his arm all the time. Briefly, she wondered if maybe Adrian was sleeping with Sandy Heller; she was pretty enough and even kind of sexy, if you liked the flashy type. And that would explain why Adrian hadn't been too turned on lately . . . Sure, another woman. Why hadn't she thought of that before? It had to be that; it couldn't be anything *she* had done, because she was exactly the same. Playing around again, that's what he was doing! Well, then, it served him right! And with a cheap little dye job like Sandy Heller! Well!

Sandy kept her eyes fixed on Adrian Winter, thinking, A tall man is a pain in the neck . . . literally a pain in the neck for someone my size. But with these doctors, you had to fix your eyes upon them and look sincere and interested, no matter how stiff your neck got or how boring they got. Not that he was difficult to look at; he was one of the better-looking men around here. Too bad he was passé.

He may not know it, she thought, but he's on his way out. So she didn't have to charm him, but what the hell, she'd do it, anyway. Her way was the gentle way. And besides, he might be on the way out, but he was still codirector of the Neonatal Nursery. She would eventually do a piece on those babies, or her name wasn't Sandra "Always Gets Her Story" Heller. A story about a two-pound infant whose life was being saved . . . Well, if she did it right, she could win a science writing award. And she would do it right. It wasn't just for the glory. This kind of story—fragile premature babies struggling for life aided by the most up-to-date equipment in the world and by the most dedicated, caring professional staff—always got to the readers, always.

Well, wasn't she helping people by letting them know what was going on at Cadman, letting them know what could be done for premies and where they could come for help?

She told him all this, being very serious, not at all like a PR person, and he looked down at her in that condescending way they had and said, "Oh, really now, Ms. Heller, do you want me to believe that you're so altruistic?"

"Why not?" she flared. "You think that doctors are the only ones dedicated to their work? I'm as much a professional as you are." And then she quickly smiled, placating, putting a light hand on his arm. "Oh, there I go, getting overenthusiastic about a possible story. You're so involved in the medical side of it, you can't realize how spectacular what you're doing looks like to the outside world."

"I realize; I promise you. But I cannot have the routine of the nursery compromised by reporters and cameramen or photographers."

"We could arrange it ahead of time . . . I mean, I'd be willing to come in after work or on weekends. I know everyone wants to know what happened to those Siamese twins, how they're doing . . ."

"Not the Siamese twins," he barked.

"Not the Siamese twins," Sandy quickly agreed, getting a bit miffed. She gave him another smile, wishing she didn't have to go through this song and dance with every goddam doctor for every goddam story. Didn't they think she was human?

If that bitch, Con Scofield thought, thinks she can pull a number on Adrian Winter, she's going to have the surprise of a lifetime. The notion of that flirty little woman tossing her hair and winking and dimpling at Adrian Winter . . . Well, it was a laugh! Adrian didn't go for girlish wiles; never had. Look who he married. Ellie was clean-cut and attractive, but she'd never been what you'd call a flirt. And even the glamorous second Mrs. Winter was a class act. But this one—!

So when Adrian left Sandy's side and headed right for her, for Con, a frown between his brows, and said, even before he got to her, "Con, I'm worried," well, she just naturally assumed that's who he was talking about.

She said, "That viper! Don't let her get to you. Just because she's so thick with Del Bello—"

"Huh? Oh, no, no. I don't mean Sandy. I'm talking about Nate. He said for sure he'd show up today for the party. He promised me. I was hoping to get him out of his apartment and get him back into Cadman, for even just a little while. I figured he's like one of those old fire horses; put him back in the traces and he's off and running."

"Oh, really?" Con instinctively looked to the entrance. "Well, maybe he's on his way."

"It's nearly over, Con. It's close to seven . . ."

"All right, so it's close to seven, and he changed his mind. What's the matter, this his first promise to you that ever got broken? Come on, Adrian, Nate's a grown man. He's allowed to change his mind."

"Yeah, but there's more. I already called him, around six. And then again at six-thirty, when he hadn't shown up. No answer. So I called his super, and he knocked, but nobody answered. Look, Con, I talked with him recently. I have good reason to be nervous. The man's in a bad depression."

Together, they left the big room and went down the hall to the staff phone. Just looking at Adrian, running, one hand through his hair, twisting his face, made her feel twitchy. He was always so cool, no matter what. There wasn't an emergency that had been invented that could shake him up—that's what she always thought. In fact, to a lot of people around here, not the patients, of course, he was known as Old Stone Face. But look at him now, so agitated.

He was obviously talking to the super again. "I'll hang on," he was saying. "Hey! And take your key! Yeah, if there's no answer, open the door. What do you mean, permission? I give you permission. I'm his doctor. That's right. Okay. I'll hang on." Unnecessarily, he said to Con, "The super's going to see what's what."

"Aw, it'll be nothing." She didn't like the gray look of him.

"I hope you're right, Con. But I have a feeling . . ."

She felt a cold chill. "What feeling?"

"Agh, nothing really. It's just . . . What? *What*?" He turned ashen, and beads of sweat sprang out on his forehead. Con thought her heart stopped for a moment; in any case, it suddenly began to hammer. "Gas! Did you turn it off and get him out of there? In the hall? Open the window? *You're not sure he's breathing*? Okay, okay." Adrian at last looked directly at her; there was anguish in his pale eyes. "Look. I'm calling from Cadman. I'm going to get into an ambulance, and we'll be over there in two minutes."

"Is he all right?" she asked. Her voice was not coming out right, somehow.

"I can't really tell, talking to the super. I wasn't even sure he understood me. I don't even know if he's breathing, goddammit. I have to get over there."

The two of them raced down the hall, toward Emergency. "We should have kept closer watch on him!" Con panted. "We should have been more careful . . . me and my big mouth!"

"You! You didn't do anything."

"Oh, every time someone said Nate needs my help, I said he's a grown man. Just before I said it . . . just before. And there he was, his head in the oven, oh, Jesus . . ."

They ran out to the ambulance. Adrian stopped and grabbed her by the shoulders. "Look, Con, I was close to him, and I *knew* he needed something from me, and I told myself he's a grown man, and I tried my best, and how much can one person do?"

Con stared into his eyes. "How much? Enough to keep him alive."

"Aw, Con—!"

"Well? Do you think I did enough? Do you think *you* did enough? Oh, hell," she quickly added as a look of pain crossed his face, "I don't want to make you feel any worse. You better get going. You did as much as anyone could."

Bitterly, he said, "Did I? Well, I'm about to find out."

229

Chapter 18

ALL THE WAY over to Nate's in the ambulance—only two miles, but it felt like fifty—Adrian sweated. Under the pin-stripe suit with its neatly buttoned vest he felt the wetness pop out all over his body. It was the sweat of panic, he knew that. He was scared of what he might find, and his adrenalin was pumping like crazy.

Nate's block was so peaceful. The siren split through the evening quiet like the scream of a wild animal, and people walking home turned to stare when he leaped out of the back, racing up the stone steps to the already open front door. He panted up the two flights of twisting stairs, cursing the darkness. These old buildings! Twelve-foot ceilings and twenty-watt bulbs for hall lights; you could hardly see where you were going.

Nate lay very very still on the floor in the hallway just outside his apartment door. You could still small gas faintly, although the hall window had been opened wide. It was freezing cold. And so damn dark! He couldn't even see the color of Nate's skin, and he couldn't see him breathe, either. *Was* he breathing? Adrian dropped to his knees, felt for the wrist pulse and put his ear to Nate's chest.

Yes, there was a faint—oh, so faint—heartbeat. Yes, he really was hearing it, not hoping it into existence. But no breathing. Jesus, no breathing. And then the calm part of him, the physician, reminded him that with methane inhalation there could be respiration as infrequent as two breaths a minute. "Nate!" he yelled. "Nate!" No response. And where the hell were the paramedics with the oxy? He bent quickly to give Nate mouth-to-mouth: four deep breaths.

"We're here, doctor."

Adrian's head snapped around. Right behind him, and he hadn't heard! Without a word, he moved over. The medic slammed the oxygen mask over Nate's face. For a moment, all was silent as they waited. And then, at last!

"He's breathing," Adrian said. "But just." The other medic appeared at the top of stairs; then, with the stretcher and swiftly, the two of them wrapped Nate tightly into it, and more quickly than Adrian would have thought possible, they were down the stairs, out into the street, and lifting him into the ambulance.

"Hop aboard, Doc, we're on our way."

"Good work," Adrian said, but they were too busy to pay attention.

He hunkered down close to Nate and held his hand. He thought the breathing was more regular now; it seemed less shallow. But he didn't like that ashy color. Nate must be sixty-two now; his body couldn't take this kind of abuse. He'd always had a strong heart; still, he wished Nate were already on the respirator in the ER.

The ambulance pulled up with a squeal of tires at the emergency entrance and again, the two young medics moved quickly, efficiently, without fuss or panic.

In the bright lights of the ER, Nate looked even sicker than before. Adrian trotted behind the medics, who shouted as they came in. "Attempted suicide! Methane!" Instantly, there was a nurse at one of the empty cots, pulling over the necessary equipment, and he heard Con's voice, saying, "Never mind, it's done, it's done; that's Dr. Levinson."

231

As from a great distance, Adrian watched the choreography of the Emergency Room, admiring all of them, noting stupid little things like the chunk of pink bubble gum stuck to the floor and that all of the nurses were wearing running shoes. He automatically noted the upward climb of Nate's blood pressure as the little nurse sang it out every couple of minutes. "Ninety over sixty, Ms. Scofield . . . one hundred over sixty . . . one ten over seventy . . ."

And then Con said, "Good. That's fine." And at the same moment, Nate took in a deep shuddering breath and let it out with a feeble groan, and Con said, "He's okay! He's kvetching." Then, and only then, did she even look over at Adrian, letting her breath out noisily. "The damn fool!" she said to him. "What did he think he was doing?"

"He's going to pull through." It was half a question.

"Sure he is. He's too stubborn not to pull through. And besides, Adrian, he wanted to be saved. His timing was perfect. Right in the middle of a party where we were all waiting for him and were bound to worry."

"He had *me* worried!"

"Tell me about it! We didn't know who we should give the oxygen to when you first came in. You looked worse than he did." She came over and put her hand on his arm. "Sit down for a minute. I'm going to get us some nice hot coffee."

"No, no, I'll—"

"Adrian, listen to an old nurse. You *need* that coffee. With plenty of sugar. Just sit. I'll be right back."

He obeyed, taking a chair where he could look at Nate, who was already looking better, the pink flush of health rising in his skin. Adrian sat back in the vinyl-covered chair. His next job was to admit Nate, but right now he was grateful just to sit and not think about anything in particular. He was drained. Without volition, his eyes closed. Behind him, the two young residents lounged against a desk, chatting.

"What is he, number ten?"

"Ten, twelve, who knows? I don't know I'm on duty if two or three old characters don't try to end it all!"

232

"What would make a guy do that?"

"You got me! *I* want to live. I'll tell you. I've got a girlfriend. She'd get awfully horny if I turned up dead."

"Well, I guess *he* doesn't have a lady!"

"Yeah, well, I guess that's a good enough reason to kill yourself. Life without a woman! Not me!"

And then one of the nurses, just as callous and careless, said, "Would you guys can it? Sex, sex, sex; that's all you think about. And don't make up your mind so fast just because someone's a geriatric. Some of these old guys are doing better than you are!"

"Oh, would you like to try us both?"

Adrian could no longer stand it. As he leaped to his feet, the young nurse added, "That's disgusting."

In his most commanding voice, he said loudly, "She's absolutely right!"

The two residents wheeled around, and two completely startled faces stared at him.

Adrian strode over to where they stood. "I'm Dr. Winter, chief of Ob/Gyn. And you are . . ." he squinted at their name tags: "Dr. O'Brien and Dr. Stahlmeyer. And I'd like to know what the hell you think you're doing, talking like that in front of the patients."

"Sorry, Dr. Winter. But the old guy is out and —"

"The old guy, as you so elegantly put it, happens to be a human being. Do I make myself clear? Yes? And furthermore, he is Dr. Nathan Levinson, who was until a short time ago the director of this hospital and very probably the man who signed the papers allowing you to come to Cadman for your graduate training."

One of them managed a sheepish smile. "Again, sorry, Dr. Winter. But listen, we didn't intend any disrespect."

"You could have fooled me!"

"I—it's just that, well, Larry and I are now into our thirty-fourth hour of on call . . . And it's true, you know, between the depressed elderly and the depressed unemployed and the depressed teenagers and the depressed junkies . . . I kid you not, Doctor. We must get seven or eight attempted suicides a month. You can't let it get to you, or you'll go nuts.''

Adrian felt a bit sheepish himself at that moment. He'd been a resident once, and he could remember the utter fatigue of being on call and the absolute necessity to distance yourself from the daily tragedies of a big hospital. He'd come down on them hard and fast—too hard and too fast.

"See, the way I figure it," the resident was going on, "where there's life, there's hope. And this is Dr. Levinson—a guy with a big rep and plenty of dough and lots of friends, right? How bad could his life be?" Now the young man rubbed his eyes, looked directly at Adrian, and shrugged. "I always figured," he said, "no matter how bad life gets, it's always better than the alternative.''

Chapter 19

"H*APPY* N*EW* Y*EAR!*" Adrian said. He stopped in the doorway and shook his head affectionately. There sat Nate in bed, fighting with his nurse. She was saying, "Come on now, Dr. Levinson, eat your nice breakfast."

And he was saying gruffly, "If you think it's so nice, here, you eat it. Take it; it's yours. I give it to you!" And then he looked up and saw Adrian, and his face changed. He looked sheepish, embarrassed.

"Yeah, yeah, the same to you. Happy New Year. You can go now, little lady."

The nurse was young enough to make a little face at that but old enough to laugh out loud. She picked up the tray and put it on the dresser.

"Of all the damn stunts!" Adrian said. "My God, Nate, I still can't believe you really tried that!"

"You're right; it was a lousy job. If I'd done it right, you wouldn't be yelling at me now. You'd be burying me instead."

From the door the nurse gave an involuntary little gasp. She turned quickly and said, "Dr. Levinson, bite your tongue."

You shouldn't talk like that—oh!'' The ''oh'' was for Con Scofield, coming through.

"He shouldn't talk like what?'' Con demanded.

"About . . . about he should be dead now.''

Con waved a hand. "Pay no attention, Carol. This man has no manners. He doesn't know any other way to talk.''

In his bed, Nate sat up straighter and folded his arms across his chest. "I guess I *am* dead. This is hell, isn't it?''

Con marched to the bedside, scowling happily, if such a thing could be; and it must be, Adrian thought, because she was doing it. "You think this is hell!'' she scolded. "I'll give you hell! First of all, you gave us all a terrible scare! Not to mention that you ruined the party for Adrian and me . . .'' As she spoke, she fussed with his blanket and his pillows, never quite touching him.

Nate heaved a sigh. "That's right. I can't do anything right these days.''

"Dammit,'' Adrian said, "I wish you'd stop that. You make me feel totally inept. You know that? I'm an obstetrician; I can only deal with *post partum* depression.''

Nate mumbled something; his head lowered. Both Con and Adrian said, "What?''

And sheepishly, he said, "Come on! You think it's wonderful, trying to commit suicide and then waking up to find you've failed and there's everybody pitying you?''

"That's not pity, you old fool. That's surprise.''

"Surprise? What for?''

She gave him a smirk. "What for? Because you haven't been around here for so long, nobody knows what in hell you look like anymore!''

"Agh! I'm not needed here anymore! I'm not so sure I'm needed *anywhere*!''

"Come on, Nate!'' Adrian exploded. "I've been begging you for months to come in and make yourself available. Especially for the ethics committee. I've told you a dozen times; we need your vote and your intelligence during those damn meetings. But you wouldn't listen, would you, and now Del Bello has done it—did I tell you his pet doctor is Art Schuster? Well, Del Bello's put him on the ethics committee, took Len Adler off—"

"Oh, no! Len *Adler*? But the man's a pro, a real thinker. Why the hell—?"

"You see what I mean? That's the kind of thing that's happening around here." And then Adrian began to laugh.

"What's so funny, all of a sudden?"

"In fact, Nate, do you know who's been assigned to your case?"

"I don't need a doctor. *I'm* a doctor."

"Well, you've got a house doctor, Doctor. And it's Art."

Nate groaned. "Oh, my God. Talk about committing suicide! They must really want me dead. I didn't do the job right? Art Schuster will finish me off, for sure."

"Nate!" Con objected, but she was laughing a little. "That's no way to talk about poor Art. You know how Art Schuster decided to be a doctor, poor thing—"

"Yeah, yeah, Con, I know how Art decided. Don't we all!" He rolled his eyes. "I mean, he only tells that story at every fund-raiser, at every cocktail party, and to nearly every patient."

"Well I think it's sad. His father said son number one is the doctor and son number two is the lawyer and son number three is the businessman . . . and poor Art got the wrong profession."

"He sure did," Adrian said.

"And I'm the one's going to be suffering for it . . ."

"Shame on both of you. Art's not a horrible doctor; he's just better at other things. Listen, he's raised so much money for Cadman—I mean, give the guy credit. He would have made a wonderful businessman; that's how his mind works . . ."

"You know," Adrian added, "he *did* tell me something last week about a business he's starting with his brothers . . . a dialysis center. He was very excited about it, and you know, it did sound good. It sounded *very* good, come to think of it. He asked if I wanted a piece of the action . . ."

"And I'm still offering. We have a couple shares left, Adrian . . ." Art Schuster, smelling of Canoë, came strolling in, smiling his professional smile. "Good morning, there, young fellow, and what are we going to do with you?"

"What did you have in mind, Arthur?"

Instead of answering Nate, Art turned to Con and Adrian and said conspiratorially, "We can't let our former presidents go around turning on the gas, now, can we?" He laughed. "Looks bad for the hospital."

Dryly, Nate said, "You're no brainier than you ever were, Schuster."

"There, there now, no need to excite yorself, Nate. We'll take care of you; don't you worry." He went to the bedside, seemingly oblivious to Nate's jibe, and felt for his pulse. "First things first," he intoned. "How are we feeling today?"

"I don't know about you, but I feel like hell. It's much too crowded in here."

Art gave a false laugh, patted Nate's arm, and checked over the chart at the foot of the bed. "Well, well, that blood pressure is way up, isn't it?"

"Better than the alternative."

"Yes, yes, of course. But this is really up further than I like to see it . . ."

"Why? What is it? I'm usually one twenty-five over eighty . . . kinda high but okay . . ."

"Now, never mind, never mind, you're supposed to rest and relax and not get yourself overwrought. You're not supposed to think about anything—"

"Like hell. I'm not turning my brain off, you know . . . And I'm not 'disturbed' just because I've been depressed lately, either! Just tell me the blood pressure reading, and we'll forget you ever said any of that stuff."

Art turned ostentatiously to Adrian and Con who were standing side by side near the window. "Will you please explain to him that *he's* a patient this time?"

Con said, "Listen, Art, I don't think—"

"He's got to take it easy this morning," Art interrupted.

"I'm sending Schlossberg in to see him this afternoon. Nothing like a good talk to clarify the problems . . ." He gave one of his hearty laughs and made a hasty exit from the room, giving them all one of his jaunty waves. "No arguing now, Nate," he called out as he left. "I know you taught me everything I know, but *I'm* the doctor now!"

No sooner had he disappeared from sight than Nate sat forward in the bed, fists clenched and face purple. "Schlossberg!" he exploded. "Schlossberg!"

Adrian had to pretend to cough, to hide the smile on his lips. Jerry Schlossberg was in for quite a time!

"Schlossberg!" Nate went on. "He's gonna send Schlossberg to me! To tell me how I feel? I need Schlossberg to tell me what my dreams mean? To clarify my problems? Let me tell you something, Con . . . Adrian . . . I was practicing medicine when Schlossberg the shrinker was still peeing in his pants! I need Schlossberg like a hole in the head! The bed-wetter!"

Adrian could no longer control himself. Perhaps it was a bit of hysteria, the hysterics of relief, but he began to laugh . . . He could not stop. Dammit, it was so good to hear Nate sound like himself once more! He hadn't carried on like that since they dumped him.

When he could speak again, he walked over to Nate and put a hand on his shoulder. "Look at you," he said. "When I first walked in here this morning, you looked like Death himself. And now look: you're sitting straight up, you're wide awake, you're complaining, you're yelling just like the old days! It's wonderful! I think you're going to recover!"

"Agh! Schuster makes me so damn mad. He's got no more bedside manner than a gorilla . . . Maybe less. What makes his patients love him so damn much, anyway?"

Con pushed herself away from the window ledge. "Now Nate, let's be fair. Not every patient likes their medicine straight and bitter. Art's patients are mostly older women from the Heights, and they need to be babied and cared for and fussed over, and he does it. You and I may know it's not exactly sincere, but they love it. And it works. Okay, so the professionals around here see what he's lacking . . . but, come on . . ." When neither of the men would answer her, she added lightly, "Okay, I've got work to do. I'll check in here from time to time to see if you need anything. And I'll send Art up, about four times a day . . ."

"What the hell you want to do that for, Con?"

"Because he makes you mad, and it looks like we're gonna have to keep you mad to keep you undepressed." She laughed.

"She's got something there, Nate," Adrian said, and the older man half smiled. "Just make sure you come by a couple of times so I can yell at *you*," he said, and waved her off.

For a few minutes, there was silence in the room. Nate sank back against the pillows and said, half to himself, "*Now* I'm tired. *Now* maybe I'd like a little nap."

"You okay?"

"Tell you something. Con's right. Getting mad did something good for me . . . made me feel alive, I guess. You know how I feel? I feel like that Dorothy Parker poem about committing suicide . . . How does it end again? 'You might as well live.' "

Adrian laughed and picked up a sheaf of papers from the windowsill. "I'm glad you decided to live, because I happen to have a couple of problems I need your help with. These are," and he shook the papers, "the minutes of the last meeting of the ethics committee, plus a couple of Xeroxes of district court opinions, plus a letter the Rev wrote and had signed by his entire flock, *plus* a copy of Del Bello's guide-lines about neonates . . . That's right, Nate. He's not a doctor, not even a Ph.D., and he's telling us how to practice medicine. When you wake up from your nap, would you take a look at this stuff?" And he put it down on the bed tray.

Nate's eyes began to sparkle. Again, he sat up straight and grabbed the papers. "Nap? Let me have a look at these!" He was already riffling through them as he said, "Where are my glasses? Get me my glasses!"

Chapter 20

OUTSIDE THE CAFETERIA windows, it was typical February—gray, gloomy, biting cold—and a nasty wind whipped the tree branches against the panes. Inside, though, the kitchen staff had done their best to brighten things up with about three hundred bright red paper hearts strung from the lights and cardboard cupids pasted on to all the cash registers.

Bobby swallowed the last dregs of his coffee and checked the time. Ten minutes to rounds. Should he just leave and go upstairs now? He was bored with the general conversation; the residents were arguing about feelings. Does a good doctor allow himself/herself to feel? Or does a good doctor seal it off for the sake of his objectivity. Feelings! Let them go on and on about it; he'd had more than enough of feelings! His head was whirling with feelings, all kinds of feelings—anger, disgust, lust, fury, guilt, worry. You name it; he was feeling it. Corinne just kept getting worse and worse; she was slowly but surely drifting right out of their marriage. They hadn't talked, really talked to each other, for months and months . . . and as for sex—well, forget it. She was no longer interested. And he might as well face it; neither was he, not with her.

With Rita, oh, yeah! Any time of the day or night, he was ready. He had to fight it all the time, to keep from running into her office, to keep from running out of the apartment all the time and heading for Henry Street . . . Oh, shit! He had to stop this. The important thing for him was to figure out where he was going to work next year. It was the end of babyhood, the end of residency. It was time to figure out the rest of your life, and he kept letting everything else get in the way.

He had to figure it out, because no matter what happened with his marriage, there was Kelly to consider. His sweet little girl, with her dimples and her active little mind and the way she had of curling her arms around his neck and burying her nose in his shoulder and saying, "I love you a million kisses, Daddy." He could hardly stand thinking about not seeing her . . . about being far away. But no court would let him have her. Corinne was a fine mother . . . And then he thought of her big belly, and his own belly gave that little lurch it always did when he thought about the baby she was carrying. She wouldn't go in for amniocentesis; shit, she wouldn't even have a sonogram to see if the head was enlarged! She wouldn't do a goddam thing! Not even a reading for Alphafeto protein levels. What if it was born really bad, really damaged, the works? Kelly plus a severely damaged baby! What kind of life would *that* make for Dr. Bobby J. Truman?

He couldn't think about it; he just couldn't think about it. He shifted in his chair, consulted his watch. Five more minutes . . . He'd like to leave at that moment, but Adrian was still sitting over there at his table, and Adrian had asked him to wait and go up together. Adrian was deep in animated conversation with Ellie and Dr. Levinson and two other doctors who had stopped by. Well, ever since Levinson had been named head of the ethics committee the previous week, doctors and nurses were always stopping by his table in the caf. To look at him, ruddy and beaming, sporting a very loud red and purple bow tie and light blue shirt under the white coat, you'd never guess that a couple of months ago he'd tried to take his own life out of despair.

"Just look at that old man," Nick Ponte said. "He's got them all shook up, hasn't he?" He laughed.

"Who? Nate Levinson?"

"Who the hell else? Those two guys are from anesthesiology? They aren't there to pass the time of day! They want to make sure he doesn't take away any of their territory with all his talk about right to die and no heroic measures and stuff . . ."

"Yeah, well, Nate's tough. And remember, he's been there."

"Agh, he's just another old doctor; nothing so magic about him. Come on, Bobby, he's an old crock. What does he know about modern medicine? When he went to medical school, they couldn't cure a damn thing! But now the two Dr. Winters have pushed him back into power, and every fucking shitless wonder in the place is gonna kiss his ass!"

"Ponte, you sure have a way with words . . ."

"Well, goddam it, it's true, isn't it? I call 'em like I see 'em."

"Yeah, well maybe you need glasses."

"You wanna convince me I'm wrong?"

"Shit, man, I don't care if you're wrong or right. But Nate Levinson isn't just an old crock who got maneuvered into the head of a committee."

"Agh!" Nick said, waving his hand in dismissal. "You're naive, Bobby. I'm a street kid. Don't you think Del Bello's shitting in his pants now? Come on! He was cutting out Winter, so Winter got back at him. That's how the game is played, my boy. And there she is, looking up at him as if he was Jesus Christ himself . . ."

"Who! Who?"

"Jesus, man, Dr. Ellie. Coming on to her ex. She wants him back, and he's eating it up with a spoon. And with that sexy little blonde waiting for him at home!"

"How do *you* know she's waiting for him at home?" God, Ponte got to him.

The response was immediate and, in its way, inevitable. "Oh, yeah? Who's she fucking?"

Bobby stood up so quickly his chair fell over with a loud clatter. "You're disgusting, you know that? Disgusting. Everything's dirty to you . . . Oh, never mind. It's time for rounds. You think you can get your mind out of the gutter and onto Janet Freedman?" Without waiting for an answer, he marched off. He caught Adrian's eye and motioned that he'd wait by the elevator.

Gary was there. "I can't believe it," he called. "I'm the first one here?"

"Well, man, you're in love, floating three feet off the ground. You're always early these days."

"Yeah, well, I don't know if it's *love*, exactly, but, you know, when Laura moved to Park Slope I missed her more than I thought I would."

Bobby grinned at him. "Gee, Weinstein, so did I, but that didn't make me start to date her regularly."

Gary blushed. "You know, all that hostility goes away once she knows you."

Bobby grimaced. "Look, man, it's none of my business. But . . . look, don't get carried away. I'm telling you, when you're horny, sometimes you see things that aren't there."

"Don't worry about me . . . Oh, hi, Dr. Levinson. Are you joining rounds this morning?"

- Nate barked a laugh. "You kidding, doctor? This is the biggest ethical issue this hospital's had for a long, long time. If heads of service are all gonna be there. then you can bet the head of the ethics committee is, too."

Janet Freedman was in a private room at the very end of the corridor on the Obstetrics floor. A notice on the door said PRIVATE. AUTHORIZED PERSONNEL ONLY. This was Room 411, a room that was often used for difficult cases.

To call Janet Freedman a difficult case was an understatement. Janet Freedman lay quietly, very quietly, on the narrow hospital bed, her eyes taped shut, her arms at her sides, breathing with the help of a respirator, fed intravenously, attached by tubes and wires to the machines that kept her body alive and the monitors that registered her vital signs.

The sight of Janet Freedman gave Bobby a *frisson* of fear. Because Janet was brain dead. No matter how hard they worked, all they could do was keep her body artificially alive. The person who was Janet Freedman was gone, forever gone. Dead, in fact. Yes, Janet Freedman was dead, he thought, and yet her chest moved, and her heart beat, and the fetus in her womb was fed and nurtured and protected and grew and thrived.

"You have to understand, ladies and gentlemen," Adrian was saying, "that this case is highly unusual." He gave a grim smile. "What we have here is a touchy and ambiguous situation. Mrs. Freedman fell down several flights of stairs and died shortly after her arrival in the Emergency Room two weeks ago. The doctors and nurses in the ER had already put her on life support, and to everyone's surprise, even after the EEG had gone totally flat, her heart and respiration were still regular and strong. And the fetal heartbeat, as well, never faltered."

"Was it then, Dr. Winter," asked the chief of radiology, "that you decided to keep her alive?"

Adrian once again gave that not quite a smile. "Well, Dr. Curtis, there seems to be a question, whether she was dead at all."

"But if there's no brain function—!"

"The ethics committee," Adrian said gently, "has ruled that brain death alone is not enough to pronounce a person dead. And besides—"

Nate interrupted. "And as you all know, I disagree with that whole concept. What is a human being if not the human mind, the human imagination, the human reasoning ability. And if that's gone—"

"Baloney!" That was Art Schuster.

"Gentlemen, gentlemen." Adrian held up a restraining hand. "This is quite beside the point. We can argue ethics in the next committee meeting. Right now, my residents and I are presenting a most unusual case—a woman, six and a half months pregnant, brain dead, otherwise perfectly healthy—and we are planning to keep her alive and healthy until the fetus has matured sufficiently so that we can deliver it and—"

"Excuse, Dr. Winter, *deliver*? Will she go into labor?"

"We won't wait for that, Doctor. We will deliver by C section as soon as the monitors show us that we have an infant capable of sustaining life outside the uterus."

A harsh voice asked, "And then what?"

All heads turned, including Bobby's. It was Nick Ponte, scowling mightily, his face flushed.

"Excuse me, Dr. Ponte. Be more explicit."

"And after we take this infant from Mrs. Freedman . . . what *then*?"

Adrian cleared his throat delicately. "We will then . . . let Mrs. Freedman go."

"Kill her, you mean!"

"No, Dr. Ponte, not kill her. She is, to all intents and purposes, already dead. We will simply—well, I can't think of a better phrase—let her go."

"Well, I think it stinks. My church, for one, doesn't agree that brain death means death . . . Hell, even our own ethics committee doesn't agree with that one . . ."

Nate Levinson quickly put in, "Gentlemen, we're becoming very loud in here. Let's not disturb the patients on the floor. If you wish to discuss this further, Dr. Ponte, please come up to my office after rounds."

"You're on, Dr. Levinson."

Bobby said, "It *is* a problem, Dr. Winter. Because no matter how modern we make our machinery, we still believe that a person's only really dead if they stop breathing. There was a girl in the city morgue this week—all you doctors must have read about it. Her respiration was so low nobody could hear or see it. And she came to life! In the morgue! Came to life! Hell, she was never dead. But some doctor thought she was, or she'd never been there. It seems crazy on some level. Her brain was intact when she came to; she was a whole person. But let a person's brain die—Hell, even if you manage to keep them on life support forever, they'll never be a human being again and . . ."

"Prove it!" Nick spat. "*You* don't know! Only God knows!"

Bobby opened his mouth, but Adrian interjected smoothly with a summing up and herded them all out the door. "We will send complete reports on her progress . . . and, of course, the minute the monitor shows anything, anything at all, amiss, we will go right in and get that baby."

As they mobbed out of the door, Bobby heard the nurse on duty. She was a small dark girl who had been sitting very quietly in the corner, glowering at them during the entire presentation. She leaned over the bed and said, "They oughtn't to talk about you that way, Janet. And I'm not going to let anyone else in today to bother you." It jolted him. The nurse was *talking* to her, just as if she were a real patient. And then he stopped walking for a moment and thought that one over. Hell, she *was* a real patient, wasn't she? And—who had said it before?—were any of them absolutely sure she couldn't hear them?

Without thinking about it, he stopped and turned to look again at Janet Freedman. He'd actually examined her a month or two ago when Adrian was busy in the delivery room. She was a tall, voluptuous woman with a wry sense of humor—now he remembered. Funny, how quickly she became the Brain-Dead Patient We're Keeping Alive So We Can Be Wonderful and Deliver a Live Baby. He'd been looking at her all morning and not seeing *her* at all. He'd been seeing a . . . thing, an object in the bed, interesting from a medical standpoint, challenging from an ethical standpoint. But a human being? He winced. He'd vowed that he would never forget the humanity common to himself and his patients.

"Bobby!" It was Adrian, who had hung back from the others apparently and was waiting in the hall. Bobby joined him. "You know," he began, "I had completely forgotten that I'd actually examined her—Remember, when you had that delivery and it turned out to be twins? Look how quickly this patient has lost her individuality for me . . ."

Adrian put a hand on his shoulder, and they started to walk down the corridor. "Yes, well, don't they say that just climbing into a hospital bed is the first step to being infantalized? I'm not so sure I totally agree with that, but—" He paused, looking a bit startled. "Do you know? I've never been in the hospital as a patient. Never!"

"Well, I have," Bobby said. "And it's true. Think about angel robes for a minute." He felt a kind of excitement rising in his chest; insights were crowding up into his head, one after the other. "Open in the back . . . too damn short . . . two little ties . . . I mean, you can't walk around in them. You can't! Your ass is hanging out. You're laughable, goddam it; you're a scream. It's demeaning! And that's only the beginning of the process of dehumanization. You're poked, you're prodded, you're stuck with needles, you're discussed, you're ignored you're condescended to . . . Jesus Christ, and we think the hospital is a place of mercy and healing!"

"Now, Bobby, you're right; of course you're right. But don't get completely carried away. That's not the whole story. Look at Janet Freedman, for instance. If we turn off the life support systems, Janet will stop breathing and will be legally dead. We're pretty sure she can't hear anybody; we're pretty sure she's unconscious. And yet . . . do you know, the nurses sing to the fetus? Yes, and they chat with Janet, all the time, and turn on her favorite TV programs . . . *just in case*."

"I guess . . ." Bobby mumbled.

"It's a good sign that you're having these thoughts, Bobby. If you weren't, I'd be disappointed. Look, I'm trying to sort out Janet Freedman's case myself. It's full of ambiguities. I don't even know if I ought to talk about it . . . But I must."

"Ambiguities?"

They were now near the nursing station, and with a motion of his head, Adrian indicated an empty room. They walked to the far end and stood looking out the window, at the children from St. Ann's playing in the park a block away.

"Ambiguities," Adrian repeated. "Above and beyond the life-death situation—which is already bizarre enough—we have . . . *Mr.* Freedman."

"I thought," Bobby said, "he was devoted. You mean he's changed his mind and doesn't want us to save his baby?"

"I wish it were that simple," Adrian said. There was a silence, and then he drew in a deep breath, letting it out noisily. "Oh, God," he said, finally. "You saw her case history . . . Three misses."

"Yeah?" Bobby was puzzled. Many women had a history of miscarriages, especially in their particular patient population. The poor and the black and the recent immigrant—all of them were prey to poor nutrition, ignorance, superstition . . . .

"Maybe you don't remember, but Janet Freedman and her husband are middle class. They live in the Heights, in that big middle-income cooperative. He's a computer programmer, and she's a dental hygienist . . . *was*, excuse me. They have a car, nice furniture, the works. And . . . three miscarriages under questionable conditions."

"Questionable . . . ?"

"The first. She fell off her bike. She bruised the whole left side of her face and body. A couple of cracked ribs. Then she was told that the next time she'd better not be so active. Okay. Number two. She tripped and fell getting out of the car on a rainy night. Again, multiple contusions and a hell of a big one on her hip, which made me begin to think."

"He beats her!"

"I can't say that. I can't know that. And yet I *do* know it. Don't quote me, of course. Number three was much the same. I can't believe a woman as competent and healthy as Janet Freedman is so clumsy . . . No, of course not. Somebody hit her and hit her and hit her . . .! Goddammit, I'm morally certain he did it to her. And now he comes in regularly every night after work; butter wouldn't melt in his mouth, eyes all filled with tears, all concern and quiet despair . . . Oh, Bobby, the man's a better actor than Barrymore.

I'm—goddammit, Bobby, the man should get an Oscar for his performance. And the hell of it is, I can't prove anything. I can't keep him away. I can't tell anybody. I can't do a damn thing. I can't even make sure he doesn't take that baby! I tell you, I'm in a dilemma . . .''

"Holy shit," Bobby breathed.

"Exactly." Adrian shifted uncomfortably and ran his fingers through his hair. "But my problem right now is Sandy Heller."

"Just tell her hands off! She's got friends in high places"— Bobby laughed—"but you're not exactly nobody."

"Correction, Bobby. My problem is Willie Freedman in *conjunction* with Sandy Heller. The man's sick; he's a classic case. We ought to send him to Schlossberg. He'd keep Jerry busy the rest of his life! But he's not really funny. I shouldn't make jokes. Willie is a well-dressed, handsome man who presents very well. And he's a talker! He just loves an audience, the bigger the better. He'll cry on cue and tell you how much she wanted this baby and how he's going to name this baby in her honor, boy or girl, and—!" He broke off and made a disgusted noise. "Sandy's been sniffing around already and complaining that she's not given access, and if Freedman were a decent guy, I'd let her in, of course. I mean, he is her husband. But the way things are, I want to keep it all under wraps. When we deliver the baby successfully, then Sandy Heller can call in her reporter friends. But, I'm telling you Bobby, it's a problem . . .''

"Does Janet have family? Parents, I mean, sibs."

"Aging parents. Her mother has hypertension and a heart problem. She came in once, took one look at her daughter, and collapsed. They're in town with friends—they live in Sacramento—but she's in no condition to deal with this. It's a mess."

"I'd call him in and face him with it."

Adrian smiled tightly. "Sure, Bobby. And he'd deny it all. At this point, I'll tell you, I'm not even so sure he hasn't forgotten it. It wouldn't be the first time an abuser used denial." Again there was silence, and then Adrian said, "Well, it was good to talk about it. I haven't put notes on any of this into her file . . . Hell, it's only speculation, even though, goddammit, I *know* it's true. So, just in case anything happens to me . . . at least you know."

They walked together out to the nursing station and said goodbye. Bobby's thoughts were whirling around. What did Adrian mean, if something happened to him? What could happen? Was he ill, or was he just referring to the political situation around here? Bobby had got the idea that things were changing, that Nate Levinson was making his way right back up to the catbird seat. Hell, they elected him to chair the ethics committee, didn't they? He'd been told that Del Bello's shrieks of agony could be heard all the way across the Brooklyn Bridge. So what was it?

And then he stopped thinking about Adrian or Nate or Del Bello. Because there at the nursing station, staring directly at him and giving him a wide-eyed smile, was a fox such as he had not seen of late. She was little, she was curved to make a man groan, she was brown, and she was sitting posed on the edge of the desk, swinging one gorgeous leg.

"Why, good morning, Doctor!" she sang. Her voice was husky, and there was no doubting the invitation in it.

He tried not to look too eager. "Well, good morning there, Miss—" And he eyed the name tag that rose and fell so sweetly on the curve of her breast. "Yvonne Duncan, R.N. Do I know you?"

"I'm new. But I've seen you. Lots. In fact, Dr. Truman, I dreamed about you last night."

He leaned in just a little, toward the warmth of her. "Not a nightmare, I hope."

She pursed her lips, licked at them lightly. "Not exactly." And then she grinned. "But it woke me up."

Oh, my god! Bobby thought, his heart beginning to thump. A real fox! "Wish I'd been there."

"Me, too."

He found himself speechless, staring at her like a dummy.

She was adorable! He wouldn't mind being in a horizontal position with her right this minute. And she was coming on to him! She made absolutely no bones about it. And while he was catching his breath, she said sweetly, "Next time, you *can*. Be there, I mean." And she scribbled something on a pad, ripped it off, and handed it to him. And then she slid off the desk and said, " 'Bye for now," and sashayed down the hall.

He knew what it was, but he looked, anyway. "Yvonne," it said, and then there was a phone number. Oh, sweet Jesus! He marched in the other direction, toward the Ob/Gyn main office, humming as he went. They were all over the goddam place! Women! White women, black women—purple women, for all he knew. His life need not be all over. No, he hadn't died along with Corinne's other personality, the one he'd married. He was going to be okay! He was going to be really okay.

Chapter 21

SANDY HELLER BOUNCED a bit as she walked. She was feeling good. Her news release on the arthritis clinic had brought in Channel 9, Channel 7, and three radio stations for interviews. Dr. Singh was out of his mind with joy. He had kissed her on the cheek—actually kissed her, when usually those Indians were so stiff and superior!—and said, "Finally, someone at Cadman has recognized the importance of what we're doing here in rheumatology." And Hank had locked the office door and given her what he called his own personal award for excellence. Big deal! A quickie from Hank Del Bello on the slippery leather couch was okay, but what she deserved was a raise and a better title. Assistant to the administrator maybe. She'd said something about it while he was still lying on her, and he mumbled something or other about "one of these days" and "keep up the good work." Men! All he could think about was the sex . . . Sex was the least of what she was doing for him. My God, he knew she had just doubled the patient load at the clinic . . . with one little news release! Singh said that if they kept getting phone calls at this rate, the

clinic would turn a profit, finally. *That* was the bottom line.
And that's what she was good at!

The elevator came, and she got on, noting who was there.
It was automatic with her; she was always aware, always
watching, always with her eyes out for a possible story.
That's why she was so good at her job. You'd think they'd
make it a vice-president's slot, but no. And she knew why,
too . . . because public relations was considered women's
work!

Well, it was . . . and a damn good thing, too. Only a
woman was smart enough to nose out all the hidden stories,
to figure out how to get around the rigidity of some of the
doctors around here. Adrian Winter, the great Dr. Winter,
said nobody could do a story on that braindead mother? Well,
that was crazy. He had no reasons, except he loved to throw
his weight around. He had no right to keep her out of Room
411. Didn't he know about freedom of the press? The man
was a martinet! It was a wonderful story; it was the ultimate
hospital story. Technology of the future in the hands of a
sensitive and caring staff . . . making a miracle. Well, it was
a miracle, that a dead woman could be kept alive and give
birth to a perfectly healthy baby . . . Well, she hoped it
would be a perfectly healthy baby. But that wasn't even the
important part. The important part was what was happening at
this very moment in that room.

It was a great story. And she was going to get it. She
wasn't allowed into Room 411? Well, you just wait and see,
Dr. Winter! She was going to get into that room, and not by
sneaking in, either. She was on her way to get herself invited
in, and tucked into her bag were her Minox and her tape
recorder, and they were both about to be used, or her name
wasn't Sandra Heller.

He was there. She wanted to smile. He was always there
by six o'clock. The nurses told her that; the father, they said,
comes every single day after work. He's so attentive, he's so
sweet. He was having a cigarette out in the hallway, leaning
against the wall, head bowed. She kept up her brisk pace but

arranged her expression to one of quiet understanding and looked him over carefully, making quick mental notes as she aproached.

He was very good-looking . . . Well, that was terrific. The nurses hadn't said anything about that, but it was a definite asset in pictures. And if any of the tv stations picked up on this one, well . . . ! He was black, but so fair that—except for the Afro hair—you wouldn't think so. His skin, in fact, was lighter than hers in the summer when she'd tanned. He was fairly tall, slim, very nicely dressed in a neat chino suit, white shirt, rep tie, brightly shined loafers. Now he heard the clacking of her heels on the floor and looked over at her. Better and better! He was really handsome, with startling green eyes. He looked straight at her without blinking and finished a last drag on his cigarette. Then he turned and walked down the hall to put it out.

Sandy stood where he had been, leaning against the wall as he had been leaning, and waited for him. He even walked nicely. Yes, indeed, William Freedman had class. Oh, boy! What a story this was going to be! Now if only he could talk half as well as he looked.

He came back, looking at her with mild curiosity. "Mr. Freedman?"

"That's right." A slight smile.

Sandy put out her hand. "Mr. Freedman, I'm Sandy Heller, head of public relations here at Cadman. I want to tell you how much I admire what you're doing . . . and to express my deep sympathy for what you're going through."

"You're very kind . . . Everyone here has been very kind. When all of this is . . . over . . ." He paused and turned his head away. Oh, my God, was the man going to cry!? And her with her camera all tucked away? He turned back almost immediately, and while there was a suspicious shininess around the eyes, he was smiling sweetly. "When all of this is over, I hope I can do something to show the staff at Cadman how much I appreciate . . . all of this."

"It must be terribly hard for you . . . the waiting, I mean."

"Well, it is, of course. But Janet wanted this baby so badly. So badly. If she could speak, I know she'd say, 'Go ahead. Save my baby. Let my baby live.' "

Sandy could hardly contain her excitement. Oh, my God! The guy was almost too good to be true! "What beautiful sentiments," she murmured. "What a beautiful story . . ." Waiting, waiting for his reaction to the word *story*. He didn't wince, and he didn't shake his head, just kept smiling. "Mr. Freedman, there are people out there, in this big city, who would be inspired by hearing the story of you and your wife and your unborn child. Would you be willing to talk with me about it? To have it in all the New York papers, perhaps?"

"Sure."

"Now, Mr. Freedman, you know this might mean that newspaper reporters would want to talk to you . . . that you might be on television . . ."

"Yes?"

"That wouldn't bother you?"

"If it'll help other people, no, it wouldn't bother me. Besides," he added, "I think what the hospital's doing is absolutely fantastic. All you read about or hear about on the news is gloomy stuff. It's always about people dying and stuff like that. This is so . . . fantastic. I mean, actually I've been wondering why they're so quiet about it. When the doctors in Utah gave that dentist his artificial heart, it was on the news every single night. I remember that. And here they are, keeping my unborn baby alive. I mean, that's as good as an artificial heart, isn't it? I can't figure it out."

Sandy hid her smile. "Neither," she said solemnly, "can I, Mr. Freedman." She reached into her shoulder bag. "Do you mind if I tape-record our conversation?"

For a moment he looked undecided, and her heart sank. She had a good memory, but she really counted on the tape recorder, especially when you were doing medical stories; you had to get all the names right. Swiftly, she added, "You put things so beautifully. I don't want to forget or inadvertently change even a single word."

Of course, he just preened. It wasn't terribly obvious—just a little smile and a little straightening of the shoulders and a little flare in the eye—but she knew her interviewees, and she knew she had him.

This was going to be beautiful . . . the best. Better even than the Susan Palko thing! That gorgeous shot she'd taken of Brian Fuller had been reproduced in both tabloids and then appeared, over and over again, on the TV news shows. The hospital had been absolutely flooded with phone calls, and a lot of them wanted an appointment with a doctor, *any* doctor, who worked in the "Hospital with a Heart." Her line! Her idea! Her picture!

Hank had fussed at her, saying, "A hospital can't afford to be known to turn people away, Sandy, goddammit." But then, later, when she had his clothes off and was caressing him and giving him the little love bites he especially liked, he relented and said yes, she'd done a damn good job. But the next day he called her in and said, very seriously, "Now look, Sandy, just between us, I'm damn proud of what you did. It shows real spirit and enterprise. But you can't go around ignoring hospital policy. I have to take the flack . . . and if the flack gets too heavy, then I'm going to have to let you go . . . And . . ." Reaching out for her and patting her bottom, "I'd hate like hell to have to do that. Even Art Schuster is furious about that picture; it was totally unauthorized."

"I know, I know . . . but I couldn't resist."

"Look, sweetheart, I'll tell you again. I think it was a stroke of genius. But you're gonna have to do your genius stuff within the rules from now on. I can't have this kind of disruption. It doesn't look good for the hospital, and it makes me look foolish. Now. You clear? You *capish*'?"

"I *capeesh*, Hank. Okay. From now on, within the rules. I promise."

She had promised, and she was going to live by it. She'd get a great interview that evening and a great picture—and it would all be within the rules, and to hell with Dr. Adrian

Winter. Just because he had old Dr. Levinson running around the place again and was pushing Hank up against the wall . . . Well, they'd see about that! She'd get the story of the year and give it right to Hank and *then* they'd talk about assistant to the administrator or vice-president for public affairs.

She and William Freedman walked down the hall together, and he said, "I can't take too long, you know. She might miss me."

"You mean—?"

He slid her a smile sideways. "I know. It sounds sentimental. I know what the doctors say; she doesn't hear or feel or know anything anymore. But *I* say they can't know for sure. So I make sure I talk to her every night. You never know . . ."

"Oh, but that's so sweet." Now, openly, she dug in her bag and took out the Sony, turning it on, checking quickly to make sure the little light went on. "You are unusually brave, Mr. Freedman. My feeling is that most people would want to stay away in a case like this."

"But how could I? We've been married for ten years, and this is her sixth pregnancy . . . Oh, yes, poor Janet, it broke her heart. She could never carry to full term."

"What a shame."

"We planned to have four or five kids. She would have made a wonderful mother. We even had names for all of them." He laughed a little, ruefully. "Lance, Lisa, Lawrence, and Louisa."

"Any reason all the names begin with L?"

He grinned sheepishly. "L for love."

Oh, my God! she thought. Unbelievable! The man was almost too good to be true! What a beautiful story! "L for Love." She had her headline.

"But this time—" she prodded.

"This time she stayed in bed. She even stopped working after we were sure she was really pregnant. She felt real bad about not being able to carry them . . . She felt guilty, felt it made her less of a woman . . . Please don't quote that, okay? But we went through a lot together . . . ten years, six miscarriages . . . Well, after all that, I couldn't possibly let her down. I just couldn't! No way! She wanted this baby so badly . . . She was so happy. After the fifth month, she went out and bought a bottle of champagne because she'd never carried even that far before.'' Once again, he turned his head a little, and Sandy reached out to put a light hand on his arm.

"I know, I know," she said. "Yours is an incredible story of hope and strength and bravery."

"Do you know what those nurses do in there? We have private nurses round the clock, you know. Do you know what they do? They lean over her belly and sing. They sing lullabies. Isn't that fabulous? And they talk to the baby. I tell you, Miss . . . uh . . . I tell you, it makes me feel so sad that Janet will never be able to hold this baby in her arms . . .'' He choked up a bit.

Sandy put in, "But *you* will," and was rewarded with a smile of such sweetness and charm that her heart constricted. Quickly she reached into her bag and took out the Minox—as usual, all ready to shoot—and snapped six pictures in rapid succession.

"Would you like to see her . . . *them*?" he said.

"I'd love to. But the doctor has said no unauthorized visitors, and I'm afraid I'm not authorized. I'm not medical, you know."

"Hell, you're with me. And now that I've spent time with you, I know you have empathy. I know I can trust you. You're with me, and anyone who's with me gets in."

Sandy hid her glee at this and said demurely, "Oh, thank you."

"Well, now that I've spent time with you, I know I can trust you. I think you'll be fair; I think you'll do a really sympathetic story."

"Oh, yes. I will. And if you like, I'll show you what I've written before it gets out, and you can change whatever bothers you."

"Hey, that's really nice." She let him go into the room ahead of her, hanging back just a bit, and heard him say to the nurse, "Okay, Gloria, why don't you take a break now? I'll stay with Janet for a while."

"Sure, Mr. Freedman." The nurse gave Sandy a brief look of curiosity as she brushed by, but there was no recognition in her eyes, and when Sandy gave her a smile, she smiled back.

And then she eased herself into the room. It was already dark outside, and the drapes had been drawn across the windows. There was a bright reading lamp on next to an easy chair in one corner and a book, laid face down and open, was on the lamp table. A bag of knitting leaned against the chair leg. The television set, mounted up on the wall, was on, turned to a rerun of "M*A*S*H." The dresser was crammed with flowers, stuck into vases and containers of all kinds.

"Hi there, honey," William Freedman said to the still figure on the bed. He bent and kissed her cheek, patting the protruding belly. "And hi to you, too, baby." Turning, he said to Sandy, "They always turn on 'M*A*S*H' . . . Janet loved it."

Sandy held her breath and took out the Minox again. She had to be very careful now. Hank said stay within hospital policy. Okay. Dr. Winter didn't want his precious patient photographed. Okay, too. She'd be very careful not to photograph Janet. But nobody said she couldn't photograph William, holding his wife's hand . . . or patting her tummy . . . or gazing down on her lovingly. Swiftly, she finished the roll of film, explaining to him that she was not including Janet. "Her doctor, Dr. Winter, has given explicit instructions, you know."

He frowned. "Yes, I know. And I don't get it, really, because I wouldn't mind. If she can hear or understand anything, she'd tell you *she* didn't mind. But"—he laughed— "he's the doctor, and I for one don't argue with doctors."

"A good idea," Sandy said, but her mind was no longer on this conversation. She was wondering if she could get one of the guys in Medical Photography to do a quick developing job . . . or should she call the *News* and get them to send a messenger over for the roll of film. *L for Love*. It could be better than the Hospital with a Heart. The papers would be sure to pick up that line. And if every TV station in New York didn't come down here at a run to get interviews with William Freedman. she'd hand in her resignation tomorrow.

Somehow she did all the right, polite things with William Freedman, shook his hand, expressed her sympathy and admiration, and got the hell out before the nurse came back and asked her what she was doing there. She walked sedately down the hall, but alone in the elevator, she hugged herself fiercely and let out a yelp. By God, she'd done it again!

Chapter 22

"B_Y G_{OD, SHE'S} done it again!" Con Scofield slammed the office door open and strode in at top speed, brandishing her folded newspaper. "Done it *again*, by God, and to hell with all of us!"

"Whoa! Done what?" Nate peered up over his half glasses, began to laugh, and then, changing his mind, frowned with concern. "Slow down, Con, slow down. Give a guy a chance, would you?"

"What do you mean, a chance?"

"I mean, tell me what you're talking about, okay? Aw, Con." He got up and walked around the desk and gently pushed her into the chair facing him. "You look like you just ate a bad pickle."

Con allowed herself to be sat and thrust the paper at him. "Read it and weep, my dear Nate. And then *you'll* look like that, too. I promise you."

The picture was good, nicely lighted, with sharp detail, and it took up half the front page. In big black letters under it was "L FOR LOVE." And then a line that said, "Life and Death Drama at Cadman, the Hospital with a Heart." Nate groaned and looked back at the picture. Now he could see what it was—the husband of the Freedman woman, gazing down tenderly and holding her hand. She was lost in shadow, but the unmistakable shape of her belly humped up at the bottom of the photograph. "Oh, God."

"Wait, Nate. Look inside."

He turned to page 4 and said, "Oh, God!" again. Before he even saw what had been written, he saw the picture of Adrian. He recognized that file photo; they'd been using it for nearly ten years. Two years ago, he'd told Adrian to have a new one taken, but somehow there'd never been the time. "Adrian's going to bust a gut."

"You said it. Where'd they get his picture, anyway?"

"They all have it, the papers. From when he was named chief of Ob/Gyn. No, it's not that. It's the whole invasion of privacy issue . . . we spent practically the whole last session of the ethics committee discussing this case. And we all agreed that under the circumstances we were going to downplay this one. When the baby is delivered—and it's healthy—then we figured we'd give it to the media." He glowered at the story, not really seeing the words, and then said, "Who did this? That Heller woman?"

"Who else?" Con threw her hands out. "That babe thinks only of herself and what's good for Sandy Heller. Well, she may not know it yet, but she is in big trouble. Adrian will have her head on a plate."

Nate paced back and forth in front of her. "Yeah. Maybe. *Maybe* Adrian will have her head on a plate. Remember, she has a very good friend in a very high place . . . And don't underestimate the power of—attraction between a man and a woman . . ." He broke off awkwardly and turned away to stare out the window.

Con knew very well why. He was remembering the night after he was brought to the hospital. It was after midnight, and the floors were all hushed. She remembered the soft squeak of her shoes on the floor as she made her way down the corridor. Nate's door was ajar slightly, and there was a soft light burning near his bed. There was also, she realized after a moment, a soft sound coming from the bed. Nate was weeping!

She hesitated at the doorway for a minute or two. She knew what she wanted to do. But what if he didn't want comforting? It had been a long time . . . years. Still, there was no way she could hear Nate Levinson crying like a baby and not do something about it.

Quietly, she slipped inside the room, quietly closing and locking the door behind her. He was hunched into a ball of misery, the sheet pulled over his head. She took off her shoes and tiptoed to the light. When she turned it off, he made a noise, and she shushed him, whispering, "It's okay, Nate. It's okay."

It didn't take her long to undress down to her slip, and then she felt her way around the bottom of the bed until she was next to him. She touched him gently, and he said grumpily, "Go away" in a choked voice.

"No, sweetie, I'm not going to go away," she said in her normal voice, and for a moment it seemed that he stopped breathing. And then she pulled the sheet down and climbed up onto the bed, saying, "Move over."

He remained tense for a minute, and then, relenting, he uncurled his legs and reached out for her in a way she still remembered vividly in spite of the years that had passed. "Oh, Con, oh, Con, you're always there when I need you."

That night, he fell asleep, deeply and contentedly asleep, his head pillowed between her breasts, his arms tightly around her, holding on for dear life.

Well, she remembered that night, too. She remembered it with warmth and pleasure. But just like all men, he found it embarrassing. She'd caught him in a weak moment, and he couldn't bring himself to acknowledge it. She understood. It hurt, but she understood it.

Now he turned from the window and looked directly at her. "Yeah," he said. "I remember. I remember it all the time. I—are you sorry you did it, Con?"

"Sorry! You old fool! Of course I'm not sorry. What kind of question is that?"

"Well . . . I know you pitied me that night. I'd hate to think . . . well . . . I don't want your pity."

"You *are* an old fool," Con said, looking right at him. Let *him* drop his eyes; she wasn't going to. "I don't pity you. If I climbed into bed with every pitiful case in this hospital, I wouldn't have time for my nursing."

"What is that supposed to mean?"

Damn it, he was irritating, Con thought. So many years gone by, so few years left . . . and he was still playing his silly little-boy games! She was going to have to do the whole thing herself, it looked like.

"Oh, Nate. Never mind. Why don't you take me to lunch today. To Rose and Sol's, not the cafeteria. And we'll discuss."

He was blushing! The man was a doctor, a grandfather, sixty-two years old, and blushing. "What'll we discuss?"

"About why, in spite of your stupidity and everything else, I still love you. Deal, Nate?"

And now he smiled. "Deal, Con."

Chapter 23

IT CAME AS no surprise to Adrian when his secretary buzzed him and said, in a patently phony, cheery tone, "Oh, Dr. Winter, Mr. and Mrs. Wilkins, Janet Freedman's parents, are here, and they need to see you right away."

"Give me two minutes, Linda."

"Right."

He used those two minutes to compose himself, to draw in several deep breaths, to hide the copies of the *News* and the *Post* in a desk drawer, and to arrange his features in what he hoped would look like the very picture of a calm but concerned physician.

But when they came bursting in, he rose to his feet involuntarily. "Please sit down," he began but was waved down by the irate and indignant man who advanced upon him as if he might throw a punch. "Mr. Wilkins!"

"I ought to wring your neck, you lousy son of a bitch! You promised! You said there'd be no publicity! And here it is! Here it is, all over the front page for the whole goddam world to look at and gossip about—!"

"Mr. Wilkins, Please! I didn't—I."

"Don't Mr. Wilkins me! And don't try to deny it! Here's your picture plastered all over the place, so there's my proof!"

"My baby! My poor baby!" Mrs. Wilkins, a plump little lady whose pretty face was distorted with crying, began to sway back and forth, and her husband immediately leaped to hold her up. With his arms supporting her, he glared pugnaciously at Adrian.

"Please, Mrs. Wilkins. Mr. Wilkins. Take a seat. Let's talk. *Wait a minute!* Hear me out, please. I'm as angry about this as you are. This story has been published and a picture taken against my very explicit instructions."

Only slightly mollified, Janet's father settled his wife into a seat, but he himself remained standing, his arms crossed tightly across his chest, his lips pressed together.

"There are things, Dr. Winter, that you don't know about Janet and her . . . husband."

"I think I—"

"No, now you hear *me* out. That man is a liar. And worse."

"Oh, James!" His wife broke into fresh sobs.

"Now, Mattie, keep a hold of yourself. It's too late now for tears . . . it's too late now for anything but saving that baby."

"My baby! My poor baby! My Janet, lying there like a dead thing! It isn't right! It just isn't right! And that man walks around, alive and well, talking to reporters and saying she couldn't go to term—!" She sobbed.

"All right, doctor, I guess it's time to tell the truth. That man is a wife beater, plain and simple. You don't look shocked . . ."

"I don't look shocked because I suspected as much. Her history was just too full of 'accidents.' But without proof."

"Oh, yes, we know about proof. We couldn't even call in the police because Janet swore she'd lie and tell them it never happened. Three times she got pregnant—"

"Not six, like he's saying! Even now he can't say a true word!" That was Mrs. Wilkins.

"I know. I'm sorry. I—"

"Never mind that now, Mother. Three times she got pregnant, and three times, Dr. Winter, three times he beat her. Beat my little girl unmercifully. Punched her in the stomach. I know . . . she told me. Finally, she told me. When she got pregnant this time, she left right away and came home to us, and she told us the whole thing. And then he came down to beg her to come back to him, and she listened. Like a woman, she listened. She loved him. She told me; she said Willie is a fine man and a good provider and a good husband. He goes a little crazy when she gets pregnant, but he wants his baby so bad. She told me. She said, every time she missed, he broke down and cried like a child. Every time, he put his arms around her and cried and swore it wasn't going to happen again and begged her to forgive him. And that's what he did when she came home to us. She told me she was determined to have this baby. 'Papa, once it's born, I just know Willie is going to love it. It'll all be different, once we're a real family.' Oh, sure. Well, you couldn't reason with her. He came to see her and sweet-talked her until she couldn't even think straight. I didn't want her to go back with him, but she wouldn't hear of anything but what he wanted. And now, look at what's happened—" His voice broke, and two tears rolled down his cheeks. "Dammit, Dr. Winter, I know as sure as I'm standing here that that man punched and pushed her down those stairs. She never tripped! She never!"

"Never!" his wife echoed.

Adrian dragged in a deep breath and allowed some of the tension to ease out of his back. He could hear in the man's voice a subtle change in his attitude. He had marched in, totally antagonistic, and now, having told his story, he was ready to call upon Adrian as an ally.

Adrian said, very distinctly and slowly, "Mr. Wilkins, I also know as sure as I'm standing here that he did it to her I can't tell you how glad I am that you told me the whole story, because you have confirmed my suspicions . . . ."

Half an hour later, they were still deep in discussion. "Yes," Adrian was saying for the fourth time, "I am going to see our administrator, Mr. Del Bello, at two-thirty, and I am going to demand the resignation of the head of public relations. I'm sure she took that picture, and I'm sure it was her who talked with Willie." What he did not say but was thinking was that he would have to do it very very carefully. It was common knowledge that Del Bello was becoming ever more deeply involved with Heller, and that it was not safe to try to cross her. Now that Nate was back and exerting some influence, he wanted to move with "all deliberate speed," meaning not too quickly and not too forcibly. It also was beginning to occur to him that if he played it right—if, for instance, he got Del Bello to *refuse* to fire her—it might work out even better. Because then Del Bello would be in complicity. It would be nice to get him out of Cadman Memorial altogether.

"Just tell me one thing, doctor," Mrs. Wilkins said. She, too, had calmed down a bit, although Adrian did not care for the extremely high color in her face . . . the woman, after all, had hypertension and had already collapsed once since the tragedy had happened.

"Anything," he said. He was now perched on the edge of his desk, and he leaned over to take her hand.

"Does that man have a legal right to take the baby?"

"I'm not a lawyer, but it's my understanding that yes, he does."

Mr. Wilkins snorted. "Well, he's no moral right, as far as I'm concerned! We're going to fight . . . that is, if Mama's doctor says it won't make her sick. We want that child. It's our grandchild . . ."

Adrian cleared his throat. "Mr. Wilkins, what if . . . what if something should go wrong . . ."

"Go wrong? What could go wrong?"

"Well, in fact, although we monitor the fetus—the baby—all the time, we cannot be sure that there hasn't been any oxygen deprivation; or, indeed, that all is well. We can only guess; we can only do our best. But, in fact, this infant might be born with severe problems . . ."

Stoutly, Mrs. Wilkins said, "We want that child, no matter what's wrong with it. It's all we have left of our daughter."

"Now, now, Mama."

Adrian was glad to have half an hour between the time Mr. and Mrs. Wilkins left and his appointment with Hank Del Bello. He had a lot to think about. He was not a fatalist, but he couldn't help thinking that poor Janet Freedman's personal tragedy might possibly be the turning point for him at Cadman. He needed some kind of wedge; he knew that now. As soon as he saw the papers that morning, he had stormed right into the administrator's office, only to be greeted by the ever-cool Nancy who insisted that her boss was not in, she didn't have the slightest notion where he was, but that she would be most happy to make an appointment with Dr. Winter for later in the day. Dammit! He saw the newspapers stuffed into a wastebasket. That meant Del Bello knew all about the whole thing. Of course he did! The bastard . . . he was stalling to have time to dream up a good lie. But there was nothing he could do. He had to smile at Nancy and pretend to believe her story and grit his teeth and make an appointment. He knew damn well he was sitting on a powder keg—and so did the administrator. He also knew—and he turned out to be absolutely right—that he'd get it from Janet Freedman's family. And sure enough, no sooner had he finished rounds and got back to his office than they stormed through.

He was going to have to be very clever to break through whatever cover-up Del Bello was planning. No matter who you were in the hospital, you couldn't call the administrator a liar—not in so many words. The best idea was to convince Del Bello that Heller would have to be sacrificed. Two birds with one stone; she'd be gone, and he'd have capitulated. Two points for our side, Adrian thought. Yes, the woman would have to go. Del Bello was stupid to get involved with her in the first place. It had given her too much control. Women tended to be too demanding sexually, anyway, and—

"Ade! Ade! I've been calling and calling."

It was Ellie, coming up behind him, slightly breathless. The minute he turned and saw her familiar face turned up to him with concern and caring, he thought, Of course, I can use Ellie. Del Bello liked Ellie and was wooing her all the time to present this, that, or the other. Yes, she was perfect . . . and then they'd have him outnumbered. Wasn't it Nate who, a long time ago, told him never to go into a confrontation without an ally? And here she was!

"Ellie! I've been thinking about you all morning!" Her face lit up with pleasure, as he knew it would, and she said, "Oh, god, and I've been thinking about you ever since one of the nurses showed me that story in the paper! I've been just waiting for a minute to talk to you . . . and then, of course, you weren't in your office. What luck that I saw you just now. You know, if there's anything at all I can do about this mess, I will. Anything at all."

Adrian smiled down at her. "Oh, I don't know, Ellie. It's something I'm going to have to handle with Del Bello myself, although—well, maybe you *could* be of help."

"Tell me!"

"You free now?" She nodded, her eyes brightening. Good old Ellie, she always did love a good battle on the side of right.

"You're going to tell him he has to fire Sandy Heller, right?"

They began to walk on together toward the administrator's office. "Right. I know damn well she took that picture," Adrian said, feeling himself getting angry again. "Against my specific orders. I told everyone—*everyone*—this story was off limits until the baby was delivered. Or until the end, anyway. Never mind why; I'm not obligated to explain my medical decisions."

"But wait a minute, Ade. That picture was only of the father. Janet wasn't in it at all."

"Clever bitch. She's hoping she can hide behind that little technicality. It doesn't matter. He talked about Janet, and it was all lies, and now her family is up in arms and wants nothing better than to splash the truth all over the papers . . . or sue us. That's what Del Bello is about to hear, Ellie. He isn't going to like it, but now, with the both of us facing him, he's going to at least have to hear it."

Where the hell is Art Schuster? Hank fumed. He banged the phone down . . . By Christ, if he had that weak sister here, he'd do that to his head. The minute anything went wrong, Art managed to disappear. Come to think of it, he'd done it before. In that last ethics meeting, as soon as they began to really ask questions, he had a patient he had to get to. An emergency, he said. Fuck his emergency. He'd told Hank one day when they'd had a couple of drinks at lunch that he had a deal with his secretary. Whenever he was stuck in a meeting that might be tough or boring or too damn long, he'd have her beep him about every forty minutes. "I call her back, and if I want out, I pretend there's something I have to do. Hell, when you're a doctor, nobody asks questions. One of the perks, Hank." And he'd laughed. Shit, they'd both laughed. Well, now Henry Francis Xavier Del Bello wasn't laughing. Now he needed that son of a bitch . . . yeah, and where the hell was he?

"Nancy," he said, into the intercom, "bring me a cup of coffee, will you?" Christ, he could use something stronger, but not today. Today he needed every bit of his brain in sharp working order. Nancy floated in with his coffee, frozen faced as usual. Christ, you couldn't get her to crack a smile hardly. But she was efficient, you had to give that to her. Give her an order, and it was done, and done right. She set the cup down on his desk, complete with spoon and napkin, and said, "Dr. Winter is here. With the other Dr. Winter."

"Oh, Christ. Both of them."

"Yes, sir. Both of them."

He checked with his watch. "Three minutes early. Well, let them wait. I need my coffee, in peace."

"Yes sir. I'll ask them to wait."

He watched her go out; she looked as if she were on wheels, like a robot. Yeah, but the coffee was strong, and it was hot, and she brought it to him right away. And now, he knew, she'd calmly tell both those Dr. Winters that Mr. Del Bello would see them as soon as he was free . . . And nothing they did, nothing they could think of, would change so much as the blank expression on her face. She was immovable. She wasn't lovable, hell, no, but she was loyal to him.

He sipped at the coffee thoughtfully. He'd just completed a half-hour conversation on the telephone with Nate Levinson. Conversation? Excuse me, Hank thought, that was no conversation; that was orders from headquarters. The little squirt! He was supposed to be all washed up. Hell, it had been easy to get him out of the hospital when he first came to take over. Just put his tail between his legs and slunk out, like a beaten mutt. And now look at him! Throwing his fucking weight around!

Look, Hank told himself, *you* did it, you chooch. You're the one who said, "Put Nate Levinson on the ethics committee . . . it sounds good, and he'll be out of the way." Shit, he thought he was sticking Nate in a drawer. Did he know that ethics was going to become the sexiest topic in all of health care? Shit! Who knew that the goddam public was going to turn against their *doctors*—against their doctors, of all the goddam people!—after so many generations of veneration and respect. He never thought there would ever come a day when people, even old people, even women, even niggers, would dare to challenge the authority of their physicians. And craziest of all, doctors were joining the enemy, turning against their own! Christ! And Levinson was the worst, with all his speeches about patient rights and the right to die . . . Christ, you'd think the man would have the decency to be ashamed of the fact that he tried to kill himself—against every church and every religion in the whole fucking world—but no. There he was, up on his fucking soapbox at every opportunity, like some old Commie, spouting off about turning off the machines and allowing people dignity and all that crap. Didn't they have enough trouble around here with patients yelling and screaming and threatening malpractice suits! Aw, shit, it gave him a headache just thinking about it.

But there was Nate, Johnny-on-the-spot, giving him the business about the invasion of Janet Freedman's rights. Jesus, the woman was dead; legally, she was dead. Her family should be damn grateful to Cadman Memorial for keeping her body alive so that the kid at least could have a chance. Instead of that, there they were, having fits because the son-in-law gave an interview.

And that reminded him. Sandy . . . Jesus Christ, Sandy! As soon as he read the story that morning—over breakfast, it was—before he even came into work, he was on the horn to her. "What the hell is the meaning of this? You know we all agreed to keep the lid on this story!"

And she was so damn cool. "All I did was talk to the father, Hank. That's all I did."

"That's not all you did, and you know it. And what about that picture?"

"He signed a release. I've got it, right in my handbag. In fact, he was eager for this story to be printed."

"Winter gave the word, and we promised."

"Oh, poo. There he was, and there I was, and he wanted to talk. And I thought the story was *beautiful*."

Well, so did he, but he wasn't about to tell *her* that. "That's besides the point. Ms. Heller . : ." Ms. Heller! Well, but there was his wife, walking in and out of the room, and if he said, "Sandy," sure as hell she'd want to know who Sandy was. If there was one thing he hated, it was telling outright lies.

"We'll discuss the point," Sandy said, and even over the phone he could hear that change in her voice. "Later, we'll discuss it. Okay, Hank? *Alone*." Christ, that's all it took; he started to get hard. She did it to him every time—a certain look or that bedroom voice or some other little trick. She was good at those little tricks.

He made his voice gruff. "Okay," he said. "We'll discuss this later. But in the meantime, remember: anyone asks you anything, anything at all, it's *no comment*. No exceptions. Got that?"

She chuckled in her huskiest voice and said, "I got it."

"Oh, and that *especially* goes for our dear friend, the Reverend Clayton. You know how he is with anyone black. He'll be breathing fire, and I for one don't intend getting burned."

"I know how to handle the Reverend Clayton."

"The way you handle me?" He lowered his voice, just in case.

"Oh, Hank!"

"Well, you better not."

Again, that chuckle. "Don't worry; I save all the best stuff for you."

He shook his head, impatient with his wandering thoughts. He really had to do something about her; she was getting too cocky.

And hadn't he been right about the Reverend. That guy had eyes and ears everywhere. On his way up the front steps that morning, there was Clayton, blood in his eye, saying, "I think we need to have a few words together, Mr. Del Bello."

"So early, Rev? What's up?"

"Come on now, Mr. Del Bello. You know what's up. You must have heard the same strange rumors I've been hearing—that the Freedman case isn't exactly what it seems . . . ?"

"No." And it was true. Other than the fact that Adrian Winter had insisted there were compelling reasons to keep this one quiet—strong ethical reasons was how he had put it—he hadn't heard anything. Damn it, anyway! What kind of administrator was he if this preacher knew more about what was going on than he did? Did Sandy know? Goddam it, if anyone should, *she* should. That was her job, for Christ's sake, to keep her finger on the goddam pulse of the goddam hospital!

"Well," the Rev said carefully, "there's some talk around . . ." He paused a moment. "From very good sources, *very* good, I might say. And the talk says that we might be dealing here with a case of wife abuse . . ."

In a flash, Hank remembered Janet Freedman's history; this was not the first time she had been hospitalized. Adrian had mentioned that, and that she had had several misses, all of them from falls, if he remembered correctly, and he was sure he did. "Holy—!" he said softly, and the Reverend nodded.

"That's right, Mr. Del Bello. This one could be a real mess. And I needn't add, need I, that once again we publicize a real mess to the whole world when it's black people!"

"Oh, come on, reverend, don't start with that. It has nothing to do with color! And besides, over half our patient population is black, as you know; statistically—"

The Reverend held up a commanding hand. "Don't quote me statistics," he said in a dangerously mild tone. "Do me that favor, Mr. Del Bello. No statistics this time. This time, we're dealing with just one family."

Well, he wished that were true. Funny the Reverend should choose to say that; he'd be the first to make a federal case out of it. One family! The minute he didn't like what was going on, he'd have half his flock out there again, marching up and down in front of the hospital, chanting, "Genocide," or some goddam thing.

Thinking about it, Hank groaned aloud. Christ, this was some can of worms. The ethics committee had already called a special meeting for the following morning, and it was going to be a doozy; he could see that. And now he had to face Adrian Winter. Oh, Christ, he's almost forgotten.

Not just Adrian but Ellie, as well. And no sign of Art Schuster.

But never mind: he could handle them with or without Schuster—who, by the way, would shortly discover what it meant around here to cross Hank Del Bello . . .

He punched the intercom button, straightened his shoulders, put a smile on his face, and said, "Nancy? Send 'em in!"

Chapter 24

SANDY TOOK A deep breath outside Hank's door and let it out slowly. She was a little nervous, she admitted it. It was like waiting to see the principal at school when you'd done something he probably wasn't going to like but you thought maybe you could convince him it was okay. Nervous, but a bit exhilarated, too. Excited. Yes, excited was how she felt right now. Horny, even. There was something . . . extra . . . about screwing the boss, something that never failed to turn her on.

But now it was time to confront him. She was already ten minutes late . . . Well, that was on purpose. Waiting put him on edge, and on edge was exactly where she wanted him. From that position he was a sure pushover. One little nudge, she thought, just one little nudge, and over he'd go.

She drew in another breath and decided to go in smiling. He was barricaded behind that oversized desk of his, looking grim and serious. Oh, her instinct had been right; just like the principal.

"So glad you could finally make it, Ms. Heller," he said. His voice was grim, too. Well, she had expected that. But she wasn't going to let him get to her. She was in control, and that's where she was going to stay.

"Sorry I'm late, Hank. I had a last-minute call. From NET. So . . ." And she shrugged.

"NET be damned," he said. "This is more important. What you did was against hospital regulations. It was against hospital procedure, it was against my direct orders, and they want your head, Sandy. They want your *head*. And you know what? I might just give it to them."

"Oh, come on, Hank. Over one little story? And you said yourself it was very well written. My God, it makes Cadman look like Florence Nightingale and Dr. Schweitzer all rolled up into one!"

"You think you're so smart. But this time you outsmarted yourself. You know that? Yeah," he repeated with satisfaction, as if the words tasted good, "outsmarted yourself."

Sandy bit her lip, thinking very fast. What was he talking about? And *why*? That was the important thing. Why was he so angry? Adrian Winter, she understood. He was a doctor, and doctors thought they were God Almighty, every one of them. Any time you defied a doctor, he was outraged . . . Hell, the women doctors were just as bad. They were nuts; they had delusions of grandeur, all of them. So Adrian Winter was easy to figure; he was bound to be furious because she had dared to go against his wishes. But, after all, so what? Every TV station in the city was after this story; Cadman Memorial would be in every living room in the metropolitan area and suburbs by six o'clock tonight. It was her job, and she'd done it. And it was what Hank wanted her to do, so what was his problem?

"What's your problem?" she asked, as lightly as she thought safe. "Your big concern is to have Cadman look good. Believe me, with this story, it looks good. *Better* than good." She edged herself farther into the room, unbuttoning the top button on her blouse ever so casually and running one finger ever so lightly up and down the swell of her breast. To her vast amusement, Hank swallowed visibly; you could see the Adam's apple move. Oh, men were funny; they were wonderful. They were so dumb you could just push them around like so many little toy soldiers.

She continued to stroll toward him, looking at him the whole time, never taking her eyes from his.

"Yeah, *now* we look good . . ." He licked his lips. She was getting to him. Still, she had to know what he meant.

"What do you mean—*now*?"

"There are things you don't know, Sandy, things I can't tell you. Privileged information. But it has to do with him, with the husband, Janet's husband. No, I can't tell you; I can't. But I can tell you that Adrian Winter wasn't just throwing his weight. He had damn good reason—what are you doing?"

She smiled at him and deliberately ran her tongue over her lips. She had unbuttoned her blouse very slowly while he talked and now had let it slip from her shoulders onto the floor.

"Jesus Christ, Sandy. This is serious stuff!"

She kept smiling and kept coming at him. She held her shoulders back so that the gently bobbing breasts stuck out. He loved to watch her walk around like that; she knew it. She knew he was probably getting a hardon, and the thought of it tightened the nipples. She could feel the shiver running through them, and even if she couldn't, the look on his face—avid and hungry—told her what was happening. Involuntarily, he pushed himself up, leaning across the desk. "Jesus Christ, Sandy. Anyone could walk in!"

Her answer was to unzip her skirt, letting it slither down her legs. Delicately, she stepped out of it. "No, they couldn't," she said softly. "I locked it behind me." The half slip went next, and now she was standing before him in nothing but sheer pantyhose. She watched his eyes move greedily from breasts to crotch and back again.

She had him! She had him now!

Weakly, he said, "I'm not kidding, Sandy. They're demanding that I fire you."

"You gonna fire me?" She moved her hips from side to side. She knew she was driving him crazy. These hot Italians, all you had to do was be a little aggressive and they were ready for rape. "You wouldn't fire me, Hank." Now she rounded the desk and came to a halt by the side of his big swivel chair. He was sitting back in it, clutching the arms, his eyes wild. Sandy glanced down, and yes, there was his cock outlined against his leg, under the fabric. She had him.

"I might have to," he muttered, but already she could hear that his mind was not on what he was saying. She knew damn well where his mind was. She stood, arms akimbo, thrust her loins out toward him, and said huskily, "You look hungry, honey. Dinner's ready, so come and get it."

With a strangled groan, he fell onto his knees, tearing at the pantyhose. On his knees, he moved close to her, biting at her thighs, pulling her hips tight into him, his mouth hot and eager.

A while later, her mouth dry, she gasped at him, "Let me down. Hank, I can't stand up; let me down." And when he had let her go, and she sank to the thick carpet, trembling and shaking, he tore his own clothes off and lunged at her, growling in his throat.

As usual, once he was in her it took only a minute or two. He came like a locomotive, pushing at her about a hundred miles an hour and yelling, as he always did when he came. He was so quick; it was a damn good thing she'd taught him to do all that good oral stuff . . . otherwise, she'd never get anything out of it. And he loved it. He was a glutton; couldn't get enough, now that he was turned on to it.

He had collapsed over her, breathing heavily into her ear. With her lips on his cheek, she murmured, "You gonna fire me, Hank?"

With a groan: "No, you know I'm not."

" 'Cause you wouldn't get this if you did."

"Shut up, will you?"

"No reason we can't continue this way for as long as you like . . . if you're real good . . ."

She felt his whole body stiffen. "Don't push, Sandy. I already said you aren't gonna be fired. This time." He pushed himself up, off her, so that he could look down at her, look directly into her eyes. "But let me tell you, I'm going to have some tough time explaining why you're not off the payroll as of yesterday. It ain't gonna be easy, baby. So don't push."

"I'm sorry, sweetie. Really I am." She pouted her lips for a kiss, a gesture that usually didn't fail to elicit an instant response; but he shook his head this time. "I'm telling you, Sandy, you pull another stunt like this—you go against hospital policy—and nothing, do you hear me, *nothing* you do will save you. Not if you fuck me in Times Square standing on your head. Understand?"

Several smart answers came to her, but there was something in his face, something in his voice. Something implacable. So she put on her sweetest little girl voice and said, "Yes, *sir*, boss."

Chapter 25

"ALL RIGHT, ALL right! Everybody quiet down, please! This is not peace talks; this is a committee!" In the midst of the general noise and arguing, there was a slight ripple of amusement. Nate, sitting at the head of a giant conference table, looked in vain for anything that might serve as a gavel and finally stood up and used his fists. Both of them.

Now several of the others laughed aloud, and Eleanor Winter called out, "Come on, people! We have important business here. And I don't know about the rest of you, but I have patients waiting downstairs."

As the room settled down, Nate looked around, taking tally. Not bad for a last-minute call. The Reverend Clayton, of course, was there, looking mighty serious. A fidgety Del Bello. Con Scofield and Tony Milano, the head of Physical Therapy. Chief of Surgery, chief of Pediatrics, chief of Internal Medicine? "I see everyone's here," Nate announced, "except Dr. Schuster." He paused a moment. "Does anyone here know where we might find Art Schuster?" From his right, from Hank Del Bello, came a barely discernible, muttered "Wish I did . . ." But when Nate looked at the administrator, he got nothing back but a blank stare. That was interesting, Nate thought, tucking it away at the back of his mind. The Terrible Two were at odds? He knew his Arthur Schuster from the old days—the first rat to desert a sinking ship and swim safely to shore. Hmmm.

"All right, then, let's get started. We are here to discuss the unfortunate . . . ah . . . *leaking* . . . of the story about Janet Freedman to the New York City press—"

Adrian Winter, halfway down the table, was on his feet, shouting. "Leak? That was no leak! There was a deliberate act on the part of someone—and I think I know who!" He glared in the direction of Hank Del Bello, who stolidly stared straight ahead, his face void of expression.

Nate held up a hand. "Doctor, Doctor, it isn't going to do anybody any good for you to lose your temper."

"I'm not—!" He stopped and grinned a little. "Okay. I'm not going to lose my temper. But that story went against all my orders. I am the physician in this case, and as long as I've been at Cadman, the physician's word is law."

Hank Del Bello's head came up immediately. "Hey! Right or wrong, Dr. Winter? Is that what you're telling us? That your word has got to be law, period?"

There was an outburst of chatter and protest and argument, and once again Nate had to pound on the table.

Adrian said, in a very level tone, "Mr. Del Bello, as I said from the very beginning, there were good and sufficient reasons to hold this story down . . ."

Del Bello smiled tightly. "I know your good and sufficient reasons. The guy beat her, right? The husband, I mean. He beat her each time she was pregnant, and that's why she miscarried . . ."

"That was our conjecture, Mr. Del Bello. And he probably caused her present condition . . . but that isn't even the point. This entire case has sensitive areas and sensitive issues . . . I felt it was best to keep it quiet until such time as a healthy, viable infant was delivered. We don't need reporters and tv personalities second-guessing our medical decisions . . . Remember what happened in the Barney Clark case . . ."

"Yeah, Dr. Winter, but that small-time hospital in Salt Lake City that nobody in the world ever heard of was on everybody's lips . . . and everybody's grants list, could I add."

Nate interrupted. "Mr. Del Bello, this is a hospital, first and foremost. In a hospital, which is for the care of the sick, those who care for the sick must be in command. Grants are important—yes, yes, I know they are—and we wouldn't be able to do a lot of what we do without them, you don't have to tell this old dog. But it's dangerous for nonmedical personnel to go against the specific instructions of the attending physician. This time all it did was cause great embarrassment to Dr. Winter and to Janet's family. But, on another occasion, on a different occasion, Mr. Del Bello, the race for publicity could very well prove fatal . . . to somebody."

Con put in, "Hold on. All this is very interesting, Dr. Levinson, but we're getting a little off the point. *I* want to know who leaked or deliberately planted or delivered this story to the papers?"

Very, very calmly, Adrian said, "Most of us here are very well aware of the identity of that person. Am I right, Mr. Del Bello?"

Hank's head thrust forward, like a bull's. "She was doing her job, doctor. Her job is to find human interest stories in this hospital and to get them printed and to make this hospital look good. As far as I'm concerned, she's doing one helluva job . . . Wait a minute, Dr. Winter. In this particular case, Mr. Freedman came to her. He *wanted* the story printed. Do I know why? No. Do I care? Not really. He came off looking tragic, and the hospital came off looking like a saint." He rose to his feet, leaning on his palms on the tabletop. "You let me finish, okay? Next. He signed a release, which I have in my pocket for anyone who doubts me. And last but not least, do you know how many phone calls we've had on this thing? At last count, seventy-seven. Seventy-seven phone calls, and four of them offering money. Eighteen baskets of flowers and a call from the post office asking us what to do with the three truckloads of mail they suddenly got for us. I call that success, doctor.''

"Janet Freedman's parents don't."

"To hell with the parents. I'm sorry they're unhappy, but come on. The woman's dead; she can't hear or feel, so it's not hurting her. There's no proof the husband ever laid a finger on her. And we might turn a profit, for a change.'' He loaded the last three words with meaning.

Now Ellie spoke. "Profit? Is that what you think we're here for?''

"Now, Dr. Ellie,''—the tone was quite different, almost deferential—"you know I don't mean profit is everything. But let's face it. The reality is that this hospital has become pretty well known. The arthritis clinic alone has tripled its patient population. Our out-of-town visitors—and I mean doctors like yourself, scientists, important people—have doubled; we're going to have to hire someone just to take them around. I know publicity is kind of a dirty word to health professionals like yourselves, but it's there to help you.''

Adrian rose to his feet. "Does this mean you refuse to fire her?''

"On what grounds would I fire her, Doctor Winter?''

"Insubordination.''

Del Bello threw his head back and laughed. In a way, Nate didn't blame him. It was such an old-fashioned word. And, in fact, Adrian wasn't her superior; he wasn't anything to her. He was just chief of Ob/Gyn, and she was head of public relations.

And then Nina Thomas, of the affirmative action office in the hospital, stood up and said in her very soft drawl, "I would like to know whether we're all picking on Ms. Heller simply because she's a woman.''

There was a general groan at this, just a murmur of a groan, and then Con snorted in derision and said, "Oh, come on, Nina, I know it's time in the meeting for you to ask the gender question, but let's not spend time on it. I know Ms. Heller. I've had dealings with her, and this isn't the first time she's put publicity ahead of any medical, ethical, or human considerations.''

"Unfair!" Del Bello blurted.

"Wrong!" Con flared back.

"If you'll excuse me, Miss Scofield . . . Con . . ." All heads turned at that sonorous voice. The Reverend Clayton had leaned forward, instantly commanding the entire table. Nate marveled. The man had charisma, and that's all there was to that. If he decided he wanted to speak, everyone just naturally shut up and listened. And no matter what he said, no matter how innocuous or how infuriating, it was all couched in that wonderful preaching rhythm that hypnotized you. "If we are going to talk about fair and unfair, then I suggest to you that we all look very carefully at what is *really* happening.'' There was a dramatic pause. "What is really happening here is that, once again, black family relationships are being held up to public ridicule. . . .'' He waited, as if he knew there would be a murmur of protest, and he smiled benevolently upon it. "Yes, brothers and sisters, *black* family relationships. Dr. Levinson, please allow me my brief moment here. Last year, a woman was brought into the hospital *in extremis* and in labor. She had been badly beaten and naturally aborted her six-month fetus and then died. Have any of you heard this story? No? I thought not. Because, brothers and sisters, that woman was named Mrs. Horace Chapman III, of Brooklyn Heights and Stonington, Connecticut, and that woman was white.'' Now there were definite squawks, and the Reverend held his hands out for silence. "I am not putting blame. I am not accusing anyone of anything. I simply put that story to you and ask you to think on it. Mr. Chapman can beat his wife and unborn child to death, and his picture does not appear in the *Daily News*. That's all.'' And he sank back into his seat, ignoring the hubbub that broke out.

Nate pounded on the table. "Ladies! Gentlemen! If I have to do this many more times this morning, I'm going to have to call upon Dr. Williams of plastic surgery to put my hands back together."

The door at the far end of the room opened, and there was Art Schuster, sidling in, just like a snake, Nate thought. Funny, how often reptile descriptions sprang to his mind where Art was concerned. And the man didn't really deserve it. So he wasn't a wonderful doctor; Nate knew at least a dozen doctors who weren't wonderful doctors. But his patients believed in him, and that was half of healing. In fact, the longer he lived, the more he was inclined to think it was maybe more than half of healing.

Art quietly took a seat and listened intently as the discussion raged on, taking some wild turns. Patients rights, women's rights, cost effectiveness, hiring policies, you name it, and they were off on it. Obviously they needed this, so for ten minutes he let it go on. He was about to pound once more for attention when Ellie Winter spoke up:

"The story is done, and it's over with. But Dr. Winter asked Mr. Del Bello a question, and Mr. Del Bello never answered it. I, for one, would like to hear that answer."

"Repeat the question," Del Bello said.

"Are you going to fire Sandy Heller?"

"No." Once again, fifteen questions and comments erupted.

And now Art Schuster held up a hand, and Nate yelled over the tumult, "Yes, Dr. Schuster." Hands turned. Probably, Nate thought, half of them hadn't noticed his late entrance.

"I've spent all day yesterday feeling out the trustees of the hospital . . . Well, not all of them but several of the more influential of them . . . We had dinner, a group of us, at the Casino. And I must say, ladies and gentlemen"—he shook his head regretfully—"the overwhelming sense I get is that we've gone too far this time. This is not the kind of publicity our trustees want for Cadman." He gave a charming toothy smile and added, "They were disturbed by the Brian Fuller picture, if you'll recall. And now this. What I was told was, if this is the kind of story that appears in the *Post* and the *News* but not in the *Times*—" A hoot went up, and he held up a patient and reproving hand. "Laugh if you like, but they call this not public relations, not 'good vibes,' but notoriety. Sensationalism. And, in fact, I find myself in agreement. I think Sandy Heller should go."

"Jesus Christ!" Hank Del Bello straightened up as if someone had just punched him in the belly. He stared at Schuster with a mixture of disbelief and fury. To himself, secretly, Nate chuckled. Oh, that Schuster. He had such an instinct for survival. Nate had no doubt that Sandy Heller was indeed on her way out and that perhaps, if he weren't careful, so was Hank Del Bello. They might not know it; hell, the trustees might not know it. But Art Schuster knew it, and Art Schuster was almost never wrong. Well, well.

Belligerently, Del Bello said in a tone of ice, "You can think what you like, Dr. Schuster. She's not going to be fired." He turned to Nate, holding out his hands, "Dr. Levinson. I appeal to you as chairman of this committee. Did the woman take a byline? No, she did not. What has she done for her own glory? Not a thing. Everything she's done has been for the sake of Cadman Memorial Hospital and not for anything else. Not for glory, not for money, not for personal aggrandizement. So, I ask you, how can I fire her? In good conscience, I cannot."

Nate half expected applause at the end of this eloquence. What happened was just as surprising—total silence. Nobody seemed to want to argue with this. Not even the Reverend Clayton, who was stroking his chin with his forefinger, looking very thoughtful.

The meeting broke up then. Nobody had anything more to say, and Nate was just as glad. Ellie was right. What was done was done. The parents would learn to live with it, and he had agreed to have a chat with William Freedman, perhaps to make an exchange: secrecy continued for the baby going with its grandparents. They'd have to wait and see; this was one, Nate thought, he'd have to play by ear.

He couldn't help but notice that Art waited for Ellie and Adrian and insinuated himself between them so that the three

289

of them were walking off down the corridor in a tight little group. Nate quietly walked behind them, not really listening to them but not drawing their attention to the fact he was there, either.

Art was saying, "It's so good to see Nate back to his old self again."

"Yes, isn't it?" Ellie sounded a trifle amused.

"He's my old mentor. Everything I know I learned from him."

Ade laughed briefly: "And a few things you taught yourself, I think."

"You think Nate Levinson isn't an old smoothie? You mean to tell me he's got you fooled with that gruff-old-doc persona of his? It couldn't be!"

"I happen to think that what you see is what you get with Nate Levinson."

"Oh, yeah, sure, he's straight as they come. But shrewd, man. I discovered that a long time ago. He gets his way a lot by seeming a bit naive, but don't you believe it."

Nate smiled to himself. Schuster had learned more from him than he had really meant to teach. He wasn't nearly as smart as he thought he was, of course, but he'd do, if you could just channel all his energies in the right direction. And he certainly had the ear of most of the trustees, thanks to Etta, who came from old Brooklyn money. He was useful. Of course he was. And that was why Del Bello had pounced on him, too.

Well, they'd have to wait, that's all. Just wait and see. Meanwhile, he'd plan his talk with Willie Freedman. And meanwhile—and here his heart lifted a bit—he'd have lunch with Con, and who knew?

Chapter 26

ELLIE WAS VERY well aware that Nate was dogging their footsteps. He was a crafty old devil, not above listening in on other people's conversations if he could get away with it, she was sure. Well, let him. He'd only hear good from this particular group. Shrewd. Clever. Strong. Not such terrible things to quote *overhear* unquote. Of course, something devilish in her wanted very badly to come to a sudden halt and turn around to grin at him and ask him how he liked the conversation so far. But of course she didn't. She got quietly on the elevator with Ade and Art Schuster, said hello to the three nurses she recognized, and noted that Dr. Levinson was no longer among them.

It wasn't until they had dropped Art off near the clinics and were both continuing to the cafeteria that she said to Adrian, "Did you see what was going on? Nate was tailing us and listening to every word."

"Was he? I didn't notice. I was too busy thinking about the meeting. All the interesting ramifications." He paused a moment and then added, "When Art Schuster switches sides, oh boy! I know what that means!"

"Really? What does that mean, Ade?"

"That means Del Bello is in such big trouble." And he looked down at her with such boyish delight that she wanted to laugh.

"Shame on you, Adrian Winter! All right, he gives you a hard time! *And* he picked somebody else to be his fair-haired boy. *And* that somebody happened to be your particular nemesis." She had stopped in the middle of the hallway, ticking off points on her fingers. "And okay, so the man has a manner that neither of us can feel comfortable with. But come on, Ade, he's doing a damn fine job as hospital administrator. And that's what he was hired for, I might remind you, not as baby-sitter to the medical staff."

"Hold on, Ellie. I'm not so sure he's such a fine administrator. Cutting my budget to ribbons! Those teenage mothers don't deserve—!"

"Nevertheless. We have a balanced budget. We're beginning to show a profit. The clinics are crowded. Looks like Tower B will actually get started within the next six months. So we don't like him! So what? Listen. Let's say you get rid of him. What do you imagine as taking his place?"

He looked puzzled. "Well, I—I don't know, exactly . . . I— Well," he finally said, sheepishly, "I guess if I thought about it at all, I figured Nate would step in."

"Wrong! Nate was not and has never been and will never be an administrator . . . Wait a minute; don't get all uptight. I'm not saying he's a dummy. He's a wonderful leader, yes, but that's not the same as shuffling people and papers and plans and making it all come out. He's too blunt, too focused on medicine, too disdainful of fund-raising and other necessities of life, and too much of a sweetie pie to fire people when it's needed."

"I guess you're right, but—"

"No buts, my darling. I'll tell you what we'll get at Cadman if Del Bello goes. We'll get one of those hospital management corporations coming in to run this place. Talk about efficiency! They won't give too hoots in hell about your pregnant teenagers, not if they don't come out on the right side of the balance sheet. And the chief administrator won't be anyone you can hate—or anyone you can love, for that matter. It'll be some faceless corporation man out in the Midwest somewhere. Or worse . . ." And she felt startled at her own thought. "Or worse, a computer somewhere in the bowels of the earth."

Now he laughed. "All right, Ellie, all right, all right. You've made your point. I don't need a whole science fiction novel to convince me." He laughed again and put his hand on her shoulder. "Just like old times," he said in a very different tone. "You always were the voice of my conscience." And he gazed down at her so tenderly that she felt tears pricking at the corners of her eyes and had to look away. He slid his arm across her shoulder so that, to the casual eye, he was all but hugging her. Ellie's heart speeded up. This wasn't typical of Adrian at all. He wasn't a hugger and squeezer, or even a toucher, not in public, and certainly not in the hospital. She hardly knew what to do.

"Come to dinner with me tonight. I have a lot of things I want to discuss with you," he said, and again she felt her pulses jolted. It was off the wall, but she could swear he was coming on to her.

"Dinner? But . . . what about your . . . what about Leslie? Won't she object?"

Was it her imagination, or did he mumble a little as he answered. "Leslie's at her sister's with Greg. In Norfolk. For a week. So it's no problem. And anyway . . ." He stopped.

"And anyway? And anyway what?"

"And anyway, I can have dinner with you if I want to. There's no law against it."

It was such a sweet, childish thing to say. "No law against it." "No, there isn't," she answered him, fighting the impulse to pat him on the hand. "And I'd be delighted to have dinner with you. Where'd you have in mind?"

"I made a reservation at Henry's End." And then he realized what he had said, and a look of total chagrin came over his face. "Oh, hell," he said. "I was counting on your saying yes . . . I was *hoping* you'd say yes." He slid her a look that said as plainly as words, "Forgive me?" Oh, she remembered that look, from the last movie. Adrian Winter never said, "I'm sorry," to her; hardly ever said *anything* emotional, in fact. Everything, come to think of it, had always been tacit, silent, understood. The strong type. Silent he had been as a young man, and as far as she could tell, the strong silent type he still was. And what fink, she thought suddenly, had sold that whole generation of men a bill of goods that said strong and silent was how a man was supposed to be. Oh, sure! And all that silence was supposed to be magically interpreted. She could remember, just offhand, a dozen different times when she totally *mis*read his unspoken messages . . . and she was a pretty smart lady, if she said so herself.

To Adrian, she said, "How could I refuse? It's been a long time since we've had a chance to really talk."

"Talk . . . yes. That's it exactly. I'll pick you up at five-thirty."

"Pick me up?"

"At your office. I figured we'd walk across Cadman Park . . . it's a nice day today."

She did not say, "Oh, you figured? Without consulting me?" She also did not say, "Had it occurred to you that I might like to change?" She didn't say anything at all, just nodded. But as she made her way down the crowded corridor to her office in the clinic, she found an old and familiar resentment rising in her. She had fantasized this moment for months now. She had known all the time it couldn't possibly happen, and yet she had hoped. One day, Adrian would realize the terrible mistake he had made, and he would try to get her back. In her fantasy, he threw his arms around her, he pleaded for her forgiveness, and he said, "Please come back to me, Ellie, I love you." And here was the reality, and what he was doing was acting as if he were still her husband—taking her acquiescence for granted, making plans without her, and assuming he was in charge. It was making her mad. It shouldn't, but it was. He was spoiling her whole dumb dream. She should have known that if he ever came on to her, it would be *his* way, the only way he knew. *This* way, in fact. Just pretend the whole divorce had never happened and go on from there.

The clinic was locked, and she was fumbling with her key when, out of the corner of her eye, she saw a familiar figure coming down the hall. She could feel the color rising in her cheeks. What idiocy! It had been so long since their breakup, and she'd seen him dozens of times—in the halls, on Montague Street, in the cafeteria. And yet it never failed to elicit this embarrassed and embarrassing response.

He saw her; she knew that he saw her. She arranged her expression and turned to him, smiling. "Why, hello, David."

"Ellie! What a nice surprise! How you doing?"

"Just fine. And you? Still liking it in Geriatrics?"

"There's nothing like the Golden Oldies." He laughed and then, more seriously, said, "Although I still think about all my kids down here and wonder how they're doing. In fact—" He looked a bit uncomfortable for a moment, then grinned. "In fact, I talk to your nurses quite a lot and get the word."

She was startled. "You *do*?"

"Well, yeah. I kinda got attached to some of them."

Ellie gazed at him, feeling oddly left out. She didn't like that feeling a bit; it was stupid. That he should call down to ask about his old patients was a wonderful, warm, and touching thing, and it was admirable. She had no business feeling whatever it was she was feeling. Was it a bit of jealousy, perhaps, because he was showing himself to be warmer and more connected to her patients than she was? Whatever it was, it was unworthy.

"David," she said warmly, "that's so nice. Really. It's that little bit extra that makes you such an outstanding nurse."

"Thank you, doctor." Was he laughing at her? If he was, she didn't want to know about it. He was so cool, so controlled. Was this the same man who, a few short years ago, all but fell on his knees, begging her to reconsider, to change her mind . . . the same man who said, his voice shaking with emotion, "I'll do *anything*, I'll go along with *anything*, except never seeing you again!"

She unlocked the door quickly and said, "I really have to go."

"Sure, doctor. I understand. See you around." She did not allow herself to look at him; instead, she let herself in, slammed the door shut, and then leaned against it, in the dark, fighting off the memories. She did not want to remember any of it; God, it had taken her six months when they broke up to—six months before she could bear the thought of anyone else's hands on her, six months before she could even start to think about dating. God, he had managed to turn her on in a way she hadn't even been able to imagine before she knew him. And once having been opened up to that kind of sensuous experience, it was painful, painful to have to give it up. She had managed to do it; of course she had. Nothing was more important than her patients, her work, the profession she had studied so hard to achieve. That's what she had told herself, that's what she believed, and that's what was the truth.

Drawing in a deep breath, she turned on the clinic lights and walked back toward her office, erasing David Powell from her thoughts. Past and done, past and done. Not like Adrian, not a marriage with three children and years of a shared life. Not the same at all. David Powell had been an interlude; Adrian Winter was real life. And, it seemed, he was coming back into *her* life, and she needed to clear her mind and prepare herself for whatever happened that evening.

She had to wait twenty minutes for him—she recalled that habit, too, from the days of their marriage—but then he took her hand when they walked across the park, a gesture he had *never* made that she could remember. When they got to the restaurant, he ordered for her without asking her what she'd like, but then he consulted with her over the wine list. The meal was delicious, as it always was, and he ordered two very different entrées, in order to share, as they'd always done in their younger days.

She found it difficult to figure out what he was up to. All this intimate behavior, and yet he kept talking about the most inane, impersonal things: should he get rid of a file clerk he didn't like . . . how he might get Nate yet another chairmanship . . . the gossip about Hank and Sandy Heller . . . an article he was trying to prepare for a journal . . . and on and on and on.

She finally had to admit to herself that she was getting impatient . . . impatient for the real stuff. She knew damn well his purpose in having dinner with her was not to chitchat . . . She knew it damn well! Didn't she? Now she began to wonder, and that made her even more impatient with him. Had she made the whole thing up?

Leaning forward and refusing a bit of his dessert, she said, "Any special reason Leslie's in Norfolk, Ade?"

"No, no, just a visit." He ducked his head a little, took a sip of his coffee, then put the cup down with a clatter and looked her straight in the eye. "Ellie, I made a terrible mistake in my marriage."

She wasn't going to help him out. "Oh, really? Well, we got a divorce, so it's okay now."

"Oh, Christ, Ellie, not *our* marriage! The other one . . . my current marriage, my marriage to Leslie."

"Oh, *that* one." She widened her eyes, all innocence.

"Ellie! Please don't! I'm serious. Our marriage—Leslie's and mine—is in terrible trouble. In fact, that's why she went to Norfolk, because we were fighting all the time. Oh, God, Ellie, I was such a fool to think I was going to find happiness with a woman so much younger than me, with such different interests."

Interesting, wasn't it, that he thought himself a fool for picking the wrong second wife, not for leaving the perfectly good first one. Even so, she felt that warm glow of satisfaction deep in her belly. She had suffered plenty for his mistake;

now he was suffering, and it was long overdue! She thought, So cry me a river! And she looked at him sympathetically, allowed him to hold her hands across the table, and tried valiantly to keep from smiling in triumph.

"It's over," he said. "It's over. There's nothing left, nothing to be salvaged."

"What are you going to do?" She sat, stunned. Was her fantasy about to come true? Was Adrian really looking her in the eye and telling her he was getting a divorce and coming back to her?

"I don't know . . . that is, I haven't worked out the details yet. But we'll separate. Actually—" He ducked his head a little. "Actually, we haven't discussed it. But I know she's as unhappy as I am."

"Separating," she echoed.

"Yes." He gripped her hands even tighter. "Ellie. Can you ever forgive me?" He didn't really wait for an answer but blurted on. "Leaving you was the worst thing I've ever done. Do you suppose . . . do you think . . ." He stopped and gave her a look of intense longing.

"Do I think what?" She felt breathless.

"Do you think that you . . . that we . . . that we could ever . . . try again?"

Now she was sure she had stopped breathing. She couldn't answer him; she could only stare. Then she said, "Oh, Ade!"

"I understand you'll have to think about it . . . I've heard rumors about you and some lawyer from Boston . . ."

"Steve? You've heard rumors about me and Steve?" Secretly, she was delighted to see him wince at the sound of the name. "I can't imagine where."

"I don't remember. Anyway, I think I saw you with him. At BAM. So . . . ?"

"So?"

"Well, is it . . . serious? Do I have a chance?"

The boyishness of the phrase totally unnerved her. She felt herself melting inside. "Oh, Ade, of course. As for Steve . . . *he* was serious. I wasn't. I haven't seen him lately."

He smiled at her radiantly, and the breath caught in her throat, so that when he said, "Let's get out of here. Now. I want to take you to bed," she could only nod her acquiescence.

Without discussing it, they went to the house—*her* house, in fact, but she understood why he headed there. Once it had been theirs.

It was all very familiar, except that *she* unlocked the front door. Without speaking of it, they went all the way up the two flights to the master bedroom. As soon as they were inside the room, he turned to her and took her in his arms, bending his head to kiss her avidly. He held her almost too tightly, and she felt she couldn't breathe; yet she did not want to pull away from him, did not want to break the mood.

Without a word, he began to undress her. There was a tiny jolt of surprise—he'd never, ever, done that when they were younger—and then a surge of excitement such as she could not recall ever having felt with him before. He stripped off her blouse and nearly ripped off the bra, kissing her neck and shoulders, his breathing ragged, then sucking at her nipples so hard it hurt.

She could feel herself getting wet. He was back, he was back, he was really back. Excitement swept over her. She pushed at him, now eager to feel his naked body crushed against her, to feel him, hard and hot, inside her. "Get undressed, Ade. Hurry!"

He pulled his clothes off, leaving them in a heap and embraced her. The feel of his skin was so shocking and familiar and lovely. His erection was a rod against her belly, and his mouth was like an oven. She couldn't remember feeling this way before . . . he was so much bigger then she recalled, so much more muscular, so much more eager.

Now he pulled them both over to the bed, and they fell on it, already entwined, their hands all over each other. "Ade," she whispered, "Ade." His answer was to kiss her more deeply, to run his hands all over her naked body, then pull her tight into him in a kind of frenzy. His heavy breathing and her moans of pleasure were the only sounds in the room.

He climbed onto her, and her thighs parted for him. "Oh, yes," she moaned. "Yes, yes, yes." And when he thrust into her, she cried aloud, her hips rising to meet his.

He was wonderful, constantly moving, moving up on her, up, up, rubbing up against her most sensitive places, and her excitement climbed and climbed and climbed. She could hear herself whimpering, could feel herself clutching at his back, throwing her loins up into his. He was better than he had ever been. She was frantic to reach her orgasm; it was right there, right there, right on the edge, but she couldn't. She was, she realized suddenly, not totally engaged in this lovemaking. She had her very own Adrian back again, and she was untouched by it. Her body was responsive, but her mind was somehow at a distance. And that hard little kernel of anger, the rage she'd so carefully kept tucked away in her head, the fury at his rejection, was all gone, suddenly. It was not there anymore. In its place was a gloating little crystal of triumph. I could have him back if I wanted him, she thought as her body moved automatically with his; but I don't want him! He can pump away in me for the next two weeks, and I'll never come. He can't make me. And he can talk till he's blue in the face, and I'll never come back to him. He can't make me.

His hands reached under her and cupped around her buttocks, bringing her in as close to him as he could and she thought, Now he's going to come. And a moment later, he did, pounding at her, sweat pouring, then collapsing over her. And all the time, she realized, he had not made a single sound. His lovemaking had been silent from beginning to end. Now she remembered. Of course, it always had been. Not for them the little words of love and affection; not for them the cries of delight; not for them the moans of passion. She'd never have to settle for that silence again. She was finished with him; it was over.

Ellie lay under him, her arms still holding him, and felt herself move away emotionally. Tears leaked out of her eyes and rolled down her cheeks. He must have felt them, against his own cheek, because then he stirred and nuzzled at her neck and murmured in her ear, "I know, I know. It was super, wasn't it? The best it's ever been." And then he rolled off her, turning his back on her, reaching his arm back to pull her close into him, spoon fashion. It was the way they had always fallen asleep together when they were married, she curled tightly around him, his legs scissored around hers. Dammit, the man intended to stay the night! Again, without so much as asking her if it was all right! Suddenly furious, she thought, He wrote the whole script, and I'm expected, as usual, to guess what my part is and what I'm supposed to do next. Well, forget that!

She pulled herself away from him and shook his shoulders angrily. "Adrian! Adrian! Wake up!"

"In the morning," he mumbled. The bastard, he was already nearly asleep. All these years apart, and he thought he could just come back one fine Tuesday night and it was going to be business as usual. The *stupid* bastard!

"No, Adrian! Not in the morning. You'd better go now."

That got him. With a grunt, he heaved himself over to face her, reaching out to her. "What do you mean?"

She backed off as subtly as she could, edging herself to her side of the bed. "I have such a big day tomorrow . . . I'm going to have to get up terribly early and shower and wash my hair and . . ." She listened to herself with interest as she babbled on, piling detail upon detail, hoping he wouldn't notice it was all a pack of lies. He was trying to argue with her— She knew Adrian Winter; she knew it wasn't that he needed to be with her so desperately but that once he came, he was overwhelmed with the need to sleep. He just didn't want to be bothered leaving right now. "And anyway," she said briskly, swinging her legs over the side of the bed and getting up as if his leave-taking were already a foregone conclusion. "And anyway, Adrian, I wouldn't want anyone to see you leaving here. Remember, you're a married man." And she smiled in the semidarkness.

"I don't feel married, not to Leslie," he said stubbornly. "I feel that here is where I belong."

To think she'd spent all those months and months, all those *years*, dreaming of this very moment, of those very words. And now that it was really happening, all she wanted was for him to get his clothes on, go home, and get the hell away from her. She was in no mood to be backed into a corner, to have to make a commitment she was longer sure she wanted.

His sexual technique had improved so much—for a fleeting moment, she toyed with the idea of sleeping with him again just to see if he could turn her on, perhaps on another night. Perhaps, she thought, she had been expecting too much from him, too much from the whole evening, and was doomed to disappointment. In any case, she did not want to deal with any of it right now; least of all, with his presence all night in her bed. "Look," she burbled as she handed him his clothes and he put them on obediently, "this is really the best idea, darling. Think: Leslie might call you from Norfolk."

Pretty soon she was ushering him out the front door and closing it softly but firmly behind him. She leaned against it, suddenly weary, as if she'd done hard physical labor; and very, very softly, just in case he had waited there outside for her to change her mind, turned the locks, all three of them.

Now she was ready for sleep. Her eyes felt very heavy, and she suddenly realized that living out your favorite fantasy took a lot out of you. Especially when it had a surprise ending. Gazing at her reflection in the dresser mirror, she was shocked at the face staring back at her. It was smooth and young looking and glowing with satisfaction. So she smiled at it and said aloud, "Well, it was a good fantasy while it lasted."

At least now the dream was over, and she could get on with her life. No more mooning over her lost love and thinking how wonderful it would all be if only he would come back. "I do not love him anymore," she told her image. "I really don't. It's really over." And her reflection smiled back at her.

Chapter 27

NEAR THE BACK entrance to Cadman Memorial, there was a line of partially enclosed telephone booths. Leslie looked at them and thought, No, what if someone overhears me? But then her only alternative was to go to the front of the hospital to call him; and she didn't want anyone she knew to see her. She shouldn't be here at all. Supposedly, she was shopping at A & S. She had even walked over to the department store and walked through the main floor, pretending to look at jewelry and handbags. But her mind was focused far away, on the Geriatrics floor, on David Powell. Where was he? Why hadn't he called her back? She'd been away for nearly two weeks—Oh, God, how she'd missed him! How many nights at her sister's she'd fallen asleep thinking of his arms around her, his mouth on her, his hands! Oh, God, how she'd dreamed of the day she'd return and talk to him on the phone and then fly into his arms! And now it was four days without a word from him. She knew damn well what that meant, but she refused to believe it. Refused! He couldn't! He couldn't dump her! She wasn't going to let him! Right there in the perfume section of A & S, she began to sweat, and her heart hammered painfully.

She had to see him, and she couldn't wait until Friday when she was doing her volunteer work. She had to see him *right now*.

She stood, indecisive, for a minute or two, chewing on a knuckle, and a passing saleslady stopped and said, "You okay, honey? Can I get you something?"

"No, no," Leslie said, putting on a bright smile. God, she must look awful. "I'm all right, really. I'm all right." And then she knew what she had to do; she had to get right over to the hospital and see him. Today. *Right now.*

And so here she was, and now she had to do it. Three of the booths were in use: two well-dressed men with their sample cases by their feet and a woman swathed in a fox stole who murmured in French into the mouthpiece, her head ducked down. That's what she'd do, Leslie decided. Turn her back and duck her head.

She knew the Geriatrics number by heart, but she made two mistakes while dialing, her hand was so slippery. She had to try three times before she got it right.

"Geriatrics." She even recognized the nurse who answered, so she disguised her voice.

"Mr. Powell, please."

"David!"

"Right."

"Let me see . . . I saw him just a minute ago. He might have taken a patient downstairs to PT. Let me check . . ." There was the clack of the phone being put down and then nothing but the background murmur of a busy hospital floor. Her heart was beating so fast she felt sick. Inside, she chanted to herself, Let him be there, let him be there, let him be there, let—

"Yes." Oh, God, it was him; it was David. At the sound of his voice, she thought she would faint. That was crazy! She was a married woman, the wife of a doctor in this hospital, and this was crazy. But oh, God, how she needed him!

"David," she croaked.

"Hello! Who is it? Hello?"

She fought to bring her voice under control. "David. It's me."

"Hi, there." His own voice was flat and expressionless. "What can I do for you?"

What could he do for her? Her eyes filled. It really was the end . . . but it couldn't be. "I've missed you," she said in her best flirtatious voice. "I wanted to make a plan with you for Friday."

"Sorry. I can't see you on Friday. You understand." His tone became loaded with meaning. Oh, yes, she understood. She got it. He was really saying I don't want to see you on Friday.

"You mean," she said, fighting more tears, "that you don't *want* to see me."

"Come on, not over the phone. We'll talk."

"When!"

"I'm on duty now, you know. This is not a good time for a discussion."

"David, I love you! I missed you so much when I was away—"

"Please. Not now. Not over the phone."

"David!" she wailed. "Please don't do this! Please!"

"I'll have to hang up now. I'll talk to you when I see you next. Really. We'll talk. But now . . . I have to say good-bye." He didn't even give her a chance to say good-bye to him; he just hung up. He just hung up, and there she was, clutching that black receiver so tightly that her fingers felt numb. She blinked her eyes rapidly . . . She couldn't cry; she couldn't, not there. A drink; she needed a drink. No, he couldn't do it. Of course he couldn't. She could go right upstairs right now and make a scene, and then he'd be sorry. But no, no, that wasn't right. He'd hate her if she did that! It was just that he hadn't seen her for so long; he'd forgotten how terrific it was with her. Or no! He couldn't have forgotten her body. He always was running his hands over her, telling her how soft and creamy her skin was, telling her how luscious he found every curve, kissing every place on her body that curved *in* and then kissing every place on her body that curved *out* and then kissing every place on her body he'd missed . . . Oh God! She couldn't stand it if she never saw him again. He was so good to her. He could spend hours making love to her, adoring her body and saying such wonderful, warm things to her. What was she going to do if she couldn't ever see him again? Her marriage was a wreck—it had been weeks and weeks since Adrian talked to her or even looked at her; he was distant and annoyed with her all the time. She couldn't do *anything* right as far as he was concerned! Well, she could handle that . . . if she had David. But if she didn't—?

Well, it didn't bear thinking of. It wasn't going to happen. Because, on Friday, she was going to put on that soft, sexy pink cashmere sweater with the matching skirt, and she was going to take an hour over her makeup and put on Opium, and when she stood next to him and looked up at him and smiled in that way she knew he loved . . . Well, he wouldn't be able to resist. He never had.

Feeling much better, she marched out of the hospital and decided she didn't really feel like going home yet. It was one-thirty, and maybe that sick feeling she'd had before was because she hadn't eaten. She needed a treat, that's what. Yes, she'd go have a nice lunch, with a nice little carafe of wine, at the Montague Street Saloon and sit there and figure out what to do.

She picked a booth at the back of the restaurant. She wanted to be alone, and with the first icy swallow of wine, she felt herself begin to relax just a little. She had to think, but her mind was just whirling around. Should it be the pink, or maybe that new cream-colored outfit . . . David always said her skin looked and felt like heavy cream, satiny and rich. And then he would lick at her skin and grin the way he had. Oh, that smile . . . it was the smile of an angel! She took another sip and scolded herself. She had to stop thinking about being in bed with him. She was so frustrated already, after all that time in Norfolk without any, and then what did she come home to! A husband who was indifferent. She hardly ever thought about Rick anymore—her first marriage had lasted less than a year—but dammit, he'd done the exact same thing! "You're boring," he told her. She was only eighteen at the time, and she had been devastated, absolutely devastated. She'd met Rick modeling; he was a photographer and very commanding and strong. She thought he was wonderful, so masterful! But after they got married, she found out he was just bossy, and then he began to stay out later and later, more and more often . . . just like Adrian. No wonder she'd turned to David Powell. Nobody in the world would ever blame her for that. She was not going to be left all alone again! And now look what was happening. Her eyes filled, and a couple of tears actually tracked down her cheeks. She gulped at the wine and gestured at the waitress for another carafe. Now David was doing it, too. Oh, no, she couldn't bear that! So maybe not the cream, but something really sexy, like her black knit with the silver threads.

The second bottle of wine came along with her lunch: a chef's salad that looked so gigantic and smelled so strongly of garlic that she pushed it far from her. She had no appetite. Her stomach felt knotted tight, and she knew if she put even one morsel into her mouth, she'd vomit. So she drank some more and regarded the enormous salad with distaste.

It was then she realized she'd been hearing the conversation behind her for quite a while, but the words hadn't penetrated. Yet half of her mind had been saying, Listen to this, Leslie. And now she knew why, because she recognized both of those voices. Art Schuster and Del Bello, the administrator. And now one of them said, "Sandy Heller," and she was immediately alert. She knew who that was; that was the little blonde public relations lady Adrian hated.

"Keep her out of this," Del Bello said. He sounded angry and defensive.

"We *can't* keep her out of this," Art said. "She's the whole problem, can't you see that?"

"The whole problem, Art, is that you doctors—yeah, and

the nurses, too, *and* any other goddam person who considers themselve a quote health professional unquote—you people just love to consider yourselves above mere publicity . . . the same way you consider yourselves above the profit motive, which is pretty goddam funny considering how much you charge your private patients! It's awfully easy to point the finger at Sandy Heller, right? It's easy to forget that what she's done is bring in new business. No, instead you guys just keep harping on those damn pictures!''

"It's not harping, Hank. It's reality. We could get sued, dammit, if she's allowed free rein around Cadman, the way you let her. The fuss Janet Freedman's parents are making is nothing compared to what might happen if Heller keeps on going. She has no sense of proportion, dammit!''

"That's unfair!''

"I don't care what the hell it is. I'm telling you what the trustees are saying . . . you know, the people who pay your considerable salary. And they're saying that yes, Cadman's getting a lot of publicity, and no, it isn't in good taste.''

Hank Del Bello gave a bark of a laugh. "Good taste! Holy shit! A bunch of uptight WASPs who haven't changed their attitudes since the nineteenth century!''

Leslie slid down so that not even the top of her head showed above the booth's high back. Oh, this was good! She could tell Adrian all about this, and then he'd have to pay attention to her.

And then Schuster said, in a very tight voice, "Fire her.''

"Fuck you.''

"Hank. Don't be an ass. She's a millstone around your neck at this point.''

"Never.''

"You *are* an ass. Because they'll get her out, and you'll go with her.''

"That's what you think.''

"That's what I heard.''

"Look, Art, enough of your threats. Can't you see I'm not

309

impressed? Sandy Heller happens to be one helluva good newswoman, a real pro.''

"That's an apt description."

"What're are you trying to say?"

"I'm saying that everyone in the goddam hospital and half of Brooklyn Heights already knows that Sandy Heller is your whore!"

There was a strangled sound from Del Bello and then a jolt against the wooden back, and he went storming past her, his face beet red, his teeth clenched, his hands fisted. His whore! Leslie thought. *His whore!* She smiled to herself and cautiously peered around. Good. Art Schuster was still sitting there, sipping from his coffee cup, and luckily his back was turned. Swiftly, she ran to the front to pay her bill. Let David Powell be difficult. She'd take care of that Friday. In the meantime, she'd have a nice little surprise for Adrian when he got home tonight.

Chapter 28

THERE WAS SOMETHING different about the apartment when she let herself in. Leslie stopped in the foyer and listened. And then she realized what it was: Adrian's voice, coming from somewhere in the back. Adrian home already! But why? She immediately felt guilty. But that was silly; she had nothing to feel guilty about. She hadn't done anything but eat lunch in a local restaurant, and all right, a couple of glasses of wine, but that was all. She stood, irresolute, in the foyer, staring blindly at herself in the mirrored wall, wondering why she wasn't running to greet her husband. Home early for the first time in about a million years.

Well, in the first place, she'd planned it all out, walking home from the Saloon. She'd figured to hell with David Powell; she'd deal with him some other time. Was David Powell a doctor? No, he wasn't. Was he rich and powerful? No. Was he handsome and important? Not at all. The first thing she had to do, she figured, was to somehow bring Adrian around . . . make him hot for her again. As he used to be.

God, before they were married, he was so passionate! How

311

he had loved her body then! Then she wouldn't have had to dig around for pieces of information in order to make him pay attention to her. Back then she joked that she never dared walk around in front of him naked, because then they never got out of the house. How good it was back then, in the beginning. Well, they'd just have to begin again, that's all. She didn't mind making all the first moves, not to save her marriage.

Darn it, she'd had it all planned! She'd come home and take a lovely perfumed bath, and she'd put on that semitransparent jumpsuit and pile her hair on top of her head and arrange a few little curling tendrils on her neck and temples. And then she'd tell the housekeeper to go home, and she'd tuck Greggy away in his little crib, and she'd have nice frosty drinks all waiting, and when she heard his key in the lock, surprise! She'd be right there. Oh, it would have been so nice, a really good new start. And now it was spoiled!

Well, all right. Make the best of it; that was her way. She checked herself in the mirror; she looked better than she would have thought. Still . . . very, very quickly, she touched up the eye shadow and the lipstick. There. Perfect. She smiled at herself, pulled her shoulders back, and then caroled, "Hello, back there!" and started down the hall.

They were in Gregory's room, Adrian and the baby, playing on the floor together with little cars. How adorable they looked together, the big handsome man and the chubby little boy, both on their stomachs, sprawled on the rug, their heads together. To her delight, Adrian was making car sounds, like motors running and horns beeping . . . it was so unlike him to be silly and loud like that. It was a sight; it really was!

"Hi, there!" she sang out. Adrian's head came up instantly, followed a second later by Greggy's. The baby broke into a beautiful smile as soon as he saw her, and cars were forgotten as he pushed himself up on his chubby little legs and ran to her. She picked him up, hugging and kissing him, waiting for Adrian to give her at least a smile.

"After all your complaints," he said quietly. "I made a

point of coming home early so we could have a supper with Gregory, only to find you're not even home."

"I only—"

"And now here you are at last and drinking again!"

Unfair! Why was he doing this! This wasn't at all what she'd had in mind! "I just had one glass of wine, Adrian, at lunch."

"Lunch?" He consulted his watch. "You just had lunch, at four P.M.?"

"No, of course . . . that was a while ago." Lord, was it that late? She'd lost track of the time. That phone call with— that phone call had been so upsetting. "Well, but it's only four," she said, keeping her smile, keeping her cool. "We can still take Greggy out to supper, for heaven's sake!" And she nuzzled the baby, making raspberries on his neck, which always made him giggle. He was such a sweetie pie; they were so lucky.

Adrian got to his feet, brushing himself off irritably. "Now I don't feel like it. Now you and I have to talk. Very seriously."

"You can't mean you're going to make a silly old fuss just because I wasn't here when you expected! I was shopping . . . um . . . I was at A & S all day. Greggy's outgrown everything, and I need some stuff, and I thought we'd redo the bedroom—"

"Redo the bedroom! Good God, Leslie, is that all you can think of! We've got far more important things to discuss than 'redoing the bedroom.' " There was such disdain in his voice, she cringed.

"All right, Adrian, all right. We'll discuss whatever it is you think needs discussing. And then," she added, "I have something to tell *you*, too."

"For god's sake, don't be coy, Leslie."

"I'm not, Adrian! I overheard something very interesting today, something important to you! What's the matter with you, anyway? Why are you so angry?"

He turned sharply, and at last that scowl disappeared from

between his eyes. Now at least he looked *friendly*. "Something important to me? What?"

"Let me get us a drink, and then I'll tell you. Greggy, honey, don't hug so tight; it hurts. Greggy! Greggy!" In the end she had to pry his little arms loose. Sometimes he seemed not to hear her at all. When he got really into something.

Adrian's face changed again. "Did you see that? Did you notice?"

"See? Notice? What, sweetheart?"

"There's something wrong with Gregory!"

"There's nothing wrong with a little boy who doesn't want to let go of his mother. He's still just a baby!"

Adrian didn't answer her. He took in a deep breath and massaged the frown between his eyes with two fingers. "Sorry, Leslie," he said after a moment. "I'm—I don't know, tired, maybe. Tell you what. Why don't you go get us those drinks, and I'll give Greg his supper, and we can sit quietly and talk. Okay?" And then he lifted his head and looked directly at her and smiled. It was such a relief, that smile; it lifted her heart. Maybe the evening wouldn't be a total disaster, after all.

Ten minutes later, she was in the living room, her hair brushed and a nice little spray of cologne—nothing heavy or suggestive like Opium, just a little Arpege. She had a pitcher of martinis, a nice bucket of ice, two glasses, lemon twists, the works. Even a wedge of Brie and some of those lovely English crackers. Now they could have a nice cozy chat, and she'd tell him everything she'd heard—she had a wonderful memory, never forgot a single word—and he'd be proud of her and pleased that Sandy Heller was in trouble.

He came in a minute later. Of course, he never said a word about the spread she'd put out; he never did anymore. He sank into one of the deep easy chairs, accepting the drink and sipping from it. Then he said, "So tell me. What was so important that you heard today?"

She wasn't at all sure she liked his tone of voice. He sounded almost condescending, and in a way she really wanted to give him hell about it. But she couldn't do that, not if she was going to start to fix up their marriage. She was going to have to tread very carefully, for a while, anyway. So she smiled at him and said, "I *over*heard it; that's what's so terrific about it. They had no idea I was there!"

"Who? Come on, Leslie. Stop playing games and just tell me, all right?"

Stung, she flared at him. "Well, it was your friend Art Schuster and Hank Del Bello, and they were having lunch in the Montague Street Saloon and they were arguing!"

"Oh, really . . ."

She told him what she'd heard, waiting for him to give some sign of excitement, or at least interest. He let her go through the whole thing, and then he smiled at her as if she were a child and said, "I'm sorry to spoil your surprise, but I already knew that." Her face must have fallen—it certainly felt as if it fell—because he very quickly added, "But thank you. For thinking of me."

"Well, sweetheart," she said, melting. "Why shouldn't I think of you. I always think of you. You're my lover and my husband and my very best friend." She thought he made a funny kind of face, but then he ducked his head. It could have been her imagination.

He got up and freshened his drink. "I haven't had a martini in—oh, God, I don't know how long. I'd forgotten how good they are."

He was acting so strangely. It was beginning to make her feel edgy. Something was up. Had he been fooling around on her? Oh, it couldn't be! Not her Adrian! Still, it had been so long since he'd turned to her.

He kept pacing around the room, restless. "Leslie, listen. This isn't going to be easy . . ." Oh, my God, she thought, panic all but choking her, he *has* been fooling around, and now he's going to leave me. She held her breath.

"I don't even know how to begin. So I'm just going to stay it. There's something wrong with Gregory."

It wasn't another woman! Relief flooded through her, leaving her lightheaded. He wasn't going away. He was— And then she focused on what he'd said. "Wrong? What do you mean, *wrong*? He's perfect! Everyone says so! The perfect little boy."

Harshly, he said, "Well, everyone's wrong. Look, I don't like saying this, Leslie, but you're going to have to stop fighting me. It isn't going to help . . . and Gregory needs all the help he can get from *both* of us."

Now she was really scared. "What do you *mean*? Why are you being so mysterious?"

"No mystery." He kept pacing back and forth, back and forth. "Look. I just spent two hours playing with him, Leslie, something I'm ashamed to say I haven't done in a long time. And so many of his responses lag . . ."

"What do you mean?"

"I mean that I talk to him, and half the time he ignores me. I explain something to him, and some of the time he understands, and some of the time he doesn't. And it may sound strange to you, Leslie, but he's too good. And also, he isn't talking!"

"He is! He says Mama and he says doggie and—"

He waved her down, impatient. "Leslie. Gregory is nearly three years old. Do you know how much most three-year-olds talk and can do? He's . . . I don't know how else to put this . . . *behind*."

"Are you trying to tell me my baby's retarded?" She had sprung to her feet without even thinking, spilling her drink all over her dress. "Well, he's not! He's smart!" He shook his head through everything she said, so she yelled louder. "He is! He's perfectly fine! I just had him at the pediatrician six weeks ago, and *he* didn't say a single word."

"Look, Leslie, I'm a doctor, and I was fooled. I didn't notice until I spent a lot of time with him."

"He's not retarded."

"I don't know what he is. I only know his development is not up to par. I'm not *saying* he's retarded, but I am saying let's find out what it is so we can help him."

She began to cry, standing there in the middle of her

beautiful living room. No, no. He couldn't do this to her. The one perfect thing in her life and he was taking it away from her. She hugged herself tightly, feeling herself begin to quiver, and shook her head over and over, wishing she could tune out the sound of his voice.

"Leslie. Please. Don't cry. I don't want you to cry. We *have* to find out what it is. I'm not saying any of this to hurt you. Believe me. It hurts me, too." She waited; the words were so warm, and she waited for him to come to her and take her in his arms. But he didn't. And when she opened her eyes, he was exactly where he had been when she closed them: across the room, remote, impersonal, distant, sipping at his martini.

She still didn't know what he meant. What could be wrong with Greggy? But somewhere in the back of her mind, she knew there really was something. The comments from the other mothers and the dozens of little things she'd noticed. There was a clutch of ice around her heart.

"What," she finally managed to say, "do you think we should do?"

"Take him to Ellie for workup."

"Take him to Ellie? Take him to your first wife? You can't be serious! I couldn't! I won't! I could never!"

"You must. She's the finest pediatric neurologist in the city."

"But Adrian, you can't ask me to do that. It would be so humiliating!"

"Grow up, Leslie. Gregory needs you."

"Not to take him to your first wife, he doesn't."

"Then I'll do it." And without looking at her again, he marched out.

Chapter 29

ADRIAN SHORTENED HIS stride, very aware of it; and very aware, too, of the chubby little hand that clung so confidently to his. It occurred to him, not for the first time that morning, that he'd rarely spent time alone with Gregory. There had never seemed to be the time, somehow. And now here they were, father and son, the little boy so very small, so very far down, trotting along, pointing at things that interested him, absolutely trusting. He loved trucks, and·at eight-thirty in the morning, there were plenty of them on Montague Street— delivery trucks, sanitation trucks, a boiler-cleaning service, a plumber, a van filled with fresh flowers. Gregory tugged at Adrian's hand and made revving-up noises, the heavy, loud sounds of the big vehicles.

"This way, Gregory," he said, and pulled gently at the little boy's hand. Gregory smiled up at him and said, "Da-da," and inwardly Adrian winced. Da-da; did children still use that baby expression at the age of three? He couldn't remember his daughters back then too clearly, but he was sure they didn't. His gut tightened, and he put all those unpleasant thoughts—the thoughts about what might be wrong with

Gregory, about what might have to be done, if anything could be done—put them all somewhere in the back of his head, to be dealt with later.

Eleanor would know. That's why they were on their way to see her right now. At first, he had thought Leslie might be right; it might be better to call Cowen at Long Island College Hospital, keep it totally impersonal. But hell, that was stupid. Ellie was the best.

"Adrian! Adrian! I've said hello three times!"

The voice startled him. Etta Schuster. Oh, Christ, of all the people! He'd have to stop and chat with her for a couple of minutes. "Etta, good morning. Sorry, but Greg and I have an early appointment, and we don't want to be late."

"Oh, Gregory, what a big boy you've become . . . and you have an appointment. How nice. Are you going to have fun?" She bent down to him, her face very close to his. Gregory stared at her intently but did not respond. Of course not, Adrian thought; he rarely did. "Gregory's three now," he said quickly. "He's a very big boy . . . very busy looking at all the trucks. He loves trucks."

Etta straightened up. "I remember that about my boy. They do love anything on wheels, don't they? I wonder what it is that makes little boys fall in love with wheels? Has medical science figured that one out yet, Adrian?"

She was looking quite well, Adrian thought. She seemed to have recovered quite nicely and was looking cheerful for a change. Was there something hysterical about her spritely chatter? No, she'd always been a bit of a ditherer; Art never allowed her to talk. "Oh, Adrian, of course, you already said . . . I wasn't thinking . . . if you have an appointment I shouldn't keep you . . . I'm so stupid . . ."

"I'd love to talk longer, Etta. It's always a pleasure to see a patient when she's doing so nicely . . . as you certainly are. You look wonderful." She colored with pleasure and started to apologize again. Poor Etta. "Say bye-bye, Gregory," he interrupted, and wagged their clasped hands. Gregory said,

"Bye-bye," which pleased him inordinately. So there *was* something there.

But as they crossed into the park and made their way along the shady path, the anxious knot tightened in his diaphragm. The doctor in him kept listing all the possibilities, good *and* bad, and the father in him—well, the father in him didn't want to think about it, not right now. How ecstatic he had been the night Gregory had been born. It began suddenly to pour as he was walking home from the hospital, and he just lifted his head to it, welcoming it, laughing aloud. He had a son, a son! And images ran through his head: throwing a ball with his son, visiting a museum with his son, taking his son to college. Hell, if the kid took after him, he might even go to medical school! He might end up being a colleague! And now . . . But no. He'd promised himself not to think about it, not to conjecture too much. He'd wait for the expert opinion: he'd just wait to see what Ellie had to say.

The clinic door was unlocked, and she was waiting for them in her office. She came right out to greet Gregory, hunkering down so their eyes were on the same level, looking intently at him, smiling. "Good morning, Gregory," she said, holding her hand out. Gregory didn't answer, but he shook her hand, and then, when Ellie had straightened up, saying, "Let's start in my office," and held out her hand, Gregory took it without question and went with her. She *was* good; he'd forgotten what a nice touch she had with kids. Not one of these new-style pediatricians, all business and tests but no heart.

She spoke slowly and carefully with Greg. Was it more slowly and more carefully than with any three-year-old? He couldn't remember. Dammit, he couldn't remember anything about small children! It wasn't his business to know! But it made him feel so . . . helpless, in a way.

She had an assortment of different kinds of toys and puzzles already out, waiting for Greg. She had him walk to her, and she watched him and said, "Good. Good," gesturing to him to keep coming toward her. Then she said, "Will you throw the ball to me?" and he took it from her, looking at her

in a perplexed way until she held out her hands and said,
"Throw it! Throw it!" Then he grinned and tossed it to her,
not quite hard enough to reach her. She put her hand on his
arm as she bent to retrieve the ball and said, "Good. Good,
Greg." And Adrian realized that he was sitting on the edge of
his chair, teeth clenched, hating that puzzled look on his
son's face, the look that said, "I don't understand."

"Ellie," he said suddenly, "I think I'm in the way here."

She turned to him and smiled in a way he had never seen,
and then he realized that it was her professional manner. He'd
never been on the receiving end, and he didn't like it. He
wanted her to look at him the way she always had. Smoothly,
she said, "Perhaps you'd like to go get a cup of coffee while
Greg and I finish up."

"Yes, yes. I have a few phone calls to make," he lied.

"That's fine," Ellie said in that impersonal tone. "Greg
and I will have a good time." She leaned forward to face
Greg. "Daddy will be back soon, Greg. Will you stay here
and play with me?"

Gregory beamed at her and turned to Adrian. "Bye-bye,"
he said and waved; Adrian left quickly. It was like a reprieve.
He couldn't bear to watch any more. He put the whole thing
right out of his mind and strode quickly to the elevator. His
desk was piled high, and he could use a few free minutes to
deal with some of it.

In fact, he lost track of time, and it was nearly an hour
before he looked at his watch again. He ran back down to the
first floor, using the stairs, and hurried through the clinic
door, apologizing as he came.

Gregory was sitting on the floor, completely engrossed in
building a highway system of brightly colored blocks and
making the loud truck and horn noises he was so fond of.
Ellie's head was bent over her paper work, and she wrote
busily. Adrian stopped talking and looked carefully at her.
Was she frowning? Did she look saddened? And then she
looked up. "Oh, there you are," she said mildly. "Take a
seat."

He did so, and then—he couldn't help himself: it just came busting out—he said, *"That's* what I mean! I've been gone for almost an hour, I come back in, and he doesn't even acknowledge my presence! A normal child would—" She was talking over his annoyed words, and he stopped.

"I said, 'Greg didn't look up when you came in because he didn't hear you.' "

"What? What do you mean exactly, Eleanor."

She smiled a little. "When you call me Eleanor, I know you're serious. I'm saying, Ade, that Gregory has a hearing deficit. No . . ." She held up a hand. "I don't know why; I don't even know exactly how profound it might be. But that's what it is. He's not retarded."

"I never said he was!"

"Come on, Ade. I've known you a long long time. You thought he was retarded, or you wouldn't have brought him to me."

"Maybe you're right. So . . . he's deaf? That's all it is?"

Gently, she said, "That's not a small matter, Ade."

"I know, I know. I'm aware of that. But frankly, Ellie, I was more than a little concerned."

"Scared, you mean."

He gave her a sharp look. "Okay. Scared. Yes, I guess I was. At least he's intelligent—he *is* intelligent, isn't he?"

Now she really smiled. "Yes, he seems very intelligent, Adrian. After all, he's taught himself how to read lips, and he's only three. That's pretty bright, I'd say."

"Then my next step is Otolaryngology—right to Spivak and his audiologist—and find out how bad it is and what we have to do. Do you think he hears anything, Ellie? He *talks* . . . a little."

"Yes, he hears some sounds. He imitates traffic, for instance. But . . . it's not my specialty. You're right; Spivak will handle it very expertly." She placed her hands on the desk and got to her feet. "You have no idea, Ade, how happy it makes me when I don't have to tell parents the dreaded news.

Gregory will be able to go to school and learn and live a normal life . . . do just about anything anyone else can do."

"Just about anything . . ." Adrian repeated.

Then Gregory looked up and saw him, and a dazzling smile lit up his face. "Da-da!" he crowed. Adrian's heart flooded. His son, his son! He reached down and picked Gregory up and held him close. "Come on, son," he said, "Let's go get you fixed up."

Chapter 30

W*HEN SHE WOKE* up from her noontime nap—the bedside clock said 1:07—Corinne found herself having a contraction. She breathed in deeply, tried to relax, and at the same time tried to remember what Dr. Winter had told her about Braxton-Hicks contractions. With Kelly, she used to have one Braxton-Hicks, and then it would go away. And she'd had them that way for months; it didn't have to mean anything.

And then the next one came, and it was 1:22, and that worried her. She prayed a little and then decided to ignore it and get up and start Kelly's snack. And fourteen minutes later, there came another one, and she leaned against the kitchen counter, breaking into a sweat.

She couldn't ignore it anymore. Sweet Jesus, let it not be real contractions. Please, Jesus, it's too soon. She dragged herself into the bedroom on leaden feet, praying very hard, and sat herself on the edge of the bed to dial Dr. Winter at the hospital.

These weren't his regular office hours. She swallowed, waiting for him to pick up, her heart hammering away in her chest like a drum. And when she heard his kind deep voice, the tears sprang to her eyes. "Oh, Dr. Winter, I've had three strong contractions!"

"Calm down now, Corinne. How far apart were they?"

"Fifteen minutes . . . and, Dr. Winter, I don't think they're Braxton-Hicks, either!" She tried to keep her voice from shaking, but the more she sat there and talked about it, the more frightened she became. It was much too early!

"Now Corinne," Dr. Winter said, and she clutched the phone as if it were his hand, listening intently to every word. "Stay calm. Don't worry. We don't know what it is. Do you have someone who can stay with Kelly?"

"Yes. Sister Rebecca."

"Good." His voice was like soothing hands, smoothing away her fears, pushing them down out of the way. "Now here's what I'd like you to do, Corinne. I'd like you to call Sister Rebecca and ask her to come in . . ."

"Right now?"

"I think that would be the best idea. I'm here in my office for the rest of the afternoon; you might as well come in right now, and we'll see what's going on with you. If you can get her, your friend, then just come on in. I'll wait for you. If for some reason you can't reach her, call me right back. I'll find Bobby and send him home. You got that?"

"Yes, Dr. Winter. I'll call Sister Rebecca and come right in, and if she's not home, I'll call you back."

"Call yourself a taxi, Corinne."

"I can walk."

"I know you can walk, and probably it would be just fine. But indulge me, would you? I'd just like to make absolutely sure." Oh, he was so wonderful, so understanding, so caring. He was the best doctor a woman could have!

Sister Rebecca was there, and God bless her, she was at the door almost as soon as Corinne had hung up. "Don't you worry about a thing, sister," she said. She even called the car service, and they wouldn't have anyone available for another hour. By this time, she'd had another contraction, and there was a heavy feeling in her heart that something was going wrong. Please, dear Jesus, don't let me lose this baby, not after all this time carrying it . . . not after all the trouble I've had with Bobby over it.

She looked out the window at Cadman Park far below. It was a cool day but brilliant with March sunshine, and a few of the trees were beginning to get that pale green haze over them. From her window she could almost see the hospital. Wasn't it silly for her to wait so long for a car when in about ten minutes she could walk across the park and be in Dr. Winter's office.

So she put on Bobby's down jacket—it was about the only thing that would zip up over her belly—and took the elevator down and walked, very slowly and very carefully, across the narrow park, breathing deeply the crisp fresh air and the damp smell of the thawing earth. She prayed all the time . . . she always felt that her prayers went winging their way to Jesus so much faster outdoors, without walls between. God would watch over her and take care of them both, both her and this dear little unborn child. She knew it.

Where the hell was Bobby? Adrian hung up his telephone and frowned at the opposite wall. They'd been paging him steadily ever since Corinne called. The minute he'd stopped talking with her, Adrian instantly dialed 6 and then Bobby's beeper code. That was fifteen minutes ago—and he still hadn't called in. And that was impossible; it shouldn't take more than a minute or two . . . five minutes at the most! Even if he was dealing with an emergency, he would have asked someone else to answer the page and find out what was up. Adrian made a face and chided himself for having morbid thoughts. No, Bobby was *not* lying somewhere in the street, hit by a truck. He had *not* been attacked in the men's room by a murderous mugger. And he was *not* in the subbasement, tied to a chair.

Nevertheless, he dialed Security and spoke to Mike Cohn, the chief, feeling rather foolish. But Mike found nobody's fears too morbid to be true. "Listen, Dr. Winter, the way it is in the city these days, you can't be too careful. You know what I mean? I'll send two of my best to look around, see if there's anything, and I'll get back to you."

Now that he'd handed over the problem, Adrian felt a bit better. But dammit, he was concerned. Bobby was too responsible to just disappear when he was supposed to be on duty. And hell, Weinstein said he'd seen him right around noon, wolfing a hero sandwich in the residents' room. So he ought to be right on the floor somewhere. His thought had been that Bobby might have fallen asleep on one of the cots in the residents' room, but that was stupid, because every young doctor learned to sleep so lightly that a mosquito walking on the wall would awaken him. And he wasn't anywhere in the cafeteria. Well, that was a stupid thought, too, because Weinstein had seen him eating. The whole thing was a mystery because he had a D & C scheduled in half an hour.

He'd turn up, he'd turn up any minute, and they'd have a good laugh about it. But he knew what kind of pressure Bobby had been under these past weeks. A pregnant at-risk wife, a troubled marriage, major career decisions looming in the near future, not to mention a full-time, heavy workload. Just one of those things could drive most men up a wall. Hell, he wouldn't be the first last-year resident to crack under the strain. And by God, now that he thought about it, Bobby had been looking extremely stressed and worn lately.

Then Corinne arrived, and he became even more concerned when he saw her. She was gray and sweating, biting her lips nervously and obviously in distress. He examined her deftly as his mind worked over his worries about Bobby. She was in labor, all right, and it was only the end of the second trimester. Not good. Gently, he said, "Corinne, I'm going to check you in."

She burst into tears. "Lord Jesus, please save my baby," she said. "Oh, Dr. Winter, I was afraid of this. Can't we stop it? Can't we stop my baby from being born too soon?"

He put his hand on her shoulder and said, "We'll do our best for both you and the baby. I promise you."

She gave him a watery smile, and he squeezed her shoulder, saying, "Good girl." Corinne might be a bit fanatic, but she was a damn good patient. Now if only Bobby would get back from wherever the hell he had gotten himself. And where the hell *was* he?

Bobby was curled around the soft, fleshy warmth of Rita Schneider's back, his arms tightly around her, each hand cradling a heavy breast, his lips buried in her hair. He groaned with pleasure and snuggled in closer, enjoying the feel of his penis as it relaxed and slipped slowly out of her. He was still breathing hard, and so was she. God, she was a hot one. He'd almost forgotten, the past weeks. He hadn't seen her for a while. She'd gone on vacation to the Bahamas for a couple of weeks, and he had just busied himself fucking everything he could get his hands on . . . or, rather, his cock into. He'd started with that foxy nurse Yvonne, and that had felt so damn good that he decided he wasn't going to stop until he'd gotten it on with as many different women as he could. And it had proved so easy! Shit, if he'd known that when he was a medical student, he'd never have even thought about marrying Corinne.

After Yvonne, there'd been Shirley, the first-year medical student who'd been making eyes at him in the cafeteria for months. And after Shirley, the girl he picked up in a local bar, whose name he never even asked. They'd flirted, and he bought her a drink, and then she said, "Would you like to come home with me and see my etchings?"

He said, "You're on," and she took him to a nice apartment in Cobble Hill—there was very nice artwork on the walls, he vaguely remembered—and took his hand and led him straight back to her bedroom and did everything she could to make him happy. What a night! And then there had been the married woman in the laundry room in his building; between the wash cycle and the spin cycle, she'd given him a blow job he'd never forget; he thought his head would come off that time. And then—but never mind, he thought now, idly caressing Rita's soft, creamy-smooth belly and edging his fingers into the crisp pubic hair; never mind what happened yesterday or last week or even five minutes ago. Now was now, and now was the only time that mattered. He was with Rita, and Rita was warm and wet, always ready for him, always eager, always orgasmic. Funny how many women weren't. Oh, they'd have a good time and writhe and moan and tell him how big it was, how good it felt. But then most of the time they didn't come. They'd pretend or tell him it didn't matter, but there was nothing like the feeling of that tight pulsation that told you you'd hit it, you'd gotten to her. Rita was so beautifully responsive; he loved it. He loved the way she glowed when she got turned on. Her skin got pink, all over her body, not just her face, and her eyes fairly sparkled.

Just thinking about it got him hard again, and he wriggled up against her in signal. She wriggled her ass back, and he turned her around to face him, pulling her close and kissing her hard with a lot of tongue. She was right with him, as always, opening her legs and putting herself into position. He got onto his knees and plunged into her. He was rigidly almost painfully erect. All his hardons lately were like this, so stiff that they hurt, just like when he was a teenager and everything made him hard . . . from Miss America to a marching band. Compelling. Demanding immediate relief. He pushed into Rita, loving the feel of her soft, moist flesh closing around him, holding him snug, pressing on him, squeezing so gently.

Ah, he loved it; he loved it. Fucking was good, fucking was wonderful. Goddam Corinne for tricking him into marriage with a sexy act and then turning herself off. Damn her, anyway, for taking all the pleasure out of it. She was his wife, for Christ's sake, and she had no right to turn the joy of this into a dirty, forbidden thing. He'd had enough of that as a kid. Everything was forbidden, everything that was fun. The main thing he'd learned from his father was that the meaning of life was to produce, to achieve, to accomplish.

You weren't supposed to play, and you certainly couldn't waste time or energy. Well, he'd done everything he was supposed to. He'd been Phi Beta Kappa at Yale, tops at Downstate Medical, and he knew he was Adrian's favorite and probably due for a really fine job at the hospital of his choice. Yes, he'd played by all the rules, and where did it get him? Trapped by Corinne and stuck in a meaningless marriage. Oh, shit, he was so goddam sick and tired of his whole life! Even the hospital, even the sanctified practice of medicine! The only way he found an escape lately was this way: with a woman, any woman, fucking her brains out. And his, too.

This way was oblivion, total and complete, all sensation, all feeling, no thought at all. He pushed in and out of Rita Schneider's soft flesh, in and out and in and out, feeling the orgasm building, building. And somewhere in the far recesses of his mind, he realized that over in the corner of Rita's bedroom, in the inside breast pocket of his jacket, his beeper was insistently calling. To hell with it. He'd been a good boy his whole life long, and he deserved this. Whatever they wanted him for could wait.

Chapter 31

"H*E'S GOT THE* whole world in his hands . . ." The melody kept running through her head, and the words, the calming words. She was in His hands, she and the babe. It hurt, just a little, because the baby was ready to be born, but she wouldn't cry out, not she. She was brave. She opened her eyes wide and smiled at the friendly brown upside-down face of the orderly who was pushing her down the hall, and he said, "There you go, mama," in a kind voice. Her head was spinning a little, and she had to concentrate on breathing deep every time her belly tightened, as the baby pushed more and more into the world. Where was Bobby? she wondered, and then she drifted off and found herself humming to herself "He's got the little-bitty babies in His hands."

Another face, framed by a nurse's cap, appeared next to the orderly, and a female voice said, "Hey, there, Doug, how's it goin'?" in that flirtatious tone so many young girls seemed to use these days.

He laughed and said, "Couldn't be better, Rosalie. I had me a weekend you wouldn't believe . . . although I'm still

331

hopin' you're gonna let me get close to you one of these days." And he laughed hugely.

"Oh, *you*!" the nurse giggled, and then her face disappeared from the world.

Where was Bobby? He was supposed to be here. He was her husband, and he was supposed to be here. But he was a doctor, too. Probably on duty in the OR—something like that. Well, she'd have a fine surprise for him in a little while. And there was another contraction, real hard this time, and as from a distance she heard herself grunt, and the nurse's face appeared again and said, "Now, honey, don't push yet," but that was stupid because *she* wasn't pushing. The baby was doing it. She could no more stop it—and then she felt a twinge of fear because vaguely she could remember that this baby wasn't supposed to be born yet. But this was labor, she remembered from the last time. This baby was not going to wait very much longer, and she started to pray. There was joy in her heart—another baby; she loved babies!—and she just knew this was a boy, a son for Bobby, and Bobby would love her again, and it would be like it used to be when they were happy. And then there was Dr. Winter's face bending over her, and it surprised her a little that he already had his mask on, and he put his hand on her cheek and said, "Here we go, Corinne" and then she knew she was in the delivery room because of the sudden bright light that made her close her eyes. She heard herself grunt again, a great loud noise, and she heard Dr. Winter say, "Miss Jackson, Now." And then there was a blur of pain, and she concentrated on the sweet face of Jesus, and they all talked a lot, and then she felt the baby, her baby, as it pushed out into the world . . . Hello, baby, she thought, and then noticed how quiet it was suddenly, and then there was a little prick on her arm and then nothing.

The Neonatal Intensive Care Unit at first glance might easily have been the playroom of a very well equipped nursery school. The walls were striped in bright primary colors, oversized teddy bears and other toys proliferated, and it was full of the sounds of music boxes and cheery voices. And then you noticed the *bleeps* and *blips* of life-support machinery that underlay all the other sounds. And then you noticed the monitors and the banks of businesslike black boxes that controlled all of that. And then you noticed the tiny, unbelievably tiny, little infants, each one in its own clear plastic box, like so many dolls in a toy store. These babies did not squirm and kick but lay very still, very quiet, tubes and wires connecting them to those black boxes.

Four white-coated figures were gathered around one of the boxes, looking down at the frail, wizened body lying on its side in a blue-and-white-checked cotton blanket.

"Did you say 860 grams?" The voice belonged to Marvin Blackman, the pediatric neurosurgeon.

"No," Adrian said, "880. Just barely made it."

Blackman sighed and said, "I can do the shunt tomorrow morning, and from the looks of it, I'd better."

Ellie said, "Isn't he a bit too small?"

"Look, Ellie, you always take a chance with a premie this size, but look at that head. You know as well as I that if I don't get the fluid out of there right away, you might as well kiss his mind good-bye. Is the mother in any shape to sign the consent form?"

Adrian frowned. "I just told her. She went into shock, and we had to put her out. But I think she understood."

"She wanted this baby so badly," Ellie put in. "I think she'll do anything to save his life."

The fourth doctor, ashen under her mask, said in an incredulous tone, "What kind of life are you saving here?"

Adrian said harshly, "We can't think about that right now. Right now our job is to keep this life going."

"But my God, look at him. Will he ever feel anything from the waist down? And look at his legs!"

Ellie said, "Have you ever seen spina bifida this severe before, Doctor Poole?"

"Never."

"Well, this is a typical L-4, and they sometimes do quite

well in spite of what looks like a considerable handicap." Her voice was very even and totally without emotion.

"But Dr. Winter!" The young resident was visibly upset, and her voice quivered. "This neonate also has a bowel obstruction. *That's* going to need surgery, too, and we can't even think about it until the infant gains more weight. And—"

"What would you have us do, Dr. Poole," Adrian interrupted. "Turn our backs? Let him die?"

"What kind of life could this child have, Dr. Winter? That's all I'm saying!"

"And I'm reminding you, Dr. Poole, that every life is of value and doctors cannot—" There was a flurry of voices out near the scrub sink, and then the main door to the unit banged open, and Bobby Truman came racing in, his face set in a grimace of pain. He pushed through them, his breathing heavy and harsh, and looked down on his son. His hands went out, gripping the sides of the bassinet tightly, his eyes closed, and he swayed a little. Ellie's hand immediately reached for him, to steady him, but he shook it off.

"Goddam her!" he rasped. "I *told* her this would happen. I told her! But would she listen? Oh, no, Jesus was gonna take care of everything. Jesus was gonna make it all right. Well, Jesus, you fucked up this time!"

Young Dr. Poole sucked her breath in sharply; but when Adrian spoke, his tone was calm; it was as if Bobby had never said anything. "I can't tell you how sorry I am, Bobby. Did anyone upstairs let you know about . . . how serious this is?"

"Yes. But goddam it, seeing is different than hearing. Oh, Christ, yes, is it ever!" He laughed, and two of the nurses turned to see what was happening.

"Easy, Dr. Truman. I realize how upset you must be . . ."

Bobby's head came up and around to face Adrian with a jerk. "Oh, really? You know how upset I am? You have a kid like this?"

Ellie grabbed his arm. "Bobby! Please. Let's go out into the hall." Again he shook her off. "No, goddam it, I'm not going to be hustled off somewhere until I behave. Oh, no. I'm not going to be the good little pet black doctor, not this time."

"Bobby! That's not fair! We're your friends! We're trying to help."

He drew in a deep breath. "I'm sorry, Ellie. I know you are. But this is—" And he ducked his head, his voice breaking. "I told her," he said in a near whisper. "But no, she had to get pregnant. She put herself in the Lord's hands instead of taking the pill, and this—this!—this is what she's done to us!" Again, he sucked in breath. Then he turned to the resident and said, "You're Beverly Poole, aren't you? You on duty here this month?"

"Yes."

"You ever seen anything like this before?" He didn't wait for her answer, but charged ahead. "Well, I'm the father of this . . . this . . . this *mistake*, and I'm here to tell you no heroic measures for this infant. In fact, Dr. Poole, no measures at all. Is that understood?"

"Hold on!" Adrian said quietly. "Dr. Truman, I'd like to remind you that as the parent you are emotionally involved and therefore cannot make objective medical decisions in this case."

Bobby's own voice became equally cool and measured. "Dr. Winter, I'd like to remind *you* that we are always seeking informed consent from our patients. You don't·get many parents as informed as I am—you may never get one again—and I'm telling you, *no consent*. No consent, Dr. Winter. I will not consent to anything being done to this infant."

The two men glared at each other, and Ellie quickly put in, "Bobby. Please. You're very informed; we all know that. But right now your emotions are obscuring your judgment. You need time—"

"No, I don't. I don't need any time at all." Once again, Bobby whirled to face Dr. Poole. "There will be no surgery on this baby," he said.

335

Now Dr. Blackman cleared his throat and looked worried, although his voice was perfectly mild. "Dr. Truman, I know what you're thinking, and—"

"You don't know what I'm thinking, Doctor. Twenty years ago—ten years ago, maybe—what happened to a spina bifida case with the opening at about the fourth lumbar? Isn't that what this is?"

Ellie nodded and said, "They died, Bobby. That's what you're getting at, isn't it?"

"That's right. They died. *As they should*, as far as I'm concerned!"

Adrian said angrily, "A physician never thinks that way. A physician's job is to prolong life, period."

"Not if it means he's playing God! None of us can afford that luxury!"

Dr. Blackman raised a restraining hand. "Gentlemen. Gentlemen. Dr. Truman. The chances are—you're right—that if we withhold treatment from this infant, he will not survive."

"That's all I ask!" Bobby said. "Just let nature take its course."

"Ah, but we can't predict nature's course, Dr. Truman. When I was a resident in Oklahoma, we had a case very much like this one, and the decision was made to do nothing. We did not put in the shunt. We—excuse me, Dr. Winter—we waited for this infant to die. But nature fooled us. The child lived, contrary to all expectation. And then, doctors, we had to live with the thought that had we done something, had we drained the fluid from the brain, at least the parents would have had more than a living vegetable to take home and care for."

There was a moment of silence. Bobby involuntarily turned to look at the baby again, and then he said, "Well, I'm going to take that chance."

"No, you're not. Because we are going to do our best to salvage this baby."

"The hell you are! I'm the father!"

"There's a mother of this child, too. Or had you forgotten?

You certainly managed to forget you were on duty today! Where the hell were you, anyway?''

"None of your business!''

Quickly, Ellie said, "Dr. Truman, Dr. Winter. You're both forgetting yourselves. We are in the neonatal nursery, to discuss this case.''

Adrian's lips were tight, and a little muscle on the side of his jaw jumped. "Quite right, Eleanor. Let's try to talk objectively.'' With an obvious effort, he calmed himself and turned to Bobby to say, "Bobby, please. We haven't time to waste. The shunt should be done, according to Dr. Blackman here, within twenty-four hours. Corinne is hysterical, and we need your consent. But"—and he held up his hand—"I can have a court order here for surgery within two hours. I don't want to do that, but—''

Bobby's eyes narrowed, and his hands balled into fists. "The hell you don't want to! You like nothing better than playing God!''

"You're forgetting yourself, Dr. Truman.''

"That's right, Dr. Winter. Up on your high horse. I have dared to disagree with the great white master. And now, I guess, I'm supposed to shuffle off like Stepin Fetchit. Yowza, yowza, yowza!''

"Bobby!'' Ellie's voice was rigid with shock.

"And don't you condescend to me, either! I've *had* it with running my life by how the white folks judge me!'' And turning on his heel, he stormed out.

There was a minute or two of total silence from the four doctors; they could not look at each other. Finally, Blackman cleared his throat and ventured, "Uh . . . what do you suppose that was all about?''

"Well, my God,'' Dr. Poole said. "How would *you* feel if your baby were born like this?''

"I know Bobby,'' Adrian said. "Yes, he's stricken over this. But there's more. That young man is in trouble, and he knows it. He went AWOL today . . .''

337

"Don't talk about it. Not here! Not now!"

"Yes, here and yes, now. He disappeared for several hours today—dammit, he was on duty, and he just left the hospital without a word to anyone. Missed a D & C he had scheduled. Luckily I was able to get Gold to take it. What I can't understand is why he didn't even get someone to cover *for* him . . . It's crazy."

"Maybe," Ellie said, and she looked very thoughtful. "Maybe crazy and maybe not crazy."

"What do you mean?"

"I don't know," she said. "I don't know exactly. But it certainly looked like guilt and remorse to me . . ."

"Guilt and remorse! He damn well better feel some of that! But he certainly didn't act it!"

"Well," she soothed, "it's over and done with. No use getting upset—"

"Oh, really? Well, I am upset, dammit, damned upset. And he's going to hear about it." His lips tightened, and without another word he wheeled and roared off.

He was angrier, Adrian realized as he stormed down the hall after Bobby, than he had been in years. He didn't know why, exactly, but he was damned if he was going to stop and analyze his feelings. Dammit, Bobby had done the unforgivable—he had ignored his responsibilities—and he had to face the music! Dammit!

Where'd he go? He was already out of sight, and it was a helluva long corridor. Adrian quickened his step and decided to just keep going straight. For some reason, he thought, The stairs, and sure enough, when he started down, there was Bobby, a flight and a half down. "Dr. Truman!" he bellowed. His voice echoed and bounced through the stairwell.

Bobby stopped suddenly mid-flight, and his face turned up. He was scowling angrily, but he waited. Adrian ran down the steps and stopped a few above Bobby.

"I want a few words with you!"

"Look, Adrian, with all due respect, this is not the optimum moment for me to talk. Not even with you. Do you mind?''

"Yes, I mind. I'm not asking to talk . . . yet. Just listen.'' When there was no response, he went on. "You've done the worst possible thing a doctor can do . . . absolutely unforgivable! To leave the hospital, without your beeper, when you're on duty—!''

Bobby's voice rasped. "Tell me, have I ever done anything like that before? No, scratch that. Have I ever done *anything*— any little thing—that was in *any* way out of line?''

Adrian was taken aback. "Why . . . no. No. That's why—''

"That's *all*, as far as I'm concerned!''

"And what about the D & C that you forgot?''

"Did that D & C get done? Yes? Okay, then. What's the beef?''

"Responsibility is—''

"I *know* what the fuck responsibility is, Doctor. And right now I've got more responsibility than I want. Right now, in case you hadn't noticed, I have a few personal problems on my mind.'' He turned away, and for some reason that made Adrian even more irate.

"Dammit, Bobby, don't you turn your back on me!''

"Fire me!''

"That's not the point!''

"Slavery ended 125 years ago, remember?'' He started on down the stairs. "So off my back, okay?''

Adrian stood very still. His heart was pounding as if he had run up several flights of stairs, and his throat burned with gall. He could strangle that Bobby. After all these years, after all the hours of working together, after all their closeness, not only working but sharing meals and playing tennis and talking shop . . . how dare he all but spit in my face!

And then the memory came back, all of a piece, all at once. Of himself, just starting out on his own at Downstate and getting a private practice going. And there was Nate, frowning a little, looking over the young Adrian's brand-new office and very sweetly, very calmly telling him this was wrong, that wasn't quite right, the other wasn't the way he'd do it. And the young Adrian, livid, gave the old man hell, absolute hell, no holds barred. It embarrassed him still to recall any of what he had said. Standing in the empty stairway, holding on to the railing, he allowed his fury at Bobby to seep away. Apparently, history was determined to repeat itself. Now he allowed himself a small smile.

He drew in a deep breath. Couldn't waste energy on petty anger, anyway. They *all* had serious problems to deal with, and there wasn't a moment to waste.

Chapter 32

BOBBY TOOK THE stairs two at a time, flying more than walking. He had to get away from Adrian before he really lost his temper. Goddammit, the man thought he was his fucking *father!* Shit, his own father was more than enough! He had to move, had to keep moving, get going, go anywhere! His head was whirling, and the pulse was pounding double time in his throat and temples.

The baby—no! His mind rejected the image. He could not think about that baby. It was utterly impossible for him to say to himself, My baby. No! Best not to think of it as a baby at all. A mistake. Premature, already dying, unable even to breathe on its own, its swollen skull filled with fluid that pressed down on the soft little brain . . . No! He would *not* think about that infant.

Ah, shit! He had been feeling so high before. Running back to the hospital from Rita's place, he had felt that he would never be unhappy again. He had found the key to his own psyche, and now he was in control of his own life again. It was so wonderful, and so simple, really. He had run easily, lightly, his feet skimming the pavement, his thoughts floating

341

in the air. He knew what he was going to do. He was going to leave Corinne, leave that marriage. But he'd never leave his little girl, never. He'd accept that job at St. Luke's-Roosevelt, and he'd come visit her nearly every day. He'd call her on the phone. He'd be such a good daddy—better than he was now—and best of all, he'd finally be free, free, free of this crazy marriage that was weighing him down.

Corinne had been such a different person before they got married. She was so wild and free and exciting. She made him laugh, and she made him put down the books, and she made him a lover. She was so good for him, so turned on. Not anything like what she was now: grim and rigid and humorless. He got a knot in his stomach every time he turned the key in their apartment door.

It was funny to think that she had loosened him up, only to backtrack. She ended up being just like his father: uptight, demanding, so positive there was only one correct answer . . . to anything. "When you're black, you have to be twice as good to get half as far." His father spoke from experience. He was a very successful insurance agent, and he never came home before nine in the evening, because from six to nine, he liked to say, were prime hours to talk to his prospects. Bobby remembered one day—he must have been eight or nine years old—when he asked, "Daddy, why can't you come home early and throw a ball with me, like the other daddies do?"

He remembered to this day the angry scowl on his father's face. "Throwing a ball is not important in this world, Bobby. Establishing yourself is. I don't come home early because I'm working for you and your mother, to give you the best. And look, you have everything you could want or need, not just food and a roof over your head but plenty of toys; you go to a fine private school and have tennis lessons, too." He remembered his father's hand, heavy on his shoulder. "You see, Bobby, I'm giving my son the very best, and in return I expect my son to give his very best."

And Jesus, did I ever! Bobby thought, turning by the nursing station and heading back up the hallway. Honor student, valedictorian, Westinghouse science finalist, tennis team in college, president of his class. You name it and Bobby Truman could do it twice as good as the next guy. And from that moment until an hour ago, being twice as good as anyone else was the most important thing in his life.

Yes, for sixty wonderful minutes today, he'd been set free—only to find himself faced now with another set of shackles. Well, he wasn't going to be trapped again. No more. No more being the good boy for Daddy. No more being the good boy for Adrian. No more being the good boy, *period*.

Now he had a destination. He realized he hadn't even seen Corinne yet. Poor Corinne. It was bound to be tough for her. Well, he had warned her. Shit, he'd done better than that. He'd *insisted* they not have any more kids. But would she listen? No, not her, not the new Corinne, not the holier-than-thou brainwashed Corinne. Oh, no, Jesus was gonna take care of everything! The woman was deaf, dumb, and blind; you couldn't reason with her at all. And this—this was the upshot of her stubborn and intransigent, so-called Christianity: a horribly damaged child who would only suffer until he died . . . who would only make all of them suffer until he died. What use was it? What good?

Bobby punched the button for the elevator angrily. What in hell had she thought she was accomplishing? A better marriage? That was a laugh. Corinne was not living in the real world anymore. Damn it, Corinne was on another planet!

The goddam elevator never came, so he took the stairs two at a time and pushed himself out on the Ob/Gyn floor, sweaty and irritated. The nurse at the desk looked at him sadly and named the room number without being asked. "We all feel so bad—" she began, but he silenced her with an abrupt wave and strode down the hall.

As soon as he opened the door, he heard Corinne sobbing and moaning. She was carrying on about "my baby" and "Jesus" and a whole lot of other stuff. Shit, he thought. Now he was to have to deal with her hysteria, on top of everything.

And he walked in and saw not only Sister Rebecca sitting on the side of the bed, holding Corinne and praying right along with her, but the Reverend Clayton himself seated in the one easy chair, hands folded and head bent, the phony! He just knew the Rev was enjoying every minute of this; it was the stuff he thrived on: suffering and sadness and helplessness. That's when he looked good, when everyone around him was in a weakened state.

"Sister Rebecca . . . reverend . . . you can go now. I'm here." He tried to keep his voice dispassionate, but even he could hear the edge on it.

"Bobby, allow me to offer my sincere sympathy in your hour of trial," the Rev said, rising immediately from the chair and extending his hand. "This is difficult for both of you, I know, and the tabernacle—"

"Excuse me, reverend, I must talk to my wife. *Alone*." That muscle on the side of his jaw was jumping. He could not stand the sound of Corinne's caterwauling; he could not stand it!

Reverend Clayton put a hand on his shoulder and said, "You're understandably upset, my son."

"I'm not your son."

The hand was instantly removed. "Sorry."

Something in their voices caught Corinne's attention, and she raised her tear-ravaged face and wailed, "Bobby, Bobby, why won't they let me see my baby?"

"Because, goddammit"—he gritted between his teeth, hating her twisted face and her childish voice—"your precious baby is on the respirator and stuck full of tubes in the neonatal ICU, that's why. Because your baby, Corinne, has everything wrong that could possibly be wrong with a baby and still live!"

There was a gasp from Sister Rebecca and a strangled sound from the Reverend. Corinne drew in a sobbing breath and ceased weeping abruptly, as if a switch had been pulled.

"What do you mean, Bobby? What do you mean?"

"Dr. Winter told you, dammit."

"All I know's that it came before its time. I prayed and prayed, but he still wanted to get born. But I know my baby was born alive; I heard him cry."

He could feel a headache, a deep dull pain, fill his skull. He swallowed and very carefully said, "Listen to me, Corinne. That baby is a lot more than premature. I *know* Dr. Winter told you. It's just as I warned you . . . the baby has spina bifida, the worst kind. Do you understand?"

Her answer was an animal cry, a wordless howl of anguish. Sister Rebecca turned quickly to comfort her, saying, "Hold on, child; it's God way of testing you. Hold firm," and Bobby turned away. He hated the sight of all of them, unctuous, self-righteous, holier than anyone! God's way to test her! Of all the crazy shit. These people were totally off the wall! "Oh, for Christ's sake!" he exploded. "Can't you leave her alone?"

"Bobby, excuse me, but I've been with Corinne awhile. And I've had dealings with this kind of thing before, and . . . well, Corinne can't really hear you right now. She can't really deal with any of this. Apparently she went into shock when Dr. Winter told her about the baby . . . Why don't we men just step into the hall and talk?"

"I don't want to talk to you. I need to talk to my—to Corinne . . ."

As if on signal, her head swung around, and she held her arms out to him. "Bobby, I want to hold my baby! Please bring me my baby!"

Now he strode over to the bed, and he must have looked like the wrath of God, because Sister Rebecca got right up from her perch and backed off. He brought his face down close to Corinne's, resting his clenched fists on the bed. He didn't want to touch her; the more he looked at her, the madder he got. She and she alone had done this to him . . . by lying and cheating. She had tricked him into marriage, and now she had tricked him into this pregnancy, and it was all her fault!

"Your baby!" His voice was full of rage. "Let me describe your baby to you, Corinne! On his back is a pouch of skin, and in that sack is the bottom of his spine and all the nerves connected to it. There's an empty space on his lower back where his spine should be . . . Do you understand me? His legs are twisted, Corinne, and he has club feet. His hips are out of alignment, and his bowels don't function. Oh, and his head, Corinne, his head is gigantic. He's hydrocephalic. He's got water on the brain, and the veins bulge out on the great big forehead . . .!'' She whimpered at him, biting her knuckles, while the tears trickled down her cheeks from wide-open, empty eyes. He ignored it all; he was the teller of truth, unflinching, unmoving, unforgiving. "And furthermore," he went on, taking a perverse pleasure in saying whatever he wanted, without thought or care or regard for anyone's feelings, "furthermore, Corinne, your baby will never walk, no, will never talk, will never have any feelings from the waist down, will never laugh or love or have children . . . He'll never even be able to *think*, Corinne. Do you understand now what you've done?''

Corinne's mouth opened, and she let out a scream, and the Reverend walked over and put himself between Bobby and the bed. "You'll forgive me, brother, but you've gone much too far. You're not helping anything; you're just being cruel.''

"You didn't help, either, Reverend Clayton.''

"Whatever do you mean?''

"I mean that this . . . this child would never have been conceived if you and your people hadn't told Corinne to stop using birth control!''

"Now, brother, we never *told* Corinne to do any such thing. The number of children we have is a matter of individual conscience.''

"Bull*shit*, Reverend!'' Again, he felt the warm surge of fury rise in his chest and into his throat. It felt so good, so releasing. "*Individual conscience*, my ass!'' He made his voice falsetto as he mimicked: " 'Jesus will take care of everything.' 'It's against God's will to take the pill.' 'It's against God's plan to interfere with what naturally happens.' ''

His voice choked, and he stopped, breathing deeply. In a quieter voice, he continued. "Well, Reverend, I invite you . . . I invite all of you to come down to the Neonatal ICU and see for yourself what God's will and God's plan has produced! A monster!"

Total silence descended, except for the sound of his own rasping breathing.

"There are no monsters in God's eyes, Bobby . . . every little baby born is precious to Jesus."

"To Jesus, maybe, but not to himself." He leaned around the Reverend's substantial bulk and shouted, "I've already told them, Corinne. We're not signing any consent forms for surgery or any other heroic measures. We're not going to keep him alive to be a vegetable!"

"I want my baby! Don't you kill my baby!"

Bobby ignored the Reverend's baleful stare and Sister Rebecca's round, sad eyes. He was totally focused on the wretched, sobbing form on the bed. *My wife*, he thought, as a test, and felt absolutely nothing. Just as he had felt nothing for the scrawny, wrinkled, light brown, only vaguely human little form in the neonatal nursery.

"Goddammit, Corinne, it's all your fault! You got yourself pregnant. You did it! You did it to us, and I'm telling you, I'm not letting you make more of a mess out of my life! Do you hear me, Corinne?"

Reverend Clayton said, "Placing blame will do no good for anyone, Bobby. Hasn't your wife suffered enough?"

"Oh? You're feeling sorry for her now? And I thought you were joyful to see God giving her such a good test of her faith!"

"That was uncalled for!"

"Well, you just butt out, Reverend. You and your religion got me into this, and so you can take you and your religion and get the hell out of here and leave us to lead our own lives!"

The Reverend spread his arms wide and closed his eyes. "Bobby Truman," he intoned, "may the Lord forgive you

347

your unjust words. And may the Lord lead you in the right path and show you how good it will be to save the life of your child.''

"No way! Nothing will be done to save that life. We'll just leave it to God. How's that, Reverend?''

The Reverend shook his head sadly. "You're a physician, Bobby. You have pledged to save life.''

"Bobby, Bobby, please save our baby!''

"No way! *No way!*''

"Bobby Truman, we'll leave now. But we're going to pray for you. Yes, I hear the voice of Lord saying, Call a pray-in for the soul and heart of Bobby Truman, M.D.''

"Fine!'' Bobby said. "Terrific. Go back to your tabernacle and pray your little hearts out.''

Reverend Clayton smiled a grim little smile. "Oh, no, I think not, Dr. Truman. I think we'll probably gather right here in the front of Cadman Memorial, and I think we'll all fall on our knees and pray very loudly, and then we'll see how the world judges this affair!''

"Even better!'' Bobby yelled. He no longer cared if anyone on the floor heard him or not. "Go right ahead. Because you know what I say about that? I say to hell with you, to hell with your pray-in, to hell with my soul!'' And he stomped out of the room, slamming the door behind him.

The last thing he heard, muffled a bit, was Corinne keening and hollering. "Bobby! Bobby! I want my baby!''

Chapter 33

I*T WAS BITTER* cold—almost freezing in spite of the budding trees and bright new grass—and a stiff wind was making everyone huddle into their coats. Adrian walked swiftly, his head down, so that when he looked up finally, the sight of the hundreds of kneeling people on the front lawn of the hospital took him by surprise. For just a moment, he couldn't figure it out, and then he saw the familiar figure of the Reverend Ezekiel Clayton looming above the crowd. And then he noticed that the Rev was not standing there all by himself, not by a long shot. He was, in fact, speaking into a hand-held mike and posing just a bit for a phalanx of TV cameras. What now? he wondered; but he knew damn well what it was. The Truman baby. Dammit, why was Bobby being so stubborn about this. It went against all of his training; dammit, it went against the Hippocratic Oath!

He paused by the front walk, wondering how he could avoid this scene—perhaps go around the back of the hospital—and then he saw Sandy Heller, and he let out an involuntary groan. Now the well-known shit was about to hit the fan, because she was definitely heading straight for him, and right on her tail was a pack of reporters. He checked around quickly. The kneelers were praying out loud and some of them held hand-lettered signs. But what did they say? SAVE THE BABY AND SAVE A SOUL. DR. TRUMAN SAVE YOURSELF. PRAY FOR BABY TRUMAN. Oh, God, yes, just as he had feared. Well, now he knew what he was going to say.

"No comment," he shouted as the group neared him. "No comment." He ducked a bit as several cameramen circled around him, shoving cameras at him. "No comment! I mean it!"

Reporter-like, nobody paid the least bit of attention to what he was saying. Instead, a barrage of questions were fired at him. "Dr. Winter, as chief of Ob/Gyn, what do you think—" "Dr. Winter, you're codirector of the Neonatal ICU; isn't there a law against—!" "Can't you get a court order—" "Is Dr. Truman going to be allowed to stay on the staff of this hospital—" and so on. God, these people knew no bounds. And as for Sandy Heller—he glared at her—she should have been gone weeks ago. Del Bello was not doing his own cause the least bit of good by ignoring the pressure being put on him to let her go. Although, to give her credit, she was trying to get the reporters to cool it. "Gentlemen, ladies, I told you we'll hold a press conference at three. Dr. Winter is a very busy man, as I have already explained." Not that they'd listen to her . . . but then, to his surprise, they did. They backed off, muttering about deadlines, schedules, editors, and all that kind of thing, but back off they certainly did, and then Heller sidled up to him and said softly, "Now's your chance, Doctor. I can only hold them at bay just so long!" And she laughed.

He did as he was bid, marveling a bit that indeed the woman seemed to have some influence and skill in her own sphere. Maybe the trustees were being a little hasty? But no. She went out of bounds too often. Her trouble was that she didn't know where her sphere ended and medicine began. And then he was inside, with the security guard giving him a deferential "Good morning, Dr. Winter," and Sandy Heller went right out of his mind. He had to find Ellie, anyway; he'd hurried in this morning purposely to discuss certain matters with her. It was just past nine; he ought to find her in the cafeteria.

And she was there; he spotted her after a minute, sitting at a corner table, deep in conversation with Con Scofield. He got a cup of coffee and made his way to their table.

"Good morning, ladies." He put his cup on the table and sat down. "How are you doing, Con? Haven't seen you for a while."

She gave him an enigmatic smile. "I took a little vacation." She and Ellie exchanged what he could only call smirks.

"Oh, good, good. We could all use a little vacation . . . Say, Con, would you mind? I need to talk to Ellie. Alone."

"Hell, no. I was just going, anyhow." Again they exchanged looks, and she hustled herself off.

"Adrian!" Ellie looked half-amused and half-annoyed. "That was rather rude, you know."

"Rude? What are you talking about? She understood what I meant. She didn't mind!"

"You never could see that in yourself—how you assume that your interests take precedence and that the rest of us will automatically defer."

"Ellie!" He was shocked. "I don't feel that way at all."

"Never mind. It's not that important. What was it you had to talk to me about, alone?"

For a moment, he felt she was laughing at him in some kind of secret way, and he was annoyed. He almost didn't want to talk to her if she was going to have that attitude.

And then she smiled and reached out and patted his hand, and the annoyance, or whatever it was, lifted. "Did you see that circus out there?" he said. "The Rev has outdone himself this time! Praying on our front lawn! It's none of their business! It's not a religious matter at all; its purely medical."

"You're not mad at the Rev, Ade," Ellie said. "You're mad at Bobby."

"That's ridiculous."

"Oh, yes. Bobby's fighting you—for the first time, and you don't like it."

"That's not true. Bobby's a grown man, and I know it. He doesn't have to agree with *me*; that's not the issue. The issue is what it means to be a doctor."

"Don't be so pompous, Ade. The issue is not just the preservation of life; we have to think about the quality of that life. You know that. What good is it to save the life of that poor little mite if it means suffering not only for him but for all of them: Corinne, who will have to care for him day and night forever; Kelly, who needs care herself and who may get pushed aside; and Bobby. For God's sake Adrian, Bobby is more than just an M.D., you know. What kind of life will it mean for him as a person, a father, a husband?"

"I didn't realize you felt so deeply about it, Eleanor."

"Ah, and now you're mad at *me*. I'm sorry, but that's how I feel." Ellie leaned back in her chair a little and regarded him. He really was angry; he was trying hard to hide it, but she knew him too well. That little flush high on his cheekbones, the tightening of his lips . . . that was enough. Actually, she should have known better than to be so frank with him. It had never done any good in the past. "I understand why you're upset," she continued. "This is a complicated issue, and it's made even worse by the fact that the father of this child is a doctor."

"You're wrong. I'm upset because now *you're* turning against me, too . . . and it happens that right now I really need . . . your support." He paused, and his eyes fell, and he took in a breath before he went on. Then he looked at her again. "Ellie, I need your support, yes—and even more." And then he stopped and looked at her expectantly, as if waiting for a particular response.

Ellie eyed him for a minute, puzzled. "And even *more*?" she repeated. "What does that mean?"

"I've been thinking about you, Ellie . . . thinking about you a lot ever since we . . . we got together . . ."

Swiftly, she said, "Ade, I don't think this line of conversation is going to take us anywhere useful—"

He held up an imperious hand. "Ellie, I still love you, and I want us to be together again . . . Why are you shaking your head like that?"

She hadn't even realized that she was. "Please don't talk about love, Ade."

"Why not? My marriage to Leslie is over. It has been for quite a while. It was a mistake from the beginning—I realize that now—the worst mistake I've ever made in my life. But there's no reason to continue. Leslie knows that we're in trouble."

She stared at him, disbelieving. The arrogance of the man!

"Wait a minute! Do I hear you correctly? Are you telling me you're about to *leave* Leslie and your baby?"

"Leslie isn't any happier than I am. It's for the best."

"Best! How can you say that? How can you even *think* it? You've just found out that your child is deaf and will need a lot of special care and training . . . How can you leave your wife to cope with that all alone? That's—that's *heartless*!"

"You know me, Ellie: I'm not heartless. The ENT people have assured me that with a hearing aid and some speech therapy he'll do just fine in a special nursery school. He's not even *profoundly* deaf, Antonelli tells me, and my God, Ellie, I thought he was *retarded*! This is a relief!"

"Relief!" Ellie repeated like an automaton. She stared at him, sitting there across the table, her thoughts racing. Here was a man she'd known since she was twenty years old. She'd lived with him, made love with him, borne him three daughters. He ought to be totally familiar to her, and yet she gazed at him and realized that she no longer knew him in certain basic ways. This self-involved person was not the man she had loved . . . at least, she didn't think so. Right now, the only emotion she felt for him was disdain. "*You're* relieved," she said finally. "Of all the self-serving—" She stopped herself; it wasn't her place to criticize him. "How

353

about Leslie? And how about Gregory?'' she asked. ''Have you forgotten that they have feelings, too?''

''Of course not! He'll have the very best of everything, I'll see to that. And as for Leslie . . . I plan to provide very generously for her. She'll never have to work or worry about money. I'm not deserting them.''

''You could have fooled me.''

''I'll even be in the same neighborhood! I can see Gregory every day!''

Ellie shook her head. She felt flooded with intense sadness. ''Oh, Adrian, what can I say? Your ideas about responsibility to your children haven't changed, not really. *Same neighborhood*! The neighborhood doesn't mean a damn thing. Don't you understand? You were never there for your daughters . . . No, no, don't look like that. I know you came home and all that. But you never changed a diaper. You never made it to a piano recital. And—don't you remember?—most evenings you required that they be fed and bathed before you and I ate our dinner. 'Like civilized human beings' was the charming way you put it. Remember? How many conversations did you ever have with your daughters? Never mind, never mind . . . What difference does it make now.''

''Ellie, Ellie, don't be so harsh with me. Please. I need you. And that's not an easy thing for me to admit!'' He gazed at her in a way she could only describe as soulful, and it made her feel embarrassed for him. ''Leslie and Gregory need *you*,'' she said. ''And you needn't look at me that way. In any case, I can never go back with you.''

''You don't really mean that,'' he said. He smirked in that condescending way. ''I know you better than you know yourself, Ellie.''

''The arrogance of you—! Well, if I had any doubts at all, they are gone forever.'' She turned on her heel, every muscle in her body clenched tight with tension, and marched away. She didn't know where she was going; all she knew was she had to move, get away from him. And the tears, unbidden and unwanted, slid unchecked down her face.

I must stop this, she thought, blinking very fast and looking down. It would be horrible to bump into someone in this state—a patient, waiting for the clinic to open. She couldn't allow anyone to see her leaking tears. Turn it off, she ordered herself, quit it, think about something else. But her mind would not move. Over and over again, she found herself railing against that arrogant assumption. How dare he! How dare he even *begin* to think he knew her so well! If he knew her so well, he'd never have left her when she needed him the most. He'd never have hurt her so deeply and then—the gall, the utter gall—come back whenever he felt like it and so casually suggest that they begin all over again! If he knew her so well, he'd have known how unsatisfying their sexual encounter had been for her. If he knew her so well, he'd have been aware that the hurt he gave her had never completely left her. If he knew her so well, he would never have—

And she stopped her rapid walking because there she was, up against a set of glass doors. She'd taken herself, without even thinking about it, to the ground-floor solarium, a place she almost never visited. It was a lovely spot, flooded with light on even the gloomiest day. The bright spring sunshine gilded the wooden benches, the shrubbery, the pots of early crocuses and daffodils. It was a popular spot with the younger people in the hospital, and that day was typical: a young nurse sat with a reflector held under her face, a beatific smile on her face. Nearby, a young black couple held hands and argued earnestly. A group of residents ate sandwiches and laughed hilariously at their own jokes. There were even a couple of ambulatory patients sitting with visitors.

Well, as long as she was there, she might as well sit for a minute and compose herself. Nobody there knew her. She picked a spot on a low wall, right in front of a circle of purple flowers, a place where the sun seemed more golden to her. She breathed deeply, letting her head fall back, willing herself to relax. She let her eyes close, let the warmth of the sunlight ease her tension. I must need a vacation, she thought.

Hell, if I let Ade get to me—Ade, who offers me no surprises, really—then I must be exhausted.

"Ellie?" The quiet voice was so unexpected on this morning, in this place . . . so unexpected and so comforting in a strange way. Tears instantly sprang up behind her closed lids; and with every bit of strength she had, she willed them not to spill over. Only then did she dare open her eyes and look at him.

"Good morning, David."

He gazed down at her with such tenderness that her heart gave a lurch. She had really thought those feelings of intimacy had dissipated with the passing of time. But the concern in his eyes brought back a surge of remembered emotion, and once again she had to blink very fast to keep from crying.

"You look sad," he said. "Would you rather be left alone?"

"No, no! *Au contraire*, as we say in French. Please, David, stay."

He sat next to her, his thigh warm against hers, and he took her hand so naturally, she could not pull it away. "Do you want to talk about it?" And he sat, patient, waiting for her to do whatever she wanted to do.

"I can't, David. It's . . . it's old business with my ex-husband . . . not really worth discussing because he and I have nothing left worth discussing. *Nothing*."

"You sound as if you just discovered that."

"I did. You're right."

"That's always a bummer. Endings . . . yeah, it's rough. But at least now you can leave all that behind you and get on with the rest of your life."

Ellie stared at him. She couldn't have said it better. My God, they hadn't even had a conversation in . . . how many years? two? . . . and right away he'd zeroed in. He was remarkable. No, wait, he was better than remarkable, he was a damn miracle: a man who notices, listens, and responds. Did she know any other man, however pleasant, however brilliant, however talented, however educated, who was capable of this? No, she did not. Only David. Only David would have noticed that she was depressed; only David would have been unafraid to ask her, and only David would have given that kind of thoughtful answer. He was a wonderful person. Funny, all this time she had been remembering their passion; but she had forgotten to remember their friendship.

At last, she said, "You're right."

David laughed and squeezed her hand. "That's twice in the past five minutes you've told me I'm right. I haven't heard that from a doctor since I moved upstairs to Geriatrics. Maybe I should come back to you."

She slid him a look and took her hand gently out of his. "David, David, you're still a devil. If you want to come back to the clinic, just call for an appointment with the head nurse."

He hesitated, and she thought she saw a shadow across his eyes. Oh, Lord. She didn't want to hurt him, just make it clear, that's all. And then he grinned at her and stood up, saying, "Well, I wasn't really on a break. I was looking for a patient who tends to wander away from time to time, looking for young people to educate." He laughed. "I'd better check the caf. See you around."

She didn't linger once he'd left. Anyway, she felt better, and she did have a clinic to run. As she made her way back, she found herself imagining David back at work with her. It would be so nice; they'd always been such a good team. Work had been fun back then, and they seemed to be on the same wavelength. Her head nurse now was a very good nurse and hard worker, but dammit, she couldn't read Ellie's mind the way he used to. And she never stayed late, working on for the sheer joy of it. Oh, it would be wonderful talking over cases with him again, walking across Cadman Plaza Park together . . . And then she realized what she was doing. She *was* in bad shape . . . Her mind kept going into the past, backward instead of forward. She and David could never be together again, never. It was a tired woman's fantasy.

And anyway, he probably had a girlfriend.

Chapter 34

S*ANDY WATCHED* A*DRIAN* Winter as he loped up the walk and up the shallow flight of steps, and she smiled to herself. I'll never get any thanks from *that* one for rescuing him, she thought, and then she gave a mental shrug. At least he didn't run away when he saw the excitement . . . came right up to give his "No comment."

Hank, the big baby, had gone sneaking in an hour ago by the garbage cans, in the back service area, leaving her on her own at the front door, besieged by a pack of rabid reporters, giving out all kinds of lies when they demanded to see him. He was late, he was in a meeting, he was leaving on the next plane for D.C. But he was on top of the situation, he was meeting with the board right now . . . whatever she could think of. Of course, they all laughed like hell.

And then out came Nancy with a note. Oh, good, a statement at last. She should have known better. The message read: "You're the spokeswoman. Do your usual and then *get in here*" There were four large heavy exclamation points. What a baby he was! But okay, she'd do her usual: put them off, give out some sort of bland, all-purpose, we're-taking-care-of-this-right-now statement, make nice to everyone, including the pickets, and stonewall it until she got the official word—whatever *that* might be.

It was 8:35 when she knocked on Hank's office door and then walked right in. "Oh, fine," she started, but he held up a hand. He was wearing his very serious, very concerned expression.

"Did you tell them we're working on it right now? That we'll have further word for them after the board of trustees meets? That—"

And now *she* interrupted, finishing up for him. "Yes, Hank, and that Mr. Del Bello will hold a press conference after that time. I did everything just the way you like it." She opened her eyes wide, the way he liked. Sure enough, a smile spread slowly across his face.

"Good girl," he said. "You sure? They're not gonna come storming in here?"

"No," she said, "they're not. First of all, Mike Cohn is out there right now with his men, and a couple of New York's finest besides. Secondly, it's a very well behaved crowd. Come on, Hank . . . they're praying out there, not throwing rocks! And finally, when we have that press conference, you are going to knock them out . . . like you always do."

His smile became less tentative, and then something changed in his eyes, and she barely had time to think, Uh-oh, here it comes, when he said huskily, "How about it, baby?"

"Oh, Hank! it would be super," she lied, "but I should get back out there, and I have a ton of messages on my desk . . ." She lowered her voice provocatively. "Let's make a date. Ten minutes after the press conference, like we always do."

"No, no, not later. Now. I really have an urge—"

She had put on her pure linen suit that morning, and every time she took it off or put it on—or even breathed, it seemed—it wrinkled. The last thing in the world she wanted to do was to go over there and have him mess her up. But she remembered his warning. She'd just better do whatever he wanted, and what the hell, it wasn't as if it were such a big deal. She knew how to make him come fast.

So she wriggled her way over to him, on automatic pilot, while her mind was busy figuring out what he ought to say to the reporters later. She'd take the skirt off herself and twist to put it carefully over the chair, while he did his thing. He was so eager, so damn hot, pulling off his pants and just flinging them across the room, then pushing her down onto the rug before she even had time to get the skirt unzipped, damn him. And then wouldn't you know, his thing just hung there. He couldn't believe it, either; he looked down at the limp little thing and swore and swore. She did her damndest—every trick in the book—but it would *not* wake up. "Well, shit," he said finally, "you might as well get up, baby. It just won't . . . Dammit, this hasn't happened to me since a whorehouse in Alabama in '56!"

She got up. Her skirt was wrinkled beyond any kind of redemption, and silently she cursed him for a selfish son of a bitch. Aloud, she said, "Oh, Hank, don't worry about it. It never happened before; it'll never happen again. My God, I'm surprised you even thought about sex; it's so crazy today, and there's so much pressure on you. Hey, you were just nervous . . ."

"Nervous?"

"Nervy is what I mean . . . on edge, you know, because of the pickets and the board meeting and all."

"Oh, yeah, sure. Well, yes, I guess I have reason to be on edge." He patted her ass lightly and said, "Go ahead; I know you have a lot of work. I'll catch you later." She fought the desire to kick him in the shins and tell him to stick it. She smiled instead.

She had taken care of about half of those phone calls, and then she looked out the front door—and she checked every ten minutes or so—and saw the Rev arriving. It was getting close to nine, and she got herself back outside just in time to save Adrian Winter from the press corps.

The Rev was everywhere at once. No matter what you thought of him personally, you had to admire him as a professional. He was as slick as they came, able to soothe and smooth things out with just a word or two. Or, as he was doing right now, pump up an event to make it more significant than it really was. "That's right," she could hear him boom, "you tell the world how Christians feel about life! That's right, you march and you sing right out and let them hear the truth. Amen!" And there was a ripple of "Amens" from all over, punctuated by a couple of "Praise the Lords!"

And then he saw her and waved to her. "Ms. Heller, just the person I've been waiting for. Do you have a minute?"

The smile appeared without her having to think about it, and the words did the same. "I always have a minute for you, Reverend Clayton. Even more, if you need it." She waited just the littlest fraction of a second to see if he would come to her, but no. So she went to him.

"Just give me a few minutes, Reverend. I'll send the press people into the cafeteria for some free coffee—that ought to get rid of them, anything free!—and then we can talk without them breathing down our necks."

Actually, she and the Rev kind of sauntered into the hospital right after them, just chatting about this and that; and before she knew it, they were at her office, and it just seemed the natural thing to do, to go in.

"I'd like to say that *I* think you do your job excellently well . . ." he began, sitting forward on his chair, his whole upper body leaning toward her, his eyes intent on hers.

She waited. He was obviously waiting for a response, so she smiled and nodded and hoped she looked pleased and waited to see what he had up his sleeve.

"You know, Ms. Heller, I am not one of the trustees who feels negatively about the attention this hospital has been getting lately."

Now she got it. "Yes?"

"To be absolutely blunt, Ms. Heller, I like what you've been doing. I think it's good. And I have fought the other members of the board on the matter of Cadman's publicity efforts." He cleared his throat delicately. "Today, the entire black community of New York is watching Cadman Memorial . . . but I'm sure you are fully aware of that fact and of the many implications for your future . . ."

"Yes?"

"Believe me, Ms. Heller, I'm on your side. I *want* this story told. Cadman is doing a wonderful thing here . . . It's the father who's being stubborn. And Adrian Winter—well, the man's got his heart in the right place. He's committed to life, just as we are, Ms. Heller. Bobby Truman is a brilliant man and a good doctor, but right now he's grief stricken and confused. If you'll forgive me for saying so, Bobby Truman is not behaving quite . . . sane. The man is obviously beside himself. In my church, Ms. Heller, we would say he has turned away from God and so has lost his way. And in this case, the case of his own natural-born son, he is morally and unequivocably *wrong*."

"Oh, I couldn't agree more," Sandy said, hoping she would remember those last few sentences. A story was beginning to shape itself in her mind; in fact, she could use some of this for Hank's statement to the press. "Morality," she added, "seems to be the issue."

"Life versus antilife," the Reverend intoned, and she quickly put a hand on his arm and said, "May I quote you?"

"Surely, surely. I'll be glad to add my voice to the voice of my people out there on the lawn, who are saying, 'Bobby Truman, give your son his chance at life.' I'll be glad to add my voice to the voice of Adrian Winter, who is saying, 'Bobby Truman, act like the doctor we've trained you to be. Preserve life; don't destroy it!' "

Sandy could hardly concentrate on the rest of what he was saying. The man was stupendous! Every phrase was a natural for a headline. She just had to write this one, but in order to get full play for it, she was going to have to get a picture of the mother. And the baby, for that matter.

"Yes, Reverend," she said, "this is a story that *must* be told to the public. But . . . well, I ought to speak to the mother first, to get her side . . ."

"Exactly, exactly," he said beaming at her. "And I know what you're thinking, Ms. Heller. You're thinking, that old board is mad at you for getting into patients' rooms and taking pictures and talking to them and all . . . and you're not going to be able to get in to talk to Corinne Truman." He patted her on the shoulder. "Well, don't you worry about it. I'm about to go up to sit and pray with Corinne right this minute . . . and I daresay if you should keep me company in the elevator, well . . ." He shrugged expressively.

"You're on, Reverend. What are we waiting for?"

Sandy found the sight of Bobby Truman's wife shocking. He was so handsome, so healthy, so boyish. The woman propped up on pillows in the bed could have been a hundred years old. The face looked sunken and grayish, and the arms lay limply on the coverlet. She was crying, not sobbing or shrieking, just quietly weeping, tears sliding down her face endlessly. And she was whispering something, her eyes closed.

A plump woman with a white turban wrapped around her head and an open Bible on her lap, sat next to the bed, looking very solid in comparison with Corinne. She turned when the door opened, but the woman in the bed gave no sign that she heard anything.

"Reverend, I'm glad you've come," the woman said. "Poor lamb, she's sick with her grief and can't seem to get herself into this world. I'm afraid if something doesn't happen real soon, we're gonna lose her."

"Sister Rebecca, make yourself clear."

"Dr. Winter was just in here with the paper for her to sign . . . the paper to operate on the poor little baby. And she couldn't even hear him. She just keeps saying over and over, 'I want to hold my baby.' Dr. Winter explained and explained to her that she can't hold the baby in her arms like she wants and as soon as she pulls herself together she can go down to the nursery and put her hands on him. But she can't seem to understand anything, Reverend, and Dr. Winter, he told me he can't possibly have her sign any papers, not when she's in the state she's in. It wouldn't be ethical, he said. I'm praying, I'm praying she'll come around."

The Reverend put his hand on her shoulder and said, "You keep right on praying, sister. This unfortunate family needs all the prayers it can get. And in the meantime, I hope Dr. Winter is getting busy on a court order." He glanced at his huge wristwatch and added, "In fact, I think I'll make a few phone calls right now on that subject. And while I'm doing that, sister, Ms. Heller here is going to take a couple of pictures of Sister Corinne. For the newspapers."

Sister Rebecca smiled at Sandy in a tentative kind of way. "You let me fix her up a little," she said. "She's just been crying and crying . . . I don't think she's stopped crying since she woke up."

"Don't disturb her," Sandy said. "This . . . is mother love. She only wants to hold her baby in her arms . . . Isn't that what all mothers want . . . ?"

"I want to bring her the other baby, her little Kelly, but they say no, she's too upset, and it would frighten Kelly. But I think Kelly already knows something's wrong. When I dressed her this morning for nursery school, she said, "Sister Becca, why isn't my mommy calling me on the phone? She said she would as soon as she got that new baby."

"Kelly is staying with you?" Sandy said.

"Yes, I'm a friend of the family, and I live right in the same building, you know. I'm taking care of Kelly until all this mess is over and they can all be together again."

"Oh, do you think they'll be able to work things out, then?"

Sister Rebecca's round, bland face registered shock. "Why, surely! When you're in the hands of the Lord, anything can be worked out."

This woman was obviously not going to be a rich vein of facts; Sandy could see that. Besides, she already had enough for a sweet little story that would make Cadman look like heaven and Dr. Winter, like God. She took several pictures of the tear-ravaged face, half in shadow, stark against the white pillows, and excused herself. It wouldn't do for her to be here alone—the Rev had long since gone out to find a telephone—not if Adrian Winter was likely to show up at any time.

But nobody saw her leave. The one nurse in the hall had her back turned, and the nurses on duty at the nursing station knew her and were incurious, anyway.

On the ground floor, on her way to her office, she saw the cause of all the furor calmly standing in the middle of the corridor, deep in conversation with Rita Schneider, the genetics counselor. Perfect! She walked right over to them and said, "Dr. Truman, please let me express my sympathy. I've just been upstairs with Mrs. Truman . . . and the Reverend Clayton. I don't like to bother you at this time, but—you understand—there's a horde of reporters in the cafeteria right this minute, waiting for a statement from the hospital, and I unfortunately must provide it for them. Of course I want to be fair—I think we should tell both sides of the story—so I wonder if you would please give me a statement . . ."

There was a moment of such deep silence that she knew she was in trouble. When he finally spoke, it was between clenched teeth, his voice shaking a bit. "You . . .must . . . be . . . crazy . . . lady!"

Rita Schneider put a hand on his arm and said, "Bobby, Bobby . . . take it easy."

He shook off her hand but then shot her a look, and Sandy had a flash that there was something going on between them. But that wasn't important now. She tucked it away into the back of her memory, saving it until it might be useful.

"I'm not taking it easy," Bobby went on, his tone implacable. "I'm taking it hard. And I have nothing—repeat, nothing—to say to you, Ms. Heller. So you can just write that Dr. Truman had no comment and to hell with the press!"

"I'm sorry," Sandy murmured, "I understand," and got away from them as fast as she could. The man looked positively murderous. "The glowering father, chief resident of Obstetrics and Gynecology, refused to speak to reporters," she wrote in her head. But wait, maybe it should be "the understandably distressed father." Yes, that might be a bit more politic.

It was time to discuss this with Hank. Oh, wouldn't he be surprised at what she'd been able to accomplish in less than an hour! He'd better stop giving her a hard time, or she'd head out for another hospital. After this story broke, after it was all over, they'd be beating down her door! Sure, she could get another job; she got at least one job offer after every big story she'd done. Sometimes, in fact, she didn't know what in hell she was doing, hanging around here, getting shat upon by that dumb board and being Hank Del Bello's part-time plaything! She deserved better, much better.

Nancy, for a change, was not behind her desk, waiting to take on all comers. The anteroom was empty, and Sandy just walked up to the door to his private office. And then she heard the voices, raised in anger, every syllable enunciated with particular care. She stood very still, holding her breath in excitement. It was Hank with Art Schuster, and they were having a *fight*! This she had to hear.

"You did it, you bastard," Hank was saying.

"I only did what needed to be done."

"Not only are you a bastard; you're a condescending bastard. Nothing *needed* to be done. We're doing a goddam good job here, and you know it. What's your game, anyway?"

"No game, my dear Mr. Del Bello. I am a member of the board and a longtime leader in the Brooklyn Heights community, and it is my duty to act upon the will of the board and the community. And that's all I've done. Listen, Hank, *I* didn't start any gossip . . . It was *there*. Believe me, it was brought to *me*."

"You're the one who could have protected me, Art. And instead of that, you made sure to undermine me . . ."

"You undermined yourself by carrying on so openly with your whore . . . and then you refused to fire her when she overstepped the bounds."

Anger so intense that it burned her chest rose up into her throat. Call her a whore, would he! The slime! Without even thinking, she burst in, straight for Dr. Art Schuster, who stood there in his tightly buttoned three-piece suit, smirking and grinning and looking so smug. She went up to him and pounded him with her fists. "You son of a bitch," she said in a fierce whisper. "You want to call names? I can think of a few for you."

"Get away," he said, backing off and making a disgusted face.

"Get away? Get away? That isn't what you said the night of the New Year's party. Or the night two weeks ago when I was working late."

"Shut your mouth, you stupid slut!"

"Sure. If that's what I am, what are you? Huh?" She took great delight in his look of discomfiture. "Backing me into the corner, putting your hands all over me, slobbering all over my face, ugh! Telling me how much you've been wanting me, how you've been watching me and having dreams about me. You couldn't stand it anymore, and Hank didn't have to know. Pleading with me just to let you put your hands for one little minute on my—"

"I said shut up with your lies!"

"Not lies! Not lies! Ha! The famous Dr. Arthur Schuster, member of the board and longtime leader of the community can't keep his fly zipped up! It's enough to make a person laugh. And it did make me laugh, didn't it, Dr. Schuster? I laughed at you—and now I'm getting paid back, aren't I? Well, you just do your worst, Dr. Schuster. And then I hope you have trouble sleeping because I'll know the way to destroy you!"

She didn't want to see what he'd say, she didn't wait to hear what Hank would say. She didn't care. She felt victorious, exultant, and invincible. She didn't care what happened in the end. For now, she had won!

Chapter 35

How dare she? The slut! Well, she had gone too far this time! She wasn't dealing with just anybody; she was dealing with Arthur Jay Schuster, M.D. A man of substance. Everyone who mattered in the Heights knew who he was: a physician; on the board of the Heights Casino; men's "B" doubles champion five years running; on the board of the Brooklyn Heights Association; chairman of the board of his co-op; chief of Internal Medicine at Cadman Memorial; on *its* board and on its ethics committee and on its residents advisory board. Not to mention plenty of other honors.

Damn the woman! To let her get to him that way was ridiculous. She was so far beneath him. She was beneath contempt, really! He punched at the elevator button furiously, and as if it knew how angry he was, the door opened immediately. Art nodded to the familiar faces, then stared straight ahead. He had to calm down before he spoke to Adrian. What that Heller woman said didn't count! Nobody would believe her, anyway. Still, it rankled. He'd never said all those things! All right, he was a man like any other man. He'd tried to cop a feel late one afternoon . . . Who wouldn't?

She was just asking for it. But that was all. He *never* had said all those things, the lying bitch. Well, let her try to harm him; just let her try. She'd find out very quickly just who she was up against.

Calm, Art, he told himself. Calm; that was the ticket. Forget her. Well, he'd handle it . . . with Adrian Winter's cooperation. The trouble was, Bobby was Adrian's protégé; it might be touchy. But there were rumors that Adrian disagreed with Bobby on this one. Good, because everything had to move quickly, and he hoped Adrian wouldn't get all stiff on him, because the trustees meeting last night was somewhat irregular. It wasn't at the hospital. It didn't have to be. As luck would have it, there was a new-members party at the Casino, and after a while, just chatting about the Truman affair, they had all realized they had a quorum.

Time was of the essence, and there they were, able to save a helluva lot of time. So, instead of talking it over where outsiders could listen in on hospital business that was none of their concern, they just all took their drinks into the Governor's Room and had their meeting sitting around the fireplace. There was a lot of concern about the Truman baby and about the kind of publicity the hospital was getting. And none of them could stomach the so-called pray-in. It wasn't exactly kosher to sit there and talk about it with the Reverend absent— after all, he was a member—but look, they did have a quorum, and their attorney was there, and he assured them that it was perfectly legal. And really, it wasn't official; it was just that everyone was there, and everyone was thinking and talking about the same problem, and there was their attorney, Joe Fredericks, at the same party . . . so why not sit down together, strictly informally, and put some questions to him. Well, they hadn't had to ask Joe a damn thing. He'd been on it already, and he had one very important thing to say to them.

And that's why Art was there at Adrian's office right now. To tell him what legal steps they had to take.

He didn't waste any time, but sat down across the desk

from Adrian and told him straight from the shoulder. "Look here, Adrian, that Truman baby has got to be operated on. Right away. No ifs, ands, or buts."

Adrian gave him that supercilious smile he reserved for people he considered beneath him. It had made Art furious years ago, and it still did. "What do you mean, Art, *got to*? There's that small matter of obtaining consent, and believe me, I'm working on it. We're all working on it."

"Fuck consent. I'm not talking consent. I'm talking murder."

"Come now, Art. Let's not get overly dramatic."

"I kid you not. We had a meeting last night at the Casino, and Joe says—"

"Hold on. Meeting? What kind of meeting?"

"Well . . ." Now that he had to put it into words, it did sound a little fishy . . . not that it *was*, really; hell, no. Joe said it was perfectly aboveboard. "Well, we were all there, the board I mean, just by chance. And everyone was troubled about this Truman thing. And luckily Joe Fredericks was there, too, with his new wife—by the way, Adrian, she is a *looker*, something like a young Lauren Bacall, and would you believe, she's a lawyer! All right, all right, I'll get on with it.

"First of all, it doesn't look good for the hospital that there's any hesitation at all about saving the life of a little baby."

"Look, Art, *I* agree. *I'm* all for the shunt . . . and then for whatever else is indicated. But Bobby—"

"Bobby," Art interrupted, holding up his hand and leaning way forward. "*Bobby*. Exactly. Exactly our point. Listen. That's what Joe wanted to tell us: Dr. Bobby Truman could be brought up on a murder charge if he allows that baby to die."

"Oh, God."

"You said it, Adrian. One of the hospital's bright young doctors, up on murder charges! Now you see that I wasn't being dramatic at all."

"Okay. If Joe Fredericks says so, it's so. What's our next move?"

"No question what we do next. We get a court order to allow the hospital to proceed with whatever it deems necessary to preserve the life of this infant, whether Bobby Truman wants it or not."

Adrian frowned. "I don't know . . . I hate going to court. Still . . ." Art hid a smile. Winter hated being at a disadvantage; it made him acutely uncomfortable. Well, tough shit. This time he *had* to do what someone else told him to do.

"Court's the only way," Art said with satisfaction.

"Okay, okay. But working under a court order is so terribly divisive . . . and Bobby is struggling with a lot of conflicting feelings; it's not as if he's *trying* to make trouble . . . Look. Let's do this. It's now ten-o-seven. Give me until eleven. Okay? Let me talk to Bobby and Corinne and see if I can get consent signed by one—or maybe both—of them. That way, we'll be able to avoid the whole court scene . . . *and*, by the way, also avoid all the press attention it would surely elicit."

"Until eleven? Okay. I'll give you until eleven. But, Adrian, time's a-wasting!"

"Don't you worry. I'll have it all under control."

How dare he? Etta Schuster scowled to herself and bit her lips. That Dr. Truman was the *father* of that baby boy, and he dared to say, "Let him die." Art told her all about it this morning. The utter gall of that Truman boy! But it was an old story, wasn't it? Doctors thought they knew everything. It was just like when she was pregnant and Art made her get an abortion. *Twice* he made her get an abortion. She cried herself to sleep every night for weeks and weeks, but did he care? No, he did not. "Oh, come on, Etta," he said to her, "you don't really care that much. You're just pretending. But you don't fool me. *I* know you're secretly relieved not to have another baby to take care of." How dared he? Telling her what she was feeling—when he didn't even know! He couldn't possibly know, because it was *her* feeling, wasn't it? Inside of her own self. But, "You have your hands full with

Lawrence," he told her. "You couldn't handle any more kids; it would be too much for you." Not a year had gone by—and it must be twelve years since the second one—that she didn't mourn those two unborn babies.

She knew *exactly* how Corinne Truman was feeling! And she was on her way to help her . . . the way she had hoped and prayed someone would come and help her all those years ago. But what could a poor woman do, helpless and alone, in the hospital . . . the *hospital*, where her husband was king and where she had absolutely nothing to say about anything.

What was it that made doctors such terrible husbands? Did they use up all of their kindness and understanding on their patients? Because their patients always loved them. Art was one of Cadman's most popular doctors; everyone said so. Maybe patients *wanted* to be told how they were feeling and what they had to do, because they were sick and helpless.

Well, Corinne Truman was feeling sick and helpless right now, and Etta was going to do something about it. She looked around quickly even as she thought it, but of course Art wouldn't be on this floor; it wasn't his service. If he ever caught her doing this, he'd kill her! He'd *murder* her! "None of your business, Etta!" he'd yell. "When will you learn to stay out of things that are too complicated for you to understand?" Too bad for him. She understood this; she was a woman, too, wasn't she? And anyway, for once in her life, she was going to do something on her own, something *she'd* thought of, something *she* felt was right. She'd explain it all to Corinne Truman: how all Corinne had to do was sign the consent form and her baby's life would be saved. Just her name at the bottom of a paper, that's all. It was so simple, she'd tell her, so simple. Corinne Truman deserved to have her baby live, no matter *what* shape it was in! A mother's love didn't see little flaws.

It was the easiest thing in the world to get into Corinne Truman's room. She just sailed on by the nursing station, saying, "Visiting," and they didn't stop her. And of course hospital doors didn't lock, so she just walked in.

Poor lamb, she looked so sad, so tired, lying there with her hands folded on top of the covers and her eyes closed. Etta walked over and put a hand over Corinne's, and Corinne's eyes opened right away. Etta smiled at her, and after a minute she smiled right back.

"I'm Etta Schuster, and my husband is a doctor here, too, just like yours. And he told me about you and your baby boy . . ."

"I want to hold my baby," Corinne said in a weak little voice. It made your heart hurt to hear it.

"Of course you do. Every mother wants to hold her baby. And every baby *needs* to be held."

Corinne's eyes opened wider, and she gripped Etta's hand with both of hers, hard. "Yes, yes, my baby needs me."

"Listen to me, Mrs. Truman. You can hold your baby, but you have to sign the papers . . . Do you understand me? So that they can save him."

Corinne smiled broadly and nodded. "Oh, yes. Oh, thank you. Save him. That's right. Save him. I'm gonna do it."

Oh, good, Etta thought. She understands. I knew she would. "That's fine," she said in her best motherly voice. "That's wonderful. I know your doctor . . . Do you understand? I know Dr. Winter; he's an old friend. So if he told you to sign, you should. You really should."

Corinne nodded again and said, "Oh, yes. Oh, thank you so much." And Etta scurried out, feeling so good. She'd done it; she'd been the one who made it all come out right. This time Art couldn't laugh at her and tell her she was a fool. This time he'd have to admit she'd been the smart one.

Corinne lay back, a smile on her face, thinking very fast. At last it had come: The sign she had been waiting and waiting for! Lord Jesus, I thank you for answering my prayers. The sign had come—right into her room, right to her very bed—and held her hand and talked to her and told her what she had to do. "Your baby needs you. Save your baby."

That's what she had to do. It was very clear now, and she felt at peace and strong.

She prayed just a few minutes, and then she got up. She was a little bit shaky in the knees, but she was okay. She could make it. There was her pretty pink duster. What did Sister Rebecca call it? Oh, yes, a model coat. "Because you're as pretty as a model." She put it on, and it did look nice, nice enough to go outside in. Nice enough to go see her baby.

There was another sign as soon as she got into the corridor—an arrow pointing that said NEONATAL ICU. She just followed it, and there it was, with great big plateglass windows, but the curtains were drawn over them now, because it wasn't visiting hours.

She knew where the door was, and when she walked in, one of the nurses looked up from some paper work and said, "Oh, Mrs. Truman, how nice. You came to see your baby. Well, he'll be glad to see *you*. First just come to the sink and scrub, okay?" And she showed Corinne how to wash properly and slipped an angel robe over her clothes. "Let me show you where he is."

She was so nervous, seeing her son for the first time. His bassinet was 'way in the corner. "He's our smallest, Mrs. Truman, so we give him the choicest spot, with the most privacy." How her heart hammered; it seemed like it took forever to walk over to that corner. She saw there was a banner taped across the bassinet that said, WELCOME, BABY BOY TRUMAN. That was so nice, and she said, "His name is Bob."

"Oh is it? How nice. We'll make a new banner right away." And she moved away to tend to another baby.

And then, at last, she was looking at her very own baby. Oh, my, he was so tiny. She didn't remember Kelly being that small. But so beautiful. He was on his tummy, wrapped in a blue and white blanket, his little face turned sideways on the mattress. Look at the sweet little nose . . . and the long lashes. And a full head of black hair. He looked just like Bobby. Oh, he was so sweet! She bent over and kissed the velvet cheek, and oh, there was a plastic tube coming out of his nose. That wasn't nice. She'd have to take that away; it must be hurting him.

When she pulled the tube out . . . oh, so gently . . . he fretted a bit, and she murmured, "It's okay, pretty baby, your mama's here. I won't let them bother and hurt you anymore. I'm here to save you, pretty boy," she crooned. And it seemed to her that he relaxed as soon as he heard her voice.

The clear plastic bassinet was neat and clean, but this wasn't the proper bed for a little baby. A little baby needed to be safe in his own little bed, in a sunny nursery, with a mobile of animals hanging over his head and a music box tinkling and his very own Mama close by to take care of him and love and keep him from harm. That's where a little baby belonged. He shouldn't be there, in an ugly plastic box with nobody who really loved him, just another baby in a row of babies that they were paid to take care of.

Look at all those hoses and tubes taped all over and stuck into him. She knew they called that the life-support system, and she knew it was to keep him alive. But was this a life? Poor little baby, unable to kick and move or even turn his head, lying all alone there. Just look at him. He couldn't be hugged; he couldn't be cuddled; he couldn't be snuggled and kissed and held close to her heart. Bobby said everything that could be wrong was wrong. Well, she loved him, anyway! He was her little baby. He was going to die. Didn't Bobby tell her that? So if he was going to die, anyway, let him do it in his mother's arms, so for the little time he had, he could feel her love. And then, when Jesus took him, he'd have His perfect love.

"Oh, yes," she said to herself. Now she knew what she had to do. Nobody was looking. Nobody was paying the least attention to her. So she removed all those hoses, carefully, all those tubes, and now, at last, she could pick him up, as a mother should. He gave a weak mewing cry, just like a little kitten, and she scooped him right up and held him close to her breasts. "Now, now, little Bobby," she whispered, "don't you cry. Your mama's taking you home."

She'd done it! With the help of the Lord, she'd walked right out of the hospital and across the park and was safe at home. And nobody had seen her. The baby was an angel; not a cry out of him the whole time, not even when she was running running so fast down the back stairs. He was so light, so tiny; he was no burden to her at all. And now here they were in the apartment with the door locked behind them and the sun streaming in the windows.

"Now we're home, baby," she murmured, smiling down at the tiny face with its perfect little features. He looked so peaceful now; this was much better, much better than that big machine-filled nursery.

Corinne looked around, making decisions; and then, without relinquishing her hold on him, she pulled the rocker out from the corner where it normally stood and placed it right in the middle of a pool of sunlight. It looked so pretty there. She took a big paisley pillow off the sofa and put it on the rocker. Now it was perfect, all soft and comfortable.

She sat in the rocker and snuggled the baby into her, rocking back and forth very, very gently. His eyes had been closed, but when she started rocking, he opened them and looked up at her. He had big, round, light eyes with thick, curling eyelashes . . . just like his daddy. She smiled down at him. He would have grown up to look just like Bobby, she thought, poor little mite.

"I'm sorry, baby," she murmured, holding him close to her. "It would have been nice, so nice, if you could have played football with your daddy. And had your big sister Kelly teach you your colors. And had your mama take you off to nursery school the first day, holding tight to your hand . . . Lordie, Lordie, it would have been wonderful. Bob Joseph Truman the fourth. Little Bobby . . ." She rocked and rocked, looking down upon him, watching the eyes close, watching the transparent lids quiver ever so slightly, watching the rosebud mouth blow a little bubble. The head turned, drooping a little, and rested even more heavily on her breast. He was sleeping. "Oh, good, baby, sleep now. Sleep, baby, sleep . . . Rest easy; you're with Mama . . ." She began to hum her favorite lullaby, very softly lest she wake him. Let him sleep, poor little thing; let him just drift away hearing his mama's heartbeat steady and secure against his little ear and feeling his mama's love all around him. "That's right, little boy, just rest now. Mama's with you. See, baby, Jesus looked down from heaven where He lives and he saw how you were suffering, and He said, 'I don't want that little Bobby to suffer anymore.' " Corinne's eyes filled, and then the tears spilled out and ran down her cheeks, but she did not wipe them away. She smiled. "That's what happened, baby," she said. "And now you're with me, and soon you'll be safe in the arms of Jesus."

Chapter 36

Y*VONNE* D*UNCAN PATTED* her nurse's cap into place and looked over at the new nurse, Erica Svendsen. She was real cute, and she seemed nice, too. A bit too Women's Lib . . . a pink pants suit and no cap. Well, okay, but Yvonne was *proud* of her cap. After all, she was the first woman in her family to have a profession, ever. But Erica didn't have to wear a cap; it didn't have a thing to do with how well she could do her job. And so far she was damn good. The way Yvonne felt about it, she could take off right now and leave Erica Svendsen in charge of the nursing station, and she would handle it just fine.

And then all hell broke loose! First there was the sound of pounding feet, and then what seemed like six or seven people came bursting through the doors, panting, shouting all at once so at first she couldn't understand a word. It wasn't six or seven, just the resident on duty, Dr. Poole, a security guard, and Joanna, one of the neonatal ICU nurses. Neonatal ICU! Alarm bells went off in Yvonne's head.

"What's wrong?" she demanded. All three of them were looking around wildly, pointing at the number indicators

378

above the elevators, giving each other instructions, talking across each other. Joanna heard her, though, and turned, and there were tears in her eyes. "Oh, God, Yvonne! She took the baby! Corinne Truman! Just took him off the support system and took him! Took him *away*! He'll die! *He'll die*!"

Then the guard whirled and said, "You didn't see her here?"

"Absolutely not. Not a living soul the past ten minutes."

"I didn't think so. Jesus, I'd love to know where she— Lemme call Mike, to cover the exits . . ." And he snatched up the red phone that connected directly to the security office downstairs, speaking into it rapidly.

"Shit!" the resident said, punching at the elevator button over and over. "*If* she took the elevator—"

"She didn't," Yvonne said. "Not from here, anyway."

The resident sighed and bit her lip. "Well, we'd never catch her, anyway . . . These damn elevators, they never come when you need them."

"She musta took the stairs," the guard said. "Come on!" And they were off, the three of them, running back the way they'd come.

Erica turned to Yvonne, her eyes wide. "Holy smoke!" she said. "Took a baby right out of the ICU? How awful!"

Yvonne shook her head sadly. "Awful is right. The whole *thing* is awful. That's the baby I told you about before, the one with everything wrong . . ."

"Dr. Truman's baby. Yes, I remember. And the mother *kidnaped* him!?"

"Hush, girl. The damn walls, doors, and windows in this place have ears! Not a word about this, not one single word."

"Sure. But . . . what difference does it make?"

"Are you kidding? You're not in Burlington, Vermont, anymore, honey. You're in the Big Apple. There must be about five million reporters around the hospital on account of the pray-in . . . And if they get wind of *this*, we'll have them all over us like Godzilla!"

"Oh . . . right! Of course."

"And remember, Dr. Truman—the father—doesn't have

any idea any of this is happening . . . And we don't want him to get any idea of it until he's finished in the OR—''

"Oh, right. They're still delivering that Freedman baby . . ." She just loved the way Erica's big blue eyes just popped wide open. Yet, Yvonne noted coolly, she stayed calm. She might be surprised, and maybe even scared, but you'd never know it. Good.

Now the elevator doors slid open, and out stepped Dr. Poole and Joanna. There was a tight look on the resident's face; Yvonne was about to ask her what had happened—she thought for a second that they'd found Corinne and the baby was dead or something. And then Hank Del Bello pushed past the two women, his face absolutely scarlet, looking as if he'd breathe fire. And was looking straight at her.

"Goddam it, how the hell could a thing like this happen?"

Erica blanched; but Yvonne was an old hand at hospital administrators. She knew what the game was. He was quickly passing the buck, and he wasn't about to do it, not to Yvonne Duncan. "Are you speaking to me?" she said, looking him square in the eyes and keeping her voice even and empty of emotion.

"You're damn right I'm speaking to you, Nurse Duncan!" What do you think you're paid to sit there for!"

"She never came out this way."

"So you say!"

Anger rose in her. "If I say so, Mr. Del Bello, then it's so."

"Goddammit, the woman has disappeared! *Disappeared*! A woman in a bathrobe carrying a baby is able to just plain disappear right off this floor . . . And isn't it interesting—" His voice was heavy with sarcasm. "Isn't it interesting how she never came this way, she never came that way, she never came any goddam way at all. And yet, goddammit, she's gone! Out of *my* hospital!"

Yvonne took a deep breath, reminding herself that he was the head honcho and that she liked her job a lot. "It's been very quiet here, Mr. Del Bello. I am a professional. If a mouse had tiptoed by this desk, I would have noticed it. She did not come out this way."

"I've heard that professional stuff before, nurse, and it doesn't impress me. Even a professional can go for a drink . . . or take a leak . . . or be busy on the telephone . . ."

"Mr. Del Bello," Yvonne said icily, "if you should discover that Corinne Truman used this elevator or even walked down this hallway, you can fire me. And I am not kidding."

"Agh!" He waved a hand in dismissal of the whole thing. "All right, all right. I'm upset. This is a terrible thing . . . a terrible thing. If that baby dies, we'll be up the well-known creek without a paddle." But now he was no longer talking to them; he was kind of giving himself a summary.

"Goddammit, Hank!" They all turned as the elevator opened again and disgorged Dr. Art Schuster, his thick hair looking as if he'd been pulling at it, his face contorted. He was shouting as he came, his voice squeaking with his outrage. Yvonne didn't know if she could keep from laughing; he was such a turkey. He even sounded like one—gobble, gobble, gobble—and come to think of it, the way he thrust his whole head out, he even looked like one!

"Nobody ever tells me anything! I have to overhear it . . . *overhear* it . . . me, a member of the board! Goddammit, Hank, I had it all fixed, had a court order in the works. We could have operated on that baby this afternoon . . . right this minute, in fact. What the hell kind of mickey-mouse security do we have around here, anyway, that a hysterical woman in a nightgown can just stroll out of the hospital with a baby . . . Dammit, Hank, where's our security? Where's Mike? Christ, those reporters are going to be all over us in about ten seconds, and that story must not, repeat, must not leak out. You hear me, Hank?"

"You think you're the only one aware of that?" Hank snarled.

"It certainly looks like it!"

"Listen," Hank said, his face getting purple again. "I think you're forgetting who you're talking to, Dr. Schuster."

"And maybe you're forgetting that the board has the power to—"

It was getting embarrassing. Worse than that, it was getting loud. Yvonne stepped out from behind the desk and walked over to them. They both towered over her, even Dr. Schuster, and they were both white men; but she didn't care. This was *her* floor; she was in charge there, and not even Jesus Christ himself could make noise and disturb patients who were under *her* supervision.

"Gentlemen, *I* think you might prefer to continue your . . . discussion somewhere more private."

They both stopped dead, and they both looked around as if they'd forgotten where they were. Del Bello shook his big head as if he needed to clear it, and then he said, "Okay. I have to see Dr.Truman . . . that's why the hell I came up here to begin with."

"He's in the delivery room."

Del Bello leaned close to Yvonne and bared his teeth in a forced smile. "Then get him *out* of the delivery room, nurse."

"I'm sorry."

"Don't sorry me, nurse. Just get him."

Now he had made her mad. "No, sir, Mr. Del Bello. No *way* is anyone disturbing those doctors while they're working on Janet Freedman!" And she gave him glare for glare, hoping to God she wouldn't blink or anything.

Once again, he gave that impatient wave as if to say, "Oh, to hell with it." Then he gestured to Dr. Schuster, and the two of them marched off, down the corridor. For a moment or two, Yvonne just stood there, catching her breath. Then Dr. Poole gave a disgusted sound and said, "Now maybe we can get back to work." She exchanged a look with Yvonne that warmed her heart. It wasn't often that any of the doctors saw you as a really competent professional; but that was a pro-to-pro look.

"At least I don't have to worry about what happens if those

reporters come up here," Dr. Poole said. "I can count on you to take care of them." And then she and Joanna went hurrying off.

"Holy smoke!" Erica said. "I hope it isn't always like this around here!"

"Of course not, nurse." Yvonne felt a bit irritated. "You think people walk out of here every day with poor sick babies?"

"Oh, no, no, Yvonne, I only meant . . . you know . . . doctors up here yelling at each other . . . And anyway, Yvonne, what *will* we do if reporters ask us questions and point those cameras at us?"

Yvonne relaxed. Erica was new; she had to remember that. "You kiddin'? They never come around the nurses, honey. Nurses are invisible; didn't you know that? Besides"—she lowered her voice—"this time the only one they're going to want to talk to is Dr. Truman."

"That poor guy. And he's such a sweetie pie."

"Sweetie pie? The man's a fox!" She paused. Could she trust Erica? She decided yes. And anyway, what the hell. "Matter of fact," she confided, "he and I had a little thing going a while back . . ." She loved the way Erica's big blue eyes just popped wide open.

"Really? Lucky you! But—oh, wait a minute, he's married."

"That's okay with me. Kept him from bothering me too often." She laughed richly at her own joke.

"Huhn! I wouldn't mind him bothering *me* too often." She paused and bit her lower lip, and then she said, "Yvonne?"

"Yeah."

"How much is there of that here? Doctors and nurses, I mean?"

"You mean foolin' around? Oh, plenty, I guess. If everything the other nurses tell me is true. In fact—" She smiled "In fact, I've heard that a couple of years ago there was a doctor fooling around with a nurse . . . only the doc was a she and the nurse was a he!" Erica thought that was funny, too. Yes, she was gonna work out just fine. "Anyway," she went on, "what I started to tell you before is, it's very important to keep this a secret, because, see, Dr. Truman doesn't know yet. About his wife and the baby."

"Oh, that's right. He's in the delivery room assisting Dr. Winter, isn't he? God! To think they're able to deliver a baby and the mother is actually dead, but the baby isn't. It's like a miracle."

"Bite your tongue, girl. We don't know yet how that baby is. You're young. When it comes to births, you don't count your babies before they're hatched. I've seen things—" She shook her head and rolled her eyes.

"Oh, Lord, if Bobby Truman doesn't know about his wife, who's going to tell him?"

"Del Bello, I guess. I figure it's the job of the head honcho to give out the bad news. I sure wouldn't want to have that job."

"Oh, Yvonne, I'll bet you could do it. You've got the guts."

"Well, thanks, Erica, that's nice to hear. I admit I've had my share of tough messages to give, believe me."

"You sure stood up to Mr. Del Bello before. He listened to you, too, Yvonne. He backed right off. He was steaming, but he backed off."

"I admit I enjoyed it myself. He's not my favorite person." She laughed. "Him *and* that turkey—Dr. Schuster. The horse's ass! Even his nurses can't stand him!"

"I'm glad Dr. Winter's our chief. I *love* Dr. Winter; he's so nice. So warm and kind."

Yvonne cogitated a moment. "I thought that for a long time, too. But I'll tell you, since he left Dr. Ellie—his first wife—he's turned cold, it seems to me."

"Oh, I don't see that at all!"

"Maybe. Maybe it's just because I like Dr. Ellie so much . . . Oh, look who's coming out of the elevator. Hello there, Reverend. May we help you in any way?"

"Afternoon, nurse, I'm looking for Dr. Truman."

"Sorry, Reverend. He's in the delivery room with Janet

Freedman.'' Yvonne looked searchingly at Reverend Clayton.
He looked sad and serious; she had a sneaking sick feeling he
was bringing real bad news. Dared she ask?

But she never got to say anything, because Dr. Winter and
Dr. Truman and some others were all coming down the
hallway in a bunch. The Freedman baby! They were finished!
She concentrated on them, looking to see what their expres-
sions were. And when Dr. Winter caught her eye, he winked
and made the A-ok sign. ''A fine, healthy boy,'' he said.
''Five pounds, eight ounces, and alert as they come. He got
an eight on the Apgar,'' he added. And then he saw the
Reverend, and he stopped. Since his arm was across Bobby's
shoulders, that stopped *him*, too. Bobby, Yvonne thought,
didn't look too wonderful. He looked sad, in fact. Well, poor
guy, his baby hadn't been fine and healthy and alert as they
come. Life was full of bad surprises.

The three men just stood there for a minute or so, staring at
each other. And then Reverend Clayton stepped forward, his
hand outstretched, and said: ''Dr. Winter . . . Dr. Truman, I
believe congratulations are in order. What you've done amounts
to a miracle . . . Life out of death . . . a wonderful thing, and
we should praise the Lord for giving some men—and women—
the heart and the skill to perform great works such as this
one.''

''Thank you, Reverend,'' Dr. Winter said. ''We're happy
to see a healthy baby, but sad, too. I've rarely felt so
ambivalent. Disconnecting the life-support systems is a terrible responsibility, and we were all very fond of Janet.''

There was a long moment of silence, and Yvonne thought
to herself, Oh, lord, now he's going to tell Bobby his wife's
gone bananas . . .

''Dr. Truman,'' the Reverend said, ''I think we'd best talk
alone for a moment.''

Bobby made a deprecating gesture. ''Anything you have to
tell me you can say in front of Dr. Winter. Dr. Winter is my
friend.''

''I'm afraid it's tragic news, Bobby.''

"That's okay, Reverend." He gave a little grimace that might have wanted to be a smile. "We don't kill the bearer of bad news anymore."

"Corinne took your baby out of the ICU earlier and—"

"She *what*? Took him out?"

"That's right. Apparently, she went to the ICU, and the nurses all figured she was visiting the baby and left her alone with him. And . . . well, she walked out with him."

"That's crazy! The alarms on the monitors—!"

"Yes, they all went off. But she slipped out somehow, and it seems she went down the stairway, and everyone figured she took the elevator, and they just kept missing her. The long and the short of it, Bobby, is, she took the baby home."

"Took . . . him . . . home." Bobby looked stunned. "Okay, and then—?"

The Reverend stepped forward and put a hand on Bobby's shoulder. "And then she sat in the rocker and held him until he was gone."

"Gone! Gone, did you say?"

"Yes, Bobby, I'm sorry to tell you your son is dead."

"Thank God."

"I'm sure He will forgive you for that. In any case, He has that little boy in His tender care, now and forever."

Bobby got a look on his face that Yvonne recognized. She half expected him to burst out with "Bull*shit*!" But he didn't. Instead, he said mildly, "Each man to his own belief, Reverend. I'm glad it's over."

Chapter 37

THERE WAS A copy of the morning tabloid at each place around the big table, page 1 facing up. As Adrian came into the board room, he winced to see, over and over again, the heavy black letters saying over and over again, LIFE . . . AND DEATH. Oh, God, hadn't they all seen it already? He certainly had; in fact, he knew the story, which began on page 3, almost by heart.

"Life and death fought to a draw yesterday at Cadman Memorial Hospital in the wealthy landmark neighborhood of Brooklyn Heights.

"Even as Corinne Truman, wife of Dr. Bobby Truman, Ob/Gyn's chief resident, tore her defective newborn infant from his life-support systems and carried him home to die in her arms, her husband was assisting Ob/Gyn chief, Adrian Winter, in the modern miracle of deliverying a healthy, live son to a mother who was already dead.

"The three-day-old Truman baby, a victim of spina bifida (open spine), breathed his last as the child of Janet Freedman gave his first cry. Shortly after, the plug was pulled and Mrs. Freedman, who had been kept alive artificially for the past seven weeks, was allowed finally to rest in peace.

"Hospital officials, asked how Mrs. Truman managed to get by security, declined comment. One of the security guards, who asked to remain anonymous, said, 'Mrs. Truman was familiar with the hospital building. She could easily duck out. Most patients wouldn't know how to do it . . .' "

In disgust, Adrian reached out and swept one of the papers off the table, watching it scatter all over the floor with pleasure. Garbage! That's all it was, anyway. And as if that weren't bad enough, every single television newscast led off with something or other about the hospital and the two cases. Oh, and the pray-in; how could he forget *that*? If he'd seen the Reverend Clayton's big handsome head once on the screen, he'd seen it a dozen times. And those damned unctuous phrases the writers kept producing: "Yesterday morning, the front lawn of Cadman Memorial Hospital was filled with kneeling and praying parishoners, demanding that Dr. Bobby Truman sign the papers that would allow lifesaving surgery for his badly crippled newborn son. Today, that vigil ended as the baby's distraught mother stole her child . . ." And on and on and on and on.

Heaving a great sigh, Adrian sat himself. God, this had turned into a mess. Already the calls were beginning to come in. From Right-to-Lifers. From-Let-Them Die-ers. From the Moral Majority. From Women's Libbers. From fringe religions. From every goddamn group that thought it had cornered the moral market!

"Morning, Adrian. Oh, Lord, that headline again!" That was Con, followed closely by Nate, followed by Ellie, Art Schuster, and several others, followed by everyone else. Except, of course, Hank Del Bello. There was none of the usual banter today; everyone looked worried. There were nods of hello but nothing more.

He found it very difficult, being in the same room with Ellie. He hadn't had to face her since that conversation in the cafeteria; in fact, it was still painful to think about it. Showed what could happen when a man let his priorities get out of their proper order. Hell, he wasn't a kid anymore; he couldn't waste time chasing after notions. He had important things to do. There was some talk of expanding the Neonatal unit; that was going to take a lot of concentration. And he'd been approached, by more than one person, with the idea that he ought to replace Del Bello. Well, it was too soon to speculate about *that*, but still, he should give some thought to it. He raised his eyes and glanced around the table, where they were all settling themselves in for the session, and met Ellie's direct gaze. She smiled a trifle and gave him a little salute, and he nodded to her. Dammit, she was the perfect wife for him; couldn't she see that! Evidently not. Of course, there always had been a recalcitrant streak in Ellie. She seemed so tough lately . . . a bit self-centered. Well, he didn't have time to fight her. He was going to have plenty to keep him busy; he could see that. And that was enough. A man really needed only meaningful work, work that contributed to his society, to feel satisfied with his life.

All the seats were filled now, save Del Bello's, and when the door opened once more, all heads turned. Hank walked in, shoulders back, a defiant thrust to his chin. He strode over to his usual chair and stood behind it.

"Okay, everybody. Who'll begin the inquisition?"

Nate cleared his throat and held up a hand. "Take a load off your feet, Hank, Who said inquisition? We're here to discuss ethics, that's all, not to crucify anyone."

"Like hell! I know damn well what you want!"

"Listen, Hank, you *don't*!"

"You want Sandy Heller's head on a plate." Del Bello looked from face to face, a sneer on his lips. "Sure! I knew it!"

"In fact, Ms. Heller *is* the focus of our discussion," Ellie put in, her voice calm and reasonable, as only Ellie could make it. "As we are all well aware. But as Nate already has put it so well, we're not here to destroy anybody. In fact, Hank, we don't have that power. You know that. All we can do is talk."

And Adrian added, "What you may *not* know, Hank, is

that this emergency meeting was requested by the board of trustees. They want our feeling on ethical considerations of the publicity generated during the last couple of days.''

''The board is not happy,'' Nate said, ''if I may be permitted the understatement of the year.''

''That damn board would only be happy with the Sleeping Beauty story without the kiss . . . because a kiss is too damn sexy!'' He laughed harshly.

''In fact,'' Nate said, ''two of the trustees used the word *sensationalism* several times.''

''Both those stories were not only exciting,'' Hank said, ''but let me remind you all . . . abolutely the truth. It's not as if she'd been making things up! Come on! And if you don't like the style, well, Sandy Heller can't be blamed for what the editors of the *Post* and *News* choose to put in their papers!''

Adrian rose to his feet. ''But she *can* be blamed for sneaking out those pictures and those interviews in the first place! As you well know, Mr. Del Bello! She's been warned on more than one occasion.''

Hank gripped the back of his chair so hard his knuckles turned white. ''Okay, everyone, let's talk about ethics, then. Let's discuss the ethics of the Reverend Clayton here—a member of the board of trustess as well as a member of this committee. Let's talk about how ethical it is for him to march his congregation over here to kneel all over our lawn and create a media event! You wanna talk about sensationalism? Why don't we start with that!''

After a beat, Nate answered. ''It might interest you to know that's also on the agenda.'' He glanced to where the Reverend sat, uncharacteristically quiet, his large hands folded on the tabletop in front of him, his face blank.

Hank stared at him belligerently. ''Well, I'd like an answer from the Reverend Clayton. How about it, Reverend? Seems to me all it needed was a word from you and they wouldn't have held that pray-in.''

''Christians believe in the sanctity of life,'' the Reverend intoned. "Each and every life, Mr. Del Bello. And so, for us, there was no choice. We had to make our voices heard, and in this city, Mr. Del Bello—" He threw his hands up dramatically. "In this city and this society, Mr. Del Bello, how do poor blacks peacefully make their voices heard?" He shrugged and looked away as if what he had said was unanswerable.

Nate pounded the table. "Excuse me, gentlemen, you're both out of order. I'm the chairman of this committee, and I say that first we discuss the fact that the story of Corinne Truman has appeared in every yellow rag and on every newscast for the past thirty-six hours . . . and it is embarrassing to this hospital and especially to the Obstetrics and Gynecology department, not to mention Dr. Truman, a brilliant young man whose career may now be in jeopardy; not to mention his wife and their living child . . . See here, Del Bello, it was Sandy Heller who created this situation by releasing that picture and story on Corinne Truman, and it's my understanding that she went in there and got that story and that picture against Dr. Winter's express orders. Goddam it, that's what we're talking about here! We don't want her head on a plate, as you put it; but goddam it, we want you to tell us how you can justify keeping her on when she's done this not once, not twice, but three times!"

"Ah," Del Bello said, leaning forward to face Nate, "now it comes out. The truth. The truth is that the issue isn't sensationalism or what stories were printed where. It's all about somebody daring to defy a doctor's orders." His voice put special emphasis on the words "doctor's orders." "And we all know that's crime number one around here."

There was a babble of raised voices. Nate pounded the table again. "Quiet, everyone. And I suggest, Del Bello, that you calm yourself. We aren't here to fight."

"It's true, though. Ever since I came here, I've seen that there are two sets of rules at Cadman Memorial: one for the doctors, the gods, and the other for the rest of us poor mortals . . . Oh, come on, the lot of you; don't deny it. Sandy Heller did a damn good job. You and your WASP-controlled board may not approve of being headlined in the *Daily News*, but face it, those headlines have resulted in increased interest in the hospital, more filled beds, more clinic visits, more grants, more invitations for house staff to lecture and speak, more private contributions, and a balance sheet printed in black!''

Con Scofield spoke now, her voice quivering with emotion. "You think the doctors are gods? Well, maybe they are. Who the hell else takes the ultimate responsibility? Dammit, Mr. Del Bello, you're not running a hotel here; you're running a hospital. And in this hospital the patients come first, not the profits. And who takes care of the patients? The medical staff. Nobody else. I don't see you or any other administration person here all hours of the day and night, making the tough decisions! That's why what the doctors say goes, period. End of discussion.''

"Oh, really? End of discussion? Doctors are perfect. Right, Ms. Scofield? Well, I happen to know one who isn't.'' He turned and bared his teeth at Art Schuster. "Your precious Dr. Art Schuster for one. Who happens to own a business on the side—did you all know that?—and is using his influence to have hospital patients referred to his dialysis center. Did you all know *that*?''

Voices were immediately raised again, and Art stood up. "That's a lie, a damn lie!'' he protested. "And furthermore, it's a red herring. We're not here to discuss me; we're here to discuss your failure to control Ms. Heller . . . And perhaps the committee would like to know *why* . . . ?''

"You bastard!'' Del Bello looked as if he might lunge across the table and grapple with Schuster, but Ellie put a restraining hand on his arm and said loudly, "None of us cares, Art.''

"You want to know something?'' Hank demanded. "I'm not answerable to this committee. You want to discuss the ethics of public relations? Talk to the head of public relations. Face *her*.''

"Face her?'' Con snorted. "*Fire* her is more like it . . .''

She immediately held up a hand and added, "I'm sorry; I'm sorry. This committee doesn't hire and fire. What I meant is, that's what the trustees are talking about, and we all know it. They want her out."

"Oh, yeah?" Hank's face turned red. "Well, I'm telling you right now. If she goes, I go!"

Nate said mildly, "Don't say too much, Hank. You may regret it."

"I got no regrets. *None*! And I'm finished with this meeting." And he slammed out of the room.

"I think we've seen the last of Mr. Del Bello," Art said in a satisfied tone.

What an ass Art is, Adrian thought, but he was probably right. Hank Del Bello had just sealed his fate with those words . . . if he meant them, of course. Hell, even if he hadn't meant them, he was too much of a hothead to be chief administrator in a volatile place like Cadman. Too apt to be swayed by emotion. No, what Cadman needed was a cool intelligence at the helm—someone who could separate his personal life from his work. A doctor would be best. Yes, the more he thought of it, the better he liked the idea. The next time they came to him asking him to take over that job, he might have a more positive answer.

Chapter 38

THE WAITING AREA for Algonquin Airlines flight 702 to Buffalo was nearly deserted at 8:35 A.M. on a Sunday in May. "Look at that," Sandy Heller said in a disgruntled tone. She thumped her carry-on case down on the floor. "Not even anyone at the check-in counter! Well, of course not. Who the hell in their right mind wants to go to Buffalo?" She plunked herself into one of the molded plastic chairs and sat very straight, her arms folded tightly across her chest, "And stop pacing, would you, Hank? You're giving me a headache!"

"You're giving yourself a headache with all your complaints. Why can't you just relax and go with it, huh?"

"But . . . *Buffalo*, of all the goddam places. In a dinky little hospital nobody's ever heard of!"

"Methodist happens to be a very fine facility with the potential for expansion. Its cystic fibrosis unit is among the best in the—"

"Can the speech, Hank. I'm not a reporter. You don't have to put on a show for me. I know damn well what Methodist is. And you know what it is? It's a dinky little hospital in the middle of nowhere that nobody's ever heard of!"

394

"Jobs don't grow on trees, you know."

"Oh, very original thought, Hank. Golly, I wish I'd thought of that one!"

He pulled in an exasperated breath, letting it out noisily, "Look, Sandy, all I'm saying is, for now we've got something. Hey, we're damn lucky. The job market stinks."

"This *job* stinks!"

Now he sat down next to her and turned, bringing his face close to hers. He spoke in a low tone, but each word was bitten off as if it tasted bad. "So what else were you offered, huh? Look, lady, if I wasn't taking you with me, you would have *zip*! And don't you forget it!"

"Big deal!" Sandy said bitterly, and turned her head away.

Now Hank grabbed her by the arm, letting his fingers dig in painfully. "Bitch! I gave up everything for you! Every fucking thing! My job, my home, my wife, family, *everything*! And *you* think you have a gripe? You belittle this job? You feel free to put me down every minute? Goddam it, you should be on your fucking knees to me—!" His voice was becoming louder and louder.

"Hank! Take it easy, will you? I'm upset, that's all. I did a good job for Cadman, and all I got was a kick in the teeth for thanks."

"You got *me*."

She put a hand on his arm. "Oh, I know that. And don't think I'm not grateful. I realize you took it on the chin for me. But God, Hank, I had a title and a big office and a secretary. And now . . . now *I'm* the secretary!" Her eyes filled, and several tears tracked down her cheeks.

"Oh, Christ, don't cry! I can't stand it when a woman cries! You're not a secretary. Jesus Christ, Sandy, I told you a hundred times. You're assistant to the president. My assistant."

Bitterly: "Your secretary! It's a fancy title, but it's still just a secretary!"

"Maybe in the beginning. But you wait. As soon as we begin expanding, I'll have a whole staff, and you'll be in charge of PR. And meantime, Jesus—you'll be doing all the news releases and stuff! It'll be fine. And if it doesn't work out . . . hell, we can move on. Give it a year—''

"Oh, God, a year! A year in Buffalo!"

"I said can it, so can it, will you? I'm getting sick and tired of hearing you bitch and bitch about fucking Buffalo. I'm the one should be complaining! I can't believe you have the goddam gall to give me such a hard time. Listen, I know it's not the first time you've been fired! You seem to have a talent for getting into trouble! So count your blessings! Jesus Christ, *I'm* the one who put my ass on the line for you. *I'm* the one who told them, 'If she goes, I go!' And I'm the one who *did* it! I can hardly believe it myself. *You* got fired, lady, not me! I quit a top job, and for what. For *you*! For you . . . so you could sit in this fucking airport and bitch me to death!''

"Oh, sure. You quit for me. Oh, sure!"

"What the hell does *that* mean?"

Sandy stood up suddenly, shaking his hand off her shoulder, looking down at him, her lip curled. "That means you know damn well that Schuster was already after you. Oh, yes, my dear Hank, your days were numbered. And you knew it! Don't you try to tell me different. I was there, remember? And I know what was going on. The board wanted you out, and Schuster wanted you out, and especially Nate Levinson and Adrian Winter wanted you out. So you just saw your chance to beat them to the punch and look noble at the same time. 'If she goes, I go!' What bullshit!"

He said, through clenched teeth, "Not bullshit." He paused a moment and then, in a different tone, added, "Look, Sandy. I quit for you. You can believe it or not. But if you don't, then I don't know if you even ought to come with me to Buffalo."

They stared at each other. Sandy's face registered in rapid succession: fear, surprise, concentration.

The sudden voice over the loudspeaker startled them both. "Flight 702, Algonquin Airlines, LaGuardia to Buffalo, is now boarding at Gate 13. Passengers should have their boarding passes ready to present to the representative at the gate.''

Hank bent and picked up his flight bag and attaché case. ''I'm going,'' he said. ''You can do whatever you damn please.''

He turned and walked away. Sandy glared after him. She opened her mouth to call out and then closed it. For perhaps ten seconds she stood irresolute, and then she grabbed up her carry-on and trailed after him.

''Nate! Stop!'' Con protested. ''I don't want any more! I'm full!''

''So what am I doing that's so terrible? I'm offering a spoonful of chopped liver. It's Rose's homemade, and it's the best!''

''You didn't offer; you dropped it on my plate. It's not a spoonful; it's a mountain. And I'm too fat as is!''

''Fat! You're not fat. Don't argue with me; I'm a doctor, remember? You're just right.''

''Well . . . maybe so. But I *will* be too fat if you keep stuffing me. Listen, I thought when I met you at Borough Hall this morning I was getting a husband, not a Jewish mother.''

. He reached across the table and put his hand over hers. ''Believe me, Con, you got a husband. And I'll prove it just as soon as we get home.''

''Shame on you, Nate! In a public place!''

''This isn't a public place, Con. This is Rose and Sol's.''

''Well, I'm awfully glad you think that way because I'm warning you I'm no cook.''

''You already told me a hundred times. Do I care? I'm terrific at eating out! I'll take good care of you.''

''I know you will.'' She smiled at him tenderly.

''So indulge me,'' Nate said, a little twinkle in his eyes. ''Eat your chopped liver.''

''Oh, Nate! You are impossible!'' But she laughed.

Rose slid two plates neatly in front of them. ''Two pastrami platters and your iced tea is on its way, Con . . . oho! what's this I see?''

Con blushed and busied herself with her napkin. "What are you talking about?''

"Isn't that a new ring on the third finger, left hand?''

"That's what it is,'' Nate said. "And why don't you shout it a little louder, Rose, and then we won't have to send announcements.'' He laughed hugely, very pleased with his own joke.

"*Mazel tov*! Listen. The lunch is on us. A little present from me and Sol, so don't argue.''

For a few minutes, Con and Nate concentrated on their food. And then Nate said, through a mouthful of pastrami, "Well, Mrs. Levinson, married ten minutes, and already the news is out. How do you feel about that?''

"I waited long enough for it to happen. If Rose doesn't tell some people pretty soon, I might just run down the street myself.''

"Let me tell Adrian,'' Nate said. "Oh, boy! When I think of the look that's gonna be on his face—! I can't wait! He'll be stupefied!''

"Talk about stupefied, I was kind of stupefied when Adrian took the job of chief administrator.''

"Why? I wasn't.''

"I thought he was a truly dedicated doctor . . . you know, the kind who would never want to give up his practice.''

"Well, you don't know Adrian the way I do. He's a dedicated doctor, all right, but he's ambitious. I know. He was really bothered when Art Schuster began to cut him out with Del Bello. He loved being the right-hand man. Oh, yeah, I always knew that. But don't get me wrong; I never minded it. You know why? Because he was damn good, that's why! I always say, when a *good* man is ambitious, you've got yourself the ideal combination!''

"I just wish I'd been a fly on the wall of Art Schuster's office when he got the memo.'' Con began to chuckle. "He must have had a apoplectic fit! Poor Art . . . he thought he had it knocked. How could he know that damn fool Del Bello would sacrifice himself for a cheap blonde like Heller—!'' Con shook her head. ''Honestly, Nate, if I live to be a hundred, I'll never figure that one.''

Nate waggled his eyebrows and said dryly, ''She had her charms.''

''Oh, that! Come on, Nate, you're talking to an old nurse. I know what grownup people do when they're alone together, but that shouldn't have been enough to make him *quit* . . . Oh, never mind. As long as he's gone, that's what matters.''

''Well, I'd like to be a fly on the wall when Art goes in to ingratiate himself with Adrian . . . oh, boy! He'll have to do a very clever song and dance to sell himself to Adrian!''

''He'll never pull it off. In fact, I don't believe he'll even try.''

Nate thrust out a hand. ''Wanna bet? Art Schuster knows no shame. Oh, no, don't argue. Remember I had him as an intern. I know him inside and out, backwards and forwards. Believe me, he'll give it the old college try. It might take a while, but I think in the end he'll be right up there again.''

''Don't you think Adrian's much too shrewd to be taken in? Well, maybe not. He let himself get taken in by his second wife. Hunh! Give up a woman like Ellie for *that*! Well, now that he finally came to his senses and wants her back . . . woops! I forgot, that's a secret.''

''It's not a secret anymore, so you might as well fill me in, Con.''

''Promise not to tell anyone . . . Oh, hell, of course you won't. It's just . . . he asked Ellie to come back to him . . .''

''Come back to him! But I thought he was happily married!''

''You guys always assume everyone's happily married. And then you're so shocked when people split. You just don't see what's right in front of you! Well, it seems he's not happily married—which, incidentally, I could've told you about six months ago; never mind how. Anyway, he asked Ellie to give him another chance, and she turned him down flat, and I don't blame her a bit!''

399

"What do you mean, you don't blame her! You always said you thought the world of Adrian!"

"Well, I do—as my doctor. As a doctor, he's just as sweet and concerned as you could want. But from what I've seen of his personal behavior, he's become a cold fish, Nate! Preoccupied with his work, distant, and uninvolved on any emotional level . . ."

Nate looked uncomfortable. "Gee, Con, I hate to hear you talk that way. *I'm* not the most demonstrative person in the world. Would you call *me* a cold fish?"

She patted his hand. "You? Never. You're demonstrative where it counts, honey . . . between the sheets . . . Oh, you're blushing, you old fool!" Now she gripped his hand in hers and squeezed. "But you *are* a wonderful lover, Nate, the best, the very best."

"Oh, Con, for God's sake! A public place! Somebody'll hear. Just eat, will you?"

"No I don't think I will, Nate. I think it's time we had our honeymoon, don't you?"

"Now that you mention it—" And he blushed even more.

"Oh, Nate!" Con said, and they laughed together. Then he gestured with a motion of his head, and together they got up from their chairs and walked out into the hazy Sunday noontime.

Bobby was sitting in the living room of their apartment watching a ballgame on the tv when Corinne came home at one-thirty after church. She walked in, unpinning the prim little hat, a broad smile on her face. He hadn't seen her smile for so long, it startled him. Without thinking about it, he got up and turned off the television set and then turned to her, waiting to see what she had to say. Since the funeral—and that was weeks ago—she had been like a little ghost, creeping about the apartment, hardly speaking and certainly never as alive as she looked right now. Something was up; but what?

"Oh, Bobby. It's finally happened. I cried. For the first time since our baby died, the spirit came to me, and I was able to cry. I *felt* something; I felt sad. It happened while they were singing. I was standing there, cold as ice, empty as a void, when suddenly my heart was moved and I saw our baby, saw him as plain as day, the way he looked the first time I saw him, and I thought to myself, Poor little thing, he never had a chance, and the tears just came, Bobby. And everyone gathered round and gave me comfort. Oh, it was wonderful!''

Bobby was moved. Poor Corinne. First it had been all the reporters. God, the phone calls and the poundings on the door and the mob of them waiting for her to just walk outside the apartment building—unbelievable. And not one of them with shame enough to fill a thimble, just pushing up close and not caring how it made her feel, asking her why she did it and how it felt to have her baby die in her arms. If he hadn't been there some of the time, he wouldn't have believed there were people in this world capable of that sort of cruelty. Luckily for her, she was in such a daze, she hardly knew what was happening. Even at the funeral—oh, God, that tiny white casket; it was so awful—even at the funeral, she stood silent and untouched. Not a tear, not a sob out of her. He went to Schlossberg—Adrian suggested it—and Schlossberg had a talk with her, and he said to give it time.

Look at that; the shrinker was absolutely right. It was a only couple of weeks, and here she was, elated because she could feel again. As a matter of fact, *he* felt pretty good about it, too. As a matter of fact, he'd been hanging around here, marking time, waiting for her to pull out of it. Jesus, he couldn't leave while she was so helpless; he couldn't! He didn't know *what* in hell might happen to Kelly while she was this way. So now he could begin to make his own plans, to think about the future, to live.

"I'm very glad for you, Corinne," he said. And he meant it. "You have to mourn before you can begin to feel better."

"That's just what the Reverend told me. 'Corinne,' he said, 'the Lord sends us tears to cleanse the spirit and ease the soul. Don't be ashamed of your tears. Look, look, I am crying, too.' Oh, Bobby, and he was. He wept for our little son. He's such a good man!''

"If you say so, Corinne.'' He couldn't talk to her, not really, not if she was going to quote the Reverend every other sentence.

"I want to talk to you, Bobby.''

"Here I am. Talk to me.''

"About taking the baby from the hospital.''

"Now Corinne, you don't have to explain yourself.'' He didn't want her to get excited. He liked this calmness, this reasonableness. Bringing it up might just reawaken all that hysteria.

"You never asked me why I did it. No, don't stop me. I want you to know what I was thinking. I know you all think I went a little crazy, and in a way I guess I did. But Bobby, when I saw that poor little baby, dying alone, suffering without the comfort of being close to his mother . . . well I couldn't leave him there, I just couldn't! Bobby, all those tv programs and those newspaper stories— Oh, I know you think I was too crazy to know what was happening, but I heard everything. I know what they said about me. Too distraught to know what I was doing. Crazed? Isn't that what some of them said? Yes, crazed by grief. But I knew; I knew exactly what I was doing. When I took him off the respirator, I realized he wasn't able to breathe very well on his own. When I took all those tubes and things out of him, I knew they were his life support. I knew. I'm not dumb. But I could tell when I looked at him that he needed me. A baby *needs* his mother; everyone knows that. My poor sick baby; he needed me even more than most. I knew he wasn't going to live long, on or off the life-support system. And I said to myself, Let him die in peace, surrounded by my love. And you know, Bobby, he died so quietly, his eyes closed. He never even cried. I rocked him and held him close to my heart and sang him lullabies, and when he went, the last thing he felt was his mother's heartbeat and her arms around him.''

Bobby stared at her. "I—I think you did exactly the right thing, Corinne."

"Of course I did." She gave him a sweet, serene smile. "Jesus told me what to do. He told me to make my baby's short life just as happy as it was possible to make it. I held him close until Jesus took him . . . took his poor little crippled body and made it whole. And today, when I thought of him, I realized with joy that now he's with Jesus, and now he's perfect."

Jesus again! Every time he fooled himself into thinking she was really okay, Bobby thought, she went off again. There was no communicating with her at all anymore.

"I'm fine now, Bobby. I'm fine now, and I'm ready to take care of my little Kelly again. I know I've been sad, but now I'm on my way. Now you can leave."

He was stunned. All he could think to say was a stammered "I'll stay as long as you need me."

She gave him a clear, direct look. "I don't need you. I have Jesus. It's for the best that you leave, Bobby. We're on two different roads of life."

"Corinne, I—"

"You've lost your way." She went on in that inexorable way. "It's like the Reverend said. I must let you go your own way. But I promise, I will keep praying for your eternal soul." She smiled gently at him, turned, and left the room. He was free.

Four o'clock already. Adrian straightened up from the boxes of books he'd been unpacking and arranging on the shelves, groaning a little and arching his back. He looked around the large bare office with pleasure. The office of the chief administrator, and although he hadn't really moved in yet, his name was on the door. Tomorrow, Monday, was his first official day. He walked around for a minute or two, unkinking his stiff muscles, and then sat in the big leather chair, his favorite, which had been moved from his old office sometime yesterday. He twirled the chair to face the big bank of windows and gazed out at the Brooklyn Bridge, silver against a rapidly darkened sky. Looked like they were in for quite a storm. It had been a stormy couple of weeks, not outside—right inside this hospital. He knew he'd just squeaked into this job; there was a contingent of Art Schuster fans on the board, and they had been quite vociferous on Art's behalf. But, in the end, common sense had prevailed. He was much more qualified by reason of experience and personality. Art was just too political, too easily swayed, and in the end the board had to recognize that. He'd use Art, no doubt about it; he'd use him where he functioned best: charming the bucks out of rich old ladies.

In the meantime, he thought, staring out the window, his first job was to clear up all the messes. Thank God Willie Freedman had just up and disappeared—to Alaska was the rumor. Janet's parents were made the legal guardians of the baby, and that was one thing he didn't have to concern himself with anymore. But there was a ton of unfinished paper work from Del Bello's time, and he was going to have to find a new PR person who would establish the proper tone for the hospital. And there must be an entirely new code of ethics. That was something he'd had to promise the board.

And once he got the old business taken care of, ah, then . . . He wanted to go after those new federal grants for testing new techniques in neurotherapy for spina bifida neonates. Ellie would do well with that, and she was pressing for it. And he had plans, big plans, plans to engage the entire catchment area of the hospital in storefront prenatal care. It would mean *everyone* could have first-class prenatal treatment; he'd put together teams to travel to churches, schools, storefronts, on a regular schedule—a resident, a nurse, a nutritionist, and a genetics counselor. That would be impressive, and he knew he could make it work if he was given the chance. Come up with enough good ideas and you could pull everyone together: the Heights and the Tillary Houses and everyone in between. And then the name of Adrian Winter would be as familiar as—

The door burst open, interrupting his reverie. Leslie came bustling in, her face alight, her arms loaded with boxes of files. "Oh, Adrian, I have the cutest office, and look at all these files. . . . Well, the last president of the auxiliary never even put them in the right order. Can you believe it? I'm going to have a month's work just getting them straightened out. And those curtains! Well, the color is disgusting, and they're so ratty . . . I guess nobody's bothered to decorate the place since the year one, but I'm there now, and it's quite a nice little space with good proportions and a lot of sunlight. . . . Oh, it's so exciting, Adrian! And just think. I'm president of the auxiliary. We're both bosses now!"

Adrian gazed at her, smiling a little. It was remarkable how much easier she was to get along with since his promotion—and hers. Apparently, she needed to be kept busy. As soon as she knew she was heading up the auxiliary, she stopped hounding him for sex all the time and nagging him to talk to her. And sad as it was, Greg's problem had focused her, had matured her. Every morning she drove him to his special school, and twice a week she brought him to Cadman to the audiologist. She worked on his exercises with him and was surprisingly competent. Yes, he was quite proud of her.

She paced about, bubbling over with her newfound enthusiasm, chatting, changing the subject mid-sentence, fussing with his furniture. Adrian watched her as if she were an actress on the stage, and he, the critic appraising her performance. He'd have to give her a good review; she was without doubt a beautiful woman who kept herself in shape. She always looked just right. A man could be proud to take her anywhere. And it wasn't only her beauty. No, she was easy with people. Crowds didn't frighten her; she was accustomed to being looked at, and she didn't mind it. Indeed, she actually enjoyed it. She was the perfect choice for a man in his position. In truth, a much better choice than Ellie. Ellie was a fine doctor, but as the wife of the chief administrator—well, she was simply not a political animal. She was too independent and too apt to say whatever she believed without thinking about the consequences. He gazed at his lovely young wife; her eyes sparkled with excitement. She *was* lovely, and he was a lucky man. Everything was working out for the best, he thought, as rain began to patter against the windows. There was no reason on earth he shouldn't be completely content with his marriage now.

Ellie sat at the kitchen table, sipping at a glass of chilled white wine. The Sunday *Times* was open in front of her, but she couldn't concentrate on it. Her eyes kept slipping right over the words. She was still feeling sad. Why, she didn't know. It had begun as a perfect day. There was a wonderful concert in Prospect Park; she'd gone with the Remsen Street Block Association, picnic basket in hand, loving the sunshine and the smell of cut grass and the light, casual conversations that drifted around the group. It was very convivial and pleasant, and she'd just enjoyed it all, without thinking about it very much.

And then, around four-thirty, it started to rain. She had come home, let herself in to her familiar beloved house, and was struck with the absolute silence, the emptiness, the aloneness that suddenly, out of nowhere, engulfed her. She stood in the hallway, still holding on to the picnic basket, and felt her heart constrict in her chest as great sobs forced their way up through her throat and tears welled in her eyes. Just like that, without any warning.

She had run into the kitchen, then, forcing herself to stop this idiotic, meaningless weeping. She had put the basket away, fighting off more tears; and she had poured herself a large goblet of wine, sniffling all the while; had turned on the radio to Jazz 88, trying to drown herself in the music. And wouldn't you know, the station was doing an all-day homage to Lady Day, Billie Holiday . . . and the husky, tragic edge of her voice just set her off again. Finally, she just gave in to it, sat at the kitchen table, put her head down on her folded arms, and boohooed. In a way, it was a wonderful release, to cry like a child, no inhibitions, just bawling.

Well, the tears had stopped, finally, after two glasses of wine, but she was unable to shake the ineffable feeling of loss. She pretended to read the paper, but when she had finished a column, she had no idea what it was about. So she ended up just sitting and sipping wine and staring at the rain pouring in dozens of little crooked streams down the kitchen window. Looking at it, teeming like that, just pouring in sheets out of the leaden sky, she felt suffused with nostalgia. Nostalgia! Why? she wondered, and then her mind shied away from it. To think nostalgically would only make her cry again, and she refused to cry again over nothing more than rain on a windowpane.

The phone rang then, and her heart gave such a leap and began to pound so hard that she put a hand involuntarily onto the sternum and pressed. As she picked up the phone, she dragged in a deep breath. "Hello?"

"Mom! I'm glad you're there!"

It was her daughter, Sonya, calling from Michigan. Calling from Michigan? Why? "Hi, Sonnie. How nice! Everything okay?"

Sonya laughed. "Stop being a mother, will you? Every phone call isn't a disaster!" Sure, Ellie thought, amused, because you don't remember when every phone call from you girls *was* an announcement that something was wrong.

It turned out that Sonya just "figured I hadn't talked to you in a while, and I don't have any time to write, so I figured I'd call and see if you were home, and you were, so hi, Mom." They chatted for a few minutes. Sonnie had a new boyfriend and was looking for a new part-time job, and graduate school was okay . . . the usual. And then they hung up, and Ellie stood there, leaning against the wall, feeling let down.

What a terrible thing! she scolded herself. Your daughter calls you long distance just to say hello, and you feel cheated. She ought to be overjoyed that Sonya's relationship with her was so good that she wanted to stay in touch. In fact, she was close to all her daughters; it could have been any one of them on the phone just now, and normally it would have warmed her. She would have walked around the house with a smile on her face for half an hour, just feeling good because she'd done a good job with her kids. So what was it, this evening? she scolded herself. First you walk in from a perfectly lovely afternoon and burst into tears, and then your daughter calls you on the telephone, and you sulk. What in hell was going on, anyway?

She walked back over to the table and picked up her wine glass, taking a tiny sip. Think about it, she told herself. You got all excited when the phone rang. Now who was it you were hoping would be on the other end? Who were you hoping to hear from? She pulled a blank. Not Adrian! Oh, surely, not Adrian. She had no regrets for turning him down. Did she? Truthfully, now, Eleanor, are you having second thoughts? Do you feel it would be nice to go back to where it was safe and secure? But no. No. Not at all. She and Ade had done all right. Actually, there was nothing horrible about him. On a scale of one to ten, he was easily a nine. It was just that when she grew and changed, he didn't. He *wouldn't*. And now number nine wasn't enough, not anymore, not for her.

So what was it? She walked around the kitchen, looking into the pantry and the refrigerator, feeling vaguely that maybe she was hungry; maybe that's what was wrong. This feeling of unease, maybe it was an empty stomach . . . or all that sun . . . or fatigue.

She drank her wine and stared at the now black window where the rain still pounded, and suddenly out of nowhere she recalled the feel of David Powell's naked body against hers as they stood, arms wound tightly around each other, breast to breast, belly to belly, thigh to thigh, just standing and hugging each other, getting as close as possible to each other. Her heart gave that jolt again. David! It had been right here, right on this spot. They had just finished making love, and she was in here, pouring him a cold drink. He had come in silently, reaching out for her, surprising her, pulling her to him and holding her so close, so tight. They had not said a word; they didn't need to. The message was so clear and strong. She had never in her life felt so close to another human being as she had at that moment.

Oh, God! David! How she missed him! It had been a night just like this one, pouring with rain, that he had appeared at the door that first time, soaked and troubled and then—! Oh, God, and then . . . Oh, David, my love, she thought, and the tears sprang into her eyes. She was a fool, an utter fool. Of course he was her love. Of course she loved him. She had never stopped loving him. She loved him—and she sent him away! And why? Because he was younger, and he was a nurse, and people would find them ridiculous together.

"I don't care!" she said aloud. And it was true; she didn't care. She didn't care anymore what anyone thought or said or did or imagined or gossiped about. "Oh, David . . ." She had to go to him. Now.

She ran to the front door, snatching a poncho from the coat rack, grabbing her keys, and the next moment she was out in the stormy night, out in the murkiness, running, running, her heart hammering in her throat, running to David. At last. Doing what she should.

She hardly noticed the puddles she splashed through, hardly noted the dark shapes of people she whizzed by, hardly noticed the cold rain pelting against her face. She knew the way! Oh, yes, she knew her way, all right. At last she knew what she wanted, what she needed. And she was going to go for it!

She was at his building, breathless, in front of the intercom when the horrid heart-stopping thought came. What if it was too late? What if he didn't want her?

To hell with it. She punched at his bell and then ruefully said to herself, He might not be home, you idiot. Why didn't you call him?

And then his voice, made flat by the intercom. "Yes?"

"David. It's me. Ellie." There was a long silence, and she stood in the rain, shivering, thinking, He doesn't want me. "David? Are you there?"

"Ellie. Don't move. Do you hear me? Don't move. The buzzer's broken. I have to come get you."

The shivering intensified, and she wrapped her arms around her body. The wait was endless, and then suddenly the door was open, and he was there, and they were in each other's arms in a frantic tight embrace. He felt so good to her; he felt so right!

"You're finally here," he said into her ear, and all she could do was nod against his cheek. She could not trust her voice.

"I'm warning you," David said. Now he released her just a little bit so that he could look into her eyes. "I'm warning you, Ellie. This time I'm not letting you go. This time I'm not keeping it a secret. This time I'm telling the world we're lovers. And this time, goddammit, we're going to live together." He stopped and raised an eyebrow in inquiry.

"Yes, David."

" 'Yes, David?' Such a meek response from my headstrong, outspoken, tough, independent, wonderful woman?"

"Yes, David."

He sucked in a breath. "Ellie. Don't play with me. I mean it. Don't fool around. I'm a very serious man at this moment. Do you mean it?"

"Yes, David."

"All of it?"

"Yes, David."

Now he grinned. "They're gonna talk, you know. They're going to say you're crazy. They're going to accuse you of robbing the cradle. They're going to say I'm a social climber. They're going to laugh at us, Ellie, and whisper and say all kinds of hurtful things. You do understand that?"

"Yes, David."

"Oh, Jesus! And this time, you don't care. This time, you admit you love me."

"Yes, David."

"Then, here's what we're going to do. We're going to go right upstairs and take off each other's clothes and love each other all night long. I mean now. I mean, let's hurry.

"Yes, David," she said. "Yes, yes, and *yes*."

About the Author

Marcia Rose is not a real person. She is *two* real persons—two women who met as young mothers and began to write books together (much to their surprise) eight years ago.

Marcia of *Marcia Rose*, a divorcee, has two teenage daughters, a teenage cat, and a teenage co-op apartment in historical Brooklyn Heights, New York. She enjoys good music, theater, and being active in her community.

Rose of *Marcia Rose* is married, has two teenage daughters, a teenage cat, and an elderly house in Brooklyn Heights. She enjoys ballet, tennis, skiing, and travel.

Marcia and Rose have written every word of their novels together. After so many years as a team, it no longer comes as a surprise when they think of the same thing at the same time, in the same words. What *is* a surprise is that something that they think is so much fun has turned out to be a full-time career.